D.

The metropolitan fifth reader

compiled for tCompiled for the use of colleges, academies, and the higher classes

of select and parish schools

D.

The metropolitan fifth reader
compiled for tCompiled for the use of colleges, academies, and the higher classes of select and parish schools

ISBN/EAN: 9783741176296

Manufactured in Europe, USA, Canada, Australia, Japa

Cover: Foto ©Andreas Hilbeck / pixelio.de

Manufactured and distributed by brebook publishing software (www.brebook.com)

D.

The metropolitan fifth reader

THE

METROPOLITAN

FIFTH READER;

COMPILED FOR THE USE OF

COLLEGES, ACADEMIES,

AND THE

HIGHER CLASSES OF SELECT AND PARISH SCHOOLS.

With an Introduction,

By RIGHT REV. DR. SPALDING.

By a Member of the Order of the Holy Cross.

NEW AND REVISED EDITION.

NEW YORK:

D. & J. SADLIER & CO., 31 BARCLAY STREET.

MONTREAL:

COR. NOTRE DAME AND ST. FRANCIS XAVIER STS.

INTRODUCTION.

THE subject of education is certainly the great question of the day. Its practical importance can scarcely be exaggerated. Upon its solution depends the future of society, whether for weal or for woe. The leading spirits of our age and country have so apprehended it; and hence school-book succeeds school-book, and method follows method, with a view to the more efficacious imparting of knowledge to youth. The activity in this department, especially among those outside the Church, has been prodigious, and it seems to be on the increase. The characteristic trait of our age seems to be the desire to seize on the child, and to mould its tender mind and heart to a particular form. Our wide-spread system of common schools is but an expression of this feeling, which is based upon a knowledge of human nature and of philosophy. The child is "the father of the man," and the character of the latter will be but a development of the impressions made upon the mind and heart of the former, while these were susceptible and plastic. If the flower be blighted, or the twig be bent, in the nursery, it will be difficult to render the matured plant either healthy or straight.

The great fault of our common-school system is found in its either wholly ignoring or greatly undervaluing the religious element in education. Without religion, education is, at best, but a doubtful boon, and it may be even a positive evil. Considering the innate tendency of our nature to evil, and the difficulty of training it up to good, the religious element is essential in the educational process. No other principle can supply an efficient curb to the headlong passions of youth; no other can effectually train up children to the practice of a sound morality, thereby making them good citizens by making them first good Christians. Without religion we may possibly succeed in making them decorous, if not decent, pagans; we cannot certainly hope to make them good, much less exemplary, Christians. The teachings of revelation, the facts of history, the lessons conveyed by our own daily observation and experience, and the frightful increase of vice whenever and wherever a contrary system has been adopted, all combine to confirm this conclusion.

We would not exclude secular education—very far from it; but we would constantly blend with it the holy influences of religion. Christian and secular instruction should go hand in hand; they cannot be consistently or safely divorced, at least among Christians. Not that we would thrust Christian teaching on the youthful mind too frequently, or on unseasonable occasions, so as to produce a feeling of weariness or disgust. This is but too common a fault among our over-zealous, but—in this respect at least—not over-wise Bible and Sabbath Christians of the day, who, but too often, in the name of religion, repress the buoyant smile of childhood, cast a gloomy shadow over the spring-tide of life, thereby infusing into the child an early, and, therefore, very deeply seated disgust for religion, and, in the end, producing an abundant harvest of in-differentists and infidels. We every day see the sad effects of this overwrought zeal and mistaken system of instruction.

We would, on the contrary, seek to make religion amiable in the eyes and dear to the hearts of the little children whom Christ so dearly loved. It should gild with its light and warm with its rays every pursuit of the school-room, even as the sun enlightens and cheers the objects of nature. We would not intrude the religious influence on the mind and heart of childhood, but we would seek to distil it gently, even as God distils the dews of heaven on the tender plants of the morning. We would carefully exclude from the reading-lessons all the poison of noxious princi-ples, and even all worldly and frivolous matter; and we would do this all the more rigidly whenever the poison would become the more dangerous, because latent, or gilded with the fascina-tions of style, or the gorgeous imagery of poetry. We would rigidly exclude Byron, in spite of his Syren Song. Thus im proved, secular instruction would put on new beauty and obtain a greatly increased influence for good; it would be "clothed with strength from on high," and the light of heaven would play around its pathway. It would then become doubly attractive to childhood; for the aroma of religion, diffused through all its departments, would lend it a charm and give it a zest which no earthly condiment could impart.

This idea, we believe, has been carried out, to a great extent a .east, in the new Series of Metropolitan Readers just issued by the Messrs. Sadlier of New York, particularly in the Fifth Reader, to which our attention has been more specially called. The matter of the lessons is varied, and though far from being exclusively religious, possesses, in general, a religious or moral tendency, and always leaves a good impression. There is no lesson without its moral.. The selection was made by a religious lady of the Order of the Holy Cross, who took care to submit her work to the judgment of gentlemen well known for their critical acumen and literary taste, and had it edited by another lady of New York, who has merited well of American Catholic literature. Under such circumstances it does not surprise us to find that the collection possesses great merit, and that it is likely to become eminently popular in our schools, and thereby to accomplish much good.

The Fifth Reader is divided into two parts: the first containing the principles and practice of elocution, and the second, well-selected and appropriate readings, both in poetry and in prose. Two things in particular strike us as distinctive of this collection of readings for children:-first, the preference given to American subjects and to American authors over those which are foreign; and, second, the copious selections from the writings of the principal Catholic writers of the day, both in Europe and in America. There is scarcely a prominent writer of this class from whose pen we have not at least one specimen. What renders this feature of the book the more valuable, is the circumstance that the writings of some of these distinguished authors are not very generally known or easily accessible to the mass of readers in this country. It is well that our children should learn that there are good and elegant works of literature in the Church as well as outside of it, and it is highly important that they should be imbued, from an early age, with a taste for this kind of reading. Among the foreign Catholic writers from whom selections are furnished, we notice the names of Cardinal Wiseman, Dr. Newman, Balmez, Chateaubriand, and Digby. Among our own writers, we perceive with pleasure the names of several of our archbishops, bishops, and clergymen, besides those of such distinguished laymen as Dr. Brownson, Dr. Huntington, McLeod, Shea, Miles, and others. The writings of these are interspersed with judicious selections from our standard American authors, Irving, Prescott, Bancroft, and Paulding.

We take pleasure in recommending this valuable series of Readers to the patronage of our Catholic colleges, schools, and academies.

CONTENTS.

PART II.

POETRY.

6   CONTENTS.

PROSE.

THE FIFTH READER.

Part I.

PRINCIPLES OF ELOCUTION.

INTRODUCTION.

THE art of reading well is one of those rare and charming powers that all wish to possess, many think they have, and others, who see and believe that it is not solely a gift of genius, labor to obtain. But it will be found that excellence in this, as in every thing else of value, is the result of well-directed effort, and the reward of unremitting industry.

To read and speak, so as at once to convey intelligence to the mind and pleasure to the ear; to give utterance to thoughts and sentiments with such force and energy as to quicken the pulse, to flush the cheek, to warm the heart, to expand the soul, and to make the hearer feel as though he were holding converse with the mighty spirit that conceived the thought and composed the sentence, is, it is true, no ordinary attainment; but it is far from being either above the power or beyond the reach of art.

To breathe life through language, to give coloring and force to the thoughts, is not merely an accomplishment; it is an acquisition of priceless value—a wondrous, omnipotent agency, when wisely and skilfully used.

But this degree of excellence is to be attained only through the assistance of sure and multiplied principles; principles that are universal; principles that are founded in nature.

Modes of delivery must inevitably vary with the suscepti-
bility of the reader to imaginative impulses, and with the
degree of his appreciation of what he reads. To prescribe
rules for what, in the nature of things, must be governed by
the answering emotion of the moment, and by a sympathizing
intelligence, may continue to be attempted, but no positive
system is likely to be the result. Language cannot be so
labelled and marked that its delivery can be taught by any
scheme of notation.

Emotional expression cannot be measured and regulated by
any elocutionary law ; and, though there has been no lack of
lawgivers, their jurisdiction has never extended far enough to
constitute them an infallible tribunal in the republic of letters
and art.

Mr. Kean does not bow to the law laid down by Mr. Kem-
ble or Mr. Macready ; Mr. Sheridan differs from Mr. Walker
and Mr. Knowles dissents from them both.

The important step, I believe, in regard to practice in ex
pressive reading, is to set before the pupil such exercises as
may at once engage his attention and be readily grasped by
his understanding. An indifferent, unsympathizing habit of
delivery is often fixed upon him, solely by accustoming him to
read what is either repulsive to his taste, or above his com-
prehension. As well might we put him to the task of reading backwards, as of reading what is too dull or difficult to
kindle his attention or awaken his enthusiasm. Reading backwards is not an unprofitable exercise, when the object is to
limit his attention to the proper enunciation of words, isolated from their sense ; but when we would have him unite an
expressive delivery to a good articulation, we must give him
for vocal interpretation, such matter as he can easily understand.

That the study and practice of *Elocution* should form a
branch in our systems of Education, is now generally con-
ceded. The true method of conveying a knowledge of this
art is, however, still open to much discussion. Experience
has confirmed me in the opinion that *elaborated* artificial rules
are almost "worse than useless," for they fetter all the natural

impulses of the Pupil, and too frequently substitute manner-
isms and affectations for a direct, earnest, natural method of
delivery. And yet *Elocution* has its rules, as essential and
as necessary to be understood and studied as are the rules
which govern a thorough knowledge of the exact sciences.
To simplify these rules, and to present only those which are
absolutely requisite to form a strictly natural and finished
reader, has been my aim in the following pages.

A knowledge of the positive rules which govern *Inflections*,
and practice on the same to enable the pupil to inflect with
ease; the general knowledge of rules governing *Emphatic
stress*, and a practice on *Modulation*, in its varieties of *level*,
emotional, and *imitative* tones, are all the necessary me-
chanical auxiliaries which Elocution, as an art, affords to the
student.

These essential rules I now present, condensed into the
briefest and most practical form, the due practice of which in
classes, accompanied by the application of the principles to the
daily *Reading* from Examples I have furnished in this work,
will, I trust, materially assist in the formation of an eminently
natural and correct style of Reading.

I claim no originality in the creation of any new system of
Elocutionary Instruction. I have only compiled and adapted
rules from acknowledged masters of the art, rejecting those
which experience has satisfied me are but superfluous and
unessential.

Proper Positions.

Whether sitting or standing, the body should be kept erect,
the head up, and the shoulders back and down. The chest
will thus be expanded, breathing be easy and full, and the vocal
organs left complete freedom of action. A *standing* position
is the best—it gives more power. Support the weight of the
body on the *left* foot; advance the *right* about three inches,
and turn the toes of both feet moderately out. This position
is termed the *second right*; it will be changed to the *first
right*, by throwing the weight of the body on the right foot,

which may sometimes be convenient for relief, where the read
ing is long continued.

HOLDING THE BOOK.

The book should be kept in the *left* hand, in a nearly hori-
zontal position from the lower point of the breast, at a distance of six or eight inches from it.   The voice will thus be
unobstructed, and the face, which is the index of the soul, in
complete view of the audience.   The right hand may be employed in turning the pages, and, in proper cases, in light, significant gesture.

RESPIRATION.

To read with elegance and power, the function of breathing
must be under entire control.   The compass and quality of the
voice depend upon it.   To secure this control, it will be found
highly useful to train the lungs to their most pliant and energetic action, on some respiratory exercise, as below:

> " The chest so exercised, improves its strength ;
> And quick vibrations through the system drive
> The restless blood."

EXERCISE.

1. Draw in the breath very slowly, until the lungs are entirely filled.

2. Emit the breath in the same manner, continuing to
breathe as long as possible.

3. Inspire in a full, quick breath, and expire it in an audible, prolonged sound of the letter *h*.

4. Inspire with a sudden, impulsive effort ; then exhale in
the manner of a strong, whispered cough.

5. Take in and give back the breath through the nostriis,
fully, but slowly, the mouth being entirely closed.

6. Exercise the lungs in the manner of violent panting.

ARTICULATION.

A perfect articulation is the great excellence of good reading and speaking.   There are other vocal qualities which rank

high in the elocutionary scale, as inflection, emphasis, and expression—but they are all inferior to this, and dependent upon it. They have no power to make clear to the mind those words or phrases which, by reason of imperfect enunciation, are not received by the ear. The student should be led, therefore, to early and persevering practice on the Elementary Sounds of the language, on difficult Consonant Combinations, and on unaccented Syllables. The effect would be almost magical. It would be marked by all the purity and completeness which Austin's Chironomia contemplates, when it says : "In just articulation, the words are not hurried over, nor precipitated syllable over syllable ; they are delivered out from the lips as beautiful coins, newly issued from the mint, deeply and accurately impressed, perfectly finished, neatly struck by the proper organs, distinct, sharp, in due succession, and of due weigh '

Defects in articulation may proceed either from over-eagerness in utterance, or from sluggishness and inattention. We will here cite some of the Vowel and Consonant sounds which are most frequently marred by a vicious articulation. The proper sound of the *a* is often too decidedly perverted in the syllables and terminations in *al, ar, ant, an, ance,* &c., as in the following words : fat*al*, particul*ar*, schol*ar*, sep*arate*, arro*gant*, honor*able*, persev*erance*, prelimin*ary*, descend*ant*, ordi-*nance*, &c., in which the *a* should be slightly obscured, but not debased into the *e* of h*er*, or the *u* in b*ut*.

Syllables and terminations in *o, ow,* and *on,* are badly articu lated by many, who say pota*tor* for pota*to,* comp*rumise* fo*r* comp*romise,* tobac*cernist* for tobac*conist,* inn*ervate* for inno*vate,* fell*er* for fell*ow,* wind*er* for wind*ow,* mell*er* for mell*ow* hist'ry for hist*ory,* hall*ered* for hall*owed,* mead*er* for mead*ow* philos*erpher* for philos*opher,* col*erny* for col*ony,* abr*urgate* fo*r* abr*ogate,* &c. The *o* in such words as horiz*on,* moti*on,* Bos-t*on,* &c., may be slightly obscured, but not dropped.

The unaccented *u* is often erroneously suppressed, or made to sound like *e,* in such words as partic*u*lar, vol*u*ble, reg*u*lar, sing*u*lar, ed*u*cate, &c. The full, diphthongal sound of the *u* in mute should be given to the above words, as well as to the following : nude, tune, tube, suit, assume, nature, mixture, moisture, vesture, vulture, geniture, structure, gesture, statue, institution, constitute, virtue, tutor, subdued, tuber, duty, duly, &c.

There are some miscellaneous vulgarisms in the rendering of Vowel sounds, to which we will but briefly allude. Do not omit the long, round sound of *o* (as it occurs in hŏme) in such words as boat, coat, &c. Do not give to the *a* in scarce the sound of *u* in purse. Do not say tremendy*ous* for tremem*lous*, or col*yume* for c*olumn* (pronounced *kollum*, the *u* short as in *us*, and not diphthongal, as in *use*). Give to the diphthong *oi* its full sound in such words as n*oi*se, p*oi*se, p*oi*nt, &c. Do not trill the *r* in the wrong place. Do not give the sound of *u* to the *a* in Indian (properly pronounced *Indyan*). Do not give the sound of *fle* or *fel* to the *ful* of aw*ful*, beauti*ful*, and the like ; of *um* to the *m* in chas*m*, pris*m*, patriotis*m*, &c. Do not dismiss the letter *d* from such words as an*d*, min*d*s, han*d*s, depen*d*s, sen*d*s, &c. Do not say g*it* for get, i*dee* for i*dea*, th*ar* for th*ere*, po'try for po*ë*try, *jest* for j*ust*, l*i*ne for jo*i*n, ketch for catch, kittle for kettle, sta*h* for star, p*i*nt for p*oi*nt, f*ur* for f*ar*, b*en* for b*een* (correctly pronounced *bin*), d*oos* for d*oes* (correctly pronounced *duz*), ag*i*n for ag*ai*n (correctly pronounced a*gen*), w*are* for w*ere* (correctly pronounced w*ur*), th*are*fore for th*ere*fore (correctly pronounced th*ur*fore), *air* for *are* (correctly pronounced *ar*, the *a* as in f*ar*). It is a common fault with careless readers to dispense with the final *g* in words of more than one syllable, ending in *ing*. Such readers tell us of their *startin' early in the mornin', seein' nobody comin'*, &c., giving us to infer that they either have a bad cold in the head, or have been but very slightly attentive to their elocutionary studies. Always avoid this vulgarism, whether in conversation, or in reading aloud.

Where consonants precede or follow the letter *s*, care should be taken to avoid the too frequent practice of improperly dropping the sound of one letter or more. For example, iu the line,—"And thou exi*st'st* and stri*v'st* as duty pro*mpts*," —the sound of the italicized consonants is often imperfectly

rendered. So we hear *acts* incorrectly pronounced *ax ; facts,
fax ; reflects, reflex ; expects, expex,* &c. Great liberties
are often taken with the letter *r*. There are speakers who
say *bust* for *burst, fust* for *first, dust* for *durst,* &c. We
also hear *Cubar* for *Cuba, lawr* instead of *law, wawr* instead
of *war, pawtial* instead of *partial, Larrence* instead of *Law-
rence, stawm* instead of *storm, mawn* instead of *morn, cawn*
instead of *corn.* The vibrant sound of the *r* should not be
muffled in such words as *rural, rugged, trophy,* &c. ; nor
should the *r* be trilled in *care, margin,* &c.

The sound of the *h*, in syllables commencing with *shr*, should
be heeded ; as in the line, " He *shrilly shrieking shrank* from
shriving him." In these and similar words the *h* is often shorn
of its due force, and, by some bad speakers, is entirely suppressed. To the preservation of its aspirate sound in such
words as *what, whale, whither, when,* &c., particular attention should be given.

Thorough and well-defined articulation will leave the hearer
in no doubt as to which word is meant in articulating the following : when, wen ; whether, weather ; what, wot ; wheel,
weal ; where, wear ; whist, wist ; while, wile ; whet, wet ;
whey, way ; which, witch ; whig, wig ; whin, win ; whine,
wine ; whirled, world ; whit, wit ; whither, wither ; white,
wight ; wheeled, wield.

Exercises.

He is content in either place ;
He is content in neither place.
They wandered weary over wastes and deserts ;
They wandered weary over waste sand deserts.
I saw the prints without emotion ;
I saw the prince without emotion.
That last still night ;
That lasts till night.
His cry moved me ;
His crime moved me.
He could pay nobody ;
He could pain nobody.

He built him an ice house ;
He built him a nice house.
My heart is awed within me ;
My heart is sawed within me.
A great error often exists ;
A great terror often exists.
He is content in either situation ;
He is content in neither situation.
Whom ocean feels through all her countless waves ;
Who motion feels through all her countless waves.
My brothers ought to owe nothing ;
My brother sought to own nothing.

In the following exercises, most of the principal difficulties in the articulation of our language have been introduced. In some of the sentences, it will be seen, that little regard has been had to the sense which they make ; the object being either to accumulate difficulties in Consonant combinations, or to illustrate varieties of Vowel sounds and their equivalents.

Exercises in Articulation.

1. A father's fate calls Fancy to beware. All in the hall here haul the awl all ways. Aunt's heart and hearth are better than her head. And shall I, sir'rah, guarantee your plaid ? Arraign his reign to-day ; the great rain gauge. And so our whaling ended all in wailing. Accent' the ac'-cent accurately always.

2. Awful the awe ; nor broad ought Tom to maul. The bulb, the bribe, the barb, the babbling bibber. Biding thou budg'dst, and budging bravely bidest. Bubbles and hubbubs barbarous and public. Canst give the blind a notion of an ocean ? Churlish chirographers, chromatic chanters. Chivalry's chief chid the churl's chaffering choice chimerical.

3. Call her ; her choler at the collar scorning. Crime craves the Czar's indictment curious. Despised despoilers tracked the dastard's doom. Diaph'anous delusions dep're-cate. Drachmas disdain dispersed despotically. Earn earth's dear tears, whose dearth the heart's hearth inurns.

4 England her men metes there a generous measure. Cæsar deceives the people from his seat. The key to that machine is in the field. Friends, heads and heifers, leopards, bury any. Examine, estimate the eggs exactly.

5. Faults? He had faults; I said he was not false. Facundious Philip's flippant fluency. Ghastly the gibbous anger gorges gnomes. Go! though rough coughs and hiccoughs plough thee through! Grudg'dst thou, and gib'dst thou, Gorgon, with thy gyves?

6. He humbly held the hostler's horse an hour. His honest rhetoric exhilarates. Hear'st thou this hermit's heinous heresy? He twists the texts to suit the several sects. Hope, boats, roads, coats, and loads of cloaks and soap. Why harass'dst thou him thus inhumanly?

7. In either place he dwells, in neither fails. Is he in life through one great terror led? In one great error rather is he not? Is there a name—is there an aim more lofty? I say the judges ought to arrest the culprit. I say the judges sought to arrest the culprit.

8. Janglingly jealous jeered the Jacobin. June's azure day sees the jay gayly jump. Knavish the knack could compass such a knot. Keep cool, and learn that cavils cannot kill. Kentucky knows the dark and bloody ground.

9. Long, lank, and lean, he illy lectured me. Lo! there behold the scenes of those dark ages. The scenes of those dark cages, did you say? Mete'orous and meteor'ic vapors Mulctedst thou him? In misery he mopes.

10. Myrrh by the murderous myrmidons was brought Man is a microcosm, a mimic world. Mute moping, maimed, in misery's murmurs whelm'd. Mammon's main monument a miscreant makes. Moments their solemn realm to Memnon give.

11. Neigh me no nays; know me now, neighbor Dobbin. Nipt now the flower is riv'n, forever fall'n. Nymphs range the forests still till rosy dawn. Nay! did I say I scream? I said ice cream. Never thou clasp'dst more fleeting triumphs here.

12. O'er wastes and deserts, waste sand deserts straying. On the hard wharf the timid dwarf was standing. Oh, note

the *occasion*, *yeoman*, *hautboy*, *beau!* Or'tho**ĕ**py precedes
orthog'raphy. Ob'ligatory *objects* then he offered.

13. *Pre'cedents* ruled *prece'dent* *Pres'idents.* Poor painted pomp of *pleasure's* proud parade. *Pharmacy* *f*ar more
*f*armers cures than kills. *Psyche* (si-kĕ) puts out the *sphinx's*
pseudo pipe. Politics ha*pp'*n to be u*pp*ermost. The room's
perfumed' with per'fumes popular.

14. *Qu̇*alp quoted *Qu*arles's *qu*iddities and *qu*irks. *Qu*eens
and co*qu*ets *qu*ickly their con*qu*ests *qu̇*it. *Qu*acks in a *qu*an-
dary were *qu*a*king* there. *Qu*ench'*d'st* thou the *qu*arrel of
the *qu̇*id'nuncs then? *Qu*iescent *Qu*ixotism and *qu*ibbl*ing*
*qu*iz*zing.*

15. *R*ave, *wr*etched *r*over, er*r*ing, *r*ash, and perjured.
*R*ude *r*ugged *r*ocks reëchoed with his *r*oar. *R*hinoceroses
armed, and *R*ussian bea*r*s. *R*ound *r*ang her *shr*ill *shar*p,
frenzied *shr*iek for mercy. *R*uin and *r*apine, *r*uthless *wr*etch,
attend thee !

16. *S*ix *sl*im, *sl*eek *s*aplings *sl*othfully he *s*awed. *S*tridulous
*s*trays the *s*tream through fore*s*ts *s*trange. *Snarl'st*s thou at
me? Vainly thou splash'*dst* and strov'*dst.* *Sh*all *sh*uffl*ing*
*sh*ift thy *shr*ink*ing*, *shr*iek*ing* *sh*ame? *S*chisms, cha*s*ms and
pri*s*ms, phanta*s*ms, and frenzies dire. *S*mith, *s*mooth, *s*mug,
*s*mart, *s*mirked, *s*mattered, *s*moked, and *s*miled. Sudd*en* he
sadd'*n'd*; *wh*erefore did he sadd'*n*?

17. The *h*eir his *h*air uncovered to the air. That la*st* *st*ill
night, that la*sts* *t*ill night's forgot ! The *st*rident trident'*s*
*st*rife *st*rides *st*renuous. The d*u*pes shall see the d*u*pe survey
the scene. The martial *corps* regarded not the *corpse.*

18. The ring*ing*, cling*ing*, blight*ing*, smit*ing* cur*s*e. The
*st*orms *st*ill *st*rove, but the ma*sts* *st*ood the *st*ruggle. The *st*eel
the*se* *st*eal *st*ill *st*er'eotypes (the *er* as in ter*r*or) their *st*igma
*T*he *st*alk the*se* *t*alkers *st*rike stands *st*rong and *st*eady. *Th*aw-
ing, it *th*ermometrically *th*rives.

19. *T*empta*t*ions *t*an*t*amoun*t* indic*t*men*t's* debtor. Ten*th* or
ten *th*ousand*th* breaks *th*e chain alike. *Th*ink'*st* *th*ou the
heig*hts*, dep*ths*, brea*dths*, *th*ou'rt *th*orough in ? The soldiers
skilled in war, a thousand men ? The soldiers *k*illed in war a
thousand men. The prin*ts* the prin*ce* selected were superb.

20 Then if thou *fall'st*, thou *fall'st* a blessed martyr. Thou *liv'st*—*liv'st* did I say? appear'*st* in the Senate! Though thy *cry* moved me, thy *crime* moved me more. These things can never make your *government*. Thou *barb'dst* the dart that wounded me, alas!

21. Thou *startl'dst* me, and still thou *startl'st* me. Thou *watch'st* there where thou *watch'dst*, sir, when I came. Thou *black'n'dst* and thou *black'n'st* me in vain. *Thought'st* thou *those thoughts* of *thine* could *thrill* me *through*? The intriguing *rogue's vague* brogue *plagues* like an *ague*.

22. Thou *slept'st*, great ocean, *hush'dst* thy myriad waves. The wolf *whose* howl, the owl *whose hoot* is heard. The *new tune* played on *Tuesday suits* the *duke*. Too soon thou *chuckl'dst* o'er the gold thou *stolest*. Twanged *short* and *sharp*, like the *shrill* swallow's cry.

23. *Use* makes *us use* it even as *usage rules* (this last *u* like the *o* in move). *Umpires usurp* the *usurer's usual custom*. *Utility's* your *ultima'tum*, then. *Untunable, untractable, unthinking. Urge* me no more; your *arguments* are *useless* The *tutor's* revolution is *reduced*.

24. *Vain, vacillating, ve'hement*, he *veers* forever. *Whetting* his scythe, the mower *singeth blithe*. *While whiling* time at *whist, why* will you *whisper? Whelmed* in the waters were the *whirling wheels. Where* is the *ware* that is to wear so well?

25. *White* were the *wights* who waggishly were winking. *Wrenched* by the hand of violence from hope. *Wouldst* thou not highly—*wouldst* not holily? With *short shrill shrieks* flits by on leathern wing. Xerxes, Xantippe, Xen'ophon, and Xanthus.

26. *Yachts yield* the *yeomen youthful* exercise. You *pay*, nobody? Do you *pain* nobody? Your kindness *overwhelms* me—makes me bankrupt. Zeuxis, Zenobia, Zeus, and Zoroäs'ter. *Zephyr* these *heifers* indolently fans.

PRONUNCIATION.

A and *the* when under emphasis have the vowel sounded *long;* as "I said â man, not thê man." But *a* when *unem-*

phatic or unaccented is always short; as, "We saw ă child playing about." The used before a vowel, takes the long sound of e, but before a consonant, the short: as, "The oranges were good, but thĕ dates bad. These distinctions deserve particular attention' in primary and intermediate schools. They are much neglected. My when emphatic takes the long sound; as, "It is my book, not yours," but in most other cases it takes the short sound. Even in reading. the Sacred Scriptures, good taste prefers the short sound, except in expressions of marked solemnity, or in connection with the Holy Name. By seldom adopts the short sound. In collo- quial phrases like the following, however, it is allowable; as, "Bȳ-the-by, or bȳ-the-way." These examples are like words of three syllables, with the accent on the third. In the word myself, the y never takes the long sound, the syllable self receiving the stress when it is emphatic, except when re- ferring to the Deity. There, when used as an adverb of place, takes the full sound of ê (long a); as, "The boy was certainly thêre;" but when merely employed to introduce a word or phrase, it takes the lighter sound of e; as, "Oh, there is the boy." So with their; as, "It is thĕir duty, not yours." "They will not neglect their duty." In the same manner your, when emphatic, sounds as the word ewer does, out unemphatic, it shortens into yŭr, having less the sound of long u. The following seven words used as adjectives always have the e sounded—aged, learned, blessed, cursed, winged, striped, streaked; as, "An agéd man; a learnéd professor; the blesséd God," not "An ag'd man, &c." When this word is compounded, however, the ed is short; as, "A full-ag'd person."

"Those who wish to pronounce elegantly" as Walker ha justly said, "must give particular attention to these syllables, as a neat pronunciation of these, forms one of the greatest beauties of speaking." But great defects are common in this respect, not only in the humbler grades of society, but among the educated and refined. In the pulpit, in the halls of legis- lation, everywhere, indeed, this is more or less the case.

The word modulation is derived from a Latin word signifying to *measure off properly*, to regulate ; and it may be applied to singing and dancing as well as speaking. It is not enough that syllables and words are enunciated properly, and that the marks of punctuation are duly observed. Unless the voice sympathetically adapts itself to the emotion or sentiment, and regulates its pauses accordingly, it will but imperfectly interpret what it utters.

The study of pronunciation, in the ancient and most comprehensive sense of that word, comprised not only the consideration of what syllables of a word ought to be accented, but of what words of a sentence ought to be emphasized. The term *Emphasis*, from a Greek word signifying to *point out* or *show*, is now commonly used to signify the stress to be laid upon certain words in a sentence. It is divided by some writers into *emphasis of force*, which we lay on almost every significant word, and *emphasis of sense*, which we lay on particular words, to distinguish them from the rest of the sentence.

The importance of emphasis to the right delivery of thoughts in speech must be obvious on the slightest reflection. " Go and ask how old Mrs. Brown is," said a father to his dutiful son. The latter hurried away, and soon returned with the report that Mrs. Brown had replied that "it was none of his business how old she was." The poor man had intended merely to inquire into the state of her health ; but he accidentally put a wrong emphasis on the word *old*.

Another instance of misapprehension will illustrate the importance of emphasis. A stranger from the country, observing an ordinary roller-rule on a table, took it up, and on asking what it was used for, was answered, "It is a rule for counting-*houses*." After turning it over and over, up and down, and puzzling his brain for some time, he at last, in a paroxysm of baffled curiosity, exclaimed : " How in the name of wonder do *you count houses with this ?*" If his informer had rightly bestowed his emphasis, the misconception of his meaning would not have taken place.

Emphasis and intonation must be left to the good sense and feeling of the reader If you *thoroughly understand*

and feel what you have to utter, and have your attention concentrated upon it, you will emphasize better than by attempting to conform your emphasis to any rules or marks dictated by one writer, and perhaps contradicted by another.

A boy at his sports is never at a loss how to make his emphasis expressive. If he have to say to a companion, " I want your *bat*, not your *ball*," or " I'm going to *skate*, not to *swim*," he will not fail to emphasize and inflect the italicized words aright. And why? Simply because he knows what he means, and attends to it. Let the reader study to know what his reading-lesson means, and he will spend his time more profitably than in pondering over marks and rules of disputed application. It is for the teacher, by his oral example, to instil a realization of this fact into the minds of the young.

Dr. Whately, in his Treatise on Rhetoric, pointedly condemns the artificial system of teaching elocution by marks and rules, as worse than useless. His objections have been disputed, but never answered. They are : first, that the proposed system must necessarily be imperfect ; secondly, that if it were perfect, it would be a circuitous path to the object in view ; and, thirdly, that even if both these objections were removed, the object would not be effectually obtained.

He who not only understands fully what he is reading, but is earnestly occupying his mind with the matter of it, will be likely to read as if he understood it, and thus to make others understand it ; and, in like manner, he who not only feels it, but is exclusively absorbed with that feeling, will be likely to read as if he felt it, and communicate his impression to his hearers.

Exercises in Emphasis.

In their prosperity, my friends shall *never* hear of me ; in their adversity, *always*.

There is no possibility of speaking properly the ladguage of any passion without feeling it.

A book that is to be read requires one sort of style ; a man that is to speak, must use another.

A sentiment which, expressed diffusely, will barely be admitted to be just, expressed concisely will be admired as spirited.

Whatever may have been the origin of pastoral poetry, it is undoubtedly a natural and very agreeable form of poetical composition.

A stream that runs within its banks is a beautiful object, but when it rushes down with the impetuosity and noise of a torrent, it presently becomes a sublime one.

Those who complain of the shortness of life, let it slide by them without wishing to seize and make the most of its golden minutes. The more we do, the more we can do; the more busy we are, the more leisure we have.

> This without those, obtains a vain employ;
> Those without this, but urge us to destroy.

> The generous buoyant spirit is a power
> .Which in the virtuous mind doth all things conquer.
> It bears the hero on to arduous deeds;
> It lifts the saint to heaven.

> To err is human; to forgive, divine.

INFLECTION.

WITH regard to the Inflections of the voice, upon which so much has been said and written—there are, in reality, but two—the *rising* and the *falling*. The compound, or circumflex inflection, is merely that in which the voice both rises and falls on the same word—as in the utterance of the word " What !" when it is intended to convey an expression of disdain, reproach, or extreme surprise.

The inflections are not termed *rising* or *falling* from the high or low tone in which they are pronounced, but from the upward or downward slide in which they terminate, whether pronounced in a high or low key. The *rising* inflection was marked by Mr. Walker with the acute accent (´);

the *falling*, with the grave accent (ˋ). The inflection mark of the acute accent must not be confounded with its use in accentuation.

In the utterance of the interrogative sentence, "Does Cæsar deserve fame' or blameˋ?" the word *fame* will have the rising or upward slide of the voice, and *blame* the falling or downward slide of the voice. Every pause, of whatever kind, must necessarily adopt one of these two inflections, or continue in a monotone.

Thus it will be seen that the *rising* inflection is that upward turn of the voice which we use in asking a question, answerable by a simple *yes* or *no;* and the falling inflection is that downward sliding of the voice which is commonly used at the end of a sentence.

Lest an inaccurate ear should be led to suppose that the different signification of the opposing words is the reason of their sounding differently, we give below, among other examples, some phrases composed of the same words, which are nevertheless pronounced with exactly the same difference of inflection as the others.

EXAMPLES.

The Rising followed by the Falling.

Does he talk rationally', or irrationallyˋ?
Does he pronounce correctly', or incorrectlyˋ?
Does he mean honestly', or dishonestlyˋ?
Does she dance gracefully', or ungracefullyˋ?

The Falling followed by the Rising.

He talks rationallyˋ not irrationally'.
He pronounces correctlyˋ not incorrectly'.
He means honestlyˋ, not dishonestly'.
She dances gracefullyˋ, not ungracefully'.

The *rising* progression in a sentence *connects* what has been said with what is to be uttered, or what the speaker wishes to be implied, or supplied by the hearer; and this with more or less closeness, querulousness, and passion, in proportion to the extent and force of the rise.

The *falling* progression *disconnects* what has been said from whatever may follow; and this with more or less completeness, exclusiveness, and passion, in proportion to the force and extent of the fall.

The *rising* inflection is thus, invariably associated with what is incomplete in sense; or if apparently complete, dependent on or modified by what follows; with whatever is relative to something expressed, or to be implied; and with what is doubtful, interrogative, or supplicatory.

The *falling* inflection, on the contrary, is invariably associated *with what is complete* and independent in sense, or intended to be received as such; with whatever is positive and exclusive; and with what is confidently assertive, dogmatical, or mandatory.

The *rising* inflection is thus, also, the natural intonation of all attractive sentiments; of love, admiration, pity, &c., as in the exclamations, "Beautiful' I Alas' I Poor thing' !" The *falling* inflection is the tone of repulsion, anger, hatred, and reproach, as in the exclamations, "Go' I Fool' I Malediction' !"

A great number of rules are given for the inflecting of sentences, or parts of sentences. To these rules there are many exceptions not enumerated by their framers. The rules, if used at all, must therefore be used with extreme caution, or they will mislead; and the reader who undertakes to regulate his elocution by them will in many instances fall into error. We give below the rules that are least liable to exception; but even these must be received rather as *hints to guide the reader where he is in doubt*, than *rules* to hold where his understanding dictates the intonation most in accordance with the sense and spirit of what he is reading.

Where the sense is complete, whether at the termination of a sentence, or part of a sentence, use the *falling* inflection.

When sentences are divisable into two parts, the commencing part is *generally* distinguished by the rising inflection.

Questions commencing with an adverb or pronoun, and

2

which cannot be answered by a simple "*yes*" or "*no*," generally terminate with the *falling* inflection.

Questions commencing with a verb, and which cannot be answered by a simple "yes" or "no," generally terminate with the *rising* inflection.

When two or more questions in succession are separated by the disjunctive particle *or*, the last question requires the *falling* and the preceding ones the *rising* inflection.

The general rule for the parenthesis is, that it must be pronounced in a lower tone, and more rapidly than the rest of the sentence, and concluded with the inflection that immediately precedes it. A simile being a species of parenthesis, follows the same rule.

The title *echo* is adopted to express a repetition of a word or phrase. The echoing word is pronounced *generally* with the rising inflection, followed by something of a pause.

EXERCISES IN INFLECTION.

In the following pieces,—the first by Sir Walter Scott, and the second and third from Ossian,—exercises in modulation for two or three voices, or sets of voices, are given. By separating an entire class, and allotting to each group its part for imultaneous utterance, a good effect, with a little drilling, may be produced. Pupils will readily perceive that where the sense is incomplete, and the voice is suspended, the rising inflection is naturally used :

For two voices, or sets of voices.

(1st) Pibroch* of Donuil Dhu', (2d) pibroch of Donuil',
(1st) Wake thy wild voice anew, (2d) summon Clan-Conuil'.
(1st) Come away', come away' ! (2d) hark to the summons' !
1st) Come in your war-array', (2d) gentles and commons'.

---

* A pibroch (pronounced *pibrok*) is, among the Highlanders, a martial ir played with the bagpipe. The measure of the verse in this stanza re- .uires that in the third line the exclamation " Come away" should be -on-.ded as if it were a single word, having the accent on the first syllable -taus, *come'away*. So in the words *hill-plaid*, and *steel blade*, in the seventh and eighth lines. The license of rhyme requires that the *ai* in *plaid* should be pronounced long, as in *maid*.

(1st) Come from deep glen', (2d) and from mountains so
rocky',

(1st) The war pipe and pennon (2d) are at Inverlochy';

(1st) Come every hill-plaid', (2d) and true heart that wears
one',

(1st) Come every steel blade', (2d) and strong hand that bears
one'.

(1st) Leave untended the herd, (2d) the flock without shelter ;

(1st) Leave the corpse uninterred, (2d) the bride at the
altar';

(1st) Leave the deer, (2d) leave the steer, (1st) leave nets and
barges' ;

(All) Come with your fighting gear', broadswords and targes'.

(1st) Come as the winds come, (2d) when forests are rended' ;

(1st) Come as the waves come, (2d) when navies are stranded' ;

(1st) Faster come, faster come, (2d) faster' and faster',

(1st) Chief, (2d) vassal', (1st) page' and groom', (2d) tenant'
and master.

(1st) Fast they come', fast they come ; (2d) see how they
gather' !

(1st) Wide waves the eagle plume (2d) blended with heather'

(1st) Cast your plaids, (2d) draw your blades', (All) forward
each man set' !

(All) Pibroch of Donuil Dhu', knell for the onset' !

In the last line but one, the two words *man set* (meaning *man set in battle array*) should be sounded as a single word of two syllables, having the
accent on the first.

For three voices, or sets of voices.

(1st voice) As Autumn's dark storm'—(2d voice) pours from
the echoing hills'—(3d voice) echoing hills',—

(1st voice) so toward each other'—(2d voice) toward each
other approached'—(3d voice) approached the heroes'.

(1st voice) As two dark streams'—(2d voice) dark streams

from high rocks'—(3d voice) meet and mix, and
roar on the plain',—

(1st voice) loud, rough, and dark'—(2d voice) dark in battle'—(3d voice) in battle met Lochlin and In'nis-
fall'.

(1st voice) Chief mixed his blows with chief—(2d voice) and
man with man'—(3d voice) steel clanging, sounded
on steel'.

(1st voice) Helmets are cleft'—(2d voice) cleft on high—
(3d voice) Helmets are cleft on high'; blood bursts
and smokes around'.

(1st voice) As the troubled noise of the ocean'—(2d voice)
the ocean when roll the waves on high'; as the last
peal of the thunder of heaven'—(3d voice) the
thunder of heaven'; such is the noise of battle.

(1st voice) The groan'—(2d voice) the groan of the people'—
(3d voice) the groan of the people spreads over the
hills'.

(1st voice) It was like—(2d voice) like the thunder'—(3d
voice) like the thunder of night'—(All) It was like
the thunder of night, when the cloud bursts on
Cona', and a thousand ghosts' shriek at once' on the
hollow wind'.

(1st voice) The morning'—(2d voice) morning was gay'—
(3d voice) the morning was gay on Cromla',—

(1st voice) when the sons—(2d voice) sons of the sea'—
(3d voice) when the sons of the sea ascended'.

(1st voice) Calmar stood forth'—(2d voice) stood forth to
meet them',—(3d voice) Calmar stood forth to
meet them in the pride of his kindling soul'.

(1st voice) But pale'—(2d voice) pale was the face'—(3d
voice) but pale was the face of the chief, as he
leaned on his father's spear'.

(1st voice) The lightning—(2d voice) lightning flies'—(3d
voice) the lightning flies on wings of fire.

(1st voice) But slowly'—(2d voice) slowly now the hero falls'
—(3d voice) but slowly now the hero falls', like

the tree of hundred roots before the driving storm.

(1st voice) Now from the gray mists of the ocean' the white sailed ships of Fingal' * appear'.—(2d voice) High' —(3d voice) high is the grove of their masts' as they nod by turns on the rolling waves'.

(1st voice) As ebbs the resounding sea through the hundred isles of Inistore'—(2d voice) so loud'—(3d voice, so vast',—(1st voice) so immense',—(All) re turned the sons of Lochlin to meet the approaching foe'.

(1st voice) But bending',—(2d voice) weeping',—(3d voice) sad, and slow'—(All) sank Calmar, the mighty chief, in Cromla's lonely wood'.

(1st voice) The battle'—(2d voice) battle is past',—(3d voice) " The battle is past," said the chief.

(1st voice) Sad is the field'—(2d voice) sad is the field of Lena' !—(3d voice) .Mournful are the oaks of Cromla' !

(All) The hunters have fallen in their strength ! The sons of the brave are no more' !

(1st voice) As a hundred winds on Morven' ;—(2d voice) as the stream of a hundred hills' ;—(3d voice) as clouds successive fly over the face of heaven';

(1st voice) so vast',—(2d voice) so terrible',—(3d voice) so roaring'—

(All) the armies mixed on Lena's echoing plain'.

(1st voice) The clouds of—(2d voice) night came rolling down' ;—(3d voice) the stars of the north arise' over the rolling waves' : they show their heads of fire through the flying mists of heaven'.

(1st voice) "Spread the sail'," said the king'—(2d voice) Seize the winds as they pour from Lena' !"—(3d voice) We rose on the waves with songs !

(All)—We rushed with joy through the foam of the deep.

The humorous ode by Thomas Hood, addressed to his son,

---

* Here the acute accent is intended as a mark of accent, not of inflection.

aged three years and five months, contains numerous examples
of the parenthesis.

Thou happy, happy elf !
(But stop !—first let me kiss away that tea)—
Thou tĭny image of myself !
(My love, he's poking peas into his ear)—
Thou mĕrry laughing sprite ! with spirits feather light
Untouch'd by sŏrrŏw, and unsoil'd by sin—
(Good heavens ! the child is swallowing a pin !)

Thou little tricksy Puck
With antic toys so funnily bestuck,
Light as the singing-bird that wings the air,
(The door ! the door ! he'll tumble down the stair !)
Thou darling of thy sire !
(Why, Jane, he'll set his pinafore afire !)
Thou imp of mirth and joy !
In love's dear chain so strong and bright a link,
Thou idol of thy parents—(Drat the boy !
There goes my ink !)

Thou cherub—but of earth !
Fit playfellow for fays bv moonlight pale,
In harmless spŏrt and mirth,
(The dog will bite him if he pulls its tail !)
Thou human humming-bee, extracting honey
From every blossom in the world that blows,
Singing in youth's Elysium ever sunny,
(Another tumble—that's his precious nose !)
Thy father's pride and hope !
(He'll break the mirror with that skipping-rope !)
With pure heart newly stamp'd from nature's mint,
(Where *did* he learn that squint !)

Tŏss the light ball—bestride the stick,
(I knew so many cakes would make him sick !)
With fancies buoyant as the thistle down,
Prŏmpting the face grotesque, and antic brisk,

With many a lamb-like frisk,
(He's got the scissors, snipping at your gown!)

Fresh as the morn, and brilliant as its star,
(I wish that window had an iron bar!)
Bold as the hawk, yet gentle as the dove—
      (I'll tell you what, my love,
I cannot write unless he's sent above!)

EXERCISES IN ELOCUTION.
Spirited Declamation.

"He woke to hear his sentry's shriek—
  'To arms! They come! The Greek! the Greek.'"

"Strike—till the last arm'd foe expires;
  Strike—for your altars and your fires;
  Strike—for the green graves of your sires,
      God, and your native land."

      "Shout, Tyranny, shout,
Through your dungeons and palaces, 'Freedom is o'er.'"

      "On, ye brave,
Who rush to glory, or the grave!
Wave, Munich, all thy banners wave!
And charge with all thy chivalry!"

"Now for the fight—now for the cannon peal!
Forward—through blood, and toil, and cloud, and fire!
On, then, hussars! Now give them rein and heel!
  Think of the orphan child, the murdered sire.
Earth cries for blood. In thunder on them wheel,
This hour to Europe's fate shall set the triumph seal.

Gay, Brisk, and Humorous Description.

"Last came Jyo's estatic trial,
  He, with viny crown advancing,
  First to the lively pipe his hand address'd;
  But soon he saw the brisk, awakening viol,
  Whose sweet, entrancing sound he loved the best."

"I come, I come !—Ye have call'd me long,
I come o'er the mountains with light and song.
Ye may trace my step o'er the wakening earth,
By the winds which tell of the violet's birth."

" Then I see Queen Mab hath been with you.
———————— She comes,
In shape no bigger than an agate stone
On the forefinger of an alderman,
Drawn by a team of little atomies
Athwart men's noses, as they lie asleep ;
Her wagon-spokes made of long spinners' legs ;
The cover, of the wings of grasshoppers ;
The traces, of the smallest spider's web ;
The collars, of the moonshine's watery beams,
Her whip, of cricket's bone ; the lash, of film ;
Her wagoner, a small, gray-coated gnat,
Her chariot is an empty hazel-nut,
Made by the joiner squirrel, or old grub,
Time out of mind the fairies' coachmakers.
And in this state she gallops, night by night.
Sometimes she gallops o'er a courtier's nose,
And then dreams he of smelling out a suit ;
And sometimes comes she with a tithe-pig's tail,
Tickling a parson's nose as he lies asleep ;
Then dreams he of another benefice.
Sometimes she driveth o'er a soldier's neck ;
And then dreams he of cutting foreign throats,
Of breaches, ambuscadoes, Spanish blades,
Of healths five fathom deep ; and then anon
Drums in his ear ; at which he starts and wakes,
And, being thus frighten'd, mutters a prayer or two
And sleeps again."

Unimpassioned Narrative.

"There was a man in the land of Uz, whose name was Job,
and that man was perfect and upright, and one that feared
God and eschewed evil."

Dignified Sentiments.

" Sir, in the most express terms, I deny the competency of parliament to do this act. I warn you, do not dare to lay your hands on the constitution. I tell you that if, circumstanced as you are, you pass this act, it will be a nullity, and no man in Ireland will be bound to obey it. I make the assertion deliberately. I repeat it, and call on any man who tears me to take down my words. You have not been elected for this purpose. You are appointed to make laws, not legislatures."

Solemn and Impressive Thoughts.

" It must be so :—Plato, thou reasonest well,
Else whence this pleasing hope, this fond desire,
This longing after immortality ?
Or whence this secret dread, and inward horror,
Of falling into naught ? Why shrinks the soul
Back on herself, and startles at destruction ?
'Tis the divinity that stirs within us,
'Tis Heaven itself that points out an hereafter,
And intimates eternity to man.
Eternity ! thou pleasing, dreadful thought !
Through what variety of untried being,
Through what new scenes and changes must we pass !
The wide, the unbounded prospect lies before me ;
But shadows, clouds, and darkness, rest upon it."

Awe and Solemnity.

" To be, or not to be, that is the question :
Whether 'tis nobler in the mind to suffer
The slings and arrows of outrageous fortune,
Or to take arms against a sea of troubles,
And, by opposing, end them ? To die,—to sleep ;
No more ;—and, by a sleep, to say we end
The heart-ache, and the thousand natural shocks
That flesh is heir to ;—'tis a consummation
Devoutly to be wished. To die ;—to sleep ;—
To sleep ! perchance to dream ; ay, there's the rub ;
3*

For in that sleep of death, what dreams may come,
When we have shuffled off this mortal coil,
Must give us pause."

Deep Solemnity, Awe, Consternation.

"In thoughts from the visions of the night, when deep
sleep falleth on men, fear came upon me, and trembling, which
made all my bones to shake. Then a spirit passed before my
face. The hair of my flesh stood up. It stood still, but I
could not discern the form thereof. An image was before
mine eyes. There was silence, and I heard a voice : 'Shall
mortal man be more just than God?'"

Besides practising the examples as they are arranged on the
preceding pages, they should be so varied as to require a sudden transition of the voice from one extreme of intervals to
another. By this practice, the pupil may at any time, by deter-
mining the depth and grade of feeling, strike the appropriate
note with as much precision as the vocalist can, when execut-
ing any note of the scale.

The elements of impassioned utterance are many and various ; and although each one must be considered in an insulated
light, yet no one of them is ever heard alone ; no one ever
exists separately in correct and varied speech. They are
always applied in combination, and several are sometimes
combined in a single act of utterance. We may have under
one syllabic impulse, a long quantity, a wide interval, aspira-
tion, and some one of the modes of stress, all simultaneous in
effecting a particular purpose of expression.

As the sister Graces produce the most pleasing effect when
arranged in one family group, so an impassioned sentiment
may be most deeply and vividly impressed by the combination
of several vocal elements. This might be clearly illustrated
in cases of deep and overwhelming emotions, where the monotone will be found one of the essential constituents, combined
with long quantity, the lowest and deepest notes, slow movement, and partially suppressed force, in expressing this condition of the soul.

MONOTONE.

The monotone may be defined as that inflexible movement of the voice which is heard when fear, vastness of thought, force, majesty, power, or the intensity of feeling, is such as partially to obstruct the powers of utterance.

This movement of the voice may be accounted for by the fact that, when the excitement is so powerful, and the kind and degree of feeling are such as to agitate the whole frame, the vocal organs will be so affected, and their natural functions so controlled, that they can give utterance to the thought or sentiment only on one note, iterated on the same unvarying line of pitch.

Grandeur of thought, and sublimity of feeling are always expressed by this movement. The effect produced by it is deep and impressive. When its use is known, and the rule for its application is clearly understood, the reading will be characterized by a solemnity of manner, a grandeur of refinement, and a beauty of execution, which all will acknowledge to be in exact accordance with the dictates of Nature, and strictly within the pale of her laws. This will clearly be exemplified in reading the following extracts:

> "Vital spark of heavenly flame,
> Quit, oh, quit this mortal frame!
> Trembling, hoping, lingering, flying—
> Oh, the pain, the bliss of dying!
> Cease, fond nature, cease thy strife,
> And let me languish into life.

> "Hark! they whisper; angels say,
> 'Sister spirit, come away.'
> What is this absorbs me quite,
> Steals my senses, shuts my sight,
> Drowns my spirit, draws my breath?
> Tell me, my soul, can this be death?"

If the reader utter the thoughts and sentiments, in the last stanza of the above extract, with a just degree of impressiveness, he will appear as if he actually heard, saw, and felt, what the poet described the Christian as hearing, seeing, and feeling.   What constituent in vocal intonation, or what element in expression, enables the reader to give force and true coloring to the thoughts and sentiments in the passage just cited?   In what way can it be explained and made clear to the understanding?

The above extract, it will seem, is descriptive of a state of inconceivable solemnity, and expressive of the deepest feelings, the most solemn thoughts, and the most profound emotions; and the natural expression of such feelings, thoughts, and emotions, requires the monotone.

Why not, then, lay it down as a principle, that passages expressive of similar sentiments are to be read in a similar manner?

If any one fail to see and acknowledge the effect of the monotone in reading the above extract, let him read it again in the key of the monotone, and then without it; and if the difference in the effect be not very perceptible, let it be read to him, first on the key of the monotone, and then with the same stress, tone, quantity, inflection, and rate of movement that would be appropriate in reading the following extract from Prior:

> "Interr'd beneath the marble stone
> Lies sauntering Jack and idle Joan.
> While rolling threescore years and one
> Did round this globe their courses run,
> If human things went ill or well,
> If changing empires rose or fell,
> The morning pass'd, the evening came
> And found this couple still the same.
> They walk'd, and ate, good folks :—What then?
> Why then they walk'd and ate again.
> They soundly slept the night away;
> They did just nothing all the day:
> Nor good, nor bad, nor fools, nor wise,
> They would not learn, nor could advise.

> Without love, hatred, joy, or fear,
> They led—a kind of—as it were ;
> Nor wish'd, nor cared, nor laugh'd, nor cried ;
> And so they lived, and so they died."

If this measure leave him in doubt, if he then do not see how the monotone may be employed with effect, further efforts will be of no avail. He may be considered as belonging to hat "kind of—as it were" class of individuals, who have not the ability either to note faults and detect blemishes, or to define beauties and enumerate graces.

The force and beauty of the monotone may be further exemplified in the reading of some portions of the following extracts :

> "The bright sun was extinguish'd, and the stars
> Did wander darkling in the eternal space,
> Rayless and pathless ; and the icy earth
> Swung blind and blackening in the moonless air."

> "Eternity ! thou pleasing dreadful thought !
> Through what variety of untried being,
> Through what new scenes and changes, must we pass !
> The wide, the unbounded prospect lies before me ;
> But shadows, clouds, and darkness rest upon it."

> "Departed spirits of the mighty dead !
> Ye that at Marathon and Leuctra bled !
> Friends of the world ! restore your swords to man,
> Fight in his sacred cause, and lead the van."

"In the beginning, God created the heavens and the earth. And the earth was without form and void ; and darkness was upon the face of the deep : and the Spirit of God moved upon the face of the waters. And God said, 'Let there be light,' and there was light."

QUANTITY.

QUANTITY consists in the extended time of utterance, without changing the standard pronunciation of words. It is produced by a well-marked radical, a full volume of sound, and a clear lessening vanish. When it is well executed, the syllable will be kept free from a vapid, lifeless drawl.

The power of giving a gracefully extended quantity to syllables is not common. The principal source of difference between a good reader and a bad one lies in their varied degrees of ability in this respect.

Although writers on elocution seem, in a measure, to have overlooked quantity as an important element of expression, still it is one of the most important which a distinguished speaker employs in giving utterance to the sentiments of sublimity, dignity, deliberation, or doubt.

When judiciously applied and skilfully executed, it seems to spread a hue of feeling over the whole sentence. It gives that masterly finish, and that fine, delicate touch to the expression, which never fails to impress the deepest feeling, or to excite the most sweet and enchanting emotions.

A well-marked stress, and a gracefully extended time, form the basis of the most important properties of the voice such as gravity, depth of tone, volume, fulness of sound, smoothness, sweetness, and strength. If the mind were a pure intellect, without fancy, taste, or passion, the above-named function of the voice, which may properly enough be termed the *signature of expression*, would be uncalled for. But the case is widely different. The impassioned speaker, overpowered by his subject, and at a loss to find words to express the strength of his feelings, naturally holds on to and prolongs the tones of utterance, and thereby supplies any deficiency in the words themselves.

EXAMPLES IN QUANTITY.

" With woful measures, wan Despair—
  Low, sullen sounds his grief beguiled ;

A solemn, strange, and mingled air ;
   'Twas sad by fits ; by starts 'twas mild."

"Thou art, O God ! the life and light
   Of all this wondrous world we see ;
Its glow by day, its smile by night,
   Are but reflections caught from thee.
Where'er we turn, thy glories shine,
And all things bright and fair are thine."

"Spirit of Freedom ! when on Phyle's brow
   Thou sat'st with Thrasybulus and his train,
Couldst thou forebode the dismal hour that now
   Dims the green beauty of thine Attic plain ?"

"The stars shall fade away, the sun himself
Grow dim with age, and nature sink in years,
But thou shalt flourish in immortal youth
Unhurt, amidst the war of elements,
The wreck of matter, and the crash of worlds."

It is apparent that one predominating sentiment pervades
the whole of the above extracts. They are of a solemn, sublime, and dignified description ; and a gracefully extended
quantity diffused over the whole with evenness and continuity,
will bring out the sentiment in the most impressive manner.

Quantity is employed in giving utterance to feelings of malignity and emotions of hatred ; also in cases of irony, and in
those of affected mawkish sentimentality, and when so managed
that the clear lessening vanish shall blend with the full opening of the succeeding word, it will give a fine effect to that
morbid sensitiveness which exaggerates every feeling.

    "That lull'd them as the north wind does the sea."

"And do you now put on your best attire ?
And do you now cull out a holiday ?
And do you now strew flowers in his way,
That comes in triumph over Pompey's blood ?"

"The languid lady next appears in state,
Who was not born to carry her own weight ;

She lolls, reels, staggers, till some foreign aid
To her own stature lifts the feeble maid.
Then, if ordain'd to so severe a doom,
She, by just stages, journeys round the room;
But, knowing her own weakness, she despairs
To scale the Alps—that is, ascend the stairs.
'My fan!' let others say, who laugh at toil;
'Fan!' 'Hood!' 'Glove!' 'Scarf!' is her laconic style
And that is spoke with such a dying fall,
That Betty rather sees than hears the call;
The motion of her lips, and meaning eye,
Piece out the idea her faint words deny.
Oh, listen with attention most profound!
Her voice is but the shadow of a sound.
And help! oh, help! her spirits are so dead
One hand scarce lifts the other to her head.
If, there, a stubborn pin it triumph's o'er,
She pants! she sinks away! she is no more!
Let the robust, and the gigantic carve;
Life is not worth so much; she'd rather starve
But chew, she must herself. Ah! cruel fate
That Rosalinda can't by proxy eat."   Pope.

----------◆----------

RATE OR MOVEMENT OF THE VOICE.

The term *rate* or *movement of the voice* has reference to the rapidity or slowness of utterance. In good reading, the voice must be adapted to the varying indication of the sentiments in the individual words, and the rate must accommodate itself to the prevailing sentiment which runs through the whole paragraph.

Every one must perceive that the rate of the voice, in the utterance of humorous sentiments and in facetious description, is vastly different from that which is appropriate on occasions of solemn invocation.

The rates of movement which are clearly distinguishable in varied sentiment, may be denoted by the terms *slow, moderate, lively, brisk,* and *rapid.*

SLOW MOVEMENT.

Slow movement is exemplified in the expression of the deepest emotions; such as awe, profound reverence, melancholy, grandeur, vastness, and all similar sentiments.

In exercising the voice on the rates of movement, the examples illustrating the extremes should be read consecutively, for reasons which must be obvious to the teacher.

As several constituents of expression are frequently blended, especially in the utterance of dignified and impressive sentiments, it may not be amiss to take the same example, to illustrate the separate functions of the voice. Thus the passage from the book of Job, which we have already used to exemplify the principles in pitch and monotone, may serve to illustrate the lowest and deepest notes, long quantity and slow movement, because all these are blended in giving force and true expression to the sentiment.

Reverence.

"Thy awe-imposing voice is heard—we hear it !
The Almighty's fearful voice ! Attend !
It breaks the silence and in solemn warning speaks."

Melancholy.

"With eyes upraised, as one inspired,.
Pale Melancholy sat retired,
And from her wild sequestered seat,
In notes by distance made more sweet,
Pour'd through the mellow hour her pensive soul."

"The hills,
Rock-ribb'd and ancient as the sun,—the vales,
Stretching in pensive quietness between,—
The venerable woods,—rivers that move
In majesty,—and the complaining brooks,
That make the meadows green,—and, pour'd round all,
Old ocean's gray and melancholy waste,—
Are but the solemn decorations all
Of the great tomb of man.'

Profound Solemnity.

" Leaves have their time to fall,
　And flowers to wither at the north wind's breath,
　And stars to set—but all,
　Thou hast all seasons for thine own, O Death !

Grandeur—Vastness.

" Roll on, thou deep and dark blue ocean, roll !
　Ten thousand fleets sweep over thee in vain. . . .

" Thou glorious mirror, where the Almighty's form
　Glasses itself in tempests ; in all time,
　Calm or convulsed—in breeze, or gale, or storm,—
　Icing the pole, or in the torrid clime
　Dark heaving,—boundless, endless, as sublime,—
　The image of Eternity, the throne
　Of the Invisible,—even from out thy slime
　The monsters of the deep are made. Each zone
　Obeys thee. Thou goest forth, dread, fathomless, alone."

MODERATE MOVEMENT.

Moderate movement is the usual rate of utterance in ordinary, unimpassioned narration, as in the following extract—

" Stranger, if thou hast learn'd a truth which needs
　Experience more than reason,—that the world
　Is full of guilt and misery,—and hast known
　Enough of all its crimes and cares
　To tire thee of it,—enter this wild wood,
　And view the haunts of Nature."

LIVELY MOVEMENT.

This rate of the voice is exemplified in giving utterance to a moderate degree of joyful and vivid emotions, as in the following extracts :

" Now, my co-mates and brothers in exile,
　Hath not old custom made this life more sweet
　Than that of painted pomp ? Are not these woods

More free from peril than the envious court?
Here feel we but the penalty of Adam,—
The seasons' difference, as, the icy fang
And churlish chiding of the wintry wind,
Which, when it bites and blows upon my body,
Even till I shrink with cold, I smile and say,
'This is no flattery.' These are counsellors
That feelingly persuade me what I am.
Sweet are the uses of adversity,
Which, like the toad, ugly and venomous,
Wears yet a precious jewel in his head;
And this our life, exempt from public haunt,
Finds tongues in trees, books in the running brooks,
Sermons in stones, and good in every thing:
I would not change it.

BRISK MOVEMENT.

This rate of the voice is employed in giving utterance to
gay, sprightly, humorous, and exhilarating emotions; as in
the following examples:

"But, oh! how alter'd was its sprightlier tone,
    When Cheerfulness, a nymph of healthiest hue,
        Her bow across her shoulder flung,
        Her buskins gemm'd with morning dew,
    Blew an inspiring air, that dale and thicket rung
The hunter's call, to Faun and Dryad known!"

"Last came Joy's estatic trial,
He, with viny crown advancing
    First to the lively pipe his hand address'd;
But soon he saw the brisk, awakening viol,
Whose sweet, entrancing voice he loved the best."

"I come, I come!—ye have call'd me long;—
I come o'er the mountain with light and song,
Ye may trace my step o'er the wakening earth
By the winds which tell of the violet's birth,
By the primrose stars in the shadowy grass,
By the green leaves opening as I pass."

"Joy, joy ! forever, my task is done,
   The gates are pass'd and heaven is won."

RAPID MOVEMENT.

This movement of the voice is the symbol of violent anger,
confusion, alarm, fear, hurry, and is generally employed in
giving utterance to those incoherent expressions which are
thrown out when the mind is in a state of perturbation ; as
may be exemplified in parts of the following extracts :

"Next Anger rush'd.   His eyes, on fire,
   In lightning owned his secret stings ;
   In one rude clash he struck the lyre,
   And swept with hurried hands the strings."

"When, doff'd his casque, he felt free air
   Around 'gan Marmion wildly stare :
   'Where's Harry Blount ? Fitz-Eustace, where ?
   Linger ye here, ye hearts of hare !
   Redeem my pennon—charge again !
   Cry, "Marmion, to the rescue !"—Vain !
   Last of my race, on battle-plain
   That shout shall ne'er be heard again !
   Yet my last thought is England's.   Fly,
   Fitz-Eustace, to Lord Surrey hie.
   Tunstall lies dead upon the field ;
   His life-blood stains the spotless shield ;
   Edmund is down—my life is reft—
   The admiral alone is left.
   Let Stanley charge, with spur of fire,
   With Chester charge, and Lancashire,
   Full upon Scotland's central host,
   Or victory and England's lost.
   Must I bid twice ?   Hence, varlets ! fly,
   Leave Marmion here alone—to die.' "

"He woke—to hear his sentry's shriek—
   'To arms ! They come ! The Greek ! the Greek !'
   He woke—to die 'midst flame and smoke,

And shout, and groan, and sabre stroke,
And death-shots falling thick and fast,
As lightnings from the mountain cloud,
And heard, with voice as trumpet loud,
    Bozzaris cheer his band ;—
  'Strike—till the last arm'd-foe expires !
  Strike—for your altars and your fires !
  Strike—for the green graves of your sires,
    God, and your native land' "

" Back to thy punishment,
  False fugitive ! and to thy speed add wings ;
  Lest, with a whip of scorpions, I pursue
  Thy lingerings, or with one stroke of this dart,
  Strange horror seize thee, and pangs unfelt before !"

" This day's the birth of sorrows ! This hour's work
Will breed proscriptions. Look to your hearths, my lords,
For there henceforth shall sit, for household gods,
Shapes hot from Tartarus !—all shames and crimes :
Wan Treachery, with his thirsty dagger drawn ;
Suspicion, poisoning his brother's cup ;
Naked Rebellion, with the torch and axe,
Making his wild sport of your blazing thrones,
'Till Anarchy comes down on you like Night
And Massacre seals Rome's eternal grave."

SEMITONE.

(Plaintiveness of speech, or the semitonic movement.)

In ascending the musical scale, if the tone of the voice, in moving from the seventh space to the eighth, be compared to the utterance of a plaintive sentiment, their identity will be perceived. The interval from the seventh to the eighth is a semitone.

Every one knows a plaintive utterance, and the pupil may at any time discriminate a semitone, and hit its interval by affecting a plaintive expression.

Subjects of pathos and tenderness, uttered on any pitch,

high or low, are capable of being sounded with this marked plaintiveness of character. Let the pupil devote much time to this subject. He must acquire the power of transferring its plaintiveness to any interval, in order to give a just coloring to expressions which call for its use.

This movement of the voice is a very frequent element in expression, and performs high offices in speech. It is used in expressions of grief, pity, and supplication. It is the natural and unstudied language of sorrow, contrition, condolence, commiseration, tenderness, compassion, mercy, fondness, vexation, chagrin, impatience, fatigue, pain, with all the shades of difference which may exist between them. It is appropriate in the treatment of all subjects which appeal to human sympathy.

When the semitone is united with quantity and tremor, the force of the expression is greatly increased. The tremulous semitonic movement may be used on a single word, the more emphatically to mark its plaintiveness of character; or it may be used in continuation through a whole sentence, when the speaker, in the ardor of distressful and tender supplication, would give utterance to the intensity of his feelings.

EXAMPLES IN PLAINTIVE UTTERANCE.

"My mother! when I heard that thou wast dead,
Say, wast thou conscious of the tears I shed?
Hover'd thy spirit o'er thy sorrowing son,
Wretch even then, life's journey just begun?
I heard the bell toll on thy burial day;
I saw the hearse that bore thee slow away;
And, turning from my nursery window, drew
A long, long sigh, and wept a last adieu.
But was it such? It was. Where thou art gone,
Adieus and farewells are a sound unknown."

"Would I had never trod this English earth,
Or felt the flatteries that grow upon it.
Ye have angels' faces, but Heaven knows your hearts,—
I am the most unhappy woman living."

"MOURNFULLY! Oh, mournfully
   This midnight wind doth sigh,
Like some sweet, plaintive melody,
   Of ages long gone by!
It speaks a tale of other years—
   Of hopes that bloom'd to die—
Of sunny smiles that set in tears,
   And loves that mouldering lie!

"Mournfully! Oh, mournfully
   This midnight wind doth moan!
It stirs some chord or memory
   In each dull, heavy tone;
The voices of the much-loved dead
   Seem floating thereupon—
All, all my fond heart cherish'd
   Ere death hath made it lone."   MOTHERWELL.

"WELL knows the fair and friendly moon
   The band that Marion leads—
The glitter of their rifles,
   The scampering of their steeds.
'Tis life our fiery barbs to guide
   Across the moonlight plains;
'Tis life to feel the night-wind
   That lifts their tossing manes.
A moment in the British camp—
   A moment—and away,
Back to the pathless forest,
   Before the peep of day.

"Grave men there are by broad Santee,
   Grave men with hoary hairs,
Their hearts are all with Marion,
   For Marion are their prayers.
And lovely ladies greet our band,
   With kindliest welcoming,
With smiles like those of summer,
   And tears like those of spring

For them we wear these trusty arms,
  And lay them down no more
Till we have driven the Briton
  Forever from our shore."   BRYANT.

ALAS! for the rarity
Of Christian charity
  Under the sun!
Oh! it was pitiful!
Near a whole city full,
  Home she had none.

Sisterly, brotherly,
Fatherly, motherly,
  Feelings had changed:
Love, by harsh evidence,
Thrown from its eminence:
Even God's providence
  Seeming estranged.

Where the lamps quiver
So far in the river,
  With many a light,
From window and casement,
From garret to basement,
She stood with amazement,
  Houseless by night.

The bleak winds of March
  Made her tremble and shiver;
But not the dark arch,
  Or the black flowing river:
Mad from life's history,
Glad to death's mystery
  Swift to be hurl'd—
Anywhere, anywhere,
  Out of the world!   T. HOOD.

THE PAST.

How wild and dim this life appears !
  One long, deep, heavy sigh,
When o'er our eyes, half closed in tears,
The images of former years
  Are faintly glittering by !
  And still forgotten while they go !
As on the sea-beach, wave on wave,
  Dissolves at once in snow,
The amber clouds one moment lie,
  Then, like a dream, are gone !
Though beautiful the moonbeams play
On the lake's bosom, bright as they,
And the soul intensely loves their stay,
Soon as the radiance melts away,
  We scarce believe it shone !
Heaven-airs amid the harp-strings dwell,
  And we wish they ne'er may fade—
They cease—and the soul is a silent cell,
  Where music never play'd !
Dreams follow dreams, thro' the long night-hours,
  Each lovelier than the last ;
But, ere the breath of morning-flowers,
  That gorgeous world flies past ;
And many a sweet angelic cheek,
Whose smiles of fond affection speak,
  Glides by us on this earth ;
While in a day we cannot tell
Where shone the face we loved so well
  In sadness, or in mirth !   WILSON.

WHERE ARE THE DEAD?

WHERE are the mighty ones of ages past,
Who o'er the world their inspiration cast,—
Whose memories stir our spirits like a blast ?
             Where are the dead ?

3

Where are old empire's sinews snapp'd and gone?
Where is the Persian? Mede? Assyrian?
Where are the kings of Egypt? Babylon?
                              Where are the dead?

Where are the mighty ones of Greece? Where be
The men of Sparta and Thermopylæ?
The conquering Macedonian, where is he?
                              Where are the dead?

THE CHARGE OF THE SIX HUNDRED.

HALF a league, half a league,
  Half a league onward,
All in the valley of Death,
  Rode the six hundred.
"Forward, the Light Brigade!"
"Charge for the guns!" he said:
Into the valley of Death
  Rode the six hundred.

"Forward, the Light Brigade!"
Was there a man dismay'd?
Not though the soldier knew
  Some one had blunder'd!
Flash'd all their sabres bare,
Flash'd as they turn'd in air,
Sabring the gunners there,
Charging an army, while
  All the world wonder'd:
Plunged in the battery smoke,
Right through the line they broke;
  Cossack and Russian
Reel'd from the sabre-stroke
  Shatter'd and sunder'd.
Then they rode back, but not—
  Not the six hundred.   TENNYSON.

GIVE ME THREE GRAINS OF CORN.

GIVE me three grains of corn, mother,
    Only three grains of corn,
It will keep the little life I have,
    Till the coming of the morn.
I am dying of hunger and cold, mother,
    Dying of hunger and cold,
And half the agony of such a death
    My lips have never told.

THE LEAVES.

THE leaves are dropping, dropping,
    And I watch them as they go ;
Now whirling, floating, stopping,
    With a look of noiseless woe.
Yes, I watch them in their falling,
    As they tremble from the stem,
With a stillness so appalling—
    And my heart goes down with them !

Yes, I see them floating round me
    'Mid the beating of the rain,
Like the hopes that still have bound me,
    To the fading past again.
They are floating through the stillness,
    They are given to the storm—
And they tremble off like phantoms
    Of a joy that has no form.   A. S. STEPHENS.

HE is gone on the mountain, he is lost to the forest,
Like a summer-dried fountain, when our need was the sorest ,
The fount, reappearing, from the rain-drops shall borrow,
But to us comes no cheering, to Duncan no morrow !
The hand of the reaper takes the ears that are hoary,
But the voice of the weeper wails manhood in glory :

The autumn winds rushing waft the leaves,that are serest,
But our flower was in flushing when blighting was nearest
Fleet foot on the correi, sage counsel in cumber,
Red hand·in the·foray, how sound is thy slumber !
Like the dew on the mountain, like the foam on the river,
Like the bubble on the fountain, thou art gone, and forever
                                                  Scott.

THE FIRST CRUSADERS BEFORE JERUSALEM.

" JERUSALEM ! Jerusalem !"   The blessed goal was won :
On Siloe's brook and Sion's mount, as stream'd the setting sun,
Uplighted in his mellow'd glow, far o'er Judea's plain,
Slow winding toward the holy walls, appear'd a banner'd
    train.

Forgot were want, disease, and death, by that impassion'd
        throng,
The weary leapt, the sad rejoiced, the wounded knight grew
        strong ;
One glance at holy Calvary outguerdon'd every pang,
And loud from thrice ten thousand tongues the glad hosannas
    rang.

But yet—and at that galling thought, each brow was bent in
        gloom—
The cursed badge of Mahomet sway'd o'er the Saviour's
        tomb :
Then from unnumber'd sheaths at once, the beaming blades
        upstream'd,
Vow'd scabbardless till waved the cross above that tomb
    redeem'd.

But suddenly a holy awe the vengeful clamor still'd,
As sinks the storm before His breath, whose word its rising
        will'd ;
For conscience whisper'd, the same soil where they so proudly
        stood,
The Son of Man had trod abased, and wash'd with tears and
        blood.

Then dropp'd the squire his master's shield, the serf dash'd
    down his bow,
And, side by side with priest and peer, bent reverently and
    low,
While sunk at once each pennon'd spear, plumed helm and
    flashing glaive,
Like some wide waste of reeds bow'd down by Nilus' swollen
    wave.

LAMENT FOR THE DEATH OF OWEN ROE O'NEILL.

THOUGH it break my heart to hear, say again the bitter words,
"From Derry against Cromwell he march'd to measure swords;
But the weapon of the Saxon, met him on his way,
And he died at Lough Oughter, upon St. Leonard's day!"

Wail, wail ye for the mighty one! wail, wail ye for the dead!
Quench the hearth and hold the breath—with ashes strew
    the head.
How tenderly we loved him! how deeply we deplore!
But to think—but to think, we shall never see him more!

Sagest in the council was he, kindest in the hall,
Sure we never won a battle—'twas Owen won them all.
Had he lived—had he lived—our dear country had been free;
But he's dead—but he's dead—and 'tis slaves we'll ever be.

Wail, wail him through the Island! Weep, weep for our
    pride!
Would that on the battle-field our gallant chief had died!
Weep the Victor of Benburb—weep him, young man and old;
Weep for him, ye women—your Beautiful lies cold!

We thought you would not die—we were sure you would
    not go,
And leave us in our utmost need to Cromwell's cruel blow—
Sheep without a shepherd, when the snow shuts out the sky—
Oh! why did you leave us, Owen? Why did you die?

Soft as woman's was your voice, O'Neill! bright was your eye.
Oh! why did you leave us, Owen? why did you die?
Your troubles are all over, you're at rest with God on high;
But we're slaves, and we're orphans, Owen!—why did you die?

THOMAS DAVIS.

THE WEXFORD MASSACRE.

They knelt around the Cross divine,
  The matron and the maid—
They bow'd before redemption's sign
  And fervently they pray'd—
Three hundred fair and helpless ones,
  Whose crime was this alone—
Their valiant husbands, sires, and sons,
  Had battled for their own.

Had battled bravely, but in vain—
  The Saxon won the fight;
And Irish corses strew'd the plain
  Where Valor slept with Right.
And now that man of demon guilt
  To fated Wexford flew—
The red blood reeking on his hilt,
  Of hearts to Erin true!

He found them there—the young, the old—
  The maiden and the wife;
Their guardians brave, in death were cold,
  Who dared for *them* the strife—
They pray'd for mercy.   God on high!
  Before Thy cross they pray'd,
And ruthless Cromwell bade them die
  To glut the Saxon blade.

Three hundred fell—the stifled prayer
  Was quench'd in woman's blood;
Nor youth nor age could move to spare
  From slaughter's crimson flood.

But nations keep a stern account
    Of deeds that tyrants do ;
And guiltless blood to Heaven will mount,
    And Heaven avenge it, too !

M. J. BARRY.

ABOU BEN ADHEM.

ABOU BEN ADHEM (may his tribe increase)!
Awoke one night from a deep dream of peace,
And saw with the moonlight in his room,
Making it rich, and like a lily in bloom,
An angel, writing in a book of gold ;
Exceeding peace had made Ben Adhem bold ;
And to the presence in the room he said,
"What writest thou?" The vision raised his head,
And, with a look made all of sweet accord,
Answer'd, "The names of those who love the Lord."
"And is mine one?" said Abou. "Nay, not so,"
Replied the angel. Abou spoke more low,
But cheerly still ; and said, "I pray thee, then,
Write me as one that loves his fellow-men."
The angel wrote and vanish'd. The next night
It came again with great awakening light,
And show'd the names whom love of God had bless'd,
And lo ! Ben Adhem's name led all the rest.

LEIGH HUNT.

THERE is a reaper, whose name is Death,
    And, with his sickle keen,
He reaps the bearded grain at a breath,
    And the flowers that grow between.

"Shall I have nought that is fair?" saith he ;
    "Have nought but the bearded grain?
Though the breath of these flowers is sweet to me,
    I will give them all back again."

He gazed at the flowers with tearful eyes,
    He kiss'd their drooping leaves ;

It was for the Lord of Paradise
    He bound them in his sheaves.

"My Lord has need of these flowerets gay,"
    The reaper said, and smiled ;
"Dear tokens of the earth are they,
    Where he was once a child.

"They all shall bloom in fields of light,
    Transplanted by my care,
And saints, upon their garments white,
    These sacred blossoms wear."

Oh, not in cruelty, not in wrath,
    The reaper came that day ;
'T was an angel visited the earth,
    And took the flowers away.   LONGFELLOW

MENTAL BEAUTY.

THE shape alone let others prize,
    The features of the fair,
I look for spirit in her eyes,
    And meaning in her air.

A damask cheek, an ivory arm,
    Shall ne'er my wishes win ;
Give me an animated form,
    That speaks a mind within.

A face where lawful honor shines,
    Where sense and sweetness move,
And angel innocence refines
    The tenderness of love.

These are the soul of Beauty's frame,
    Without whose vital aid,
Unfinish'd all her features seem,
    And all her roses dead.   AKENSIDE.

THE SOLILOQUY OF KING RICHARD III.

GIVE me another horse :—bind up my wounds :—
Have mercy, Jesu :—soft : I did but dream ?—
O coward conscience, how dost thou afflict me !
The lights burn blue. It is now dead midnight.
What do I fear ? Myself ? There's none else by.
Richard loves Richard ; that is, I am I.
Is there a murderer here ? No : yes ; I am.
Then fly. What ? From myself ? Great reason ; why ?
Lest I revenge. What ? Myself on myself ?
I love myself. Wherefore ? For any good
That I myself have done unto myself ?
Oh, no ; alas ! I rather hate myself,
For hateful deeds committed by myself.
I am a villain : yet I lie ; I am not.
Fool, of thyself speak well :—fool, do not flatter :—
My conscience hath a thousand several tongues ;
And every tongue brings in a several tale ;
And every tale *condemns* me for a villain.
Perjury, perjury, in the highest degree,
Murder, stern murder, in the direst degree,
Throng to the bar, crying all, Guilty ! guilty !
I shall despair.—There is no creature loves me,
And, if I die, no soul will pity me :
Nay, wherefore should they ; since that I myself
Find in myself no pity to myself ?—
Methought the souls of all that I had murdered
Came to my tent, and every one did threat
To-morrow's vengeance on the head of Richard.

SHAKSPEARE

SPRING FLOWERS.

WHILE the trees are leafless,
    While the fields are bare,
Buttercups and daisies
    Spring up here and there.

3*

Ere the snow-drop peepeth,
  Ere the crocus bold,
Ere the early primrose
  Opes its paly gold,
Somewhere on a sunny bank,
  Buttercups are bright :
Somewhere 'mong the frozen grass
  Peeps the daisy white ;
Little hardy flowers,
  Like to children poor
Playing in their sturdy health
  By their mother's door ;
Purple with the north wind,
  Yet alert and bold ;
Fearing not and caring not,
  Though they be a-cold.   HOWITT.

THE MODERN BLUE-STOCKING.

In all the modern languages, she was
Exceedingly well versed, and had devoted
To their attainment, far more time than has,
By the best teachers, lately been allotted ;
For she had taken lessons, twice a week,
For a full month in each ; and she could speak
French and Italian, equally as well
As Chinese, Portuguese, or German ; and,
What is still more surprising, she could spell
Most of our longest English words, off hand :
Was quite familiar in low Dutch and Spanish,
And thought of studying modern Greek and Danish.

INVOCATION.

Tell me, my secret soul,
  Oh ! tell me, Hope and Faith,
Is there no resting-place
  From sorrow, sin, and death ?—

Is there no happy spot,
   Where mortals may be bless'd,
Where grief may find a balm,
   And weariness, a rest?
Faith, Hope, and Love, best boons to mortals given,
Waved their bright wings, and whisper'd,—"YES, IN HEAVEN!"
                    MACKAY.

TIME.

              THE year
Has gone, and, with it, many a glorious throng
Of happy dreams. Its mark is on each brow,
Its shadow in each heart. In its swift course,
It waved its sceptre o'er the beautiful,
And they are not. It laid its pallid hand
Upon the strong man, and the haughty form
Is fallen, and the flashing eye is dim.
It trod the hall of revelry, where throng'd
The bright and joyous, and the tearful wail
Of stricken ones, is heard where erst the song
And reckless shout resounded.
              G. D. PRENTICE.

POETASTERS.

"Shut, shut the door, good John!" fatigued, I said;
"Tie up the knocker; say I'm sick—I'm dead!"
The dog-star rages! nay, 'tis past a doubt
All Bedlam or Parnassus is let out:
Fire in each eye, and papers in each hand,
They rave, recite, and madden round the land.
What walls can guard me, or what shades can hide?
They pierce my thickets, through my grot they glide;
By land, by water, they renew the charge,
They stop the chariot, and they board the barge.
No place is sacred, not the church is free,
Even Sunday shines no Sabbath-day to me;
Then from the Mint walks forth the man of rhyme,
Happy to catch me just at dinner-time.
              POPE.

RICHARD'S RESIGNATION.

K. RICH. Too well, too well thou tell'st a tale so ill,
Where is the Earl of Wiltshire? Where is Bagot?
What is become of Bushy? Where is Green?
No matter where; of comfort no man speak;
Let's talk of graves, of worms, and epitaphs;
Make dust our paper, and with rainy eyes
Write sorrow on the bosom of the earth.
And yet not so—for what can we bequeath,
Save our deposed bodies to the ground?
Our lands, our lives, and all are Bolingbroke's;
And nothing can we call our own but death,
And that small morsel of the barren earth,
Which serves as paste and cover to our bones.
For heaven's sake, let us sit upon the ground,
And tell sad stories of the death of kings—
How some have been deposed; some slain in war;
Some haunted by the ghosts they have deposed;
Some poison'd by their wives; some sleeping, kill'd;
All murder'd. For within the hollow crown,
That rounds the mortal temples of a king,
Keeps Death his court; and there the antic sits,
Scoffing his state, and grinning at his pomp;
Allowing him a breath, a little scene
To monarchize, be fear'd, and kill with looks;
Infusing him with self and vain conceit,
As if this flesh, which walls about our life,
Were brass impregnable; and humor'd thus,
Comes at the last, and with a little pin
Bores through his castle walls; and, farewell, king!
Cover your heads, and mock not flesh and blood
With solemn reverence; throw away respect,
Tradition, form, and ceremonious duty,
For you have but mistook me all this while.
I live on bread, like you; feel want, like you;
Taste grief, need friends. Subjected thus,
How can you say to me, "I am a king?" SHAKSPEARE.

EVE'S REGRETS ON QUITTING PARADISE.

MUST I thus leave thee, Paradise ? thus leave
Thee, native soil ? these happy walks and shades,
Fit haunt of gods ! where I had hoped to spend,
Quiet, though sad, the respite of that day
That must be mortal to us both ! O flowers,
That never will in other climate grow,
My early visitation and my last
At even, which I bred up with tender hand
From the first opening bud, and gave ye names !
Who now shall rear ye to the sun, or rank
Your tribes, and water from the ambrosial fount ?
Thee, lastly, nuptial bower ! by me adorn'd
With what to sight or smell was sweet ! from thee
How shall I part, and whither wander down
Into a lower world, to this obscure
And wild ? How shall wo breathe in other air
Less pure, accustom'd to immortal fruits ? MILTON.

LOVE DUE TO THE CREATOR.

AND ask ye why He claims our love ?
   Oh, answer, all ye winds of even,
Oh, answer, all ye lights above,
   That watch in yonder darkening heaven ;
Thou earth, in vernal radiance gay
   As when His angels first array'd thee,
And thou, O deep-tongued ocean, say
   Why man should love the Mind that made thee !

There's not a flower that decks the vale,
   There's not a beam that lights the mountain,
There's not a shrub that scents the gale,
   There's not a wind that stirs the fountain,
There's not a hue that paints the rose,
   There's not a leaf around us lying,
But in its use or beauty shows
   True love to us, and love undying ! G. GRIFFIN

A Child's first Impression of a Star.

She had been told that God made all the stars
That twinkled up in heaven, and now she stood
Watching the coming of the twilight on,
As if it were a new and perfect world,
And this were its first eve.   How beautiful
Must be the work of nature to a child
In its first fresh impression !   Laura stood
By the low window, with the silken lash
Of her soft eye upraised, and her sweet mouth
Half parted with the new and strange delight
Of beauty that she could not comprehend,
And had not seen before.   The purple folds
Of the low sunset clouds, and the blue sky
That look'd so still and delicate above,
Fill'd her young heart with gladness, and the eve
Stole on with its deep shadows, and she still
Stood looking at the west with that half smile,
As if a pleasant thought were at her heart.
Presently, in the edge of the last tint
Of sunset, where the blue was melted in
To the first golden mellowness, a star
Stood suddenly.   A laugh of wild delight
Burst from her lips, and, putting up her hands,
Her simple thought broke forth expressively,—
" Father, dear father, God has made a star."

WILLIS.

The Carrier-Pigeon.

The bird, let loose in Eastern skies, when hastening fondly
    home,
Ne'er stoops to earth her wing, nor flies where idle warblers
    roam ;
But high she shoots through air and light, above all low delay,
Where nothing earthly bounds her flight, nor shadow dims
    her way.

So grant me, God, from every care and stain of passion free,
Aloft, through Virtue's purer air, to hold my course to thee;
No sin to cloud, no lure to stay my soul, as home she
    springs ;—
Thy sunshine on her joyful way, thy freedom in her wings !
                                                    MOORE.

POLYCARP, one of the fathers of the Christian Church, suffered martyr
dom at Smyrna, in the year of our Lord 167, during a general persecution
of the Christians.

"Go, lictor, lead the prisoner forth, let all the assembly stay,
For he must openly abjure his Christian faith to-day."
The prætor spake ; the lictor went, and Polycarp appear'd,
And totter'd, leaning on his staff, to where the pile was rear'd.
His silver hair, his look benign, which spake his heavenly lot,
Moved into tears both youth and age, but moved the prætor not.

The heathen spake : "Renounce aloud thy Christian heresy !"—
"Hope all things else," the old man cried, "yet hope not this
    from me."—
"But if thy stubborn heart refuse thy Saviour to deny,
Thy age shall not avert my wrath ; thy doom shall be—to
    die !"—
"Think not, O judge ! with menaces, to shake my faith in God ;
If in His righteous cause I die, I gladly kiss the rod."—

"Blind wretch ! doth not the funeral pile thy vaunting faith
    appall ?"—
"No funeral pile my heart alarms, if God and duty call."—
"Then expiate thy insolence ; ay, perish in the fire !
Go, lictor, drag him instantly forth to the funeral pyre !"
The lictor dragg'd him instantly forth to the pyre ; with bands
He bound him to the martyr's stake, he smote him with his
    hands.

"Abjure thy God," the prætor said, "and thou shalt yet be
    free."—
"No," cried the hero, "rather let death be my destiny !"

The prætor bow'd ; the lictor laid with haste the torches nigh ;
Forth from the fagots burst the flames, and glanced athwart
      the sky ;
The patient champion at the stake with flames engirdled stood,
Look'd up with rapture-kindling eye, and seal'd his faith in
      blood.

To the Passion Flower.

What though not thine the rose's brilliant glow,
   Or odor of the gifted violet,
   Or dew with which the lily's cheek is wet ;
Though thine would seem the pallid streaks of woe,
The drops that from the fount of sorrow flow,
   Thy purple tints·of shame ; though strange appear
   The types of torture thou art doom'd to wear ;
Yet blooms for me no hue like thine below.
   For from thee breathes the odor of a name;
Whose sweetness melts my soul and dims my eyes ;
   And in thy mystic leaves of woe and shame
I read a tale to which my heart replies
In voiceless throbbing and devoted sighs ;
   Death's darkest agony and mercy's claim,
And love's last words of grief are written in thy dyes.

To spend too much time in studies is sloth ; to use them
too much for ornament is affectation ; to make judgment
wholly by their rules is the humor of a scholar. They perfect nature, and are perfected by experience ; for natural
abilities require study, as natural plants need pruning ; and
studies themselves do give forth directions too much at
large, except they be bounded in by experience. Crafty
men contemn studies, simple men admire them, and wise men
use them ; for studies teach not their own use—this wise
men learn by observation. Read not to contradict and refute, not to believe and take for granted, but to weigh and
consider.   BACON.

ADVICE TO AN AFFECTED SPEAKER.

WHAT do you say?—What? I really do not understand you. Be so good as to explain yourself again.—Upon my word, I do not.—Oh, now I know: you mean to tell me it is a cold day. Why did you not say at once, "It is cold to-day?" If you wish to inform me it rains or snows, pray say, "It rains," "It snows;" or, if you think I look well, and you choose to compliment me, say, "I think you look well." "But," you answer, "that is so common, and so plain, and what everybody can say." Well, and what if they can? Is it so great a misfortune to be understood when one speaks, and to speak like the rest of the world? I will tell you what, my friend; you and your fine-spoken brethren want one thing—you do not suspect it, and I shall astonish you—you want common sense.

Nay, this is not all: you have something too much; you possess an opinion that you have more sense than others. That is the source of all your pompous nothings, your cloudy sentences, and your big words without a meaning. Before you accost a person, or enter a room, let me pull you by your sleeve and whisper in your ear, "Do not try to show off your sense; have none at all—that is your part. Use plain language, if you can; just such as you find others use, who, in your idea, have no understanding; and then, perhaps, you will get credit for having some." La Bruyère.

REMARKS TO TEACHERS.

It is of the utmost importance, in order to acquire a cor rect and elegant style of reading, frequently to refer the pupil to the Principles of Elocution, given in the First Part. These should be frequently reviewed, and the direc tions applied to the selections in Part Second.

THE FIFTH READER.

Part II.

SELECT LITERARY EXERCISES IN READING

1. CHARACTER OF COLUMBUS.

IRVING.

WASHINGTON IRVING was born in New York, April 3, 1783—died, 1860. As an historian and essayist, Irving had no superior and few equals among the men of his time. His "History of New York," written under the assumed name of Diedrich Knickerbocker; his "History of Columbus," and the "Sketch-Book," were among the earlier triumphs of his genius; but his last and greatest work is the "Life of Washington," concluded just before his death.

COLUMBUS was a man of great and inventive genius. The operation of his mind were energetic, but spasmodic; bursting forth at times with that irresistible force which characterizes intellect of such an order. His mind had grasped all kinds of knowledge connected with his pursuits; and though his information may appear limited at the present day, and some of his errors palpable, it is because knowledge, in his peculiar department of science, was but scantily developed in his time. His own discoveries enlightened the ignorance of that age; guided conjecture to certainty; and dispelled numerous errors with which he himself had been obliged to struggle.

2. His ambition was lofty and noble. He was full of high aspirations, and eager to wreathe his name with great achievements. It has been said that a mercenary feeling mingled with his views, and that his stipulations with the Spanish court were selfish and avaricious. The charge is inconsiderate and unjust. He aimed at dignity and wealth in the same lofty spirit which urged him to seek renown; but he staked them on

his discoveries, and measured them by the importance of the territories ceded to the Crown.

3. He asked nothing of the sovereigns but a command of the countries he hoped to give them, and a share of the profits to support the dignity of his command. The gains that promised to arise from his discoveries, he intended to appropriate in the same princely and pious spirit in which they were obtained. He contemplated works and achievements of benevolence and religion, vast contributions for the relief of the poor of his native city ; the foundation of churches, where masses should be said for the souls of the departed ; and armies for the recovery of the holy sepulchre in Palestine.

4. Columbus was a man of quick sensibility, liable to great excitement, to sudden and strong impressions, and powerful impulses. He was naturally irritable and impetuous, and keenly sensible to injury and injustice ; yet the quickness of his temper was counteracted by the benevolence and generosity of his heart. The magnanimity of his nature shone forth through all the troubles of his stormy career. Though continually insulted in his dignity, and braved in the exercise of his command ; though foiled in his plans and endangered in his person by the seditions of turbulent and worthless men, and that, too, at times when suffering under anxiety of mind and anguish of body sufficient to exasperate the most patient, he restrained his valiant and indignant spirit ; and, by the strong powers of his mind, brought himself to forbear, and reason, and even to supplicate : nor should we fail to notice how free he was from all feeling of revenge, how ready to forgive and forget, on the least signs of repentance and atonement. He has been extolled for his skill in controlling others ; but far greater praise is due to him for the firmness he displayed in mastering himself.

5. His magnanimous benignity made him accessible to all kinds of pleasurable sensations from external objects. In his letters and journals, instead of detailing circumstances with the technical precision of a mere navigator, he depicts the beauties of nature with the enthusiasm of a poet or a painter.

6. His piety was sincere ; religion mingled with the whole course of his thoughts and actions, and shines forth in all his

most private and unstudied writings. Whenever he made any great discovery, he celebrated it by solemn thanks to God. The voice of prayer and melody of praise rose from his ships when they first beheld the New World, and his first action on landing was to prostrate himself upon the earth and return hanks.

7. With all the visionary fervor of his imagination, its fondest dreams fell short of reality. He died in ignorance of the real grandeur of his discovery. Until his last breath he entertained the idea that he had merely opened a new way to the old resorts of opulent commerce, and had discovered some of the wild regions of the East. He supposed Hispaniola to be the ancient Ophir which had been visited by the ships of Solomon, and that Cuba and Terra Firma were but remote parts of Asia.

8. What visions of glory would have broken upon his mind could he have known that he had indeed discovered a new continent, equal to the whole of the Old World in magnitude, and separated by two vast oceans from all the earth hitherto known by civilized man! And how would his magnanimous spirit have been consoled, amidst the afflictions of age and the cares of penury, the neglect of a fickle public, and the injustice of an ungrateful king, could he have anticipated the splendid empires which were to spread over the beautiful world he had discovered; and the nations, and the tongues, and languages which were to fill its lands with his renown, and to revere and bless his name to the latest posterity!

---

2. The Landing of Columbus.

ROGERS.

Samuel Rogers was born in England, in 1765, and died in 1855. His poetry has no strong claim to originality; but it is eminently characterized by the merits of good taste, refinement, and careful composition.

1. The sails were furl'd; with many a melting close,
   Solemn and slow the evening anthem rose,—
   Rose to the Virgin. 'Twas the hour of day
   When setting suns o'er summer seas display

A path of glory, opening in the west
To golden climes and islands of the blest;
And human voices on the silent air
Went o'er the waves in songs of gladness there!

2. Chosen of men! 'Twas thine at noon of night
First from the prow to hail the glimmering light:
(Emblem of Truth divine, whose secret ray
Enters the soul and makes the darkness day!)
"Pedro! Rodrigo! there methought it shone!
There—in the west! and now, alas, 'tis gone!—
'Twas all a dream! we gaze and gaze in vain!
But mark and speak not, there it comes again!
It moves!—what form unseen, what being there
With torch-like lustre fires the murky air?
His instincts, passions, say, how like our own!
Oh, when will day reveal a world unknown?"

3. Long on the deep the mists of morning lay;
Then rose, revealing as they rolled away
Half-circling hills, whose everlasting woods
Sweep with their sable skirts the shadowy floods:
And say, when all, to holy transport given,
Embraced and wept as at the gates of heaven,—
When one and all of us, repentant, ran,
And, on our faces, bless'd the wondrous man,—
Say, was I then deceived, or from the skies
Burst on my ear seraphic harmonies?

4. "Glory to God!" unnumber'd voices sung,—
"Glory to God!" the vales and mountains rung,
Voices that hail'd creation's primal morn,
And to the shepherds sung a Saviour born.
Slowly, bareheaded, through the surf we bore
The sacred cross, and kneeling kiss'd the shore.

---

3. PHILANTHROPY AND CHARITY.

DR. BROWNSON.

Dr. O. A. Brownson was born at Stockbridge, Vermont, Sept. 16, 1903.
He comes of an old New-England stock, and was brought up in the ways

of his Puritan ancestors. His youth and early manhood were passed in the
vain quest of religious truth, with his powerful intellect as his sole guide,
until, at length, by the blessing of God, he made his way to the saving
portals of the true Church. Since then, Dr. Brownson has devoted his
great talents to the service of Catholicity, and few men have done more
than he to make the truths of faith manifest to the unbeliever. As a
Catholic reviewer, he holds a high place in the world of letters; but it is
as a Christian philosopher, logician, and metaphysician, that he is known
to the learned of all nations. His fame is, indeed, universal, and his authority of the highest rank, as well east as west of the Atlantic.

1. THE natural *sentiment* of philanthropy is, at best, only
human love. This answers very well, when the work to be
done is simply to concoct grand schemes, make brilliant and
eloquent speeches, or when there are no disagreeable duties to
be performed, no violent natural repugnances to be overcome;
but it fails in the hour of severe trial. Your philanthropist
starts with generous impulses, with an ardent enthusiasm; and
so long as there are no great discouragements, no disgusting
offices in his way, and he has even a small number of admiring
friends to stimulate his zeal, applaud his eloquence, flatter his
vanity, and soften the rebuffs which a hard world gives him, he
may keep on his course, and continue his task.

2. But let him find himself entirely alone, let him have no
little public of his own, which is all the world to him, let him
be thwarted on every point, let him be obliged to work in
secret, unseen by all but the All-seeing Eye, encounter from
men nothing but contradiction, contempt, and ingratitude, and
he will soon begin to say to himself, Why suffer and endure so
much for the unworthy?   He who loves man for man's sake,
loves only a creature, a being of imperfect worth, of no more
worth than himself,—perhaps not so much; and why shall he
love him more than himself, and sacrifice himself for him?
The highest stretch of human love is, to love our neighbor *as*
we love ourselves; and we do injustice to ourselves, when we
love them more than we do ourselves.

3. Nay, philanthropy itself is a sort of selfishness. It is a
sentiment, not a principle. Its real motive is not another's
good, but its own satisfaction according to its nature. It
seeks the good of others, because the good of others is the
means of its own satisfaction, and is as really selfish in its
principle as any other of our sentiments; for there is a broad·

distinction between the *sentiment* of philanthropy, and the *duty* of doing good to others,—between seeking the good of others from sentiment, and seeking it in obedience to a law which binds the conscience.

4. The measure of the capacity of philanthropy, as a sentiment, is the amount of satisfaction it can bring to the possessor. So long as, upon the whole, he finds it more delightful to play the philanthropist than the miser, for instance, he will do it, but no longer. Hence, philanthropy must always decrease just in proportion to the increase of the repugnances it must encounter, and fail us just at the moment when it is most needed, and always in proportion as it is needed. It follows the law so observable in all human society, and helps most when and where its help is least needed. Here is the condemnation of every scheme, however plausible it may look, that in any degree depends on philanthropy for its success.

5. The principle the Associationists want for their success is not philanthropy,—the love of man for man's sake,—but divine charity, not to be had and preserved out of the Catholic Church. Charity is, in relation to its subject, a supernaturally infused virtue; in relation to its object, the supreme and exclusive love of God for his own sake, and man for the sake of God. He who has it, is proof against all trials; for his love does not depend on man, who so often proves himself totally unamiable and unworthy, but on God, who is always and everywhere infinitely amiable and deserving of all love. He visits the sick, the prisoner, the poor, for it is God whom he visits; with tenderness he clasps the leprous to his bosom, and kisses their sores, for it is God whom he embraces and whose wounds he kisses. The most painful and disgusting offices are sweet and easy, because he performs them for God, who is love, and whose love inflames his heart. Whenever there is a service to be rendered to one of God's little ones, he runs with eagerness to do it; for it is a service to be rendered to God himself.

6. "Charity never faileth." It is proof against all natural repugnances; it overcomes earth and hell; and brings God down to tabernacle with men. Dear to it is this poor beggar,

for it sees in him only our Lord who had "not where to lay his head ;" dear are the sorrowing and the afflicted, for it sees in them Him who was "a man of sorrows and acquainted with infirmity ;" dear are these poor outcasts, for in them it beholds Him who was "scorned and rejected of men ;" dear are the wronged, the oppressed, the down-trodden, for in them it beholds the Innocent One nailed to the Cross, and dying to atone for human wickedness.

7. And it joys to succor them all ; for in so doing, it makes reparation to God for the poverty, sufferings, wrongs, contempt, and ignominious death which he endured for our sakes ; or it is his poverty it relieves in relieving the poor, his hunger it feeds in feeding the hungry, his nakedness it clothes in throwing its robe over the naked, his afflictions its consoles in consoling the sorrowing, his wounds into which it pours oil and wine and which it binds up. "Inasmuch as ye did it unto the least of these, my brethren, ye did it unto me."

8. It does all things for God, whom it loves more than men, more than life, and more than heaven itself, if to love Him and heaven were not one and the same thing. This is the principle you need ; with this principle, you have God with you and for you, and to fail is impossible. But with this principle, Association is, at best, a matter of indifference ; for this is sufficient of itself at all times, under any and every form of political, social, or industrial organization. He who has God can have nothing more.

---

4. LOVE FOR THE CHURCH.

DR. BROWNSON.

1. God, in establishing his Church from the foundation of the world, in giving his life on the cross for her, in abiding always with her, in her tabernacles, unto the consummation of the world, in adorning her as a Bride with all the graces of the Holy Spirit, in denominating her his Beloved, his Spouse, has taught us how he regards her, how deep and tender, now infinite and inexhaustible, his love for her, and with what love and

4

honor we should behold her. He loves us with an infinite love
and has died to redeem us ; but he loves us and wills our sal
vation, only in and through his Church. He would bring us
to himself, and he never ceases as a lover to woo our love;
but he wills us to love, and reverence, and adore him only as
children of his Beloved. Our love and reverence must redound
to his glory as her Spouse, and gladden her maternal heart,
and swell her maternal joy, or he wills them not, knows them not.

2. Oh, it is frightful to forget the place the Church holds
in the love and providence of God, and to regard the relation
in which we stand to her as a matter of no moment ! She is
the one grand object on which are fixed all heaven, all earth,
ay, and all hell. Behold her impersonation in the Blessed
Virgin, the Holy Mother of God, the glorious Queen of heaven.
Humble and obscure she lived, poor and silent, yet all heaven
turned their eyes towards her ; all hell trembled before her ;
all earth needed her. Dear was she to all the hosts of heaven ;
for in her they beheld their Queen, the Mother of grace, the
Mother of mercies, the channel through which all love, and
mercies, and graces, and good things were to flow to man, and
return to the glory and honor of their Father.

3. Humblest of mortal maidens, lowliest on earth, under
God, she was highest in heaven. So is the Church, our sweet
Mother. Oh, she is no creation of the imagination ! Oh, she
is no mere accident in human history, in divine providence, divine grace, in the conversion of souls ! She is a glorious, a
living reality, living the divine, the eternal life of God. Her
Maker is her Husband, and he places her, after Him, over all
in heaven, on the earth, and under the earth. All that he can
do to adorn and exalt her, he has done. All he can give he
gives ; for he gives himself, and unites her in indissolubl
union with himself. Infinite love, infinite wisdom, infinite power,
can do no more.

4. All hail to thee, dear and ever-blessed Mother, thou
chosen one, thou well-beloved, thou Bride adorned, thou chaste,
immaculate Spouse, thou Universal Queen ! All hail to thee !
We honor thee, for God honors thee ; we love thee, for God
loves thee ; we obey thee, for thou ever commandest the will

of thy lord. The passers-by may jeer thee ; the servants of
the prince of this world may call thee black ; the daughters of
the uncircumcised may beat thee, earth and hell rise up in
wrath against thee, and seek to despoil thee of thy rich ornaments and to sully thy fair name ; but all the more dear art
thou to our hearts ; all the more deep and sincere the homage
we pay thee ; and all the more earnestly do we pray thee to
receive our humble offerings, and to own us for thy children,
and watch over us that we never forfeit the right to call thee
our Mother.

---

5. MARY, QUEEN OF MERCY.

MANGAN.

JAMES CLARENCE MANGAN.—Among the poets whom Ireland has produced within the last ten or fifteen years, Clarence Mangan deservedly
occupies a high place. As a translator, he was unequalled: he translated
from the Irish, the French, the German, the Spanish, the Italian, the Danish, and the Eastern languages, with such a versatile facility as not only
to transfuse into his own tongue the substance of the original, but the
graces of style and ornament, and idiomatic expression, which are peculiar
to the poetry of every country. He frequently surpassed the originals in
the fluency of his language. Many of the poems called " translations," are
entirely his own.—*Ballads of Ireland.*

1. THERE lived a knight long years ago,
     Proud, carnal, vain, devotionless ;
   Of God above, or hell below,
       He took no thought, but, undismay'd,
     Pursued his course of wickedness.
       His heart was rock ; he never pray'd
     To be forgiven for all his treasons ;
     He only said, at certain seasons,
         " O Mary, Queen of Mercy !"

2. Years roll'd, and found him still the same,
     Still draining Pleasure's poison-bowl ;
   Yet felt he now and then some shame ;
       The torment of the Undying Worm
     At whiles woke in his trembling soul ;
       And then, though powerless to reform,

Would he, in hope to appease that sternest
Avenger, cry, and more in earnest,
  "O Mary, Queen of Mercy!"

8. At last Youth's riotous time was gone,
   And Loathing now came after Sin.
   With locks yet brown, he felt as one
       Grown gray at heart; and oft, with tears,
     He tried, but all in vain, to win
       From the dark desert of his years
   One flower of hope; yet, morn and evening,
   He still cried, but with deeper meaning,
       "O Mary, Queen of Mercy!"

4. A happier mind, a holier mood,
   A purer spirit ruled him now:
   No more in thrall to flesh and blood,
       He took a pilgrim-staff in hand,
     And, under a religious vow,
       Wended his way to Pommerland;
   There enter'd he an humble cloister,
   Exclaiming, while his eyes grew moister,
       "O Mary, Queen of Mercy!"

5. Here, shorn and cowl'd, he laid his cares
   Aside, and wrought for God alone.
   Albeit he sang no choral prayers,
       Nor matin hymn nor laud could learn,
     He mortified his flesh to stone;
       For him no penance was too stern;
   And often pray'd he on his lonely
   Cell-couch at night, but still said only,
       "O Mary, Queen of Mercy!"

6 They buried him with mass and song
   Aneath a little knoll so green;
   But, lo! a wonder-sight!—Ere long
       Rose, blooming, from that verdant mound
     The fairest lily ever seen;
       And, on its petal-edges round

Relieving their translucent whiteness,
Did shine these words, in gold-hued brightness,
 " O Mary, Queen of Mercy !"

7. And, would God's angels give thee power,
 Thou, dearest reader, mightst behold
The fibres of this holy flower
 Upspringing from the dead man's heart,
 In tremulous threads of light and gold ;
 Then wouldst thou choose the better part,
And thenceforth flee Sin's foul suggestions ;
Thy sole response to mocking questions,
 " O Mary, Queen of Mercy !"

6. Religious Memorials.

SIR HUMPHREY DAVY.

Sir Humphrey Davy—an eminent English philosopher and chemist of the present century. Author of some very interesting books of travel.

1. The rosary, which you see suspended around my neck, is a memorial of sympathy and respect for an illustrious man. I was passing through France, in the reign of Napoleon, by the peculiar privilege granted to a *savant*, on my road to Italy. I had just returned from the Holy Land, and had in my possession two or three of the rosaries which are sold to pilgrims at Jerusalem, as having been suspended in the Holy Sepulchre. Pius VII. was then in imprisonment at Fontainebleau. By a special favor, on the plea of my return from the Holy Land, I obtained permission to see this venerable and illustrious pontiff. I carried with me one of my rosaries.

2. He received me with great kindness. I tendered my services to execute any commissions, not political ones, he might think fit to intrust me with, in Italy, informing hi 1 that I was an Englishman : he expressed his thanks, but declined troubling me. I told him that I was just returned from the Holy Land ; and, bowing, with great humility, offered him my rosary from the Holy Sepulchre.

3. He received it with a smile, touched it with his lips, gave

his benediction over it, and returned it into my hands, supposing, of course, that I was a Roman Catholic. I had meant to
present it to his Holiness ; but the blessing he had bestowed
upon it, and the touch of his lips, made it a.precious relic to
me ; and I restored it to my neck, round which it has ever
since been suspended. . . . . "We shall meet again ; adieu :"
and he gave me his paternal blessing.

4. It was eighteen months after this interview, that I went
out, with almost the whole population of Rome, to witness and
welcome the triumphal entry of this illustrious father of the
Church into his capital. He was borne on the shoulders of
the most distinguished artists, headed by Canova : and never
shall I forget the enthusiasm with which he was received ; it
is impossible to describe the shouts of triumph and of rapture
sent up to heaven by every voice. And when he gave his
benediction to the people, there was a universal prostration, a
sobbing, and marks of emotion and joy, almost like the bursting of the heart. I heard everywhere around me cries of
"The holy father ! the most holy father ! His restoration is
the work of God !"

5. I saw tears streaming from the eyes of almost all the
women about me, many of whom were sobbing hysterically,
and old men were weeping as if they were children. I pressed
my rosary to my breast on this occasion, and repeatedly
touched with my lips that part of it which had received the kiss
of the most venerable pontiff. I preserve it with a kind of
hallowed feeling, as the memorial of a man whose sanctity,
firmness, meekness, and benevolence, are an honor to his
Church and to human nature : and it has not only been useful
to me, by its influence upon my own mind, but it has enabled
me to give pleasure to others ; and has, I believe, been some
times beneficial in insuring my personal safety.

6. I have often gratified the peasants of Apulia and Cala-
bria, by presenting them to kiss a rosary from the Holy Sepulchre, which had been hallowed by the touch of the lips and
benediction of the Pope : and it has even been respected by,
and procured me a safe passage through, a party of brigands,
who once stopped me in the passes of the Apennines.

7. The Convert.

BURNETT.

Mr. P H. Burnett has filled, with much honor, the highest position in the judiciary of Oregon Territory; and later, the gubernatorial chair of California. As a writer, he is learned, clear-sighted, calm, and exact. On his conversion to the Catholic Church, he published his work entitled, "The Path which led a Protestant Lawyer into the Church," a book of considerable merit.

1. He has embraced a higher grade of faith, has been brought into closer and holier communion with the unseen world, and has adopted a more just and charitable estimate of human veracity. He has taken a step towards the Celestial City, from the low, murky valleys of discord, where the fogs of error do love to dwell. He shakes hands with the brethren of every kind, name, and tongue. He worships with the people of every nation. He joins his prayers with those who speak the varied languages of earth. On every shore, in every land, beneath every sky, and in every city, he meets his brethren of the universal Church. He is at home everywhere, and bows down with the millions who have worshipped, and still worship, at the same altar, and hold the same faith.

2. This is not all. He traverses the records of all history, and goes back, link after link, by an indubitable chain, to the apostolic day. He has no chasms to leap, no deserts to cross. At every step in this progress he finds the same Old Church— the same faith—the same worship still pre-eminent in the Christian world. He sees the rise and fall of empires and sects; but the same Old Church always pre-eminent. The records of the past are with him. He has the sanction of antiquity. Time tells for him a glorious story. He meets with myriads of brethren all along the slumbering ages. The old martyrs and saints are his brethren. He claims companionship with them. Their memories are beloved by him.

3. And Blandina, the poor slave, but noblest of martyrs, was his sister. And old Ignatius, and Polycarp, and Justin, and Irenæus, are also his brethren. And she, the humblest of the humble—the purest of the pure—the stainless Virgin Mother of his Lord, whom all generations call "blessed," is

revered by him as the noblest of creatures. And the old Apostles—the noble and the true—the holy and the just—the despised and persecuted—they, too, are his brethren. In short, the saints and martyrs of the olden time held the same faith, worshipped at the same altar, and used the same form of worship that he does. He loves and venerates their memory, admires their virtues, calls them brethren, and asks their prayers in heaven. He has no accusations to bring against them—no crimes to lay to their charge.

4. But besides all this, his faith is sustained by a logical power, and a Scriptural proof, that cannot be fairly met and confuted. It is sustained by every plain and luminous principle upon which society and government are founded. His reason, his common sense, the best feelings of his nature, the holiest impulses of his heart, all satisfy him beyond a doubt, that he is in the right.

> "When all the blandishments of life are gone—
> When tired dissimulation drops her mask,
> And real and apparent are the same;"

when eternity, with all its mighty consequences, rolls up its endless proportions before the dying vision—ah! then, no Catholic asks to change his faith! Oh, give me the last sacraments of the Church! Let me die in her holy communion! Let me be buried in consecrated ground! Let my brethren pray for me!

---

8. LANGUAGE OF A MAN OF EDUCATION.

COLERIDGE.

SAMUEL TAYLOR COLERIDGE, an English poet, died in 1834, aged 62. He was one of the remarkable men of his times, and exerted a wide and deep intellectual influence on minds of the highest class. He was decidedly an original poet, and a critic of unrivalled excellence. Coleridge's life was not what the admirers of his genius could have wished.

1. WHAT is that which first strikes us, and strikes us at once, in a man of education? and which, among educated men, so instantly distinguishes the man of superior mind, that (as was observed with eminent propriety of the late Edmund

Burke) "we cannot stand under the same archway during a shower of rain, *without finding him out?*"

2. Not the weight or novelty of his remarks; not any unusual interest of facts communicated by him; for we may suppose both the one and the other precluded by the shortness of our intercourse, and the triviality of the subjects The difference will be impressed and felt, though the conversation should be confined to the state of the weather or the pavement.

3. Still less will it arise from any peculiarity in his words and phrases. For, if he be, as we now assume, a *well-educated man*, as well as a man of superior powers, he will not fail to follow the golden rule of Julius Cæsar, *Avoid an unusual word as you would a rock;* unless where new things necessitate new terms. It must have been among the earliest lessons of his youth, that the breach of this precept, at all times hazardous, becomes ridiculous in the topics of ordinary conversation.

4. There remains but one other point of distinction possible; and this must be, and in fact is, the true cause of the impression made on us. It is the unpremeditated and evidently habitual *arrangement* of his words, grounded on the habit of foreseeing, in each integral part, or, more plainly, in every sentence, the whole that he then intends to communicate. However irregular and desultory his talk, there is *method* in the fragments.

5. Listen, on the other hand, to an ignorant man, though perhaps shrewd and able in his particular calling; whether he be describing or relating. We immediately perceive that his memory alone is called into action; and that the objects and events recur in the narration in the same order, and with the some accompaniments, however accidental or impertinent, as they had first occurred to the narrator.

6. The necessity of taking breath, the efforts of recollection, and the abrupt rectification of its failures, produce all his pauses; and with exception of the "*and then,*" the "*and there,*" and the still less significant "*and so,*" they constitute likowise all his connections.

9. LANGUAGE.

HOLMES.

O. W. HOLMES—an American poet of the day. He possesses much humor and genial sentiment, and his style is remarkable for its purity and exquisite finish. He possesses the happy talent of blending ludicrous ideas with fancy and imagination. His lyrics sparkle with mirth, and his serious pieces arrest the attention by touches of genuine pathos and tenderness. "Terpsichore," "Mania," and "Poetry," are among his longest and best pieces.

1. SOME words on Language may be well applied ;
   And take them kindly, though they touch your pride.
   Words lead to things ; a scale is more precise,—
   Coarse speech, bad grammar, swearing, drinking, vice
   Our cold Northeaster's icy fetter clips
   The native freedom of the Saxon lips :
   See the brown peasant of the plastic South,
   How all his passions play about his mouth !
   With us, the feature that transmits the soul,
   A frozen, passive, palsied breathing-hole.

2. The crampy shackles of the ploughboy's walk
   Tie the small muscles, when he strives to talk ;
   Not all the pumice of the polish'd town
   Can smooth this roughness of the barnyard down ;
   Rich, honor'd, titled, he betrays his race
   By this one mark—he's awkward in the face ;—
   Nature's rude impress, long before he knew
   The sunny street that holds the sifted few.

3. It can't be help'd ; though, if we're taken young,
   We gain some freedom of the lips and tongue :
   But school and college often try in vain
   To break the padlock of our boyhood's chain ;
   One stubborn word will prove this axiom true—
   No late-caught rustic can enunciate *view*.[1]

---

[1] The poet here humorously alludes to the difficulty which many persons, bred in retirement, find in pronouncing this word correctly. It will be difficult to express in letters the manner in which it is fre-

4. A few brief stanzas may be well employ'd
To speak of errors we can all avoid.
Learning condemns beyond the reach of hope
The careless churl that speaks of sŏap for sōap ;
Her edict exiles from her fair abode
The clownish voice that utters rŏad for rōad ;
Less stern to him who calls his cŏat a cōat,
And steers his bŏat believing it a bōat.
She pardon'd one, our classic city's boast,
Who said, at Cambridge, mŏst instead of mōst ;
But knit her brows, and stamp'd her angry foot,
To hear a teacher call a root[1] a root.[2]

5. Once more : speak clearly, if you speak at all ;
Carve every word before you let it fall ;
Don't, like a lecturer or dramatic star,
Try over hard to roll the British R ;
Do put your accents in the proper spot ;
• Don't—let me beg you—don't say " How ?" for " What ?"
And when you stick on conversation's burs,
Don't strew the pathway with those dreadful urs.[3]

---

10. THE INDIANS.

STORY.

JOSEPH STORY.—In 1811, Joseph Story was appointed Associate Justice of the Supreme Court of the United States, and held the office with
much ability until his death in 1845. His principal literary writings are
contained in a collection of his discourses, reviews, and miscellanies.

1. THERE is, in the fate of these unfortunate beings, much
to awaken our sympathy, and much to disturb the sobriety of

---

quently mispronounced, but it is a sound somewhat similar to vŏ.
The proper pronunciation is vŭ. They, also, who give the second
sound of o in the words soap, road, coat, boat, and most, come in for a
small share of his lash.
[1] Rŏot.   [2] Root (rŭt).
[3] The drawling style in which many persons are in the habit of
talking, heedlessly hesitating to think of a word, and the mean-
while supplying its place by the unmeaning syllable "ur," is here

our judgment; much which may be urged to excuse their own atrocities; much in their characters which betray us into an involuntary admiration. What can be more eloquent than their history? By a law of nature they seemed destined to a slow but sure extinction. Everywhere at the approach of the white man they fade away. We hear the rustling of their footsteps, ike that of the withered leaves of autumn, and they are gone forever.

2. They pass mournfully by us, and they return no more. Two centuries ago, and the smoke of their wigwams, and the fires of their councils rose in every valley, from the Hudson Bay to the farthest Florida, from the ocean to the Mississippi and the lakes. The shouts of victory and the war-dance rang through the mountains and the glades. The thick arrows and the deadly tomahawk whistled through the forests; and the hunter's trace and dark encampment startled the wild beasts in their lairs. The warriors stood forth in their glory. The young listened to the song of other days. The mothers played with their infants, and gazed on the scene with warm hopes of the future. The aged sat down, but they wept not; they should soon be at rest in finer regions, where the Great Spirit dwells, in a home prepared for the brave beyond the western skies.

3. Braver men never lived; truer men never drew the bow. They had courage, and fortitude, and sagacity, and perseverance beyond most of the human race. They shrank from no dangers, and they feared no hardships. If they had the vices of savage life, they had its virtues also. They were true to their country, their friends, and their homes. If they forgave not injury, neither did they forget kindness. If their vengeance was terrible, their fidelity and generosity were unconquerable also. Their love, like their hatred, stopped not this side of the grave.

4. But where are they? Where are the villagers and war-

---

happily condemned. Such habits may easily be corrected by a little presence of mind, and particularly by following the direction, Think twice before you speak once.

riors and youth; the sachems and the tribes; the hunters and their families? They have perished; they are consumed. The wasting pestilence has not alone done the mighty work. No, nor famine—nor war; there has been a mightier power; a moral canker, which has eaten into their heart cores---a plague, which the touch of the white man communicated--a poison which betrayed them to lingering ruin. The winds of the Atlantic fan not a single region which they may call their own. Already the last feeble remnant of their race are preparing for their journey beyond the Mississippi. I see them leave their miserable homes—the aged, the helpless, the men, and the warriors—"few and faint, yet fearless still." ·

5. The ashes are cold upon their native hearths. The smoke no longer curls around their lowly cabins. They move on with slow unsteady steps. The white man is upon their heels for terror or dispatch, but they heed him not. They turn to take a last look of their desolate villages. They cast a last glance upon the graves of their fathers. They shed no tears; they utter no cry; they heave no groans. There is something in their hearts which passes speech. There is something in their looks, not of vengeance or submission, but of hard necessity, which stifles both; which chokes all utterance; which has no aim or method. It is courage absorbed by despair. They linger but a moment. Their look is onward.

6. They have passed the fatal stream. It shall never be repassed by them, no—never. Yet there lies not between us and them an impassable gulf. They know and feel that there is for them still one remove farther, not distant nor unseen. It is to the general burial-ground of their race.

7. Reason as we may, it is impossible not to read in such a fate much which we know not how to interpret; much of provocation to cruel deeds and deep resentments; much of apology for wrong and perfidy; much of pity mingling with indignation; much of doubt and misgiving as to the past much of painful recollections, much of dark forebodings.

11. INDIAN NAMES.

SIGOURNEY.

MRS. LYDIA H. SIGOURNEY is a popular American poetess. She has written no poem of length, but many of her fugitive pieces evince a light and agreeable poetic talent.

1. YE say, they all have pass'd away,
    That noble race and brave,
  That their light canoes have vanish'd
    From off the crested wave ;
  That 'mid the forests where they roam'd
    There rings no hunter's shout ;
  But their name is on your waters,
    You may not wash it out.

2. 'Tis where Ontario's billow
    Like Ocean's surge is curl'd,
  Where strong Niagara's thunders wake
    The echo of the world ;
  Where red Missouri bringeth
    Rich tributes from the West,
  And Rappahannock sweetly sleeps
    On green Virginia's breast.

3. Ye say, their cone-like cabins,
    That cluster'd o'er the vale,
  Have fled away like wither'd leaves
    Before the autumn gale ;
  But their memory liveth on your hills,
    Their baptism on your shore,
  Your everlasting rivers speak
    Their dialect of yore.

4. Old Massachusetts wears it
    Within her lordly crown,
  And broad Ohio bears it,
    Amid her young renown ;

Connecticut hath wreathed it
   Where her quiet foliage waves,
And bold Kentucky breathes it hoarse,
   Through all her ancient caves.

5. Wachusett hides its lingering voice
   Within his rocky heart,
And Alleghany graves its tone
   Throughout his lofty chart;
Monadnock on his forehead hoar
   Doth seal the sacred trust;
Your mountains build their monuments,
   Though ye destroy their dust.

---

12. St. Vincent, Deacon and Martyr.

MRS. ANNA JAMESON.

Mrs. Jameson was born in Dublin, A. D. 1797. "Her father, Mr. Murphy, an artist of merit, was painter in ordinary to the Princess Charlotte; and from his conversation and example she derived her enthusiasm for art and intimate acquaintance with its technicalities." Mrs. Jameson's numerous works on art are the most attractive in the English language. Her splendid series (one of the latest efforts of her genius), "Sacred and Legendary Art," "Legends of the Monastic Orders," and "Legends of the Madonna," has established her reputation, both as an artist and an author, beyond all competition in her own peculiar department. Mrs. Jameson is a Protestant, but her inspiration is of the loftiest and most Catholic. In her devoted and life-long researches she has attained to the sublime heights which the old masters trod, and there pays her graceful homage to the religion which was their inspiration.

1. This renowned saint and martyr of the early Christian Church has been most popular in Spain, the scene of his history, and in France, where he has been an object of particular veneration from the sixth century. It is generally allowed that the main circumstances of the history of Vincent, deacon of Saragossa, of his sufferings for the cause of Christ, and his invincible courage, expressed by his name, rest on concurrent testimony of the highest antiquity, which cannot be rejected.

2. He was born in Saragossa, in the kingdom of Aragon. Prudentius, in his famous Hymn, congratulates this city on

having produced more saints and martyrs than any other city
in Spain. During the persecution under Diocletian, the cruel
proconsul Dacian, infamous in the annals of Spanish martyrdom, caused all the Christians of Saragossa, men, women,
and children, whom he collected together by a promise of
immunity, to be massacred. Among these were the virgin
Engracia, and the eighteen Christian cavaliers who attended
her to death.

3. At this time lived St. Vincent : he had been early in
structed in the Christian faith, and with all the ardor of youth
devoted himself to the service of Christ. At the time of the
persecution, being not more than twenty years of age, he was
already a deacon. The dangers and the sufferings of the
Christians only excited his charity and his zeal ; and after
having encouraged and sustained many of his brethren in
the torments inflicted upon them, he was himself called to
receive the crown of martyrdom.

4. Being brought before the tribunal of Dacian, together
with his bishop, Valerius, they were accused of being Christians and contemners of the gods. Valerius, who was very
old, and had an impediment in his speech, answered to the
accusation in a voice so low that he could scarcely be heard.
On this, St. Vincent burst forth, with Christian fervor,—
"How is this, my Father ! canst thou not speak aloud, and
defy this pagan dog? Speak, that all the world may hear ;
or suffer me, who am only thy servant, to speak in thy
stead !"

5. The bishop having given him leave to speak, St. Vincent
stood forth, and proclaimed his faith aloud, defying the tortures with which they were threatened ; so that the Christians
who were present were lifted up in heart and full of gratitude
o God, and the wicked proconsul was in the same degree
filled with indignation. He ordered the old bishop to be
banished from the city ; but Vincent, who had defied him, he
reserved as an example to the rest, and was resolved to bend
him to submission by the most terrible and ingenious tortures
that cruelty could invent.

6. The young saint endured them unflinchingly. When his

body was lacerated by iron forks, he only smiled on his tormentors : the pangs they inflicted were to him delights ; thorns were his roses ; the flames a refreshing bath ; death itself was but the entrance to life.

7. They laid him, torn, bleeding, and half consumed by fire, on the ground strewn with potsherds, and left him there ; but God sent down his angels to comfort him ; and when his guards looked into the dungeon, they beheld it filled with light and fragrance ; they heard the angels singing songs of triumph, and the unconquerable martyr pouring forth his soul in hymns of thanksgiving. He even called to his jailers to enter and partake of the celestial delight and solace which had been vouchsafed to him ; and they, being amazed, fell upon their knees and acknowledged the true God.

8. But Dacian, perfidious as he was cruel, began to consider what other means might remain to conquer his unconquerable victim. Having tried tortures in vain, he determined to try seduction. He ordered a bed of down to be prepared, strewn with roses ; commanded the sufferer to be laid upon it, and allowed his friends and disciples to approach him. They, weeping, stanched his wounds, and dipped their kerchiefs in his flowing blood, and kissed his hands and brow, and besought him to live. But the martyr, who had held out through such protracted torments, had no sooner been laid upon the bed, than his pure spirit, disdaining as it were these treacherous indulgences, fled to heaven : the angels received him on their wings, and he entered into bliss eternal and ineffable.

---

13. THE SEVEN SLEEPERS OF EPHESUS.

MRS. JAMESON.

1. DURING the persecution under the Emperor Decius, there lived in the city of Ephesus seven young men, who were Christians : their names were Maximian, Malchus, Marcian, Dionysius, John, Serapion, and Constantine ; and as they refused to offer sacrifice to the idols, they were accused before the tribunal. But they fled and escaped to Mount Cœlian, where

they hid themselves in a cave. Being discovered, the tyrant ordered that they should roll great stones to the mouth of the cavern, in order that they might die of hunger. They, embracing each other, fell asleep.

2. And it came to pass in the thirtieth year of the reign of the Emperor Theodosius, that there broke out that dangerous heresy which denied the resurrection of the dead. The pious emperor, being greatly afflicted, retired to the interior of his palace, putting on sackcloth and covering his head with ashes: therefore, God took pity on him, and restored his faith by bringing back these just men to life—which came to pass in this manner :

3. A certain inhabitant of Ephesus, repairing to the top of Mount Cœlian to build a stable for his cattle, discovered the cavern ; and when the light penetrated therein, the sleepers awoke, believing that their slumbers had only lasted for a single night. They rose up, and Malchus, one of the number, was dispatched to the city to purchase food. He, advancing cautiously and fearfully, beheld to his astonishment the image of the cross surmounting the city gate. He went to another gate, and there he found another cross. He rubbed his eyes, believing himself still asleep, or in a dream ; and entering the city, he heard everywhere the name of Christ pronounced openly : and he was more and more confounded.

4. When he repaired to the baker's, he offered in payment an ancient coin of the time of the Emperor Decius, and they looked at him with astonishment, thinking that he had found a hidden treasure. And when they accused him, he knew not what to reply. Seeing his confusion, they bound him and dragged him through the streets with contumely ; and he looked round, seeking some one whom he knew, but not a face in all the crowd was familiar to him.

5. Being brought before the bishop, the truth was disclosed, to the great amazement of all. The bishop, the governor, and the principal inhabitants of the city, followed him to the entrance of the cavern, where the other six youths were found. Their faces had the freshness of roses, and the brightness of a holy light was around them. Theodosius himself, being in

formed of this great wonder, hastened to the cavern ; and one of the sleepers said to him, " Believe us, O Emperor ! for we have been raised before the Day of Judgment, in order that thou mightest trust in the Resurrection of the Dead !" And having said this, they bowed their heads and gave up their spirits to God. They had slept in their cavern for 196 years

6. Gibbon, in quoting this tradition, observes that it may be traced to within half a century of the date of the miracle. About the end of the sixth century, it was translated from the Syriac into the Latin, and was spread over the whole of western Christendom. Nor was it confined to the Christian world. Mahomet has introduced it, as a divine revelation, into the Koran. It has penetrated into Abyssinia. It has been found in Scandinavia ;—in fact, in the remotest regions of the Old World this singular tradition, in one form or another, appears to have been known and accepted.

7. The Seven Sleepers of Ephesus, extended in their cave side by side, occur perpetually in the miniatures, ancient sculpture, and stained glass of the thirteenth and fourteenth centuries. Thus they are represented in the frieze of the chapel of Edward the Confessor, at Westminster. In general, the name of each is written overhead.

14.—TIMES GO BY TURNS.

SOUTHWELL.

ROBERT SOUTHWELL was born, A. D. 1560, and underwent his martyrdom, A. D. 1595. Of all the hundred and twenty-eight Catholic priests put to death in Elizabeth's reign, not one was more worthy of pious commemoration. Descended from an ancient family in Norfolk, he was educated on the Continent, and became a Jesuit at Rome. While on the English mission, he resided chiefly at the house of Anne, countess of Arundel, who died in the Tower of London. He was thrown into prison in 1592, where he remained three years, during which time he was put on the rack ten several times. Nothing could be proved against him, except what he confessed :—that he was a Catholic priest, and prepared to die for his faith. Such was the condition of the dungeon in which Southwell suffered his long captivity, that his own father petitioned that he might be released from it, although but to die. On the 21st of February, 1595, he was hung, drawn, and quartered at Tyburn, being subjected, during a prolonged death, to those horrible tortures commonly undergone by the martyrs of that reign, tortures to which he replied only by repeatedly making the sign of the cross. Besides his poems, which possess a solid energy of diction, as well as a noble spiritual elevation, Southwell left behind him two works in prose, which abound in beauty and pathos, *Mary Magdalene's Funeral Tears,* and the *Triumphs over Death.*

1. THE lopped tree in time may grow again,
      Most naked plants renew both fruit and flower,
    The sorriest wight may find release of pain,
      The driest soil suck in some moistening shower.
    Time goes by turns, and chances change by course,
    From foul to fair, from better hap to worse.

2. The sea of Fortune doth not ever flow;
      She draws her favors to the lowest ebb;
    Her tides have equal times to come and go;
      Her loom doth weave the fine and coarsest web
    No joy so great but runneth to an end,
    No hap so hard but may in fine amend.

3. Not always fall of leaf, nor ever spring;
      Not endless night, yet not eternal day;
    The saddest birds a season find to sing;
      The roughest storm a calm may soon allay.
    Thus, with succeeding turns God tempereth all,
    That man may hope to rise, yet fear to fall.

4. A chance may win that by mischance was lost;
      That net that holds no great takes little fish;
    In some things all, in all things none are cross'd;
      Few all they need, but none have all they wish.
    Unmingled joys here to no man befall;
    Who least, hath some; who most, hath never all.

——————

15. CATHOLIC MISSIONS IN THE NORTHWEST.

EXTRACTS FROM BANCROFT'S HISTORY OF THE UNITED STATES.

GEORGE BANCROFT has written the only work that deserves the title of History of the United States. From a Catholic point of view some objections can be made to the first volumes, but on the whole it is a noble monument of the genius of the author and the genius of his country.—*Dr Brownson.*

Bancroft was born at Worcester, Massachusetts, October 3, 1800.

1. Religious zeal not less than commercial ambition had influenced France to recover Canada; and Champlain, its governor, whose imperishable name will rival with posterity the fame of Smith and Hudson, ever disinterested and compassionate, full of honor and probity, of ardent devotion and burning zeal, esteemed "the salvation of a soul worth more than the conquest of an empire."

2. Thus it was neither commercial enterprise nor royal ambition which carried the power of France into the heart of our Continent; the motive was religion. Religious enthusiasm founded Montreal, made a conquest of the wilderness of the upper lakes, and explored the Mississippi. The Roman (Catholic) Church created for Canada its altars, its hospitals, and its seminaries. . . . The first permanent efforts of French enterprise in colonizing America preceded any permanent English settlement on the Potomac.

3. Years before the pilgrims landed in Cape Cod, the Roman (Catholic) Church had been planted, by missionaries from France, in the eastern moiety of Maine; and Le Caron, an unambitious Franciscan, had penetrated the land of the Mohawks, had passed to the north of the hunting-grounds of the Wyandots, and, bound by his vows to the life of a beggar, had, on foot, or paddling a bark canoe, gone onward, and still onward, taking alms of the savages, till he reached the rivers of Lake Huron.

4. While Quebec contained scarcely fifty inhabitants, priests of the Franciscan Order—Le Caron, Fiel, Lagard —had labored for years as missionaries in Upper Canada, or made their way to the neutral Huron tribe that dwelt o the waters of the Niagara.

5. To confirm the missions, the first measure was the establishment of a college in New France, and the parents of th Marquis de Gamache, pleased with his pious importunity, assented to his entering the Order of the Jesuits, and added from their ample fortunes the means of endowing a Seminary for education at Quebec. Its foundation was laid, under happy auspices, in 1635, just before Champlain passed from among the living; and two years before the emigration of John Har-

vard, and one year before the General Court of Massachusetts had made provisions for a College.

6. The fires of charity were at the same time enkindled. The Duchess D'Aguillon, aided by her uncle, the Cardinal Richelieu, endowed a public hospital dedicated to the Son of God, whose blood was shed in mercy for all mankind. Its doors were opened, not only to the sufferers among the emigrants, but to the maimed, the sick, and the blind, of any of the numerous tribes between the Kennebec and Lake Superior; it relieved misfortune without asking its lineage. From the hospital nuns of Dieppe, three were selected, the youngest but twenty-two, to brave the famine and rigors of Canada in their patient mission of benevolence.

7. The same religious enthusiasm, inspiring Madame de la Peltier, a young and opulent widow of Alençon, with the aid of a nun of Dieppe and two others from Tours, established the Ursuline Convent for girls. . . . . Is it wonderful that the natives were touched by a benevolence which their poverty and squalid misery could not appall? Their education was attempted ; and the venerable ash-tree still lives beneath which Mary of the Incarnation, so famed for chastened piety, genius, and good judgment, toiled, though in vain, for the education of the Huron children.

8. The life of the missionary on Lake Huron was simple and uniform. The earliest hours, from four to eight, were absorbed in private prayer. The day was given to schools, visits, instructions in the catechism, and a service for proselytes. Sometimes, after the manner of St. Francis Xavier, Brebeuf would walk through the village and its environs ringing a little bell, and inviting the Huron braves and counsellors to a conference. There, under the shady forest, the most solemn mysteries of the Catholic faith were subject to discussion.

9. Yet the efforts of the Jesuits were not limited to the Huron race. Within thirteen years, the remote wilderness was visited by forty-two missionaries, members of the Society of Jesus, besides eighteen others, who, if not initiated, were yet chosen men, ready to shed their blood for their faith. Twice or thrice a year they all assembled at St. Mary's; during

the rest of the time they were scattered through the infidel tribes.

· 10. The first missionaries among the Hurons—Fathers De Brebeuf, Daniel, and Lallemand—all fell glorious martyrs to their devoted zeal. . . . . Father Reymbault soon after fell a victim to the climate, and died in Quebec (1642). His associate, Father Jogues, who with him had first planted the cross 'n Michigan, was reserved for a still more disastrous, though glorious, fate. He was taken prisoner by the fierce Mohawks, and was made to run the gauntlet at three different Mohawk villages.

11. For days and nights he was abandoned to hunger and every torment which petulant youth could contrive. But yet there was consolation;—an ear of Indian corn on the stalk was thrown to the good Father; and see, to the broad blade there clung little drops of dew, or of water—enough to baptize two captive neophytes. He had expected death; but the Mohawks, satisfied, perhaps, with his sufferings, or awed at his sanctity, spared his life, and his liberty was enlarged.

12. On a hill apart, he carved a long cross on a tree; and there, in the solitude, meditated the Imitation of Christ, and soothed his griefs by reflecting that he alone, in that vast region, adored the true God of earth and heaven. Roaming through the stately forests of the Mohawk valley, he wrote the name of Jesus on the bark of trees, engraved the cross, and entered into possession of these countries in the name of God—often lifting up his voice in a solitary chant. Thus did France bring its banner and its faith to the confines of Albany. The missionary himself was humanely ransomed from captivity by the Dutch, and sailing for France, soon returned to Canada.

13. Similar was the fate of Father Bressani. Taken prisoner while on his way to the Hurons; beaten, mangled, mutilated; driven barefoot over rough paths, through briers and thickets; scourged by a whole village; burned, tortured, wounded, and scarred;—he was an eye-witness to the fate of one of his companions, who was boiled and eaten. Yet some mysterious awe protected his life, and he, too, was humanely rescued by the Dutch.

16. Catholic Missions—*continued.*

1. In 1655, Fathers Chaumont and Dablon were sent on a mission among the tribes of New York. They were hospitably welcomed at Onondaga, the principal village of that tribe. A general convention was held at their desire ; and before the multitudinous assembly of the chiefs and the whole people gathered under the open sky, among the primeval forests, the presents were delivered ; and the Italian Jesuit, with much gesture after the Italian manner, discoursed so eloquently to the crowd, that it seemed to Dablon as if the word of God had been preached to all the nations of that land. On the next day, the chiefs and others crowded round the Jesuits with their songs of welcome.

2. "Happy land," they sang, "happy land, in which the Jesuits are to dwell !" and the chief led the chorus, "Glad tidings ! glad tidings ! It is well that we have spoken together : it is well that we have a heavenly message." At once a chapel sprung into existence, and by the zeal of the nation was finished in a day. "For marble and precious stones," writes Dablon, "we employed only bark ; but the path to heaven is as open through a roof of bark as through arched ceilings of silver and gold." The savages showed themselves susceptible of the excitements of religious ecstasy ; and there, in the heart of New York, the solemn services of the Roman (Catholic) Church were chanted as securely as in any part of Christendom.

3. The Cayugas also desired a missionary, and they received the fearless René Mesnard. In their village a chapel was erected, with mats for the tapestry ; and there the pictures of the Saviour and of the Virgin mother were unfolded to the admiring children of the wilderness. The Oneidas also listened to the missionary ; and early in 1657, Chaumont reached the most fertile and densely peopled lands of the Senecas. . . . . . The Jesuit priests published their faith from the Mohawk to the Genesee. . . . . The Missions stretched westward along Lake Superior to the waters of the Mississippi. Two young fur-traders, having travelled to the

West five hundred leagues, returned in 1656, attended by a number of savages from the Mississippi valley, who demanded missionaries for their country.

4. Their request was eagerly granted; and Gabriel Drenillettes, the same who carried the cross through the forests of Maine, and Leonard Gareau, of old a missionary among the Hurons, were selected as the first religious envoys to a land of sacrifices, shadows, and deaths. The canoes are launched; the tawny warriors embark; the oars flash, and words of triumph and joy mingle with their last adieus. But just below Montreal, a band of Mohawks, enemies to the Ottawas, awaited the convoy: in the affray Gareau was mortally wounded, and the fleet dispersed.

5. But the Jesuits were still fired with zeal to carry the cross westward. . . . . "If the Five Nations," they said, "can penetrate these regions, to satiate their passion for blood; if mercantile enterprise can bring furs from the plains of the Sioux; why cannot the cross be borne to their cabins!" . . . The zeal of Francis de Laval, the Bishop of Quebec, kindled with a desire himself to enter on the mission; but the lot fell to René Mesnard. He was charged to visit Green Bay and Lake Superior, and on a convenient inlet to establish a residence as a common place of assembly for the surrounding nations.

6. His departure was immediate (A. D. 1660), and with few preparations; for he trusted—such are his words—"in the Providence which feeds the little birds of the desert, and clothes the wild flowers of the forests." Every personal motive seemed to retain him in Quebec; but powerful instincts impelled him to the enterprise. Obedient to his vows, the aged man entered on the path that was red with the blood of his predecessors, and made haste to scatter the seeds of truth through the wilderness, even though the sower cast his seed in weeping. "In three or four months," he wrote to a friend, "you may add me to the *memento* of deaths."

7. His prediction was verified. Several months after, while his attendant was employed in the labor of transporting the canoe, he was lost in the forest, and never seen more. Long

afterwards, his cassock and breviary were kept as amulets
among the Sioux. . . . . . Similar was the death of the great
Father Marquette, the discoverer of the Mississippi. Joliet
returned to Quebec to announce the discovery. . . . . . The
unaspiring Marquette remained to preach the gospel to the
Miamis, who dwelt in the north of Illinois around Chicago.
Two years afterwards (A. D. 1675), sailing from Chicago to
Mackinaw, he entered a little river in Michigan.

8. Erecting an altar, he said mass after the rites of the
Catholic Church; then, begging the men who conducted his
canoe to leave him alone for a half-hour,

> "In the darkling wood,
> Amid the cool and silence, he knelt down
> And offered to the Mightiest solemn thanks
> And supplication."

At the end of half an hour they went to seek him, and he
was no more. The good missionary, discoverer of a new
world, had fallen asleep on the margin of the stream which
bears his name. Near its mouth the canoe-men dug his grave
in the sand. Ever after, the forest rangers, if in danger on
Lake Michigan, would invoke his name. The people of the
West will build his monument.

17. MARY STUART'S LAST PRAYER.

SMYTHE.

Rev. J. G. SMYTHE has written some of the sweetest ballads in the English language; those particularly in connection with the House of Stuart, are distinguished for their beauty and pathos.

1. A LONELY mourner kneels in prayer before the Virgin's face
   With white hands clasp'd for Jesus' sake—so her prayer
        may not be vain;
   Wan is her cheek, and very pale—her voice is low and faint,
   And tears are in her eyes the while she makes her humble
        plaint ·
   Oh, little could you deem, from her sad and humble mien,
   That she was once the Bride of France, and still was Scot
        land's Queen !

2. "O Mary mother! Mary mother! be my help and stay!
   Be with me still as thou hast been, and strengthen me
       to-day;
   For many a time, with heavy heart, all weary of its grief,
   I solace sought in thy blest thought, and ever found relief:
   For thou, too, wert a Queen on earth, and men were harsh
       to thee!
   And cruel things and rude they said, as they have said to me!

3. "Oh, gentlemen of Scotland! oh, cavaliers of France!
   How each and all had grasp'd his sword and seized his
       angry lance,
   If lady-love, or sister dear, or nearer, dearer bride,
   Had been like me, your friendless liege, insulted and belied!
   But these are sinful thoughts, and sad—I should not mind
       me now
   Of faith forsworn, or broken pledge, or false or fruitless vow!

4. "But thou, dear Mary—Mary mine! hast ever look'd the
       same,
   With pleasant mien and smile serene, on her who bore thy
       name:
   Oh, grant that when anon I go to death, I may not see
   Nor axe, nor block, nor headsman—but thee, and only thee!
   Then 'twill be told, in coming times, how Mary gave her
       grace
   To die as Stuart, Guise, should die—of Charlemagne's fear
       less race!"

18. The Discovery of America.

THOMAS D'ARCY McGEE.

T. D. McGee is a native of Carlingford, county Louth, Ireland. Though still comparatively young, he has achieved an immense amount of literary labor. As an orator he has few, if any, superiors at the present day. As a prose writer his works are chiefly historical and biographical, many of them possessing a high order of merit, such as his *Popular History of Ireland, Irish Settlers in America, Catholic History of America, Gallery of Irish Writers, &c., &c.* As a statesman and politician he has already attained the first rank in the Canadian House of Assembly, where he represents the city of Montreal.

1. In the foreground of American history there stand these three figures—a lady, a sailor, and a monk. Might they not be thought to typify Faith, Hope, and Charity? The lady is especially deserving of honor. Years after his first success, the Admiral (Columbus) wrote: "In the midst of general incredulity, the Almighty infused into the Queen, my lady, the spirit of intelligence and energy. While every one else, in his ignorance, was expatiating on the cost and inconvenience, her Highness approved of it on the contrary, and gave it all the support in her power."

2. And what were the distinguishing qualities of this foster-mother of American discovery? Fervent piety, unfeigned humility, profound reverence for the Holy See, a spotless life as a daughter, mother, wife, and queen. "She is," says a Protestant author, "one of the purest and most beautiful characters in the pages of history." Her holy life had won for her the title of "the Catholic." Other queens have been celebrated for beauty, for magnificence, for learning, or for good fortune; but the foster-mother of America alone, of all the women of history, is called "the *Catholic*."

3. As to the conduct of the undertaking, we have first to remark, that on the port of Palos the original outfit depended, and Palos itself depended on the neighboring convent. In the refectory of La Rabida the agreement was made between Columbus and the Pinzons. From the porch of the Church of St George, the royal orders were read to the astonished townsfolk.

4. The aids and assurances of religion were brought into requisition to encourage sailors, always a superstitious generation, to embark on this mysterious voyage. On the morning of their departure, a temporary chapel was erected with spars and sails on the strand; and there, in sight of their vessels riding at shortened anchors, the three crews, numbering in all one hundred and twenty souls, received the blessed sacrament. Rising from their knees, they departed with the benediction of the Church, like the breath of heaven, filling their sails

19. The Discovery of America—*continued.*

1. On the night before the discovery of the first land, after the *Salve Regina* had been chanted, according to his biographers, the Admiral made an impressive address to his crew. His speech must have been one of the most Catholic oratio. s ever delivered in the New World. It has not been recorded, it can never be invented. We can, indeed, conceive what a lofty homily on confidence in God and His ever Blessed Mother such a man so situated would be able to deliver.

2. We can imagine we see him as he stands on the darkened deck of the *Santa Maria*, his thin locks lifted by the breeze already odorous of land, and his right hand pointing onward to the west. We almost hear him exclaim, "Yonder lies the land! Where you can see only night and vacancy, I behold India and Cathay! The darkness of the hour will pass away, and with it the night of nations. Cities more beautiful than Seville, countries more fertile than Andalusia, are off yonder.

3. "There lies the terrestial paradise, watered with its four rivers of life ; there lies the golden Ophir, from which Solomon, the son of David, drew the ore that adorned the temple of the living God ; there we shall find whole nations unknown to Christ, to whom you, ye favored companions of my voyage, shall be the first to bring the glad tidings of great joy proclaimed ' of old by angels' lips to the shepherds of Chaldea.' " But, alas ! who shall attempt to supply the words spoken by such a man at such a moment, on that last night of expec tation and uncertainty—the eve of the birthday of a new world ?

4. Columbus and his companions landed on the morning of the 12th of October, 1492, on the little island which they called San Salvador. Three boats conveyed them to the shore ; over each boat floated a broad banner, blazoned with "a green cross." On reaching the land the Admiral threw himself on his knees, kissed the earth, and shed tears of joy. Then, raising his voice, he uttered aloud that short but fervent prayer, which, after him, all Catholic discoverers were wont to repeat.

5. It is in these words : "O Lord God, Eternal and Omnipotent, who by thy Divine Word hast created the heavens, the earth, and the sea, blessed and glorified be thy name, and praised thy majesty, who hast deigned, by me, thy humble servant, to have that sacred name made known and preached in this other part of the world !"

6. The nomenclature used by the great discoverer, like all his acts, is essentially Catholic. Neither his own nor his patron's name is precipitated on cape, river, or island. San Salvador, Santa Trinidada, San Domingo, San Nicolas, San Jago, Santa Maria, Santa Marta—these are the mementoes of his first success. All egotism, all selfish policy, was utterly lost in the overpowering sense of being but an instrument in the hands of Providence.

7. After cruising a couple of months among the Bahamas, and discovering many new islands, he returns to Spain. In this homeward voyage two tempests threaten to ingulf his solitary ship. In the darkest hour he supplicates our Blessed Lady, his dear patroness. He vows a pilgrimage barefoot to her nearest shrine, whatever land he makes ; a vow punctually fulfilled. Safely he reaches the Azores, the Tagus, and the port of Palos. His first act is a solemn procession to the church of St. George, from which the royal orders had been first made known.

8. He next writes in this strain to the Treasurer Sanchez : "Let processions be made, let festivities be held, let churches be filled with branches and flowers, for Christ rejoices on earth as in heaven, seeing the future redemption of souls." The court was, at the time, at Barcelona, and thither he repaired with the living evidences of his success. Seated on the royal dais, with the aborigines, the fruits, flowers, birds, and metals spread out before them, he told to princes his wondrous tale.

9. As soon as he had ended, "the King and Queen, with all present, prostrated themselves on their knees in grateful thanksgiving while the solemn strains of the *Te Deum* were poured forth by the choir of the royal chapel as in commemoration of some great victory !" To place beyond any sup-

position of doubt the Catholicity of this extraordinary event, one evidence is still wanting—the official participation of the sovereign Pontiff. That it had from the outset.

———◆———

20. THE VIRGIN MARY'S KNIGHT.

A BALLAD OF THE CRUSADES.

THOS. D'ARCY MCGEE.

[In "the middle ages," there were orders of knights especially devoted to our Blessed Lady, as well as many illustrious individuals of knightly rank and renown. Thus the order called Servites, in France, was known as *les esclaves de Marie*; and there was also the order of "Our Lady of Mercy," for the redemption of captives; the Templars, too, before their fall, were devoutly attached to the service of our Blessed Lady.]

1. BENEATH the stars in Palestine seven knights discoursing
        stood,
    But not of warlike work to come, nor former fields of blood,
    Nor of the joy the pilgrims feel prostrated far, who see
    The hill where Christ's atoning blood pour'd down the
        penal tree ;
    Their theme was old, their theme was new, 'twas sweet and
        yet 'twas bitter,—
    Of noble ladies left behind spoke cavalier and ritter,
    And eyes grew bright, and sighs arose from every iron
        breast,
    For a dear wife, or plighted maid, far in the widow'd
    West

2 Toward the knights came Constantine, thrice noble by his
        birth,
    And ten times nobler than his blood his high out-shining,
        worth ;
    His step was slow, his lips were moved, though not a word
        he spoke,
    Till a gallant lord of Lombardy his spell of silence broke.
    "What aileth thee, O Constantine, that solitude you seek !
    If counsel or if aid you need, we pray thee do but speak ;

Or dost thou mourn, like other freres, thy lady-love afar,
Whose image shineth nightly through yon European star?"

3. Then answer'd courteous Constantine—"Good sir, in sim
    ple truth,
I chose a gracious lady in the hey-day of my youth ;
I wear her image on my heart, and when that heart is cold,
The secret may be rifled thence, but never must be told.
For her I love and worship well by light of morn or even
I ne'er shall see my mistress dear, until we meet in heaven
But this believe, brave cavaliers, there never was but one
Such lady as my Holy Love, beneath the blessed sun."

4. He ceased, and pass'd with solemn step on to an olive grove,
    And, kneeling there, he pray'd a prayer to the lady of his
        love.
    And many a cavalier whose lance had still maintain'd his
        own
    Beloved to reign without a peer, all earth's unequalled one,
    Look'd tenderly on Constantine in camp and in the fight ;
    With wonder and with generous pride they mark'd the
        lightning light
    Of his fearless sword careering through the unbelievers'
        ranks,
    As angry Rhone sweeps off the vines that thicken on his
        banks.

5. "He fears not death, come when it will ; he longeth for
    his love,
    And fain would find some sudden path to where she dwells
        above.
    How should he fear for dying, when his mistress dear is
        dead ?"
    Thus often of Sir Constantine his watchful comrades said ;
    Until it chanced from Zion wall the fatal arrow flew,
    That pierced the outworn armor of his faithful bosom
        through ;
    And never was such mourning made for knight in Palestine,
    As thy loyal comrades made for thee, belovèd Constantine

6 Beneath the royal tent the bier was guarded night and day,
  Where with a halo round his head the Christian champion
      lay ;
  That talisman upon his breast—what may that marvel be
  Which kept his ardent soul through life from every error free!
  Approach ! behold ! nay, worship there the image of his love,
  The heavenly Queen who reigneth all the sacred hosts above,
  Nor wonder that around his bier there lingers such a light,
  For the spotless one that sleepeth *was the Blessed Virgin's
      Knight !*

---

21. THE YOUNG CATHOLIC.

ABBÉ MARTINEZ.

Abbé Martinez—a native of France. His writings bear the stamp of the French national genius. His works are worthy of being ranked next to those of Moehler and Balmez. His " Religion in Society," as a popular manual against the discordant but numerous errors of the day, is unrivalled

1. WHAT commands his attention most in the temple, is the mysterious person of the priest, the spiritual father of the whole parish, and with whom he is about to form the most intimate relations,—at catechism, where, during many years, he is to receive, with children of his own age, the milk of the divine word ; or in the confessional, where he will reveal the most secret movements of his heart.

2. It is to the priest he is indebted—and he is reminded of it by the sight of the sacred font—for the sublime title of the child of God and of the Church ; it is from his sacred hand that he awaits the mysterious sacrament which is to unite him intimately to his Creator. Great is the influence of his pastor over his spiritual children. Napoleon, on his death-bed, confessed to his companions in exile, that the presence of the priest had always spoken to his heart. Here let every one recall the impression of his early days.

3. But to the eye of the young Catholic, the religious horizon extends, and gradually reveals itself with age.

Around his parish other parishes are gathered. The common father of priests and people—the priest emphatically

— the bishop, appears in the midst of joyful chants. His sacred hand touches the young brow, and the union, before so close, of our youth with the mystical body of the Church becomes still closer.

4. Beyond and above bishops, universal veneration points out to him the Bishop of bishops, the universal pontiff, seated upon the immovable chair of St. Peter, and forming of the one hundred and sixty millions of Catholics, scattered throughout the world, one only body, animated with the same spirit, nourished with the same doctrine, moving towards the same end.

5. He sees in the clear light of history this vast society, which no visible hand has formed or supports ; and for the destruction of which, all the known forces of the physical and moral world have conspired,—surviving all human societies, resisting the most frightful tempests, and constantly bringing the immense majority of Christians into subjection to its laws so unyielding to the passions of men.

6. Who are the enemies, in every age, rising up against the *House of the living God?* He sees odious tyrants, the enemies of all restraint ; proud dreamers, who pretend to substitute their thought of a day for universal faith ; sectarians without a past, without a future, with no tie to bind them to each other but their common hatred to Catholic society ;—and all confessing, by the name they bear, their descent from one man, and their religious illegitimacy.

7. What a powerful guarantee against the assaults of doubt is presented to the young Catholic by this fact, which is as clear as the sun, and the evidence of which is more convincing every step we advance in the knowledge of the present and the past. He cannot refuse to believe in the Church, without saying: "In matters of religion I see more plainly, I alone, than a hundred and sixty millions of my cotemporaries and the eight or ten thousand millions of Catholics who preceded me, all as interested as I am in knowing the truth, and most of them with better advantages of becoming acquainted with it."

22. The Children of the Poor.

LAMB.

CHARLES LAMB, a native of England, died in 1834, aged 59. He was both a prose and poetical writer, but his fame rests chiefly on his Essays of ELIA; these are distinguished by a most delicate vein of humor and exquisite pathos. The following extract is from a series of his papers, written with much humor and taste, against the truth of certain popular proverbs—the subject in the present instance being, "Home is home, be it ever so homely."

1 THE innocent prattle of his children takes out the sting of a man's poverty. But the children of the very poor do not prattle. It is none of the least frightful features in that condition, that there is no childishness in its dwellings. "Poor people," said a sensible old nurse to us once, "do not bring up their children; they drag them up." The little careless darling of the wealthier nursery, in their hovel, is transformed betimes into a premature, reflecting person. No one has time to dandle it, no one thinks it worth while to coax it, to soothe it, to toss it up and down, to humor it. There is none to kiss away its tears. If it cries, it can only be beaten.

2. It has been prettily said that "a babe is fed with milk and praise." But the aliment of this poor babe was thin, un-nourishing; the return to its little baby tricks, and efforts to engage attention, bitter, ceaseless objurgation. It never had a toy, or knew what a coral meant. It grew up without the lullaby of nurses; it was a stranger to the patient fondle, the hushing caress, the attracting novelty, the costlier plaything or the cheaper off-hand contrivance to divert the child, the prattled nonsense (best sense to it), the wise impertinences, the wholesome fictions, the apt story interposed, that puts a stop to present sufferings, and awakens the passions of young wonder.

3. It was never sung to; no one ever told it a tale of the nursery. It was dragged up, to live or to die as it happened. It had no young dreams. It broke at once into the iron realities of life. A child exists not for the very poor as an object of dalliance; it is only another mouth to be fed, a pair of little hands to be betimes inured to labor. It is the rival, till it can be the co-operator, for food with the parent. It is never his

mirth, his diversion, his solace ; it never makes him young
again, with recalling his young times.   The children of the
very poor have no young times.

4. It makes the very heart to bleed to overhear the casual
street-talk between a poor woman and her little girl, a woman
of the better sort of poor, in a condition rather above the
squalid beings which we have been contemplating.   It is not
of toys, of nursery books, of summer holidays (fitting that
age), of the promised sight or play, of praised sufficiency at
school.   It is of mangling and clear-starching, of the price of
coals, or of potatoes.   The questions of the child, that should
be the very outpourings of curiosity in idleness, are marked
with forecast and melancholy providence.   It has come to be
a woman—before it was a child.   It has learned to go to
market ; it chaffers, it haggles, it envies, it murmurs ; it is
knowing, acute, sharpened ; it never prattles.   Had we not
reason to say, that the home of the very poor is no home ?

--- --- ---

23. My Life is like the Summer Rose.

WILDE.

R. H. WILDE was born in 1789; he passed his childhood in Baltimore,
and subsequently removed to Georgia ; and, although engaged in law and
political life, devoted a sufficient portion of his time to literature to make
it evident that he had the talents to assume a proud position in its ranks.
He died, in 1847, a most edifying death, in the bosom of the Catholic Church.

1. My life is like the Summer rose,
     That opens to the morning sky,
 But ere the shades of evening close,
     Is scatter'd on the ground to die!
 Yet on the humble rose's bed,
 The sweetest dews of night are shed ;
 As if she wept the waste to see;—
 But none shall weep a tear for me!

2. My life is like the Autumn leaf

Its hold is frail, its date is brief,
   Restless, and soon to pass away!
Yet ere that leaf shall fall and fade,
The parent tree will mourn its shade,
The winds bewail the leafless tree,—
But none shall breathe a sigh for me!

8. My life is like the prints, which feet
   Have left on Tampa's desert strand,
Soon as the rising tide shall beat,
   All trace will vanish from the sand!
Yet, as if grieving to efface
All vestige of the human race,
On that lone shore loud moans the sea,—
But none, alas, shall mourn for me!

---

24. THE BLESSED SACRAMENT.
FABER.

FREDERICK WILLIAM FABER, one of the Oxford divines, is a man of great literary attainments. His works, "Growth in Holiness," "Blessed Sacrament," "Mary at the Foot of the Cross," and the "Conferences," show that he is eminently an ascetic writer. He is also a poet of high order:— "The Cheswell Water-Lily," "Sir Launcelot," "Rosary," "Styrian Lake," and many other poems, rank among the noblest and purest of the English bards; he awakens anew the lyre of the martyr Southwell and the pious Canon Crashaw.—*Metropolitan.*

1. LET us suppose it to be the Feast of Corpus Christi. We have risen with one glad thought uppermost in our minds. It gives a color to every thing around about us. It is health to us even if we are not well, and sunshine though the skies be dull. At first there is something of disappointment to us, when we see our dear country wearing the same toilsome look of commonplace labor and of ordinary traffic. We feel there is something wrong, something out of harmony in this.

2. Poor London! if it knew God, and could keep holydays for God, how it might rejoice on such a day, letting the chains of work fall from off its countless slaves of Mammon, and giving one whole sun to the deep, childlike joy in a mystery which is

the triumph of faith over sight, of spirit over matter, of grace
over nature, and of the Church over the world. But somehow
our very disappointment causes us to feel more touchingly the
gift of faith, and the sense of our own unworthiness, which
makes it such a wonder that God should have elected us to so
great a gift.

3. Oh, sweet Sacrament of Love! we belong to thee, for
thou art our Living Love himself. Thou art our well of life,
for in thee is the Divine Life himself—immeasurable, compassionate, eternal. To-day is thy day, and on it there shall not
be a single thought, a single hope, a single wish, which shall
not be all for thee!

4. Now the first thing we have to do is to get the spirit of the
Feast into us. When this is once accomplished, we shall be better
able to sound some of the depths of this salutary mystery.
Nay, the whole theology of the grand dogma of the Eucharist
is nothing less than angelic music made audible to mortal ears;
and when our souls are attuned to it we shall the better understand the sweet secrets which it reveals to our delighted minds.

5. But we must go far away in order to catch the spirit of
the Feast. We must put before ourselves, as on a map, the
aspect which the whole Church is presenting to the eye of God
to-day. Our great city is deafened with her own noise; she
cannot hear. She is blinded with her own dazzle; she cannot
see. We must not mind her; we must put the thoughts of
her away, with sadness if it were any other day than this, but
to-day, because it is to-day, with complete indifference.

6. Oh, the joy of the immense glory the Church is sending up
to God this hour, verily, as if the world was all unfallen still !
We think, and as we think, the thoughts are like so many
successive tide-waves, filling our whole souls with the fulness
of delight, of all the thousands of masses which are being
said or sung the whole world over, and all rising with one note
of blissful acclamation from grateful creatures to the Majesty
of our merciful Creator.

7. How many glorious processions, with the sun upon their
banners, are now winding their way round the squares of
mighty cities, through the flower-strewn streets of Christian

villages, through the antique cloisters of the glorious cathedral, or through the grounds of the devout seminary, where the various colors of the faces, and the different languages of the people, are only so many fresh tokens of the unity of that faith which they are all exultingly professing in the single voice of the magnificent ritual of Rome !

8. Upon how many altars of various architecture, amid sweet flowers and starry lights, amid clouds of humble incense, and the tumult of thrilling song, before thousands of prostrate worshippers, is the blessed sacrament raised for exposition, or taken down for benediction ! And how many blessed acts of faith and love, of triumph and of reparation, do not each of these things surely represent !

9. The world over, the summer air is filled with the voice of song. The gardens are shorn of their fairest blossoms, to be flung beneath the feet of the Sacramental God. The steeples are reeling with the clang of bells ; the cannon are booming in the gorges of the Andes and the Apennines ; the ships of the harbors are painting the bays of the sea with their show of gaudy flags ; the pomp of royal or republican armies salutes the King of kings.

10. The Pope on his throne, and the school-girl in her village, cloistered nuns and sequestered hermits, bishops and dignitaries and preachers, emperors and kings and princes, are all engrossed to-day with the Blessed Sacrament. Cities are illuminated ; the dwellings of men are alive with exultation.

11. Joy so abounds, that men rejoice they know not why ; and their joy overflows on sad hearts, and on the poor and the imprisoned and the wandering and the orphaned and the homesick exiles. All the millions of souls that belong to th royal family and spiritual lineage of St. Peter, are to-day en gaged, more or less, with the Blessed Sacrament, so that the whole Church militant is thrilling with glad emotion, like the tremulous rocking of the mighty sea. Sin seems forgotten ; tears even are of rapture rather than of penance. It is like the soul's first day in heaven, or as if earth itself were passing into heaven, as it well might do, for sheer joy of the Blessed Sacrament.

25. THE BLIND MARTYR.

CARDINAL WISEMAN.

His Eminence CARDINAL WISEMAN, the first Archbishop of Westminster, was born at Seville, in Spain, of Irish parents, August 2, 1802. He was ordained priest in 1825, and was for some years Rector of the English College at Rome. He was elevated to the episcopate in 1840, being made Coadjutor to Dr. Walsh, Vicar Apostolic of the Midland District. In 1848, e was made Pro-Vicar Apostolic of the London District, on the death of Dr. Griffiths; and subsequently, Vicar Apostolic. On the 29th of September, 1850, his Holiness Pope Pius IX. re-established the Catholic Hierarchy in England, when Dr. Wiseman was made Archbishop of the new See of Westminster; and on the following day he was raised to the dignity of a Cardinal Priest of the Holy Roman Church.

"Few of the great men of our day will, in the pages of Church history, occupy a more conspicuous place than Cardinal Wiseman, as a learned and brilliant controversialist, or as a writer abounding in erudition, a knowledge of the Oriental languages, manners, and customs, the life of the primitive Christians, and all their remains, as well as in a thorough knowledge alike of theology, and of the times in which he lived. His Lectures on Revealed Religion are acknowledged to be the best and most complete answer in the language to the infidel doctrines of the day."—*Metropolitan*.

These form but a small portion of his learned labors. We give below an extract from his unequalled tale of "Fabiola," the scene of which is laid in Rome during the reign of the tyrant Diocletian.

[Cæcelia, a poor, blind young girl, warns the Christians, who had assembled in the Catacombs to assist at the Holy Sacrifice of the Mass, that they have been betrayed to the Prefect of Rome.]

1. CÆCELIA, already forewarned, had approached the cemetery by a different but neighboring entrance. No sooner had she descended than she snuffed the strong odor of the torches. "This is none of our incense, I know," she said to herself; "the enemy is already within." She hastened, therefore, to the place of assembly, and delivered Sebastian's note; adding also what she had observed. It warned them to disperse, and seek the shelter of the inner and lower galleries; and begged of the Pontiff not to leave till he should send for him, as his person was particularly sought for.

2. Pancratius urged the blind messenger to save herself too. "No," she replied, "my office is to watch the door, and guide the faithful safe."

"But the enemy may seize you."

"No matter," she answered, laughing; "my being taken may save much worthier lives. Give me a lamp, Pancratius."

3. "Why, you cannot see by it," observed he, smiling.

"True ; but others can."

"They may be your enemies."

"Even so," she answered ; "I do not wish to be taken in the dark. If my Bridegroom come to me in the night of this cemetery, must he not find me with my lamp trimmed ?"

Off she started, reached her post, and hearing no noise except that of quiet footsteps, she thought they were those of friends, and held up her lamp to guide them.

4. When the party came forth, with their only captive, Fulvius was perfectly furious. It was more than a total failure —it was ridiculous—a poor mouse come out of the bowels of the earth. He rallied Corvinus till the wretch winced and foamed ; then suddenly he asked, "And where is Torquatus ?" He heard the account of his sudden disappearance, told in as many ways as the Dacian guards' adventures ; but it annoyed him greatly. He had no doubt, whatever, in his own mind, that he had been duped by his supposed victim, who had escaped into the unsearchable mazes of the cemetery. If so, this captive would know, and he determined to question her. He stood before her, therefore, put on his most searching and awful look, and said to her, sternly, "Look at me, woman, and tell me the truth."

5. "I must tell you the truth without looking at you, sir," answered the poor girl, with her cheerfulest smile, and softest voice ; "do you not see that I am blind ?"

"Blind !" all exclaimed at once, as they crowded to look at her. But over the features of Fulvius there passed the slightest possible emotion, just as much as the wave that runs, pursued by a playful breeze, over the ripe meadow. A knowledge had flashed into his mind, a clue had fallen into his hands.

6. "It will be ridiculous," he said, "for twenty soldiers to march through the city, guarding a blind girl. Return to your quarters, and I will see you are well rewarded. You, Corvinus, take my horse, and go before to your father, and tell him all. I will follow in a carriage with the captive."

"No treachery, Fulvius," he said, vexed and mortified.

7. "Mind you bring her. The day must not pass without a sacrifice."

"Do not fear," was the reply.

Fulvius, indeed, was pondering whether, having lost one spy, he should not try to make another. But the calm gentleness of the poor beggar perplexed him more than the boisterous zeal of the gamester, and her sightless orbs defied him more than the restless roll of the toper's ; still, the first thought that had struck him he could still pursue. When alone in a carriage with her, he assumed a soothing tone, and addressed her. He knew she had not overheard the last dialogue.

"My poor girl," he said, "how long have you been blind ?"

8. "All my life," she replied.

"What is your history ? Whence do you come ?"

"I have no history. My parents were poor, and brought me to Rome, when I was four years old, as they came to pray, in discharge of a vow made for my life in early sickness, to the blessed martyrs Chrysanthus and Daria. They left me in charge of a pious lame woman, at the door of the title of Fasciola, while they went to their devotions. It was on that memorable day when many Christians were buried at the tomb, by earth and stones cast down on them. My parents had the happiness to be among them."

9. "And how have you lived since ?"

"God became my only Father then, and his Catholic Church my Mother. The one feeds the birds of the air, the other nurses the weaklings of the flock. I have never wanted for any thing since."

"But you can walk about the streets freely and without fear, as well as if you saw."

"How do you know that ?"

10. "I have seen you. Do you remember very early on morning in the autumn, leading a poor lame man along the Vicus Patricus ?"

She blushed and remained silent. Could he have seen her put into the poor old man's purse her own share of the alms ! "You have owned yourself a Christian ?" he asked, negligently.

11. "Oh, yes; how could I deny it ?"

"Then that meeting was a Christian meeting ?"

"Certainly; what else could it be ?"

He wanted no more; his suspicions were verified. Agnes, about whom Torquatus had been able or willing to tell him nothing, was certainly a Christian. His game was made. Sh must yield, or he would be avenged.

12. After a pause, looking at her steadfastly, he said, "Do you know whither you are going ?"

" Before the judge of earth, I suppose, who will send me to my Spouse in heaven."

" And so calmly ?" he asked, in surprise; for he could see no token from the soul to the countenance but a smile.

" So joyfully, rather," was her brief reply.

13. Having got all that he desired, he consigned his prisoner to Corvinus at the gates of the Æmilian basilica, and left her to her fate. It had been a cold and drizzling day, like the pre ceding evening. The weather, and the incidents of the night, had kept down all enthusiasm; and while the prefect had been compelled to sit in-doors, where no great crowd could collect, as hours had passed away without any arrest, trial, or tidings, most of the curious had left, and only a few more persevering remained past the hour of afternoon recreation in the public gardens. But just before the captive arrived a fresh knot of spectators came in, and stood near one of the side-doors, from which they could see all.

---

26. THE BLIND MARTYR—*continued*.

1. As Corvinus had prepared his father for what he was to expect, Tertullus, moved with some compassion, and imagining there would be little difficulty in overcoming the obstinacy of a poor, ignorant, blind beggar, requested the spectators to re main perfectly still, that he might try his persuasion on her, alone, as she would imagine, with him; and he threatened heavy penalties on any one who should presume to break the silence.

2. "What is thy name, child?"

"Cæcelia."

'It is a noble name; hast thou it from thy family?"

"No; I am not noble; except because my parents, though poor, died for Christ. As I am blind, those who took care of me called me Cæca,* and then, out of kindness, softened it into Cæcelia."

3. "But, now, give up all this folly of the Christians, who nave kept thee only poor and blind. Honor the decrees of the divine emperors, and offer sacrifice to the gods; and thou shalt have riches, and fine clothes, and good fare; and the best physicians shall try to restore thee thy sight."

"You must have better motives to propose to me than these; for the very things for which I most thank God and his Divine Son, are those which you would have me put away."

4. "How dost thou mean?"

"I thank God that I am poor and meanly clad, and fare not daintily; because by all these things I am the more like Jesus Christ, my only Spouse."

"Foolish girl!" interrupted the judge, losing patience a little; "hast thou learnt all these silly delusions already? At least thou canst not thank thy God that he has made thee sightless?"

"For that, more than all the rest, I thank him daily and hourly with all my heart."

"How so? dost thou think it a blessing never to have seen the face of a human being, or the sun, or the earth? What strange fancies are these?"

5. "They are not so, most noble sir. For in the midst of what you call darkness, I see a spot of what I must call light, it contrasts so strongly with all around. It is to me what the sun is to you, which I know to be local from the varying direction of its rays. And this object looks upon me as with a countenance of intensest beauty, and smiles upon me as ever And I know it to be that of Him whom I love with undivided

---

* Blind.

affection. I would not for the world have its splendor dimmed
by a brighter sun, nor its wondrous loveliness confounded with
the diversities of other features, nor my gaze on it drawn
aside by earthly visions. I love him too much, not to wish
to see him always alone."

6. "Come, come; let me hear no more of this silly prattle
Obey the emperor at once, or I must try what a little pain
will do. That will soon tame thee."

"Pain !" she echoed, innocently.

"Yes, pain. Hast thou never felt it? hast thou never been
hurt by any one in thy life ?"

"Oh, no ; Christians never hurt one another."

7. The rack was standing, as usual, before him ; and he
made a sign to Catulus to place her upon it. The executioner
pushed her back on it by her arms ; and as she made no resistance, she was easily laid extended on its wooden couch.
The loops of the ever-ready ropes were in a moment passed
round her ancles, and her arms drawn over the head. The
poor sightless girl saw not who did all this ; she knew not but
it might be the same person who had been conversing with her.
If there had been silence hitherto, men now held their very
breath, while Cæcelia's lips moved in earnest prayer.

8. "Once more, before proceeding further, I call on thee to
sacrifice to the gods, and escape cruel torments," said the
judge, with a sterner voice.

"Neither torments nor death," firmly replied the victim, tied
to the altar, "shall separate me from the love of Christ. I
can offer up no sacrifice but to the one living God, and its
ready oblation is myself."

9. The prefect made a signal to the executioner, and he gav
one rapid whirl to the two wheels of the rack, round th
windlasses of which the ropes were wound ; and the limbs o·
the maiden were stretched with a sudden jerk, which, thoug!
not enough to wrench them from their sockets, as a further
turn would have done, sufficed to inflict an excruciating, or
more truly, a racking pain, through all her frame. Far more
grievous was this from the preparation and the cause of it
being unseen, and from that additional suffering which dark

ness inflicts. A quivering of her features and a sudden pale-
ness alone gave evidence of her suffering.

10. "Ha ! ha !" the judge exclaimed, "thou feelest that !
Come, let it suffice ; obey, and thou shalt be freed."

She seemed to take no heed of his words, but gave vent to
er feelings in prayer : "I thank thee, O Lord Jesus Christ,
that thou hast made me suffer pain the first time for thy
sake. I have loved thee in peace ; I have loved thee in
comfort ; I have loved thee in joy ; and now in pain I love
thee still more. How much sweeter it is to be like thee,
stretched upon thy cross even, than resting upon the hard
couch at the poor man's table !"

11. "Thou triflest with me !" exclaimed the judge, thoroughly vexed, "and makest light of my lenity. We will try
something stronger. Here, Catulus, apply a lighted torch to
her sides."

A thrill of disgust and horror ran through the assembly,
which could not help sympathizing with the poor blind creature. A murmur of suppressed indignation broke out from
all sides of the hall.

12. Cæcelia, for the first time, learnt that she was in the midst
of a crowd. A crimson glow of modesty rushed into her brow,
her face, and neck, just before white as marble.

The angry judge checked the rising gush of feeling ; and all
listened in silence, as she spoke again, with warmer earnestness than before :

"O my dear Lord and Spouse ! I have been ever true and
faithful to thee ! Let me suffer pain and torture for thee ;
but spare me confusion from human eyes. Let me come to
thee at once ; not covering my face with my hands in shame,
when I stand before thee."

13. Another muttering of compassion was heard.

"Catulus !" shouted the baffled judge, in fury, "do your
luty, sirrah ! What are you about, fumbling all day with that
torch ?"

"It is too late. She is dead."

"Dead !" cried out Tertullus ; "dead, with one turn of the
wheel ? Impossible !"

14. Catulus gave the rack a turn backwards, and the body remained motionless. It was true ; she had passed from the rack to the throne, from the scowl of the judge's countenance to her Spouse's welcoming embrace. Had she breathed out her pure soul, as a sweet perfume, in the incense of her prayer ? or had her heart been unable to get back its blood, 'rom the intensity of that first virginal blush ?

15. In the stillness of awe and wonder, a clear, bold voice cried out, from the group near the door, " Impious tyrant, dost thou not see that a poor blind Christian hath more power over life and death than thou or thy cruel masters ?"

" What ! a third time in twenty-four hours wilt thou dare to cross my path ? This time thou shalt not escape."

16. These were Corvinus' words, garnished with a furious imprecation, as he rushed from his father's side, round the inclosure before the tribunal, towards the group. But as he ran blindly on he struck against an officer of herculean build, who, no doubt quite accidentally, was advancing from it. He reeled, and the soldier caught hold of him, saying :

" You are not hurt, I hope, Corvinus ?"

" No, no ; let me go, Quadratus, let me go."

17. " Where are you. running to in such a hurry ? Can I help you ?" asked his captor, still holding him fast.

" Let me loose, I say, or he will be gone."

" Who will be gone ?"

" Pancratius," answered Corvinus ; " who just now insulted my father."

" Pancratius !" said Quadratus, looking round, and seeing that he had got clear off ; " I do not see him." And he let him go ; but it was too late. The youth was safe at Diogenes' in Suburra.

18. While this scene was going on, the prefect, mortified, ordered Catulus to see the body thrown into the Tiber.

But another officer, muffled in his cloak, stepped aside and beckoned to Catulus, who understood the sign, and stretched out his hand to receive a proffered purse.

" Out of the Porta Capena, at Lucina's villa, an hour after sunset," said Sebastian.

19. "It shall be delivered there, safe," said the executioner
"Of what, do you think, did that poor girl die?" asked a
spectator from his companion, as they went out.

"Of fright, I fancy," he replied.

"Of Christian modesty," interposed a stranger, who passed
them.

---

27. PEACE TRIBUNALS.

ARCHBISHOP KENRICK.

FRANCIS PATRICK KENRICK, D. D., archbishop of Baltimore, was born in
Dublin, in 1797. In biblical and theological learning, he has no superior
among the hierarchy of the Church. His "Dogmatic Theology" and
"Primacy of the Apostolic See," and others of his voluminous works, are
everywhere received as standard authorities. His greatest work, however,
is his Translation of the Holy Bible, with notes and comments. It is
worthy of remark that the brother of this eminent prelate is Archbishop
of St. Louis, and has also written some works of merit.

1. PHILANTHROPISTS often speculate on the propriety of establishing a peace tribunal, to settle, without the proud control
of fierce and bloody war, the various controversies which may
arise among nations; yet they seldom reflect that such a tribunal existed in the middle ages, in the person of the sovereign
pontiff. The warlike spirit of the northern barbarians, which
still survived in their descendants, should be understood in order to fully appreciate the services which the popes in restrain-
ing it rendered to society.

2. Their efforts were not always successful, but their merit
was not, on that account, the less in endeavoring to stem the
torrent of human passion; and their success was sufficient to
entitle them to the praise of having effectually labored to
substitute moral and religious influence for brute force.

3. As ministers of the Prince of Peace, they often interposed spontaneously, and with arms powerful before God,
opposed the marauders who rushed forward to shed human
blood. The fathers of the Council of Rheims, in 1119, under
the presidency of Calistus II., were engaged in ecclesiastical
deliberations, when the pontiff communicated to them over-
tures of peace which had reached him from Henry V.

4. He informed them that he must repair to the place which the emperor had appointed for an interview, promising to return and close the Council. "Afterwards," said he, "I shall wait on the King of England, my godchild and relative, and exhort him, Count Theobald his nephew, and others who are at variance, to come to a reconciliation, that each, for the love of God, may do justice to the other, and according to the law of God, all of them being pacified, may abandon war, and with their subjects enjoy the security of perfect peace."

5. Leibnitz regarded this mediatorial office of the pope as one among the most beautiful evidences of Christian influence on society, and expressed the desire, which, however, he did not hope to see realized, that a peace tribunal were established anew at Rome, with the Pontiff as its president, that the controversies of princes, and the internal dissension of nations might, by the mild influence of religion, be decided without bloodshed. "Since we are allowed to indulge fancy," said he, " why should we not cherish an idea that would renew among us the golden age ?"

28. Song of the Union.

CUMMINGS.

Reverend Dr. Cummings, the learned and accomplished pastor of St. Stephen's Church, New York, has, in his leisure moments, contributed to the polite literature of the day, both in prose and poetry. Many of his poems are real gems ; such as prove the author, had he devoted himself to poetry, might have taken the first rank among the poets of his country.— *Dr. Brownson.*

1. Ere peace and freedom, hand in hand,
   Went forth to bless this happy land
   And make it their abode,
   It was the footstool of a throne ;
   But now no master here is known—
   No king is fear'd but God.

2. Americans uprose in might,
   And triumph'd in the unequal fight,
   For union made them strong ;

6

Union ! the magic battle-cry,
That hurl'd the tyrant from on high,
 And crush'd his hireling throng !

3. That word since then hath shone on high,
In starry letters to the sky— •
 It is our country's name !
What impious hand shall rashly dare
Down from its lofty peak to tear
 The banner of her fame ?

4. The spirits of the heroic dèad,
Who for Columbia fought and bled,
 Would curse the dastard son
Who should betray their noble trust,
And madly trample in the dust,
 The charter which they won.

5. From vast Niagara's gurgling roar
To Sacramento's golden shore,
 From east to western wave,
The blended vows of millions rise,
Their voice re-echoes to the skies—
 "The Union we must save !"

6. The God of nations, in whose name
The sacred laws obedience claim,
 Will bless our fond endeavor
To dwell as brethren here below ;
The Union, then, come weal, come woe,
 We will preserve forever !

---

29. THE SPIRIT OF THE AGE.
CUMMINGS.

1. A WONDERFUL genius is this Spirit of the Age ! No mat
ter how true or how much needed a maxim may be, one is re
minded of the danger he incurs in uttering it, by the awful
warning that it is not in accordance with the Spirit of the

Age. The Spirit of the Age knows all things, and has an opinion to express on all subjects—past, present, or future. It is a thousand pities that so learned a spirit can never be tangibly taken hold of and made to speak for himself. But, like certain other spirits, though always busy at work, he is never seen, and though quoted by everybody, never speaks himself. Still, as we do not bear him unlimited veneration, we take the liberty sometimes to bring him fairly before us, in the form we imagine his vague and unsettled nature would choose, were he to become visible.

2. In these instances the great Genius presents himself adorned with a face very much like that of an ape, for his speech imitates wisdom and truth precisely as a monkey imitates a man. The body, half human and half Satanic, winds off in a serpentine manner, emblematic of the crookedness of his philosophy. On his head, in lieu of the Socratic bays, we discern a little Red Republican cap dashed slightly on one side, to make him look interesting; under his arm he carries a wonderful dictionary, compiled from the leading socialist, progressive, ultra-democratic periodicals of the day.

3. From this book of wisdom, the obliging Genius answers, without stopping to take breath, all the possible difficulties of every art, science, and creed, in a manner which would put all the gray-beard philosophy of olden times to the blush. Nothing is too high or too profound for him. Yet, to tell the truth, whenever he affirms a thing, we have a shrewd suspicion that he knows he ought to deny it; and whenever we hear him cry loudly for a measure as good, we feel pretty sure that secretly he understands it to be an evil.

4. What he says may often seem plausible enough, but we prefer to look at his professions more searchingly, and discover what he means. Thus, for example, when he opens his dictionary at the word Liberty, and reads a brilliant passage descriptive of its greatness and glory, we marvel at his keeping a serious face, and suspect that, were he to state honestly what he means, it would sound very much in this fashion: "Gentlemen, Liberty means leave for me to pick your pocket, and for you—not to complain."

5. He turns over a leaf of his book, and tells us of the philosophy of his enlightened school. We translate his definition of philosophy, and it avers that philosophy is the art of proving that two and two, not unfrequently, make five ; that black in many cases looks exceedingly like white, and that persons who wish to preserve their countenances from being burnt by the sun ought to wear a thick veil, especially at twelve o'clock at night. Does the Genius speak of the upwardness of modern progress? Then, to our understanding, he means that progress is a faithful imitation of the motion of a crab going down hill. He descants upon the comforts of equality.

6. Understood as he means it, no matter what he may say, equality consists in the very pleasant process of cutting off the heads of the tall men, and in pulling out the small men, as one might do a spy-glass, so that both become of a size. And when he searches his dictionary to give us the true meaning of his favorite word, Fraternity, his warm description of the peace which it produces puts us in mind of the famous Kilkenny cats, who fought until they had eaten each other up, all except the tips of their respective tails, which they still wagged in token of defiance.

7. Guided by this key to the true meaning of the learned Genius of the Age, we look to him for an answer to the questions proposed higher up, and we have no doubt that his true view of the case would embody itself in solutions equivalent to the following : "Religion and society," he would say, "are two orders, one opposed to the other. Religion was made, of course, by the Almighty ; it begins at the altar, ends at the holy-water font at the door, and is bounded by the four walls of the church. The period of its duration is from Sunday morning until Sunday evening. Society was invented by the Devil, and it rules the week from Monday morning until Saturday night. Business, politics, and amusements, are things that lie beyond the verge of morality, and the control of religion. He who pretends to be religious anywhere but inside of the church is a bigot, a hypocrite, a man of the Dark Ages ; and he who outside of the church suits his convenience by cunningly cheating, smoothly lying—playing, in short, the

confidence man—is a smart man ; in fact, something of an honorable man ; and, in fact—if he take care not to be found out—he may be one of the most remarkable men of his age and country."

---

30. DEATH OF ALONZO DE AGUILAR.

PRESCOTT.

WM. H. PRESCOTT—a distinguished American historian, born in 1796. While all due praise is given him for the merits of his two great works, "Ferdinand and Isabella," and the "Conquest of Mexico," it is much to be regretted that religious prejudices have in many instances betrayed him into grievous error, as well as into gross injustice. "We say it the more freely, as it is almost the only stain on an otherwise faultless book—a dark spot, or rather a collection of spots, on the sun. We regret this fault the more, as such prejudice is wholly unworthy the enlightened and moderate mind of Mr. Prescott."—*Rt. Rev. Dr. Spalding.*

1. FOR a long period, the south of Spain was occupied by the Moors, the city of Granada being their capital. They were finally conquered by Ferdinand the Catholic, to whom Granada was surrendered on the twenty-fifth day of November, 1491 ; but many of the inhabitants of the mountain regions received with great reluctance the Christian yoke, and in December, 1500, an insurrection broke out among them.

2. Orders were issued to the principal chiefs and cities of Andalusia to concentrate their forces at the city of Ronda, in the south of Spain, and thence to march against the insurgent Moors. Several distinguished noblemen and officers of Spain accordingly assembled with their troops at the city. Among them were Alonzo de Aguilar, the Conde de Ureña, and the Conde de Cifuentes. The historian's narrative then proceeds as follows :

3. It was determined by the chiefs to strike into the heart of the Red Sierra, as it was called, from the color of its rocks rising to the east of Ronda, and the principal theatre of insurrection. On 18th March, 1501, the little army encamped before Monarda, on the skirts of a mountain, where the Moors were understood to have assembled in considerable force. They had not been long in these quarters before the enemy were seen hovering along the slopes of the mountain,

from which the Christian camp was divided by a narrow river
—the Rio Verde, probably, which has gained so much ce
lebrity in the Spanish song.

4. Aguilar's[1] troops, who occupied the van, were so much
rousod at the sight of the enemy, that a small party, seizing
a banner, rushed across the stream, without orders, in pursuit
of them. The odds, however, were so great, that they would
have been severely handled, had not Aguilar, while he bitterly
condemned their temerity, advanced promptly to their support
with the remainder of his corps. The Count of Ureña[2] fol-
owed with the central division, leaving the Count of Cifuentes,[3] with the troops of Seville, to protect the camp.

5. The Moors fell back as the Christians advanced, and retiring nimbly from point to point, led them up the rugged
steep far into the recesses of the mountains. At length they
reached an open level, encompassed on all sides by a natural
rampart of rocks, where they had deposited their valuable
effects, together with their wives and children. The latter, at
sight of the invaders, uttered dismal cries, and fled into the
remoter depths of the sierra.

6. The Christians were too much attracted by the rich
spoils before them to think of following, and dispersed in
every quarter in quest of plunder, with all the heedlessness
and insubordination of raw, inexperienced levies. It was in
vain that Alonzo de Aguilar reminded them that their wily
enemy was still unconquered, or that he endeavored to force
them into the ranks again and restore order. No one heeded
his call, or thought of any thing beyond the present mc-
ment, and of securing as much booty to himself as he could
carry.

7. The Moors, in the mean while, finding themselves n
longer pursued, were aware of the occupations of the Christians, whom they, not improbably, had purposely decoyed into
the snare. They resolved to return to the scene of action and
surprise their incautious enemy. Stealthily advancing, therefore, under the shadows of night now falling thick around,

---

[1] Pronounced A·ghe-lar.   [2] U-rane'-ya.   [3] Thee-fuen'-tea.

they poured through the rocky defiles of the inclosure on the astonished Spaniards.

8. An unlucky explosion, at this crisis, of a cask of powder into which a spark had accidentally fallen, threw a broad glare over the scene, and revealed for a moment the situation of the hostile parties—the Spaniards in the utmost disorder many of them without arms, and staggering under the weight of their fatal booty; while their enemy were seen gliding, like so many demons of darkness, through every crevice and avenue of their inclosures, in the act of springing on their devoted victims.

9. This appalling spectacle, vanishing almost as soon as seen, and followed by the hideous yells and war-cries of the assailants, struck a panic into the hearts of the soldiers, who fled, scarcely offering any resistance.

10. The darkness of the night was as favorable to the Moors, familiar with all the intricacies of the ground, as it was fatal to the Christians, who, bewildered in the mazes of the sierra, and losing their footing at every step, fell under the swords of their pursuers, or went down the dark gulfs and precipices which yawned all around.

31. DEATH OF ALONZO DE AGUILAR—*continued*.

1. AMIDST this dreadful confusion, the Count of Ureña succeeded in gaining a lower level of the sierra, where he halted, and endeavored to rally his panic-struck followers. His noble comrade, Alonzo de Aguilar, still maintained his position on the heights above, refusing all entreaties of his followers to attempt a retreat. "When," said he, proudly "was an Aguilar ever known to fly from the field?" His eldest son the heir of his house and honors, Don Pedro de Cordova, a youth of great promise, fought at his side. He had received a severe wound on the head from a stone, and a javelin had pierced quite through his leg. With one knee resting on the ground, however, he made a brave defence with his sword.

2. The sight was too much for his father, and he implored him to suffer himself to be removed from the field. "Let not the hopes of our house be crushed at a single blow," said he. "Go, my son; live as becomes a Christian knight: live, and cherish your desolate mother!" All his endeavors were fruitless, however; and the gallant boy refused to leave his father's side till he was forcibly borne away by the attendants, who fortunately succeeded in bringing him in safety to the station occupied by the Count Ureña.

3. Meantime, the brave little band of cavaliers who remained true to Aguilar had fallen one after another; and the chief, left almost alone, retreated to a huge rock in the middle of the plain, and, placing his back against it, still made fight, though weakened by a loss of blood, like a lion at bay, against his enemies. In this situation, he was pressed so hard by a Moor of uncommon size and strength, that he was compelled to turn and close with him in a single combat.

4. The strife was long and desperate; till Don Alonzo, whose corselet had become unlaced in the previous struggle, having received a severe wound in the breast, followed by another on the head, grappled closely with his adversary, and they came rolling on the ground together. The Moor remained uppermost; but the spirit of the Spanish cavalier had not sunk with his strength, and he proudly exclaimed, as if to intimidate his enemy, "I am Don Alonzo de Aguilar!" to which the other rejoined, "And I am the Feri de Ben Estepar!"—a well-known name of terror to the Christians.

5. The sound of his detested name roused all the vengeance of the dying hero; and, grasping his foe in mortal agony, he rallied his strength for a final blow. But it was too late; his hand failed, and he was soon dispatched by the dagger of his more vigorous rival. Thus fell Alonzo Hernandez de Cordova, or Alonzo de Aguilar, as he is commonly called, from the land where his family estates lay.

6. "He was of the greatest authority among the grandees of his time," says Father Abarea, "for his lineage, personal character, large domains, and the high posts which he filled both in peace and war. More than forty years of his life he

served against the infidel ; under the banner of his house in boyhood, and as leader of that same banner in later life, as viceroy of Andalusia and commander of the royal armies.

7. "He was the fifth lord of his warlike and pious house who had fallen fighting for their country and religion against he accursed sect of Mahomet. And there is good reason to relieve," continues the same orthodox authority, "that his soul has received the reward of a Christian soldier, since he was armed on that very morning with the blessed sacraments of confession and communion."

---

32. GENTLE RIVER.

The sad death of Alonzo de Aguilar and his brave companions, as related in the foregoing lesson, fell mournfully upon the national heart of Spain, and was kept in fresh remembrance by the many expressions of sympathy and admiration which it called forth from the popular literature of the country. The following poem is a translation by the Rev. Thomas Percy, Protestant Bishop of Dromore, in Ireland (born 1728, died 1811), of one of the ballads in which the fate of the hero is commemorated. The translation is found in the "Reliques of Ancient English Poetry," a work edited by Bishop Percy with great taste and judgment, and originally published in 1765. It has since been frequently reprinted, and has exerted a most favorable influence upon English poetical literature of a date subsequent to its publication.

1. GENTLE river,* gentle river,
   Lo, thy streams are stain'd with gore;
   Many a brave and noble captain
   Floats along thy willow'd shore.

2. All beside thy limpid waters,
   All beside thy sands so bright,
   Moorish chiefs and Christian warriors
   Join'd in fierce and mortal fight.

3 Lords, and dukes, and noble princes
   On thy fatal banks were slain;

---

* The original is *Rio Verde*, that is, River Verde. But *verde* is Spanish also means *green ;* and the translator, not being aware that it was a proper name, substituted *gentle ;*—an epithet not well suited to a mountain stream.

Fatal banks, that gave to slaughter
All the pride and flower of Spain.

4. There the hero, brave Alonzo,
   Full of wounds and glory, died ;
There the fearless Urdiales
   Fell a victim by his side.

5. Lo, where yonder Don Saavedra*
   Through their squadrons slow retires;
Proud Seville, his native city,
   Proud Seville his worth admires.

6. Close behind, a renegado
   Loudly shouts, with taunting cry,
" Yield thee, yield thee, Don Saavedra!
   Dost thou from the battle fly?

7. " Well I know thee, haughty Christian;
   Long I lived beneath thy roof;
Oft I've in the lists of glory
   Seen thee win the prize of proof.

8. " Well I know thy aged parents,
   Well thy blooming bride I know;
Seven years I was thy captive,
   Seven years of pain and woe.

9. " May our prophet grant my wishes,
   Haughty chief, thou shalt be mine;
Thou shalt drink that cup of sorrow
   Which I drank when I was thine."

10. Like a lion turns the warrior,
   Back he sends an angry glare;
Whizzing came the Moorish javelin,
   Vainly whizzing, through the air.

---

* Don Saavedra is an imaginary personage, no nobleman of that
name having really been engaged in the battle.

11. Back the hero, full of fury,
Sent a deep and mortal wound;
Instant sank the renegado,
Mute and lifeless, on the ground.

12. With a thousand Moors surrounded,
Brave Saavedra stands at bay;
Wearied out, but never daunted,
Cold at length the warrior lay.

13. Near him fighting, great Alonzo
Stout resists the paynim bands,
From his slaughter'd steed dismounted,
Firm intrench'd behind him stands.

14. Furious press the hostile squadron,
Furious he repels their rage;
Loss of blood at length enfeebles;
Who can war with thousands wage ?

15. Where yon rock the plain o'ershadows,
Close beneath its foot retired,
Fainting sank the bleeding hero,
And without a groan expired.

---

33. St. Peter's Entry into Rome.

ARCHBISHOP HUGHES.

Most Reverend JOHN HUGHES, D. D., first Archbishop of New York, born in Tyrone, Ireland, in 1798. A few years after his ordination he was brought before the American public by a controversy and oral discussion with Rev. Mr. Breckinridge, a Presbyterian minister, which established his reputation as one of the ablest controversialists of the day. Indeed, his life since then has been almost a continual controversy, owing to the perpetual attacks made upon the Church through him. Soon after he became Bishop of New York, he was called on to maintain, in a long-protracted struggle, the freedom of education. His "Debates on the School Question," his "Letters to Kirwan," and his "Letters to Brooks," on the management of church property, are excellent specimens of close reasoning, keen wit, and polished sarcasm. Innumerable lectures and letters on various subjects connected with Catholic interests have kept the Archbishop in the front rank of the champions of the Church.

1. It must have been during the latter portion of the reign of

Tiberius Nero Drusus, or in the beginning of the reign of Nero, that a traveller, dressed in Eastern costume, was seen approaching one of the entrances of the imperial city of Rome. He was weary and wayworn. The dust of travel had incrusted itself on the perspiration of his brow He bore in his hand a staff, but not a crosier. His counterance was pale, but strik. ng and energetic in its expression. Partially bald, what re mained of his hair was gray, crisp, and curly.

2. Who was he ? No one cared to inquire, for he was only one of those approaching the gates of Rome, within the walls of which, we are told, the population numbered from three to four millions of souls. But who was this pilgrim? He was a man who carried a message from God and his Christ, and who had been impelled to deliver that message in the very heart and centre of Roman corruption and of Roman civiliza- tion, such as it was.

3. His name at that time was Peter. His original name had been Simon, but the Son of God having called him and his elder brother, Andrew, from the fisherman's bank on the Sea of Galilee, to be His apostles, changed the name of Simon and called him in the Syriac language, Cephas, which in Latin and English is translated Peter. In Syriac the word signifies a rock, and our Saviour, by changing his name, declared the mission for which he was especially selected.

4. He said to him : "Thou art Cephas, and upon this rock I will build my church, and the gates of hell shall not prevail against it." He was an Apostle, like his brother and the other ten. But he was more—he was the Rock on which the Church was to be built—he was the prince of the Apostolic College. And this was the man who was approaching the gates of the city of Rome. Where he slept that night, whether on or under the porch of some princely palace, his· tory has not informed us. But he soon began to proclaim the message which he had from God. To human view the attempt would appear to be desperate. Rome, at that pe- riod, was divided into two principal classes—masters and slaves—both of the same color, and, in many instances, both of the same country.

5. The higher class of those who were not slaves were, at that time, gorged to repletion with the wealth and the plunder which the triumphant armies of Rome had brought to the Imperial capital from the conquered tribes and nations of the then known world. These conquered nations, after having been plundered, as we might say, once for all, were still retained as perpetual tributaries to the exchequer of the Cæsars and of their satellites. The superstitions and idolatries of those nations were all inaugurated in the pagan temples of the Imperial city. Their corruption of morals was also introduced, spreading from freemen to slaves, although such was the state of local morals that no imported corruption could add much to the universal depravity.·

6. Such was Rome when this eastern stranger entered its inclosures. He preached the Word of Christ, and his preaching, even in that polluted atmosphere, brought forth many souls to acknowledge and adore the Crucified. He was subsequently joined by St. Paul, and both labored with a common zeal to propagate the doctrine of salvation. They had already made such an impression that the tyrant Nero had them arrested and condemned to death.

7. Peter was crucified, it is generally supposed, on the very spot on which St. Peter's church now stands. The cross was the instrument of punishment for the man of Hebrew origin. But Paul of Tarsus, having been born a Roman citizen, was entitled to a less ignominious death; and accordingly he was beheaded at a place called the Three Fountains, some distance from Rome. Nero made the distinction, which is now so popular, between what is called temporal and spiritual. The body was temporal; and Nero did not pretend to go farther than its destruction.

---

34 IF THOU COULDST BE A BIRD.

FADER.

1. IF thou couldst be a bird, what bird wouldst thou be?
A frolicsome gull on the billowy sea,

Screaming and wailing when stormy winds rave,
Or anchor'd, white thing! on the merry green wave?

2. Or an eagle aloft in the blue ether dwelling,
Free of the caves of the hoary Helvellyn,
Who is up in the sunshine when we are in shower,
And could reach our loved ocean in less than an hour?

3. Or a heron that haunts the Wallachian edge
Of the barbarous Danube, 'mid forests of sedge,
And hears the rude waters through dreary swamps
    flowing,
And the cry of the wild swans and buffaloes lowing?

4. Or a stork on a mosque's broken pillar in peace,
By some famous old stream in the bright land of Greece.
A sweet-manner'd householder! waiving his state,
Now and then, in some kind little toil for his mate?

5. Or a murmuring dove at Stamboul, buried deep
In the long cypress woods where the infidels sleep.
Whose leaf-muffled voice is the soul of the seas,
That hath pass'd from the Bosphorus into the trees!

6. Or a heath-bird, that lies on the Cheviot moor,
Where the wet, shining earth is as bare as the floor;
Who mutters glad sounds, though his joys are but few—
Yellow moon, windy sunshine, and skies cold and blue?

7. Or if thy man's heart worketh in thee at all,
Perchance thou wouldst dwell by some bold baron's hall
A black, glossy rook, working early and late,
Like a laboring man on the baron's estate?

8. Or a linnet who builds in the close hawthorn bough,
Where her small, frighten'd eyes may be seen looking
        through;
Who heeds not, fond mother! the ox-lips that shine
On the hedge-banks beneath; or the glazed celandine?

9. Or a swallow that flieth the sunny world over,
 The true home of spring and spring-flowers to discover;
 Who, go where he will, takes away on his wings
 Good words from mankind for the bright thoughts he
  brings ? ·

10. But what! can these pictures of strange winged mirth
 Make the child to forget that she walks on the earth?
 Dost thou feel at thy sides as though wings were to start
 From some place where they lie folded up in thy heart?

11. Then love the green things in thy first simple youth,
 The beasts, birds, and fishes, with heart and in truth
 And fancy shall pay thee thy love back in skill ;
 Thou shalt be all the birds of the air at thy will!

35. NOVEL READING.

ANON.

1. It is argued in favor of novel reading, that works of fiction of the present day are, in their general character, so correct in principle, so unexceptionable in narrative, sometimes even so high-toned in morality, and, in the case of some particular authors, so finished in style, and rich in the varied beauties of good compositions, that they may be perused not only without injury, but actually, under some aspects, with positive advantage. As clever delineations of character, too, they are said to afford so deep an insight into human nature, and so profitable a knowledge of the world and its ways, as to be in those respects a useful study for the inexperienced.

2. There can be no doubt of the vast improvement of the present period in that description of literary production emphatically called light. We know by hearsay that the romances of former days were not calculated to promote the health either of mind or heart ; and that they should have been superseded by fictitious works of a more refining tendency,

and a more enlightened character, canno; but be deemed an advantage. Yet, according to all the merit they can possibly claim, and viewing them under their very best and most favorable aspect, they are in many ways, to say the least, extremely dangerous.'

3. Novels are in general pictures, and usually very highly wrought pictures, of human passions; and it has been remarked, that although the conclusion of the tale frequently awards signal punishment and degradation to some very gross offender, yet that in a far greater number of instances passion is represented as working out its ends successfully, and attaining its object even by the sacrifice of duty—an evil lesson for the heart yet unacquainted with vice, and uncontaminated by the world. It may indeed be safely questioned whether the knowledge of human nature thus acquired is of a profitable kind, and whether experience of life might not, for all practical purposes, be derived from other and purer sources than the teachings of romances.

4. Again, novels, as a class, present false views of life; and as it is the error of the young to mistake those for realities, they become the dupes of their own ardent and enthusiastic imaginations, which, instead of trying to control and regulate, they actually strengthen and nourish with the poisonous food of phantoms and chimeras. When the thirst for novel reading has become insatiable, as with indulgence it is sure to do, they come at last to live in an unreal fairy-land, amid heroes and heroines of their own creation. The taste for serious reading and profitable occupation is destroyed—all relish for prayer is lost. In addition to their other disadvantages, many of these books unfortunately teem with maxims subversive of simple faith, and in cordial irreverence for the truths of religion; and so it but frequently happens, as the climax of evil, that faith suffers to a greater or lesser extent from their habitual, indiscriminate perusal.

5. As a recreation, light works may, of course, be occasionally resorted to; but so many and so great are their attendant dangers, that extreme care should be taken to neutralize their poison by infallible antidotes The selection of such works

should always be left to a religious parent, or a pious and intelligent friend. They should never be made an occupation, but merely serve as a pastime, and that occasionally. They should never be perused in the early part of the day, but only in the evening hour, specially laid aside for relaxation. They should never be continued beyond the moderate length of time to which, under prudent and pious direction, you have limited yourself—never resumed after night prayers, and never read on Sundays.

6. They should not be allowed to engross the mind to the exclusion of all other thoughts; but more especially during their perusal should the sweet, refreshing, invigorating thought of God's presence be often recalled, and our aspirations ascend to His Throne, that He who is the Author of all the happiness we enjoy may bless and sanctify even our amusements.

7. The observance of these conditions no doubt requires some self-control; but if you cannot exercise that control, neither can you expect to peruse works of fiction without material, perhaps fatal, injury to your precious soul. If you cannot exercise that control, you should never read novels. If there be one more than another of these conditions to which your are recommended strict fidelity, it is to the first. By referring, for directions in your reading, to a pious, experienced guide, you will be secured against making selections among that class of fictitious works impregnated with the venom of anti-catholic maxims.

8. And, as the spirit of impiety and infidelity so prevalent in the literary world, seeks a medium for its venom no less in works of science than in works of fiction, you will find the advantage of applying the foregoing rule in the one case as in the other, never reading a suspected author without having ascertained how far your doubts are well founded.

86. Death of Father Marquette.

J. G. SHEA.

JOHN GILMARY SHEA is a native of New York. He has made many valuable contributions to American Catholic literature. His writings are chiefly on historical and archæological subjects. His original "History of the Catholic Missions in America," and his translation (with additions) of De Courcy's "History of the Church in the United States," are works of great value to the student of ecclesiastical history. Mr. Shea, has also written "The First Book of History," and a short "History of the United States," for the use of schools.

1. CALMLY and cheerfully he saw the approach of death, for which he prepared by assidious prayer; his office he regularly recited to the last day of his life; a meditation on death, which he had long since prepared for this hour, he now made the subject of his thoughts; and as his kind but simple companions seemed overwhelmed at the prospect of their approaching loss, he blessed some water with the usual ceremonies, gave his companions directions how to act in his last moments, how to arrange his body when dead, and to commit it to the earth with the ceremonies he prescribed.

2. He now seemed but to seek a grave;—at last perceiving the mouth of a river which still bears his name, he pointed to an eminence as the place of his burial. . . . . His companions then erected a little bark cabin, and stretched the dying missionary beneath it as comfortably as their wants permitted them. Still a priest, rather than a man, he thought of his ministry, and, for the last time, heard the confessions of his companions and encouraged them to rely with confidence on the protection of God—then sent them to take the repose they so much needed.

3. When he felt his agony approaching, he called them, and taking his crucifix from around his neck he placed it in thei hands, thanking the Almighty for the favor of permitting him to die a Jesuit, a missionary, and alone. Then he relapsed into silence, interrupted only by his pious aspirations, till at last, with the names of Jesus and Mary on his lips, with his eyes raised as if in an ecstasy above his crucifix, with his face radiant with joy, he passed from the scene of his labor to God who was to be his reward.

4. Obedient to his directions, his companions, when the first outbursts of grief were over, laid out the body for burial, and to the sound of his little chapel bell, bore it slowly to the spot which he had pointed out. Here they committed his body to the earth, and, raising a cross above it, returned to their now desolate cabin. Such was the edifying and holy death of th illustrious explorer of the Mississippi, on Saturday, 18th of May, 1675.

37. The Cross in the Wilderness.

MRS. HEMANS.

FELICIA D. HEMANS was born in England in 1794; died in 1835. Her poetry has an elevated tone, with a fine appreciation of the beauty of nature and expresses the domestic affections with tenderness and truth.

1. SILENT and mournful sat an Indian chief,
   In the red sunset, by a grassy tomb;
His eyes, that might not weep, were dark with grief,
   And his arms folded in majestic gloom,
And his bow lay unstrung beneath the mound,
Which sanctified the gorgeous waste around.

2. For a pale cross above its greensward rose,
   Telling the cedars and the pines, that there
Man's heart and hope had struggled with his woes,
   And lifted from the dust a voice of prayer,—
Now all was hush'd; and eve's last splendor shone,
With a rich sadness, on the attesting stone.

3. There came a lonely traveller o'er the wild,
   And he, too, paused in reverence by that grave,
Asking the tale of its memorial, piled
   Between the forest and the lake's bright wave;
Till, as a wind might stir a wither'd oak,
On the deep dream of age his accents broke.

4. And the gray chieftain, slowly rising, said—
   " I listen'd for the words which, years ago,

Pass'd o'er these waters ; though the voice is fled,
    Which made them as a singing fountain's flow,
Yet, when I sit in their long-faded track,
Sometimes the forest's murmur gives them back.

5. "Ask'st thou of him whose house is lone beneath ?
    I was an eagle in my youthful pride,
When o'er the seas he came with summer's breath,
    To dwell amidst us on the lake's green side.
Many the times of flowers have been since then;
Many, but bringing naught like him again.

6. "Not with hunter's bow and spear he came,
    O'er the blue hills to chase the flying roe;
Not the dark glory of the woods to tame,
    Laying their cedars, like the corn stacks, low;
But to spread tidings of all holy things,
Gladdening our souls as with the morning's wings.

7. "Doth not yon cypress whisper how we met,
    I and my brethren that from earth are gone,
Under its boughs to hear his voice, which yet
    Seems through their gloom to send a silvery tone ?
He told of one the grave's dark lands who broke,
And our hearts burn'd within us as he spoke !

8. "He told of far and sunny lands, which lie
    Beyond the dust wherein our fathers dwell:
Bright must they be! for there are none that die,
    And none that weep, and none that say 'Farewell ?'
He came to guide us thither;—but away
The happy call'd him, and he might not stay.

9. "We saw him slowly fade—athirst, perchance,
    For the fresh waters of that lovely clime;
Yet was there still a sunbeam in his glance,
    And on his gleaming hair no touch of time;
Therefore we hoped—but now the lake looks dim,
For the green summer comes and finds not him

10 "We gather'd round him in the dewy hour
    Of one still morn, beneath his chosen tree:
From his clear voice at first the words of power
    Came low, like moanings of a distant sea;
But swell'd, and shook the wilderness ere long,
As if the spirit of the breeze grew strong.

11. "And then once more they trembled on his tongue,
    And his white eyelids flutter'd, and his head
Fell back, and mists upon his forehead hung—
    Know'st thou not how we pass to join the dead?
It is enough! he sank upon my breast,—
Our friend that loved us, he was gone to rest!

12. "We buried him where he was wont to pray,
    By the calm lake, e'en here, at eventide;
We rear'd this cross in token where he lay,
    For on the cross, he said, his Lord had died!
Now hath he surely reach'd, o'er mount and wave,
That flowery land whose green turf hides no grave!

13 "But I am sad—I mourn the clear light taken
    Back from my people, o'er whose place it shone,
The pathway to the better shore forsaken,
    And the true words forgotten, save by one,
Who hears them faintly sounding from the past,
Mingled with death-songs, in each fitful blast."

14 Then spoke the wanderer forth, with kindling eye:
    "Son of the wilderness, despair thou not,
Though the bright hour may seem to thee gone by,
    And the cloud settled o'er thy nation's lot;
Heaven darkly works,—yet where the seed hath been
There shall the fruitage, glowing, yet be seen."

38. EARLY DAYS AT EMMETTSBURG.

MRS. SETON.

Mrs. E. A. SETON, foundress of the Sisters of Charity in the United States, was a convert to the Catholic faith. The following letters were written to two of her friends, shortly after she had commenced the establishment of St. Joseph's, Emmettsburg—the Mother House of the Sisters of Charity. Her life has been beautifully written by Rev. Dr. White.

1. "IF you have received no other letters than those you mention, you do not perhaps know of the happy conversion and subsequent death of our Harriet Seton. Cecilia's death Mr. Zocchi must have mentioned particularly. Harriet's was also every way consoling. I have them both lying close by our dwelling, and there say my *Te Deum* every evening. O Antonio, could you and Filippo know half the blessing you have procured us all !

2. "My Anna now treads in their steps, and is an example of youth, beauty, and grace, internally and externally, which must be and is admired as a most striking blessing not only to her mother, but to many. My two little girls are very good, and know no other language or thoughts but of serving and loving our dear Lord—I do not mean in a religious life, which cannot be judged at their age, but of being his wherever they may be.

3. "The distant hope your letter gives that there is a possibility of your coming to this country, is a light to my gloomy prospects for my poor children ; not for their temporal good : our Lord knows I would never grieve to see them even beggars, if they preserve and practise their faith ; but their prospect, in case of my death, is as desolate as it can be, unless they are given up to their old friends, which would be almost their certain ruin of principle.

4. "I give all up, you may be sure, to Him who feeds the birds of heaven, as you say; but in the weak and decaying state of my health, which is almost broken down, can I look at the five without the fears and forebodings of a mother whose only thought or desire is for their eternity ? Our blessed Cheverus seemed to have many hopes of them when he came to see us last winter, and encouraged me to believe he

would do all he could for their protection. To him and your
Filicchi hearts I commit them in this world.

5. "Our success in having obtained the confidence of so
many respectable parents, who have committed the whole
charge of their children to us, to the number of about fifty,
besides poor children who have not means of education, has
enabled us to get on very well without debt or embarrassment,
and I hope onr Adored has already done a great deal through
our establishment.

6. "The Rev. Superior òf St. Mary's in Baltimore, who was
our first director, has zealously endeavored to do a great deal
more; but he did not find me as ready as converts generally
are, as I had to include the consideration of my poor children
in my religious character, which has greatly pleased and satisfied our blessed Cheverus and Archbishop Carroll, who is now
more my protector than ever,—more truly attached to us, and
finally takes the superior charge of our house, which at first
he had bestowed on another: so that every thing I do or act,
even in points less material, is and will be solely directed by
them. . . . O Filicchi! how is the blessing you most love increased and increasing in our wooden land, as you used to call
it! Blessed, a thousand times blessed, be His holy name
forever!

7. "You direct your letter to Baltimore, but we are fifty
miles from it, in the midst of woods and mountains. If we
had but the dear Christian children and their father and mother,
it would be an earthly paradise to me. No wars or rumors
of wars here, but fields ripe with harvest; the mountain
church, St. Mary's, the village church, St. Joseph's, and our
spacious log-house, containing a private chapel (our Adored
always there), is all our riches; and old Bony would not covet
them; though one of the most eloquent and elegant orators at
the bar of New York wrote our poor Harriet, among other
reasons why she should not listen 'to the siren voice of her
sister,' that in a few years every Catholic building should be
razed to the ground, and our house shortly be pulled about
our ears. That would be odd enough in the land of liberty.

8. "Will you tell your most honored brother that my

prayers shall not now go beyond the grave for him, but will be equally constant ? All the children go to communion once a month, except little Rebecca (Annina once a week), and believe me their mother's example and influence is not wanting to excite every devotion of gratitude and lively affection for their true and dearest friends and best of fathers, through whom they have received a real life, and been brought to the light of everlasting life. Our whole family, sisters and all, make our cause their own, and many, many communions have been and will be offered for you both, by souls who have no hope of knowing you but in heaven.

9. "Eternity, eternity, my brother !♥ Will I pass it with you ? So much has been given, which not only I never deserved, but have done every thing to provoke the adorable hand to withhold from me, that I even dare hope for *that*, that which I forever ask as the dearest, most desired favor. If I never write you again from this world, pray for me continually. If I am heard in the next, O Antonio, what would I not obtain for you, your Filippo, and all yours ! . . . . May the blessings you bestow on us be rewarded to you a thousand times ! Ever yours."

10. The blessings, however, enjoyed by the inmates of St. Joseph's, and the usefulness of the institution, would not have been permanent, without increased and strenuous exertions on the part of Mother Seton. The maintenance of the house found a provision in the income from the board and tuition of the pupils ; but the debts contracted by the improvement of their property were yet to be liquidated, and threatened to place it in a very embarrassing position.

11. To avert the destruction of the institution, Mother Seton privately appealed to the liberality of friends, among whom General Robert G. Harper was conspicuous, both for the interest he manifested in the welfare of St. Joseph's house, and for the eminence of his position in society.[1] The following

---

[1] General Harper, son-in-law of Charles Carroll of Carrollton, was one of the most gifted orators of the American Bar. Some of his speeches have been published in 3 vols., 8vo.

letter, addressed to him by Mother Seton, will serve to show the difficulties she had to contend with, and the eloquence of her pen in pleading the cause of religion and humanity:

12. "Will you permit the great distance between us to be forgotten, for a moment, and suffer the force of those sentiments which your liberality and kindness to us have created, to act without reserve in speaking to you on a subject I believe you think interesting? The promising and amiable perspective of establishing a house of plain and useful education, retired from the extravagance of the world, connected also with the view of providing nurses for the sick and poor, an abode of innocence and refuge of affliction, is, I fear, now disappearing under the pressure of debts contracted at its very foundation.

13. "Having received the pensions of our boarders in advance, and with them obliged not only to maintain ourselves, but also to discharge the endless demands of carpenters and workmen, we are reduced now to our credit, which is poor indeed. The credit of twenty poor women, who are capable only of earning their daily bread, is but a small stock, particularly when their flour-merchant, grocer, and butcher, are more already in advance than they are willing to afford.

14. "What is our resource? If we sell our house to pay our debts, we must severally return to our separate homes. Must it be so, or will a friendly hand assist us, become our guardian protector, plead our cause with the rich and powerful, serve the cause of humanity, and be a father to the poor? Would Mrs. Harper be interested for us, or is this an extravagant dream of female fancy? Oh, no; Mrs. Harper has a heart of pity,—she has proved it, unsolicited. If we were relieved but from a momentary embarrassment, her name would be blessed by future generations; for, so simple and unpretending is our object, we cannot fail of success if not crushed in our beginning. The Rev. Mr. Dubourg has exerted himself continually for us, and bestowed all he could personally give. From him we are to expect no more.

15. "What shall we do? How dare I ask you, dear sir, the question? But, if addressing it to you gives you a mo-

7

ment's displeasure, forgive ; and, considering it as any other occurrence of life which is differently judged of according to the light in which it is viewed, then blot it out, and be assured, whatever may be your impression of it, it arose from a heart filled with the sentiment of your generosity, and overflowing with gratitude and respect. Dear Mrs. Harper, tell your sweet nieces to look at the price of a shawl or veil, and think of the poor family of St. Joseph's. December 28th, 1811."

16. Happily for religion and society, the institution was rescued from its impending danger by the timely aid of its friends ; and though it had to struggle on amidst difficulties and trials, it gradually became more and more consolidated, and an instrument of great and extensive good in the hands of Divine Providence.

39. THE PARROT.

CAMPBELL.

THOMAS CAMPBELL, a native of Scotland, died in 1844. His principal poems are the "Pleasures of Hope," and "Gertrude of Wyoming;" but his genius is seen to greater advantage in his shorter poems, such as "The Exile of Erin," "O'Connor's Child," "Lochiel's Warning," "Hohenlinden," "The Battle of the Baltic," &c. These are matchless poems, containing a magic of expression that fastens the words forever upon the memory. No poet of our times has contributed so much, in proportion to the extent of his writings, to that stock of established quotations which pass from lip to lip and from pen to pen, without thought as to their origin.

1. THE deep affections of the breast,
   That Heaven to living things imparts,
   Are not exclusively possess'd
   By human hearts.

2. A parrot, from the Spanish Main,
   Full young, and early caged, came o'er,
   With bright wings, to the bleak domain
   Of Mulla's shore.

3. To spicy groves where he had won
   His plumage of resplendent hue,
   His native fruits, and skies, and sun,
   He bade adieu.

4 For these he changed the smoke of turf,
   A heathery land and misty sky,
And turn'd on rocks and raging surf
   His golden eye.

5. But, petted, in our climate cold
   He lived and chatter'd many a day;
Until with age, from green and gold,
   His wings grew gray.

6. At last, when, seeming blind and dumb,
   He scolded, laugh'd, and spoke no more,
A Spanish stranger chanced to come
   To Mulla's shore.

7 He hail'd the bird in Spanish speech;
   The bird in Spanish speech replied,
Flapp'd round his cage with joyous screech,
   Dropp'd down, and died.[1]

---

40. PORTRAIT OF A VIRTUOUS AND ACCOMPLISHED WOMAN.

FÉNELON.

FRANCIS DE SALIGNAC DE LA MOTHE FENELON, archbishop of Cambray, in France, was born at Perigord, 1651; died, at Cambray, 1715. No prelate of the Church, in any age, has left behind a greater name than Fénelon. It was truly said of him, that he was one of the meekest and most amiable of men. His works are numerous, and in high repute. They are chiefly on spiritual subjects. Those best known to the English reader, are the "Adventures of Telemachus," "Treatise on the Education of a Daughter," and "Treatise on the Love of God."

1. ANTIOPE is mild, simple, and wise; her hands despise not labor; she foresees things at a distance; she provides against all contingencies; she knows when it is proper to be silent; she acts regularly and without hurry; she is continually employed, but never embarrassed, because she does every thing in its proper season.

---

[1] The above poem records an incident which actually took place.

2. The good order of her father's house is her glory, it adds greater lustre to her than beauty. Though the care of all lies upon her, and she is charged with the burden of reproving, refusing, retrenching (things which make almost all women hated), yet she has acquired the love of all the household; and this, because they do not find in her either passion, or conceitedness, or levity, or humors as in other women. By a single glance of her eye, they know her meaning, and are afraid to displease her.

3. The orders she gives are precise; she commands nothing but what can be performed; she reproves with kindness, and in reproving encourages. Her father's heart reposes upon her as a traveller, fainting beneath the sun's sultry ray, reposes himself upon the tender grass under a shady tree.

4. Antiope is a treasure worth seeking in the most remote corners of the earth. Neither her person nor her mind is set off with vain ornaments; and her imagination, though lively, is restrained by her discretion. She never speaks but through necessity; and when she opens her mouth, soft persuasion and simple graces flow from her lips. When she speaks, every one is silent; and she is heard with such attention, that she blushes, and is almost inclined to suppress what she intended to say; so that she is rarely ever heard to speak at any length.

41. EXECUTION OF MARY, QUEEN OF SCOTS.

MISS AGNES STRICKLAND.

AGNES STRICKLAND is the author of "Lives of the Queens of England and Scotland." As a biographer, she is noted for her careful and erudite researches, and is generally considered impartial. In her "Life of Mary Stuart," she forcibly vindicates the persecuted, traduced, and beautiful queen from the dark imputations from which even Mary's friends have not always sufficiently defended her memory. Miss Strickland is a native of England.

1. BEFORE Mary proceeded further in her preparations for the block, she took a last farewell of her weeping maidens, kissing, embracing, and blessing them, by signing them with the cross, which benediction they received on their knees.

2. Her upper garments being removed, she remained in her

petticoat of crimson velvet and camisole, which laced behind, and covered her arms with a pair of crimson-velvet
sleeves. Jane Kennedy now drew from her pocket the gold-
bordered handkerchief Mary had given her to bind her eyes
With this she placed a Corpus Christi cloth—probably the
ame in which the consecrated wafer sent to her by the Pope
iad been enveloped. Jane folded it corner-wise, kissed i',
nd with trembling hands prepared to execute this last office;
but she and her companion burst into a fresh paroxysm of
hysterical sobbing and crying.

3. Mary placed her finger on her lips reprovingly. "Hush !"
said she ; "I have promised for you. Weep not, but pray for
me." When they had pinned the handkerchief over the face
of their beloved mistress, they were compelled to withdraw
from the scaffold ; and "she was left alone to close up the
tragedy of life by herself, which she did with her wonted
courage and devotion." Kneeling on the cushion, she repeated, in her usual clear, firm voice, *In te Domine speravi*—
"In thee, Lord, have I hoped ; let me never be put to confusion."

4. Being then guided by the executioners to find the block,
she bowed her head upon it intrepidly, exclaiming, as she did
so, *In manus tuas*—"Into thy hands, O Lord, I commend
my spirit." The Earl of Shrewsbury raised his baton, in performance of his duty as Earl Marshal, to give the signal for
the *coup-de-grâce ;* but he averted his head at the same time,
and covered his face with his hand, to conceal his agitation
and streaming tears.

5. A momentary pause ensued ; for the assistant-execu-
tioner perceived that the queen, grasping the block firmly
with both hands, was resting her chin upon them, and that
they must have been mangled or cut off if he had not removed them, which he did by drawing them down and holding
them tightly in his own, while his companion struck her with
the axe a cruel, but ineffectual blow. Agitated alike by the
courage of the royal victim, and the sobs and groans of the
sympathizing spectators, he missed his aim and inflicted a
deep wound on the side of the skull

6. She neither screamed nor stirred, but her sufferings were too sadly testified by the convulsion of her features, when, after the third blow, the butcherwork was accomplished, and the severed head, streaming with blood, was held up to the gaze of the people. "God save Queen Elizabeth!" cried the executioner. "So let all her enemies perish!" exclaimed the Dean of Peterborough. · One solitary voice alone responded "Amen!"—it was that of the Earl of Kent. The silence the tears, and groans of the witnesses of the tragedy, yea, even of the very assistants in it, proclaimed the feelings with which it had been regarded.

7. Mary's weeping ladies now approached and besought the executioners "not to strip the corpse of their beloved mistress, but to permit her faithful servants to fulfil her last request, by covering it as modesty required, and removing it to her bedchamber, where themselves and her other ladies would perform the last duties." But they were rudely repulsed, hurried out of the hall, and locked into a chamber while the executioners, intent only on securing what they considered their perquisites, began, with ruffian hands, to despoil the still warm and palpitating remains.

8. One faithful attendant, however, lingered, and refused to be thrust away. Mary's little Skye terrier had followed her to the scaffold unnoticed, had crept closer to her when she laid her head on the block, and was found crouching under her garments, saturated with her blood. It was only by violence he could be removed, and then he went and lay between her head and body, moaning piteously.

9. Some barbarous fanatic, desiring to force a verificatio of Knox's favorite comparison between this unfortunate prin cess and Jezebel, tried to tempt the dog to lap the blood of his royal mistress; but, with intelligence beyond that of his species, the sagacious creature refused; nor could he be induced to partake of food again, but pined himself to death.

10. The head was exposed on a black velvet cushion to the view of the populace in the court-yard for an hour, from the large window in the hall. No feeling but that of sympathy for her and indignation against her murderers was elicited by

this woful spectacle. The remains of this injured princess were contemptuously covered with the old cloth that had been torn from the billiard-table, and carried into a large upper chamber, where the process of embalming was performed the following day by surgeons from Stamford and Peterborough.

---

42 THE CONSTANCY OF NATURE.

DANA.

R. H. DANA, born at Cambridge, Mass., 1787, ranks high as a poet, and is surpassed by none of our prose writers in the clearness, purity and classic grace of his style and diction.

1. How like eternity doth nature seem
   To life of man—that short and fitful dream !
   I look around me : nowhere can I trace
   Lines of decay that mark our human race.
   These are the murmuring waters, these the flowers
   I mused o'er in my earlier, better hours.
   Like sounds and scents of yesterday they come.
   Long years have past since this was last my home !
   And I am weak, and toil-worn is my frame;
   But all this vale shuts in is still the same:
   'Tis I alone am changed; they know me not:
   I feel a stranger—or as one forgot.

2. The breeze that cool'd my warm and youthful brow
   Breathes the same freshness on its wrinkles now.
   The leaves that flung around me sun and shade,
   While gazing idly on them, as they play'd,
   Are holding yet their frolic in the air;
   The motion, joy, and beauty still are there,
   But not for me;—I look upon the ground:
   Myriads of happy faces throng me round,
   Familiar to my eye; yet heart and mind
   In vain would now the old communion find.
   Ye were as living, conscious beings then,
   With whom 1 talk'd--But I have talk'd with men !

With uncheer'd sorrow, with cold hearts I've met;
Seen honest minds by harden'd craft beset.
Seen hope cast down, turn deathly pale its glow;
Seen virtue rare, but more of virtue's show

---

43. THE HUMMING-BIRD.

AUDUBON.

JOHN J. AUDUBON was born in Louisiana, in 1780. His "Birds of America," in seven imperial octavo volumes, was pronounced by the great Cuvier the most splendid monument which art has erected to ornithology. He died in 1851.

1. WHERE is the person, who on observing this glittering fragment of the rainbow, would not pause, admire, and instantly turn his mind with reverence towards the Almighty Creator, the wonders of whose hand we at every step discover, and of whose sublime conceptions we everywhere observe the manifestations in his admirable system of creation? There breathes not such a person; so kindly have we all been blessed with that intuitive and noble feeling—admiration.

2. No sooner has the returning sun again introduced the vernal season, and caused millions of plants to expand their leaves and blossoms to his genial beams, than the little humming-bird is seen advancing on fairy wings, carefully visiting every opening flower-cup, and, like a curious florist, removing from each the injurious insect that otherwise would ere long cause their beauteous petals to droop and decay.

 3. Poised in the air, it is observed peeping cautiously, and with sparkling eye, into their innermost recesses, while the ethereal motions of its pinions, so rapid and so light, appear to fan and cool the flower, without injuring its fragile texture, and produce a delightful murmuring sound, well adapted for lulling the insects to repose. . . . . . The prairies, the fields, the orchards, the gardens, nay the deepest shades of the forest, are all visited in their turn, and everywhere the little bird meets with pleasure and with food.

4. Its gorgeous throat in brilliancy and beauty baffles all competition. Now it glows with a fiery hue, and again it is

changed to the deepest velvety black. The upper parts of its delicate body are of resplendent changing green; and it throws itself through the air with a swiftness and vivacity hardly conceivable. It moves from one flower to another like a gleam of light, upward, downward, to the right, and to the left. In this manner it searches the extreme northern portions of our country, following, with great precaution the advances of the season, and retreats, with equal care, at the approach of Autumn.

---

44. DESCRIPTION OF NATURE IN THE CHRISTIAN FATHERS.

HUMBOLDT.

ALEXANDER VON HUMBOLDT, a German baron, born in Berlin, 1769, and died in 1859, the most distinguished *savant* of the nineteenth century. He was the author of many profound and erudite works on natural and scientific subjects.

1. At the period when the feeling died away which had animated classical antiquity, and directed the minds of men to a visible manifestation of human activity rather than to a passive contemplation of the external world, a new spirit arose. Christianity gradually diffused itself, and wherever it was adopted as the religion of the State, it not only exercised a beneficial influence on the condition of the lower classes by inculcating the social freedom of mankind, but also expanded the views of men in their communion with nature. The eye no longer rested on forms of the Olympic gods. The Fathers of the Church, in their rhetorically correct and often poetically imaginative language, now taught that the Creator showed himself in inanimate no less than in animate nature, and in the wild strife of the elements, no less than in the still activity of organic development.

2. At the gradual dissolution of the Roman dominion, creative imagination, simplicity, and purity of diction, disappeared from the writings of that dreary age; first in the Latin territories, and then in Grecian Asia Minor. A taste for solitude, for mournful contemplation, and for a moody absorption of mind, may be traced simultaneously, in the style and coloring of the language.

3. Whenever a new element seems to develop itself in the feelings of mankind, it may almost invariably be traced to an earlier, deep-seated, individual germ. Thus the softness of Mimnermus has often been regarded as the expression of a general sentimental direction of the mind. The ancient world is not abruptly separated from the modern, but modifications in the religious sentiments and the tenderest social feelings of men, and changes in the special habits of those who exercise an influence on the ideas of the mass, must give a sudden predominance to that which might previously have escaped attention.

4. It was the tendency of the Christian mind to prove from the order of the universe, and the beauty of nature, the greatness and goodness of the Creator. This tendency to glorify the Deity in his works gave rise to a taste for natural descriptions. The earliest and most remarkable instances of this kind are to be met with in the writings of Minucius Felix, a rhetorician and lawyer at Rome, who lived in the beginning of the third century, and was the contemporary of Tertullian and Philostratus.

5. We follow with pleasure the delineation of his twilight rambles on the shore near Ostia, which he describes as more picturesque, and more conducive to health, than we find it in the present day. In the religious discourse entitled Octavius, we meet with a spirited defence of the new faith against the attacks of a heathen friend.

6. The present would appear to be a fitting place to introduce some fragmentary examples of the descriptions of nature, which occur in the writings of the Greek fathers, and which are probably less known to my readers than the evidences afforded by Roman authors, of the love of nature entertained by the ancient Italians.

7. I will begin with a letter of Basil the Great, for which I have long cherished a special predilection. Basil, who was born at Cesarea, in Cappadocia, renounced the pleasures of Athens when not more than thirty years old, and, after visiting the Christian hermitages in Caelo-Syria and Upper Egypt, retired to a desert on the shores of the Armenian river Iris. He thus writes to Gregory of Nazianzen:

8. "I believe I may at last flatter myself with having found the end of my wanderings. The hopes of being united with thee—or I should rather say, my pleasant dreams, for hopes have been justly termed the waking dreams of men—have remained unfulfilled. God has suffered me to find a place, such as has often flitted before our imaginations; for that which fancy has shown us from afar is now made manifest to me. A high mountain, clothed with thick woods, is watered to the north by fresh and overflowing streams; at its foot lies an extended plain rendered fruitful by the vapors with which it is moistened; the surrounding forest, crowded with trees of different kinds, incloses me as in a strong fortress.

9. "This wilderness is bounded by two deep ravines: on the one side the river rushing in foam down the mountain, forms an almost impassable barrier; while on the other, all access is impeded by a broad mountain ridge. My hut is so situated on the summit of the mountain, that I can overlook the whole plain, and follow throughout its course, the Iris, which is more beautiful, and has a more abundant body of water, than the Strymon near Amphipolis.

10. "The river of my wilderness, which is more impetuous than any other that I know of, breaks against the jutting rock, and throws itself foaming into the abyss below; an object of admiration to the mountain wanderer, and a source of profit to the natives, from the numerous fishes that are found in its waters. Shall I describe to thee the fructifying vapors that rise from the moist earth, or the cool breezes wafted over the rippled face of the waters?

11. "Shall I speak of the sweet song of the birds, or of the rich luxuriance of the flowering plants? What charms me beyond all else, is the calmness of this spot. It is only visited occasionally by huntsmen; for my wilderness nourishes herd of deer and wild goats, but not bears and wolves. Wha other spot could I exchange for this? Alemacon, when he had found the Echinades, would not wander farther."

12. In this simple description of scenery and of forest life, feelings are expressed which are more intimately in unison with those of modern times, than any thing that has been transmitt-

ed to us from Greek or Roman antiquity. From the lonely Alpine hut, to which St. Basil withdrew, the eye wanders over the humid and leafy roof of the forest below. The place of rest, which he and his friend Gregory of Nazianzen had long desired, is at length found. The poetic and mythical allusion t the close of the letter falls on the Christian ear like an echo rom another and earlier world.

13. Basil's Homilies on the Hexæmeron also give evidence of his love of nature. He describes the mildness of the constantly clear nights of Asia Minor, where, according to his expression, the stars, " those everlasting blossoms of heaven," elevate the soul from the visible to the invisible.

14. When in the myth of the Creation, he would praise the beauty of the sea, he describes the aspect of the boundless ocean-plain, in all its varied and ever-changing conditions, " gently moved by the breath of heaven, altering its hue as it reflects the beams of light in their whiter blue, or roseate hues, and caressing the shores in peaceful sport." We meet with the same sentimental and plaintive expressions regarding nature in the writings of Gregory of Nyssa, the brother of Basil the Great.

15. "When," he exclaims, "I see every ledge of rock, every valley and plain, covered with new-born verdure; the varied beauty of the trees, and the lilies at my feet decked by nature with the double charms of perfume and of color; when in the distance I see the ocean, toward which the clouds are onward borne, my spirit is overpowered by a sadness not wholly devoid of enjoyment.

16. "When in autumn, the fruits have passed away, the leaves have fallen, and the branches of the trees, dried and shrivelled, are robbed of their leafy adornments, we are instinctively led, amid the everlasting and regular change of nature, to feel the harmony of the wondrous powers pervading all things. He who contemplates them with the eye of the soul, feels the littleness of man amid the greatness of the Universe."

17. While the Greek Christians were led by their adoration of the Deity, through the contemplation of his works, to a

poetic delineation of nature, they were at the same time, during the earlier ages of their new belief, and owing to the peculiar bent of their minds, full of contempt for all works of human art. Thus Chrysostom abounds in passages like the following :

18. " If the aspect of the colonnades of sumptuous buildings would lead thy spirit astray, look upward to the vault of heaven, and around thee on the open fields, in which herds graze by the water's side. Who does not despise all the creations of art, when, in the stillness of his spirit, he watches with admiration the rising of the sun, as it pours its golden light over the face of the earth ; when, resting on the thick grass beside the murmuring spring, or beneath the sombre shade of a thick and leafy tree, the eye rests on the far-receding and hazy distance ?"

19. Antioch was at that time surrounded by hermitages, in one of which lived Chrysostom. It seemed as if Eloquence had recovered her element—freedom—from the fount of nature in the mountain regions of Syria and Asia Minor, which were then covered with forests.

---

45. THE VIRGIN MARTYR.

MASSINGER.

PHILIP MASSINGER was born at Salisbury, A. D. 1584. The "Virgin Martyr," the first printed of Massinger's works, appeared in 1622; but there can be little doubt that he had written much before that period. His literary career was a constant struggle, for fortune never smiled upon him. His writings breathe a spirit incomparably nobler and manlier than that of his contemporaries generally ; they are wholly free from the servile political maxims; and, in a large measure, from the grave offences against religion and morals with which the stage in his time abounded. Their merit consists less in the vigor with which they delineate passion they in their dignity and refinement of style, and the variety of their versification. To wit they have no pretensions.

The place of execution. Antonius, Theophilus, Dorothea, &c.

Ant.   See, she comes ;—
How sweet her innocence appears ! more like
To Heaven itself than any sacrifice
That can be offer'd to it. By my hopes
Of joys hereafter, the sight makes me doubtful

In my belief; nor can I think our gods
Are good, or to be served, that take delight
In offerings of this kind ; that, to maintain
Their power, deface this masterpiece of nature,
Which they themselves come short of.   She ascends,
And every step raises her nearer heaven !

            *   *   *   *   *

                                  She smiles,
Unmoved, by Mars ! as if she were assured
Death, looking on her constancy, would forget
The use of his inevitable hand.
   Theo. Derided too !   Dispatch, I say !
   Dor.   Thou fool !
Thou gloriest in having power to ravish
A trifle from me I am weary of.
What is this life to me ?   Not worth a thought,
Or, if it be esteem'd, 'tis that I lose it
To win a better : even thy malice serves
To me but as a ladder to mount up
To such a height of happiness, where I shall
Look down with scorn on thee and on the world ;
Where, circled with true pleasures, placed above
The reach of death or time, 'twill be my glory
To think at what an easy price I bought it.
There's a perpetual spring, perpetual youth ;
No joint-benumbing cold, or scorching heat,
Famine nor age, have any being there.
Forget for shame your Tempè ; bury in
Oblivion your feign'd Hesperian orchards :—
The golden fruit, kept by the watchful dragon,
Which did require a Hercules to get it,
Compared with what grows in all plenty there,
Deserves not to be named.   The Power I serve
Laughs at your happy Araby, or the
Elysian shades ; for He hath made his bowers
Better, indeed, than you can fancy yours.

            *   *   *   *   *

Enter Angelo, in the Angel's habit.

Dor. Thou glorious minister of the Power I serve
(For thou art more than mortal), is't for me,
Poor sinner, thou art pleased awhile to leave
Thy heavenly habitation, and vouchsafest,
Though glorified, to take my servant's habit?
For, put off thy divinity, so look'd
My lovely Angelo.

    Angelo.   Know, I am the same:
And still the servant to your piety.
Your zealous prayers and pious deeds first won me
(But 'twas by His command to whom you sent them)
To guide your steps. I tried your charity,
When, in a beggar's shape, you took me up,
And clothed my naked limbs, and after fed,
As you believed, my famished mouth. Learn all,
By your example, to look on the poor
With gentle eyes; for in such habits often
Angels desire an alms. I never left you,
Nor will I now; for I am sent to carry
Your pure and innocent soul to joys eternal,
Your martyrdom once suffer'd.

---

46. Queen Elizabeth of Hungary.

MONTALEMBERT.

Count Montalembert is one of the most distinguished statesmen and noblemen of France. He is cherished by every Catholic heart for his defence of Catholic principles, his opposition to godless education, and steady devotion to the interests of the Church.

1. Generosity to the poor, particularly that exercised by princes, was one of the most remarkable features of the age in which she lived; but we perceive that in her, charity did not proceed from rank, still less from the desire of acquiring praises or purely human gratitude, but from an interior and heavenly inspiration. From her cradle, she could not bear the sight of a poor person without feeling her heart pierced with grief, and

now that her husband had granted her full liberty in all that concerned the honor of God and the good of her neighbor, she unreservedly abandoned herself to her natural inclination to solace the suffering members of Christ.

2. This was her ruling thought each hour and moment: to the use of the poor she dedicated all that she retreuched from the superfluities usually required by her sex and rank. Yet, notwithstanding the resources which the charity of her husband placed at her disposal, she gave away so quickly all that she possessed, that it often happened that she would despoil herself of her clothes in order to have the means of assisting the unfortunate.

3. Elizabeth loved to carry secretly to the poor, not alone money, but provisions and other matters which she destined for them. She went thus laden, by the winding and rugged paths that led from the castle to the city, and to cabins of the neighboring valleys.

4. One day, when accompanied by one of her favorite maidens, as she descended by a rude little path (still pointed out), and carried under her mantle bread, meat, eggs, and other food to distribute to the poor, she suddenly encountered her husband, who was returning from hunting. Astonished to see her thus toiling on under the weight of her burden, he said to her, "Let us see what you carry," and at the same time drew open the mantle which she held closely clasped to her bosom ; but beneath it were only red and white roses, the most beautiful he had ever seen—and this astonished him, as it was no longer the season of flowers.

5. Seeing that Elizabeth was troubled, he sought to console her by his caresses; but he ceased suddenly, on seeing over her head a luminous appearance in the form of a crucifix. He then lesired her to continue her route without being disturbed by him, and he returned to Wartbourg, meditating with recollection on what God did for her, and carrying with him one of these wonderful roses, which he preserved all his life.

6. At the spot where this meeting took place, he erected a pillar, surmounted by a cross, to consecrate forever the remembrance of that which he had seen hovering over the head of

his wife. Among the unfortunate who particularly attracted her compassion, those who occupied the greatest part in her heart were the lepers; the mysterious and special character of their malady rendered them, throughout the middle ages, objects of a solicitude and affection mingled with fear.

---

47. AGES OF FAITH.

BY KENELM H. DIGBY.

KENELM H. DIGBY, in his "Compitum, or Meeting of the Ways," and his "Mores Catholici, or Ages of Faith," devotes all the resources of his profound erudition to the middle ages. The latter work is one of the most remarkable literary productions of our times, for its varied learning, its deep, reverential tone, its sincere and fervent piety, and its noble appreciation of Catholic honor and Catholic heroism. K. H. Digby is a native of England.

1. IN the third stage of this mortal course, if midway be the sixth, and on the joyful day which hears of the great crowd that no man could number, I found me in the cloister of an abbey, whither I had come to seek the grace of that high festival. The hour was day's decline; and already had "Placebo Domino" been sung in solemn tones, to usher in the hours of special charity for those who are of the suffering Church. A harsh sound from the simultaneous closing of as many books, cased in oak and iron, as there were voices in that full choir, like a sudden thunder-crash, announced the end of that ghostly vesper.

2. The saintly men, one by one, slowly walked forth, each proceeding to his special exercise. Door then shutting after door gave long echoes, till all was mute stillness, and I was left alone, under cloistered arches, to meditate on the felicity of blessed spirits, and on the desire which presses both the living and the inmates of that region in which the soul is purged from sinful stain, to join their happy company. Still, methought I heard them sing of the bright and puissant angel ascending from the rising of the sun—and of the twelve times twelve thousand that were signed; and of the redeemed from every nation and people and language; and of the angels who stood around the throne of Heaven.

3. It seemed now as if I heard a voice like that which said to Dante, "What thou heardst was sung that freely thou mightst open thy heart to the waters of peace, that flow diffused from their eternal fountain." What man is there so brutish and senseless, to things divine, as not to have sometimes experienced an interval like that which is described by him who sung of Paradise, to whom the world appeared as if stretched far below his feet, and who saw this globe—

> " So pitiful of semblance, that perforce
> It moved his smiles ; and him in truth did hold
> For wisest, who esteems it least—whose thoughts
> Elsewhere are fix'd, him worthiest call'd and best ?" [1]

4. But soon the strained sense will sink back to it—for the human spirit must perforce accomplish, in the first place, its exercise in that school which is to prepare it for the home it anticipates above. Yet I felt not disconsolate nor forgetful of the bright vision. My thoughts were carried backwards to ages which the muse of history had taught me long to love; for it was in obscure and lowly middle-time of saintly annals that multitudes of these bright spirits took their flight from a dark world to the Heavens.

5. The middle ages, then, I said, were ages of highest grace to men—ages of faith—ages when all Europe was Catholic ; when vast temples were seen to rise in every place of human concourse, to give glory to God, and to exalt men's souls to sanctity ; when houses of holy peace and order were found amidst woods and desolate mountains — on the banks of placid lakes, as well as on the solitary rocks in the ocean ; ages of sanctity which witnessed a Bede, an Alcuin, a Bernard, a Francis, and crowds who followed them as they did Christ ; ages of vast and beneficent intelligence, in which it pleased the Holy Spirit to display the power of the seven gifts in the lives of an Anselm, a Thomas of Aquinum, and the saintly flocks whose steps a cloister guarded : ages of the highest civil virtue, which gave birth to the laws and institutions of an Edward, a Lewis, a Suger ; ages of the noblest

---

[1] Cary's *Dante.*

art, which beheld a Giotto, a Michael Angelo, a Raffaelo, a
Dominichino ; ages of poetry, which heard an Avitus, a Caed-
mon, a Dante, a Shakspeare, a Calderon ; ages of more than
mortal heroism, which produced a Tancred and a Godfrey ;
ages of majesty, which knew a Charlemagne, an Alfred, and
the sainted youth who bore the lily ; ages, too, of England'
glory, when she appears, not even excluding a comparison
with the Eastern empire, as the most truly civilized country
on the globe ; when the sovereign of the greater portion of
the western world applied to her schools for instructors—
when she sends forth her saints to evangelize the nations of
the north, and to diffuse spiritual treasure over the whole
world—when heroes flock to her court to behold the models
of reproachless chivalry, and emperors leave their thrones to
adore God at the tombs of her martyrs ! as Dante says,

> " No tongue
> So vast a theme could equal, speech and thought
> Both impotent alike."

6. In a little work which embodied the reflections, the
hopes, and even the joys of youthful prime, I once attempted
to survey the middle ages in relation to chivalry ; and though
in this we had occasion to visit the cloister, and to hear as a
stranger who tarries but a night, the counsels of the wise and
holy, we were never able to regard the house of peace as our
home ; we were soon called away from it to return to the
world and to the courts of its princes.   Now I propose to
commence a course more peaceful and unpretending, for it
only supposes that one has left the world, and withdrawn
from these vain phantoms of honor and glory, which distract
so often the morning of man's day.   Thus we read that in
youth many have left the cloister, dazzled by the pomp and
circumstance of a wild, delusive chivalry, who, after a littl
while, have hastened back to it, moved by a sense of earthly
vanity ; there

> " To finish the short pilgrimage of life,
> Still speeding to its close on restless wing.'

---

[1] Dante, *Purg.* 20.

7. Yes, all is vanity but to love and serve God! Men have found by long experience that nothing but divine love can satisfy that restless craving which ever holds the soul, ' finding no food on earth ;" that every beauty, every treasure, every joy, must, by the law which rules contingency, vanish like a dream : and that there will remain for every man, sooner or later, the gloom of dark and chaotic night, if he is ot provided with a lamp of faith. Those men who, reasoning, went to depth profoundest, came to the same conclusion ; they found that the labors of the learned, and the visions of the poet, were not of their own nature different in this respect from the pleasures of sense :

> " 'Tis darkness all : or shadow of the flesh,
> Or else its poison."   .

48. AGES OF FAITH—*continued.*

1. THIS was their experience. That labor of the mind, or that fond ideal ecstasy, did not necessarily secure the one thing needful—the love of Jesus. In a vast number of instances it led to no substantial good : its object was soon forgotten, or the mind recurred to the performance with a sense of its imperfections.

2. Still the heart cried, Something more! What, said they, can be given to it? What will content it? Fresh labor? fresh objects? Ah! they had already begun to suspect how little all this would avail; for, in hearkening to "the saintly soul, that shows the world's deceitfulness to all who hear him," they had learned to know that it might indeed be given to their weakness to feel the cruel discord, but not to set it right—to know that it was but a vain, delusive motive which would excite them to exertion from a desire of pleasing men ; for men pass rapidly with the changing scene of life, and the poor youth, who, mistaking the true end of human labor, had fondly reckoned upon long interchange of

respect and friendship, at the moment when his hopes are brightest and his affections warmed into ecstasy, wakens suddenly from his sweet protracted dream, and finds himself without honor, without love, without even a remembrance, and virtually in as great solitude as if he were already in his grave!

3. Well might they shudder at the thought of this eternal chilliness, this spiritual isolation, this bitter and unholy state! Truly it was fearful, and something too much for tears! Sweet Jesus, how different would have been their state, if they had sought only to love and serve thee! for thy love alone can give rest and comfort to the heart—a sure and lasting joy :—

> Other good
> There is, where man finds not his happiness;
> It is not true fruition; not that blest
> Essence of every good, the branch and root.

4. Changed, then, be the way and object of our research, and let the converse to that which formerly took place hold respecting our employment here; and if we shall again meet with knights and the world's chivalry, let it be only in the way of accident, and, as it were, from the visit of those who pass near our spot of shelter; and let our place of rest henceforth be in the forest and the cell.

5. Times there are, when even the least wise can seize a constant truth—that the heart must be devoted either all to the world, or all to God. When they, too, will pray, and make supplications urged with weeping, that the latter may be their condition in the mortal hour, that they may secure the rest of the saints for eternity.

6. Returning to that cloisteral meditation, how many thought I, throughout the whole world, have heard this day the grounds and consummation of the saints' felicity! how many have been summoned onward, and told the steps were near, and that now the ascent might be without difficulty gained? and yet,

> A scanty few are they, who, when they hear
> Such tidings, hasten. Oh, ye race of men!

Though born to soar, why suffer ye a wind
So slight to baffle ye ?"[1]

7. But for those who seemed to feel how sweet was that
solemn accent, eight times sung, which taught them who were
blessed, would it not be well, when left alone, and without
distraction, if they were to take up histories, and survey the
course which has been trod by saintly feet, and mark, as if
from the soul-purifying mount, the ways and works of men on
earth, keeping their eyes with fixed observance bent upon the
symbol there conveyed, so as to mark how far the form and
acts of that life, in ages past, of which there are still so
many monuments around them, agreed, not with this or that
modern standard of political and social happiness and grandeur, but with what, by Heaven's sufferance, gives title to
divine and everlasting beatitude?

8. Such a view would present a varied and immense horizon, comprising the manners, institutions, and spirit of many
generations of men long since gone by. We should see in
what manner the whole type and form of life were Christian,
although its detail may have often been broken and disordered;
for instance, how the pursuits of the learned, the consolations
of the poor, the riches of the Church, the exercises and dispositions of the young, and the common hope and consolation
of all men, harmonized with the character of those that sought
to be poor in spirit.

9. How, again, the principle of obedience, the Constitution
of the Church, the division of ministration, and the rule of
government, the manners and institutions of society, agreed
with meekness and inherited its recompense. Further, how
the sufferings of just men, and the provisions for a penitential
spirit were in accordance with the state of those that were to
mourn and weep there.

10. How the character of men in sacred orders, the zeal of
the laity, and the lives of all ranks, denoted the hunger and
thirst after justice. Again, how the institutions, the foundations, and the recognized principle of perfection, proclaimed

---

[1] Dante *Parad.* 12. Carey's translation.

ᴚᴇn merciful Moreover, how the philosophy which prevailed,
and the spiritual monuments which were raised by piety and
genius, evinced the clean of heart.

11. Still further, how the union of nations, and the bond
of peace which existed even amid savage discord, wars, and
confusion; as also, how the holy retreats for innocence, which
hen everywhere abounded, marked the multitude of pacific
men. And, finally, how the advantage taken of dire events,
and the acts of saintly and heroic fame, revealed the spirit
which shunned not suffering for sake of justice.

49. THE SHEPHERD'S SONG.

TASSO.

Torquato Tasso—an Italian poet of the sixteenth century. He wrote
much, but his "Jerusalem Delivered" gained him the greatest renown;
during his life it excited universal favor, and has ever since been justly
regarded as one of the great poems of the world. "Jerusalem Delivered"
is a history of the crusades, related with poetic license.

Clement VIII. invited Tasso to Rome, that he might receive the laurel
crown—an honor which had not been conferred upon any one since the
days of Petrarch. But scarcely was the day of coronation about to dawn
when the poet felt his dissolution approaching. He requested liberty
to retire to the monastery of St. Onofrio. On hearing that his last hour
was near, he joyfully returned thanks to God for having brought him to so
secure a haven. A few days before his death, one of the monks sought to
raise his spirits by speaking to him of the triumphal honors preparing for
him at the Capitol. Tasso replied—"Glory, glory, nothing but glory. Two
idols have reigned in my heart and decided my life—love and that vapor
you call glory. The one has always betrayed me; the other, after fleeing
me for forty years, is ready to-day to crown—what?—a corpse. Laurels for
Tasso! It is a winding sheet he requires! I feel too well to-day that on earth
all is vanity, all but to love and serve God. But," he added, as his head sunk
on his breast, "all the rest is not worth a quarter of an hour's trouble."
On receiving a plenary indulgence from the Pope, he said—"This was
the chariot on which he hoped to go crowned, not with laurel as a poet into
the Capitol, but with glory, as a saint, to Heaven." Feeling his mortal
agony at hand, he closely embraced the crucifix, and murmuring, "Into
thy hands, O Lord!" peacefully resigned his spirit.

1. SAFE stands our simple shed, despised our little store;
   Despised by others, but so dear to me,
      That gems and crowns I hold in less esteem;
   From pride, from avarice, is my spirit free,
      And mad ambition's visionary dream.
   My thirst I quench in the pellucid stream,

Nor fear lest poison the pure wave pollutes ;
  With flocks my fields, my fields with herbage teem ;
My garden-plot supplies nutritious roots ;
And my brown orchard bends with Autumn's wealthiest
    fruits.

2. Few are our wishes, few our wants ; man needs
  But little to preserve the vital spark :
These are my sons ; they keep the flock that feeds,
  And rise in the gray morning with the lark.
Thus in my hermitage I live ; now mark
The goats disport amid the budding brooms ;
  Now the slim stags bound through the forest dark ;
The fish glide by, the bees hum round the blooms ;
And the birds spread to heaven the splendor of their plumes

3. Time was (these gray hairs then were golden locks),
  When other wishes wanton'd in my veins ;
I scorn'd the simple charge of tending flocks,
  And fled disgusted from my native plains.
Awhile in Memphis I abode, where reigns
The mighty Caliph ; he admired my port,
  And made me keeper of his flower-domains ;
And though to town I rarely made resort,
Much have I seen and known of the intrigues of court.

4. Long by presumptuous hopes was I beguiled,
  And many, many a disappointment bore ;
But when with youth false hope no longer smiled,
  And the scene pall'd that charm'd so much before,—
I sigh'd for my lost peace, and brooded o'er
The abandoned quiet of this humble shed ;
  Then farewell State's proud palaces ! once more
To these delightful solitudes I fled ;
And in their peaceful shades harmonious days have led.

50. BISHOP BRUTÉ.

BAYLEY.

JAMES ROOSEVELT BAYLEY, D. D., first bishop of Newark, was born in New York, on the 23d of August, 1814. Being by birth and education, a Protestant, he spent some years in the ministry of the Episcopal Church. He was received into the Catholic Church, by the Rev. Father Esmonde, S. J., at Rome, April 26, 1842. On the 4th of March, 1843, he was ordained priest, by Bishop (now Archbishop) Hughes, and on the 30th of October, 1853, was consecrated by the most Reverend Archbishop Bedini, Bishop of Newark, which had been erected into an Episcopal See, by his Holiness Pope Pius IX., on the 29th of July, 1853. Bishop Bayley is the author of a very useful and interesting work on the history of the Catholic Church in New York. It may be interesting to observe, that the Right Reverend prelate is a nephew of Mother Seton, the founder of the Sisters of Charity in this country, also a convert to the Catholic Church.

[Extract from the forthcoming Memoirs of the Right Reverend Simon Wm. Gabriel Bruté, D. D., by the Right Reverend Dr. Bayley.]

1. HE turned from it (the medical profession), only because he had higher and more important objects in view. His eleven thousand classmates in medicine, told him that it was easy to find physicians for the body, but the Revolution had made it more difficult to find physicians for the souls of men. For ten years the houses of religious education and seminaries had been shut up. The guillotine, and prisons, and privations of exile, had spared but a comparatively small number of the former clergy, and of these many were occupied in foreign missions.

2. Dreadful as had been the ravages of infidelity and impiety, and the almost entire privation of all spiritual succor, an immense number of the French people still remained faithful to their religion, and a new supply of Levites, to fill the places of those who had perished, was called for on every side. One of the first matters to which the new bishops turned their attention, was the re-establishment of Diocesan Seminaries, in order to provide for these pressing wants.

3. These were the circumstances which induced Mr. Bruté to seek admission into the sanctuary. Such a determination could surprise no one who knew him. His whole life, even in the world, had already been a preparation for it. At a different time, it would probably have been his first choice, and having chosen it now, he gave himself wholly to the work.

He always studied with his pen in his hand, and his manu
scripts again mark the exactness and extent of his new studies.
Theology was a science for which his mind was admirably
fitted. He loved his religion, and it evidently became his
delight thoroughly to explore the very foundations of it.

4. In note books, made at this time, each subject is devel
ped and illustrated, as if his place had been that of a teach
r, instead of a scholar. Bishop Bruté was never a surface
tudent, but now he became, emphatically, a foundation one.
The works of the fathers of the Church, the acts and canons
of her councils, as marking her tradition, were carefully
studied by him. From this time until the end of his life,
every thing that he read or studied was with this view.

5. His voluminous memoranda show how carefully he recorded
every thing which might serve to defend or illustrate the truth,
or to expose and confute error. He made the principles of the
various sects his careful study, after he came to this country,
and could have written a philosophical history of them, if he
had seen fit. No one ever made a more faithful and exact
use of every moment of his time. He never was idle, and as
a consequence of this, his tenacious memory enabled him to
bring forth from the treasure-house of his mind, things new
and old.

51. Loss and Gain.

DR. NEWMAN.

JOHN HENRY NEWMAN, D.D., superior of the Oratory in England, born
21st February, 1901. In 1845 he became a convert to the Catholic faith,
and was ordained priest in Rome, May 26, 1847. He was appointed first
rector of the Catholic University of Ireland, which office he filled for several years. Dr. Newman is undoubtedly one of the leading minds of the
present century. His English style is unrivalled in any age for majesty,
copiousness, and long-drawn but sustained harmony. His learning is
quite a marvel among Englishmen, and is united with a profound and subtle analytic genius. "Loss and Gain," and "Callista," are works of fiction in which he has displayed as singular a versatility.

1. THE conversation flagged ; Bateman was again busy with
his memory, and he was getting impatient, too ; time was
slipping away, and no blow struck. Moreover, Willis was
beginning to gape, and Charles seemed impatient to be re

leased. "These Romanists put things so plausibly," he said
to himself, "but very unfairly, most unfairly ; one ought to
be up to their dodges. I dare say, if the truth were known,
Willis has had lessons ; he looks so demure. I dare say he
s keeping back a great deal, and playing upon my ignorance.
Who knows ? perhaps he's a concealed Jesuit."

2. It was an awful thought, and suspended the course of his
reflections some seconds. "I wonder what he does really think ;
it's so difficult to get at the bottom of them ; they won't tell
tales, and they are under obedience ; one never knows when
to believe them. I suspect he has been wofully disappointed
with Romanism, he looks so thin; but of course he won't
say so: it hurts a man's pride, and he likes to be consistent ;
he doesn't like to be laughed at, and so he makes the best of
things.

3. I° wish I knew how to treat him ; I was wrong in
having Reding here ; of course Willis would not be confidential before a third person. He's like the fox that lost his
tail. It was bad tact in me ; I see it now ; what a thing it
is to have tact ! it requires very delicate tact. There are so
many things I wish to say about Indulgences, about their so
seldom communicating; I think I must ask him about the
Mass." So, after fidgeting a good deal within, while he was
ostensibly employed in making tea, he commenced his last assault.

4. "Well, we shall have you back again among us by next
Christmas, Willis," he said ; " I can't give you greater law ;
I am certain of it; it takes time, but slow and sure. What
a joyful time it will be ! I can't tell what keeps you ; you
are doing nothing ; you are flung into a corner ; you are
wasting life. *What* keeps you ?" Willis looked odd ; and
then simply answered, ".Grace." Bateman was startled, but
recovered himself ; " Heaven forbid," he said, " that I should
treat these things lightly, or interfere with you unduly.

5. "I know, my dear friend, what a serious fellow you are;
but do tell me, just tell me, how can you justify the Mass, as
it is performed abroad? how can it be called a 'reasonable
service,' when all parties conspire to gabble it over; as if it

mattered not a jot who attended to it, or even understood it!
Speak, man, speak," he added, gently shaking him by the
shoulder.

6. "These are such difficult questions," answered Willis;
"must I speak? Such difficult questions," he continued, rising into a more animated manner, and kindling as he went on;
"I mean, people view them so differently; it is so difficult to
convey to one person the idea of another. The idea of worship is different in the Catholic Church from the idea of it in
your Church ; for, in truth, the *religions* are different. Don't
deceive yourself, my dear Bateman," he said tenderly, "it is
not that ours is your religion carried a little farther—a little
too far, as you would say. No, they differ in kind, not in degree ; ours is one religion, yours another.

7. "And when the time comes, and come it will for you, alien
as you are now, to submit yourself to the gracious yoke of Christ,
then, my dearest Bateman, it will be *faith* which will enable you
to bear the ways and usages of Catholics, which else might perhaps startle you. Else, the habits of years, the associations
in your mind of a certain outward behavior, with real inward
acts of devotion, might embarrass you, when you had to conform yourself to other habits, and to create for yourself other
associations. But this faith, of which I speak, the great gift
of God, will enable you in that day to overcome yourself, and
to submit, as your judgment, your will, your reason, your
affections, so your tastes and likings, to the rule and usage of
the Church.

8. "Ah, that faith should be necessary in such a matter,
and that what is so natural and becoming under the circumstances, should have need of an explanation ! I declare, to
me," he said, and he clasped his hands on his knees, and
looked forward as if soliloquizing, "to me nothing is so consoling, so piercing, so thrilling, so overcoming, as the Mass,
said as it is among us. I could attend masses forever, and
not be tired. It is not a mere form of words—it is a great
action, the greatest action that can be on earth. It is not
the invocation merely, but, if I dare use the word, the evoca-
tion of the Eternal. He becomes present on the altar in flesh

and blood, before whom angels bow and devils tremble. This is that awful event which is the end, and is the interpretation, of every part of the solemnity.

9. "Words are necessary but as means, not as ends ; they are not mere addresses to the throne of grace, they are in truments of what is far higher—of consecration, of sacrifice They hurry on as if impatient to fulfil their mission. Quick y they go, the whole is quiek; for they are all parts of one in tegral action. Quickly they go; for they are awful words o. sacrifice, they are a work too great to delay upon; as when it was said in the beginning, 'What thou doest, do quickly.' Quickly they pass; for the Lord Jesus goes with them, as He passed along the lake in the days of His flesh, quickly calling first one and then another.

10. "Quickly they pass ; because as the lightning which shineth from one part of the heaven unto the other, so is the coming of the Son of Man. Quickly they pass ; for they are as the words of Moses, when the Lord came down in a cloud, calling on the Name of the Lord as He passed by, 'The Lord, the Lord God, merciful and gracious, long suffering, and abun- dant in goodness and truth.' And as Moses on the mountain, so we, too, 'make haste and bow our heads to the earth, and adore.' So we, all around, each in his place, look out for the great Advent, 'waiting for the moving of the water.'

11. "Each in his place, with his own heart, with his own wants, with his own thoughts, with his own intestions, with his own prayers, separate but concordant, watching what is going on, watching its progress, uniting in its consummation ; not painfully and hopelessly following a hard form of prayer from beginning to end, but like a concert of musical instru- ments, each different, but concurring in a sweet harmony, we take our part with God's priest, supporting him, yet guided by him.

12. "There are little children there, and old men, and simple laborers, and students in seminaries, priests preparing for mass, priests making their thanksgiving ; there are innocent maidens, and there are penitents ; but out of these many minds rises one eucharistic hymn, and the great Action is the measure and

the scope of it. And oh, my dear Bateman," he added, turning to him, "you ask me whether this is not a formal, unreasonable service? It is wonderful!" he cried, rising up, "quite wonderful. When will these dear good people be enlightened? O Wisdom, strongly and sweetly disposing all things! O Adonai! O Key of David, and Expectation of nations—come and save us, O Lord our God!"

13. Now, at least, there was no mistaking Willis. Bateman started, and was almost frightened at a burst of enthusiasm which he had been far from expecting. "Why, Willis," he said, "it is not true, then, after all, what we heard, that you were somewhat dubious, shaky, in your adherence to Romanism? I'm sure I beg your pardon; I would not for the world have annoyed you, had I known the truth." Willis's face still glowed, and he looked as youthful and radiant as he had been two years before.

14. There was nothing ungentle in his impetuosity; a smile, almost a laugh, was on his face, as if he was half ashamed of his own warmth; but this took nothing from its evident sincerity. He seized Bateman's two hands, before the latter knew where he was, lifted him up out of his seat, and raising his own mouth close to his ear, said in a low voice, "I would to God, that not only thou, but also all who hear me this day, were both in little and in much such as I am, except these chains." Then, reminding him it had grown late, and bidding him good-night, he left the room with Charles.

15 Bateman remained awhile with his back to the fire after the door had closed; presently he began to give expression to his thoughts. "Well," he said, "he's a brick, a regular brick; he has almost affected me myself. What a way those fellows have with them! I declare his touch has made my heart beat; how catching enthusiasm is! Any one but I might really have been unsettled. He is a real good fellow; what a pity we have not got him! he's just the sort of man we want. He'd make a splendid Anglican; he'd convert half the dissenters in the country. Well, we shall have them in time; we must not be impatient   But the idea of his talking

of converting *me;* ' in little and in much,' as he worded it !
By the by, what did he mean by ' except these chains ?'"

16. He sat ruminating on the difficulty; at first he was
inclined to think that, after all, he might have some misgiv-
ings about his position; then he thought that perhaps he had
a hair shirt or a catenella on him; and lastly, he came to the
conclusion that he had just meant nothing at all, and did but
finish the quotation he had begun. After passing some little
time in this state, he looked towards the tea-tray; poured
himself out another cup of tea; ate a bit of toast; took the
coals off the fire; blew out one of the candles, and taking up
the other, left the parlor, and wound like an omnibus up the
steep twisting staircase to his bedroom.

52. ADVICE TO A YOUNG CRITIC.

POPE.

ALEXANDER POPE will always be popular while the English language
remains as it is. One of his merits was to mould the language of poetry
into pliancy and softness:—before his time there was much ruggedness in
the diction even of the most celebrated poets. Some of his pieces are repulsive to the sentiments of religion and morals. He died in 1744.

1. 'Tis not enough, taste, judgment, learning join;
   In all you speak, let truth and candor shine ;
   That not alone what to your sense is due
   All may allow, but seek your friendship too.
   Be silent always, when you doubt your sense,
   And speak, though sure, with seeming diffidence.

2. Some positive, persisting fops we know,
   Who, if once wrong, will needs be always so :
   But *you*, with pleasure, own *your* errors past,
   And make each day a critic on the last.
   'Tis not enough your counsel to be true :
   Blunt truths more mischief than slight errors do ;
   Men must be taught, as if you taught them not,
   And things unknown proposed, as things forgot.

3. Without good breeding truth is disapproved ;
   That only makes superior sense beloved.
   Be niggard of advice on no pretence ;
   For the worst avarice is that of sense.
   With mean complacence ne'er betray your trust
   Nor be so civil as to prove unjust.
   Fear not the anger of the wise to raise ;
   Those best can bear reproof, who merit praise.

4. But where's the man who counsel can bestow,
   Still pleased to teach, and yet not proud to know ;
   Unbiass'd, or by favor, or by spite ;
   Not dully prepossess'd, nor blindly right ;
   Though learn'd, well-bred; and, though well-bred, sincere
   Modestly bold, and humanly severe ;
   Who to a friend his faults can freely show,
   And gladly praise the merit of a foe ?

5. Blest with a taste exact, yet unconfined ;
   A knowledge both of books and human kind ;
   Generous converse, a soul exempt from pride,
   And love to praise with reason on his side ;
   Careless of censure, nor too fond of fame ;
   Still pleased to praise, yet not afraid to blame ;
   Averse alike to flatter or offend ;
   Not free from faults, nor yet too vain to mend ?

---

53. God's Share.

McLEOD.

DONALD McLEOD is a convert to the Catholic faith. He has written a
'Life of Mary, Queen of Scots," a "Life of Sir Walter Scott," both admirable specimens of biography. He has contributed several other works
to the stock of American literature.

1. At the distance of some leagues from Fribourg, in the
ancient county of Gruyère, lived, in the good old time, the
excellent Count Peter III ; and when his race was run, he

departed this life in a good Christian manner, leaving his memory and his property to his widow Wilhelmette.

2. The lady Wilhelmette had, in her province, a certain mountain, fruitful in snows and torrents, very grand to look at, but very unproductive. To this she joined some acres of ood pasture-land, and gave it all to the Carthusians, asking hem to pray for her, for her young son, and for good Count Peter the departed. To it she gave the name of *Theil-Gottes*, or *Pars-Dieu*—the share of God; and got Bochard, monk of Val Saint, appointed the first Prior.

3. The monks went stoutly to work; they cleared the forest, they terraced parts of the mountain-side, they brought soil thither with much labor, and sowed abundantly, and planted. ' And soon the voice of prayer made sweet the solitudes, and alms were ready for the wandering poor; and the cross upon the tower and the mellow bell told the poor mountaineer that God was beside him.

4. Little by little, the people gathered round and built their humble houses there; and the wilderness smiled, and there was another home of torrents won from rough Nature for a house of prayer. This was in A. D. 1308. In the year 1800, the ancient convent was burned down; but the monks contrived to build it up again, without diminishing their alms. And so it stood until that melancholy Revolution, lifting up radicalism, drove the good fathers from their home, and left the empty halls of "God's Share" to tell to the wandering stranger the story of their benevolence.

54. The Last Hours of Louis XVI.

ALISON.

Sir Archibald Alison—son of the well-known author of the "Essay on Taste," was born in Scotland, in 1792. His great work is "The History of Europe, from the commencement of the French Revolution, to the restoration of the Bourbons." His style is rich and flowing, and he writes like a man who has no wish to be unfair; but his point of view is always that of an Englishman and a tory. His History has been written too rapidly, and often betrays marks of haste, which destroy its value as an authority

1. His last interview with his family presented the most heart-rending scene. At half-past eight, the door of his apartment opened, and the Queen appeared, leading by the hand the Princess Royal, and the Princess Elizabeth; they all rushed into the arms of the King. A profound silence ensued for some minutes, broken only by the sobs of the afflicted family.

2. The King took a seat, the Queen on his left, the Princess Royal on his right, Madame Elizabeth in front, and the young Dauphin between his knees. This terrible scene lasted nearly two hours, the tears and lamentations of the royal family, frequently interrupting the words of the King, sufficiently evinced that he himself, was communicating the intelligence of his condemnation. At length, at a quarter-past ten, Louis arose; the Royal parents gave, each of them, their blessing to the Dauphin, while the Princess still held the King embraced around the waist. As he approached the door, they uttered the most piercing shrieks. "I assure you," said he, "I will see you again in the morning at eight o'clock." "Why not at seven?" they all exclaimed. "Well, then, at seven," answered the King. "Adieu, adieu!"

3. These words were pronounced with so mournful an accent, that the lamentations of the family were redoubled, and the Princess Royal fell fainting at his feet. At length, wishing to put an end to so trying a scene, the King embraced them all in the tenderest manner, and tore himself from their arms.

4. The remainder of the evening he spent with his confessor, the Abbé Edgeworth, who, with heroic devotion, discharged the perilous duty of assisting his monarch in his last moments. At twelve he went to bed, and slept peacefully till five. He then gave his last instruction to Cléry, and put into his hands, the little property that still remained in his hands, a ring, a seal, and a lock of hair. "Give this ring," said he, "to the Queen, and tell her with how much regret I leave her; give her also the locket containing the hair of my children; give this seal to the Dauphin, and tell them all what I suffer at dying without receiving their last embrace, but I

wish to spare them the pain of so cruel a separation." He then received the Holy Sacrament, from the hands of his confessor, from a small altar erected in his chamber, and heard the last service of the dying, at the time when the rolling of the drums, and the agitation in the streets, announced the preparation for his execution.

5. At nine o'clock, Santerre presented himself in the Temple. "You come to seek me," said the King. "Allow me a minute." He went into his closet, and immediately returned with his Testament in his hand. "I pray you," said he, " give this packet to the Queen, my wife." "That is no concern of mine," replied the representative of the municipality. "I am here only to conduct you to the scaffold." The King then asked another to take charge of the document, and said to Santerre, "Let us be off." In passing through the court of the Temple, Louis cast a last look at the tower which contained all that was most dear to him on earth, and immediately summoning all his courage, seated himself calmly in the carriage beside his confessor, with two gendarmes on the opposite side. During the passage to the place of execution, which occupied two hours, he never failed reciting the psalms which were pointed out to him by the good priest. Even the soldiers were astonished at his composure.

6. The streets were filled with an immense crowd, who beheld in silent dismay the mournful procession. A large body of troops surrounded the carriage. A double file of National Guards, and a formidable array of cannon, rendered hopeless any attempts at rescue. When the procession arrived at the place of execution, between the gardens of the Tuileries and the Champs Elysées, he descended from the carriage, and undressed himself without the aid of the executioners, but testified a momentary look of indignation, when they began to bind his hands. M. Edgeworth exclaimed with almost inspired felicity, "Submit to this outrage as the last resemblance to the Saviour, who is about to recompense your sufferings."

7 At these words, he resigned himself, and walked to the foot of the scaffold Here he received that sublime benedic-

tion of his confessor, "Son of St. Louis, ascend to heaven!" He no sooner mounted, than advancing with a firm step to the front of the scaffold, with one look he imposed silence on twenty drummers, placed there to prevent him from being heard, and said with a loud voice: "I die innocent of all crimes laid to my charge. I pardon the authors of my death, and pray God that my blood may not fall upon France. And you, my people—" At these words, Santerre ordered the drums to beat; the executioners seized the King, and the descending axe terminated his existence. One of the assistants seized the head, and waved it in the air; the blood fell on the heroic confessor, who was on his knees by the lifeless body of his sovereign.

55. OLD TIMES.

GRIFFIN.

GERALD GRIFFIN, a distinguished novelist and dramatist of the present century, was born near Limerick, in 1808. At an early age, when his talents were winning him fame and popularity in London, whither he had repaired, as he pleasantly expresses it in one of his letters, " with the modest desire of rivalling Scott and throwing Shakspeare into the shade," he suddenly withdrew from the path of literature, and became a devoted Brother of the Christian Schools, in which sphere of usefulness he died, in 1840, at the early age of 37. Some of Griffin's novels, and especially "The Collegians," "Suil Dhu," "Tracy's Ambition," and "Tales of the Five Senses," are equal to any thing of the kind in our language. His great historical novel of "The Invasion" contains a mine of antiquarian research. His tragedy of "Gysyppus" holds one of the first places in the modern drama. As a poet, Griffin was also eminently successful.

1. OLD times ! old times ! the gay old times !
   When I was young and free,
And heard the merry Easter chimes,
   Under the sally tree ;
My Sunday palm beside me placed,
   My cross upon my hand,
A heart at rest within my breast,
   And sunshine on the land !
      Old times ! old times !

2. It is not that my fortunes flee,
   Nor that my cheek is pale,
I mourn whene'er I think of thee,
   My darling native vale !
A wiser head I have, I know,
   Than when I loiter'd there ;
But in my wisdom there is woe,
   And in my knowledge care,
                 Old times ! old times !

3. I've lived to know my share of joy,
   To feel my share of pain,
To learn that friendship's self can cloy,
   To love, and love in vain—
To feel a pang and wear a smile,
   To tire of other climes,
To like my own unhappy isle,
   And sing the gay old times !
                 Old times ! old times !

4. And sure the land is nothing changed,
   The birds are singing still ;
The flowers are springing where we rang'd,
   There's sunshine on the hill ;
The sally waving o'er my head,
   Still sweetly shades my frame,
But ah, those happy days are fled,
   And I am not the same !
                 Old times ! old times !

5. Oh, come again, ye merry times !
   Sweet, sunny, fresh, and calm ;
And let me hear those Easter chimes,
   And wear my Sunday palm.
If I could cry away mine eyes,
   My tears would flow in vain ;
If I could waste my heart in sighs,
   They'll never come again !
                 Old times ! old times !

56. CHARACTER OF THE IRISH PEASANTRY.

BARRINGTON.

SIR JONAH BARRINGTON was born in Queen's county, Ireland, in 1717; died, 1834. He was a Judge of the Court of Admiralty, and a member of the Irish Parliament. He has left behind a valuable work on a most interesting period of Irish history, entitled " Rise and Fall of the Irish Nation." His *Personal Sketches* of the men of his times are inimitable in their way.

1. THE Irish people have been as little known, as they have been grossly defamed, to the rest of Europe. The lengths to which English writers have proceeded in pursuit of this object would surpass all belief, were not the facts proved by histories written under the immediate eye and sanction of Irish governments; histories replete with falsehood, which, combined with the still more mischievous misrepresentations of modern writers, form all together a mass of the most cruel calumnies that ever weighed down the character of a meritorious people.

2. This system, however, was not without its meaning. From the reign of Elizabeth, the policy of England has been to keep Ireland in a state of internal division : perfect unanimity among her inhabitants has been considered as likely to give her a population and a power incompatible with subjection ; and there are not wanting natives of Ireland, who, impressed with that erroneous idea, zealously plunge into the same doctrine, as if they would best prove their loyalty to the king by vilifying their country.

3. The Irish peasantry, who necessarily compose the great body of the population, combine in their character many of those singular and repugnant qualities which peculiarly designate the people of different nations ; and this remarkable contrariety of characteristic traits pervades almost the whole current of their natural dispositions. Laborious, domestic, accustomed to want in the midst of plenty, they submit to hardships without repining, and bear the severest privations with stoic fortitude. The sharpest wit, and the shrewdest subtility, which abound in the character of the Irish peasant, generally lie concealed under the semblance of dulness, or the appearance of simplicity ; and his language, replete with the

keenest humor, possesses an idiom of equivocation, which never fails successfully to evade a direct answer to an unwelcome question.

4. Inquisitive, artful, and penetrating, the Irish peasant learns mankind without extensive intercourse, and has an instinctive knowledge of the world, without mingling in its societies ; and never, in any other instance, did there exist a people who could display so much address and so much talent in the ordinary transactions of life as the Irish peasantry.

5. The Irish peasant has, at all periods, been peculiarly distinguished for unbounded but indiscriminate hospitality, which, though naturally devoted to the necessities of a friend, is never denied by him even to the distresses of an enemy.* To be in want or misery, is the best recommendation to his disinterested protection ; his food, his bed, his raiment, are equally the stranger's and his own ; and the deeper the distress, the more welcome is the sufferer to the peasant's cottage.

6. His attachment to his kindred are of the strongest nature. The social duties are intimately blended with the natural disposition of an Irish peasant : though covered with rags, oppressed with poverty, and perhaps with hunger, the finest specimens of generosity and heroism are to be found in his unequalled character.

7. An enthusiastic attachment to the place of their nativity is another striking trait of the Irish character, which neither time nor absence, prosperity nor adversity, can obliterate or diminish. Wherever an Irish peasant was born, there he wishes to die ; and, however successful in acquiring wealth or rank in distant places, he returns with fond affection to renew his intercourse with the friends and companions of his youth and his obscurity.

---

* It has been remarked that the English and Irish people form their judgment of strangers very differently:—an Englishman suspects a stranger to be a rogue, till he finds that he is an honest man ; the Irishman conceives every person to be an honest man till he finds him out to be a rogue ; and this accounts for the very striking difference in their conduct and hospitality to strangers.

8. An innate spirit of insubordination to the laws has been strongly charged upon the Irish peasantry: but a people to whom the punishment of crimes appears rather as a sacrifice to revenge than a measure of prevention, can never have the same deference to the law as those who are instructed in the principles of justice, and taught to recognize its equality. It .as, however, been uniformly admitted by every impartial writer on the affairs of Ireland, that a spirit of strict justice has ever characterized the Irish peasant.*

9. Convince him by plain and impartial reasoning, that he is wrong; and he withdraws from the judgment-seat, if not with cheerfulness, at least with submission: but, to make him respect the laws, he must be satisfied that they are impartial; and, with that conviction on his mind, the Irish peasant is as perfectly tractable as the native of any other country in the world.

10. An attachment to, and a respect for females, is another characteristic of the Irish peasant. The wife partakes of all her husband's vicissitudes; she shares his labor and his miseries, with constancy and with affection. At all the sports and meetings of the Irish peasantry, the women are always of the company: they have a great influence; and, in his smoky cottage, the Irish peasant, surrounded by his family, seems to forget all his privations. The natural cheerfulness of his disposition banishes reflection; and he experiences a simple happiness, which even the highest ranks of society might justly envy.

---

* Sir John Davis, attorney-general of Ireland, who, in the reign of James the First, was employed by the king to establish the English laws throughout Ireland, and who made himself perfectly acquainted with the character of the inhabitants, admits that "there were no people under heaven, who loved equal and impartial justice better han the Irish."

57. St. Frances of Rome.

LADY FULLERTON.

LADY G. FULLERTON—Born in England, in 1812. She is a convert to the Catholic faith, and a writer of considerable merit. Her "Ellen Mid lle ton" and "Grantly Manor" were written previous to her conversion. Her "Lady Bird," and her beautiful "Life of St. Frances of Rome," are the works of a later period, and bear the unmistakable stamp of faith-inspired genius.

1. THERE have been saints whose histories strike us as particularly beautiful, not only as possessing the beauty which always belongs to sanctity, whether exhibited in an aged servant of God, who for threescore years and more has borne the heat and burden of the day, or in the youth who has offered up the morning of his life to his Maker, and yielded it into His hands before twenty summers have passed over his head; whether in a warrior king like St. Louis, or a beggar like Benedict Labré, or a royal lady like St. Elizabeth, of Hungary; but also as uniting in the circumstances of their lives, in the places they inhabited, and the epochs when they appeared in the world, much that is in itself poetical and interesting, and calculated to attract the attention of the historian and the man of letters, as well as of the theologian and the devout.

2. In this class of saints may well be included Francesca Romana, the foundress of the religious order of the Oblates of Tor di Specchi. She was the model of young girls, the example of a devout matron, and finally a widow, according to the very pattern drawn by St. Paul. She was beautiful, courageous, and full of wisdom, nobly born, and delicately brought up. Rome was the place of her birth, and the scene of her labors; her home was in the centre of the great city, in the heart of the Trastevere; her life was full of trials and hair-breadth 'scapes, and strange reverses.

3. Her hidden life was marvellous in the extreme. Visions of terror and of beauty followed her all her days; favors such as were never granted to any other saint were vouchsafed to her; the world of spirits was continually thrown open to her sight; and yet, in her daily conduct, her character, and her

ways, minute details of which have reached us, there is a
simplicity as well as a deep humility, awful in one so highly
gifted, touching in one so highly favored.

4. Troubled and wild were the times she lived in. Perhaps,
if one had to point out a period in which a Catholic Christian
would rather not have had his lot cast,—one in which there was
most to try his faith and wound his feelings,—he would name
the end of the fourteenth century, and the beginning of the
fifteenth. War was raging all over Europe; Italy was torn
by inward dissensions, by the rival factions of the Guelphs
and the Ghibellines.

5. So savage was the spirit with which their conflicts were
carried on, that barbarism seemed once more about to over-
spread that fair land; and the Church itself was afflicted not
only by the outward persecutions which strengthen its vitality,
though for a while they may appear to cripple its action, but
by trials of a far deeper and more painful nature. Heresy had
torn from her arms a great number of her children, and repeated schisms were dividing those who, in appearance and
even in intention, remained faithful to the Holy See.

6. The successors of St. Peter had removed the seat of
their residence to Avignon, and the Eternal City presented
the aspect of one vast battle-field, on which daily and hourly
conflicts were occurring. The Colonnas, the Orsinis, the Sa-
vellis, were every instant engaged in struggles which deluged
the streets with blood, and cut off many of her citizens in the
flower of their age. Strangers were also continually invading
the heritage of the Church, and desecrated Rome with mas-
sacres and outrages scarcely less deplorable than those of the
Huns and the Vandals.

7. In the capital of the Christian world, ruins of recent date
lay side by side with the relics of past ages; the churches
were sacked, burned, and destroyed; the solitary and in
destructible basilicas stood almost alone, mournfully erect
amidst these scenes of carnage and gloom; and the eyes of the
people of Rome were wistfully directed towards that tutelary
power which has ever been to them a pledge of prosperity
and peace, and whose removal the signal of war and of misery

58. SPRING.

LONGFELLOW.

MR. LONGFELLOW is an accomplished American poet and scholar; born in 1807. "Evangeline," "The Golden Legend," and "The Song of Hiawatha" are his longest and most finished poems. He is also popular as a prose writer.

1. It was a sweet carol, which the Rhodian children sang of old in Spring, bearing in their hands, from door to door, a swallow, as herald of the season :

"The swallow is come!
The swallow is come!
Oh, fair are the seasons, and light
Are the days that she brings
With her dusky wings,
And her bosom snowy white!"

2. A pretty carol, too, is that, which the Hungarian boys, on the islands of the Danube, sing to the returning stork in Spring :

"Stork! stork! poor stork!
Why is thy foot so bloody?
A Turkish boy hath torn it :
Hungarian boy will heal it
With fiddle, fife, and drum."

But what child has a heart to sing in this capricious clime of ours, where Spring comes sailing in from the sea, with wet and heavy cloud-sails, and the misty pennon of the East wind nailed to the mast?

3. Yes, even here, and in the stormy month of March even, there are bright warm mornings, when we open our windows to inhale the balmy air. The pigeons fly to and fro, and w hear the whirring sound of wings. Old flies crawl out of th cracks, to sun themselves, and think it is Summer. They die in their conceit; and so do our hearts within us, when the cold sea-breath comes from the eastern sea, and again,

"The driving hail
Upon the window beats with icy flail."

4. The red-flowering maple is first in blossom : its beautiful purple flowers unfolding a fortnight before the leaves. The moosewood follows, with rose-colored buds and leaves ; and the dogwood, robed in the white of its own pure blossoms. Then comes the sudden rain-storm ; and the birds fly to and fro, and shriek. Where do they hide themselves in such storms? at what firesides dry their feathery cloaks ? At the fireside of the great, hospitable sun ; to-morrow, not before : they must sit in wet garments until then.

5. In all climates, Spring is beautiful : in the South it is intoxicating, and sets a poet beside himself. The birds begin to sing : they utter a few rapturous notes, and then wait for an answer from the silent woods. Those green-coated musicians, the frogs, make holiday in the neighboring marshes. They, too, belong to the orchestra of nature, whose vast theatre is again opened, though the doors have been so long bolted with icicles, and the scenery hung with snow and frost like cobwebs.

6. This is the prelude which announces the opening of the scene. Already the grass shoots forth. The waters leap with thrilling pulse through the veins of the earth, the sap through the veins of the plants and trees, and the blood through the veins of man. What a thrill of delight in Spring-time ! what a joy in being and moving !

7. Men are at work in gardens, and in the air there is an odor of the fresh earth. The leaf buds begin to swell and blush ; the white blossoms of the cherry hang upon the boughs, like snow-flakes ; and ere long our next door neighbors will be completely hidden from us by the dense green foliage. The May flowers open their soft blue eyes. Children are let loose in the fields and gardens ; they hold buttercups under each thers' chin, to see if they love butter ; and the little girls dorn themselves with chains and curls of dandelions, pull out the yellow leaves, and blow the down from the leafless stalk.

8. And at night so cloudless and so still ! Not a voice of living thing, not a whisper of leaf or waving bough, not a breath of wind, not a sound upon the earth nor in the air ! And overhead bends the blue sky, dewy and soft and radiant

with innumerable stars, like the inverted bell of some blue
flower, sprinkled with golden dust, and breathing fragrance ;
or if the heavens are overcast, it is no wild storm of wind and
rain ; but clouds that melt and fall in showers.   One does not
wish to sleep, but lies awake to hear the pleasant sound of the
dropping rain.   It was thus the Spring began in Heidleberg

---

95. WHAT IS A CHURCH?

HECKER.

REV. ISAAC THOMAS HECKER—was born in New York, in 1819.   In 1845,
he became a convert to Catholicity, in 1847 joined the Redemptorists, and
in 1849, was ordained priest by His Eminence Cardinal Wiseman.   Having
spent some years with the Redemptorists, he with the consent of the supreme pontiff, and in conjunction with some other zealous fathers, established the new missionary order of St. Paul the Apostle.
  His published works are *Questions of the Soul*, and *Aspirations of Nature*,
both of which are addressed to the thinking portion of the American people, and are calculated to do much good.

1. RELIGION is a question between God and the Soul.   No
numan authority, therefore, has any right to enter its sacred
sphere.   The attempt is sacrilegious.

Every man was made by his Creator to do his own thinking.
What right then has one man, or a body of men, to dictate
their belief, or make their private convictions, or sentiments,
binding upon others?

2. There is no degradation so abject, as the submission of
the eternal interests of the soul to the private authority or
dictation of any man, or body of men, whatever may be their
titles.   Every right sentiment in our breast rises up in abhor-
rance against it.

A Church which is not of divine origin, and claims assen
to its teachings, or obedience to its precepts, on its own
authority, is an insult to our understandings, and deserves the
ridicule of all men, who have the capacity to put two ideas
together.

3. A Church that claims a divine origin, in order to be
consistent, must also claim to be unerring; for the idea of
teaching error in the name of the Divinity, is blasphemous.

A Church, if it deserves that title, must yield us assistance, and not we the Church. The Church that needs our assistance, we despise. Only the Church which has help from above for mankind, and is conscious of. it, is a divine institution.

4. A Church that has its origin in heaven, is an organ of divine inspiration and life to humanity. For Religion is not only a system of divinely given truths, but also the organ of a divine life. Life, and its transmission, is inconceivable, independent of an organism. The office of the Church, therefore, is not only to teach divine truths, but also to enable men to actualize them.

If entrance into the Church is not a step to a higher and holier life, the source of a larger and more perfect freedom, her claims do not merit a moment's consideration. Away with the Church that reveals not a loftier manhood, and enables men to attain it.

5. The object of the Church authority is not to lay restraints on man's activity, but to direct it aright; not to make him a slave, but to establish his independence; the object of Church authority is to develop man's individuality, consecrate and defend his rights, and elevate his existence to the plane of his divine destiny.

Divine Religion appeals to man's holiest instincts, and inspires the soul with a sublime enthusiasm. A Church without martyrs, is not on equality with the institution of the family or state; for they are not wanting in heroes. A Church that ceases to produce martyrs is dead.

6. Hearts are aching to be devoted to the down-trodden and suffering of the race. Breasts are elated with heroic impulses to do something in the noble cause of Truth and God; and shall all these aspirations and sentiments, which do honor to our nature, be wasted, misspent, or die out for want of sanction and right direction? Who can give this sanction? Who can give this direction? No one but God's Church upon earth. This is her divine mission.

In concert with the voice of all those who are conscious of their humanity, we demand a visible and divine authority, to anite and direct the aspirations and energies of individuals and nations to great enterprises for the common welfare of men upon earth, and for eternity.

7. If the Religion we are in search of does not exist, and we remain in darkness, we shall be found standing upright, ooking heavenward, our Reason unshackled, in all the dignity and energy of our native manhood.

> " Better roam for aye, than rest
> Under the impious shadow of a roof unbless'd." [1]

60. The Wild Lily and the Passion Flower.

ROUQUETTE.

Rev. A. Rouquette is a native of New Orleans. His French poems, under the title of *Les Savanes*, were received with much encouragement in France. He has written a beautiful and poetical treatise on the solitary life, entitled *La Thébaïde en Amerique*, and a volume of English poems, called " Wild Fowers." He is a perfect master of the melody of the English; and that he is a poet by nature appears in every line, and more strikingly in his prose than in his verse. Mr. Rouquette was ordained a priest in 1845.

1.   Sweet flower of light,
    The queen of solitude,
      The image bright
    Of grace-born maidenhood,

      Thou risest tall
    Midst struggling weeds that droop :—
      Thy lieges all,
    They humbly bow and stoop.

2.   Dark color'd flower,
    How solemn, awful, sad !—
      I feel thy power,
    O king, in purple clad !

      With head recline,
    Thou art the emblem dear

---

[1] De Vere.

Of woes divine ;
The flower I most revere !

8.   The lily white,
The purple passion flower ,
Mount Thabor bright,
The gloomy Olive-bower.

Such is our life,—
Alternate joys and woes,
Short peace, long strife,
Few friends and many foes !

4.   My friend, away
All wailings here below :
The royal way
To realms above is woe !

To suffer much
Has been the fate of Saints ;
Our fate is such :—
Away, away all plaints !

---

61. ILLUMINATION AT ST. PETER'S.

DR. ENGLAND.

Right Reverend JOHN ENGLAND, D.D., first Bishop of Charleston, S. C., was born in Cork, in 1786, died in Charleston in 1842. Dr. England was a man of great natural abilities, and profound and varied attainments. He was one of the greatest prelates the American Church has yet had. As a writer and an orator he had no superior, and few equals. He has enriched our literature with essays on almost every subject bearing upon the interests of Catholicity in this country. His works were collected and published, in five octavo volumes, by his successor, Dr. Reynolds.

1. IN my last I gave a brief description of the procession and first vespers of the festival of St. Peter and Paul, on the 28th ult. Preparations had been made for illuminating the exterior of the church of St. Peter's as soon as night should fall. No description can convey to your readers a

adequate idea of the spectacle which this presents. The dome is somewhat larger than the church of St. Mary of the Martyrs, which is the old Pantheon ; and this is not only surmounting the roof, but raised considerably above it. This Pantheon is much larger than the Circular.Church,[1] in Meeting-street. Imagine this as only one of three domes, of which it is indeed far the largest, elevated considerably above the roof of a church, the façade of which is a grand pile of architecture ; this dome is half surrounded by columns, and the one by which the entablature over them is crowned, is closely ribbed to its summit ; over this is a ball, in which I was one of eight persons, standing erect, and we had room for at least four others, and this ball surmounted by a cross.

2. From the sides of the front two wings of splendid architecture project forward, upwards of eighty feet ; at their extremities are lofty columns, over which run the proper entablatures, crowned by pediments ; from these the immense colonnades recede almost semicircularly from each wing, sweeping with their hundreds of pillars round the immense piazza, capable of containing probably one hundred thousand human beings upon the area within their embrace.

3. In the centre of this is a rich Egyptian obelisk, resting upon the backs of four lions *couchant* upon the angles of a fine pedestal. Half way from this obelisk, at each side toward the colonnade, are the two magnificent fountains, probably the most superb in the world. Each appears to be a spacious marble vase, elevated upon a sufficiently strong, but gracefully delicate stem ; the summit of this vase is at the elevation of about twelve feet. From its centre rises to nearly the same height another still more slender and delicately-shaped stem, from whose summit is projected to a considerable height, a water-spout, which gracefully bending near its summit, and yielding to the direction of the wind, as it forms its curve and descent, is separated into a sort of sparkling spray of pearls and silver intermixed; twelve other simi-

---

[1] The Circular Church, one of the principal buildings in Charleston, South Carolina

9

lar spouts shoot round this central liquid column, diverging from it on every side as they rise, and falling with a similar appearance at somewhat of a less elevation.

4. They seem in the distance to be like rich plumes of some gigantic ostrich, gracefully waving in the breeze, while the descending shower is received in the capacious vase, from whose interior it is conducted to various fountains in the city. Hundreds of statues lift their various forms, appearing larger than life, over the frieze and cornice of the colonnade ; while at the foot of the majestic flight of steps by which you ascend to the portico of the church, two ancient statues of St. Peter and St. Paul have for centuries rested upon their pedestals.

5. The façade of the church itself is surmounted by the colossal statues of the Twelve Apostles. The illumination consisted of two parts. The lamps for the first part were disposed closely, in colored paper, along the architectural lines of this mighty mass, along the ribs of the domes, around the ball, and on the cross.

6. To me, as I looked from the bridge of St. Angelo, the scene appeared like a vision of enchantment. It seemed as if a mighty pile of some rich, black, soft material, was reared in the likeness of a stupendous temple, and the decorations were broad lines of burning liquid gold. The ball and the cross were seen as if detached and resting in the air above its summit. It was indeed a becoming emblem of the triumph of a crucified Redeemer over this terrestrial ball. After I had passed the bridge, and as I approached the piazza, the front of the church, and the expanse of the colonnade, exhibited their lines of light. The specks which formed those lines glowed now more distinct and separate, and though their continuity was lost, their symmetry was perfect and magnificent.

7. The immense piazza was thronged with carriages, and persons on foot; while a division of the Papal dragoons, one of the finest and best disciplined bodies of cavalry in existence, moved in sections and single files through the multitude, calmly, but steadily and firmly, preserving order in a kind, polite, but determined manner. Scarcely a word is heard

above a whisper; an accident is of so rare an occurrence as not to be calculated upon.

8. The cardinal secretary of state has a gallery in front of the church, to which foreign ambassadors, and a few other strangers of distinction are invited. I observéd Captain Reed and his lady in this gallery, and many of our officers were promenading below. About an hour elapsed from the commencement, when the motion of a brighter light was observed towards the summit of the cupola, a large star seemed to shoot upwards to the cross, and, as if by a sudden flash from heaven, the whole edifice appeared to blaze in the glare of day.

9. A thousand lights, kindled by some inconceivably rapid communication, shed their beams upon every part of the building. Pillars and pilasters, with their vases, shafts, and capitals; mouldings, friezes, cornices, pediments, architraves, panels, doors, windows, niches, images, decorations, enrichments, domes—all, all with their faint lines of golden light, now softened to a milder lustre, revealed in brilliant relief to the enraptured eye.

62. Illumination at St. Peter's—*continued.*

1. The fountains were magnificently grand, and richly pure, and softened into a refreshing white. The multitude was silent. The horses were still. The glowing cross, elevated above the Vatican hill, beamed to the wide plains and distant mountains its augury of future glory, because of past humiliations. The crowd began to move; the low buzz of conversation, and then the horses' tramp; then followed the rattling of wheels.

2. And while tens of thousands remained yet longer, other thousands moved in various directions to their homes, or to distant elevated points, for the sake of a variety of views. I went to the magnificent Piazza del Popolo. It was literally a desert; but in its stillness, and the dereliction of its obelisk, its fountains, and its statues, by the very contrast to the scene that I had left, there arose a feeling of new sublimity It

was more deep, it was more solemn; but it was less elevated,
not so overpowering, nor so impressive as that to which it
succeeded.

3. My object was to ascend from this place to the Monte
Pincio, the commanding view from which would enable me to
look over the city at the great object which attracted every
eye. But the gates of the avenue at this side were closed,
and I had to go to the Piazza di Spagna, and there to ascend
by the immense and beautiful flight of steps to the Trinita
del Monti. Standing here, in front of the convent of the Ladies of the Sacred Heart, the view of St. Peter's was indeed
superb.

4. I proceeded up towards the public gardens lately formed
on the summit of this ancient residence of so many of the remarkable men of five-and-twenty ages. At various intervals,
I stopped and turned to view the altered appearance presented
by the mass of light, as seen from those different positions.
As I contemplated it, I reflected that it must soon be extinguished, like the transient glories of the philosophers, the heroes, the statesmen, the orators, who successively passed over
the spot on which I stood.

5. An humble fisherman from Galilee, and an obscure tent-
maker from Tarsus, were confined in the dungeons of this city
Seventeen hundred and sixty-eight years had passed away
since one of them was crucified with his head downwards on
the Vatican Hill, and the other was beheaded on the Ostian
Way. They had been zealously faithful in discharging the
duties of their apostleship.

6. In the eyes of men, their death was without honor; but
it was precious in the sight of God. Grateful and admiring
millions from year to year proclaim their praises, while the
Church exhibits their virtues as proofs of the Saviour's
grace, as models for the imitation of her sons. Oh, let my
soul die [the death of] the just, and let my last end be like
to theirs! Translated from this earth, they live in heaven.
Tried for a time, and found faithful, they enjoy a glorious
recompense!

7. The God that we serve is merciful in bestowing his

grace, and is exceedingly bountiful in crowning his own gifts, by giving to us, through the merits of his Son, a recompense for those acts of virtue which he enables us to perform. I found myself again near the summit of the steps. I descended, and retired to my home, reflecting upon the wonders wrought by the Most High, through the instrumentality of those two great saints, the celebration of whose festival had thus commenced.

8. The ardent Peter and the active Paul. The name changed to signify the office to which he should be raised. The vicegerent of Heaven's King, bearing the mystic keys, with powers of legislation and of administration rested upon him; who of himself weak, but who, sustained by Christ, was strong. "Before the cock shall crow twice this night, thou shall thrice deny me. Yes! Satan hath desired to have thee, that he might sift thee as wheat; but I have prayed for thee, that thy faith fail not. And thou once converted, confirm thy brethren."

9. The strongest power that hell can muster in its gates to make a furious assault upon that Church, the weighty administration of which shall rest upon you, and upon those that shall succeed you, shall from time to time be marshalled and sent forth for the destruction of that body which the Saviour organized, like a well-ordered kingdom upon earth, for the attainment of heaven; but the gates of hell shall not prevail against it. The dynasties of nations have perished, the palaces of the Cæsars are in ruins, their tombs have mouldered with the bodies they contained, but the successors of Peter continue.

10. Under the orders of Nero, the two apostles were consigned to what was imagined to be destruction. The vaults of the tyrant's golden palace are covered with vegetation. Standing on the unseemly ruins of the remnant of this monster's monument, by the side of the Flaminian Way, through the obscurity of the night the Christian peasant looks towards that blaze of light which, from the resting-place where the relics of the head of the Church and of the doctor of the Gentiles are found, breaks forth and irradiates the Eternal

City and its monumental environs. If Peter is elevated in
station, Paul is not less glorious in merit.

11. He, too, looked back with sorrow on that day
when he held the clothes of those who slew Stephen. But
how nobly did he redeem his error! A vessel of election to
bear the good odor of Christ into the palaces of kings! a torrent of eloquence flowing into the barren fields of a vain philosophy, to fertilize and adorn! A rich exhibition of virtue,
winning by its beauty, attracting by its symmetry, and exciting to activity by emulation! A glowing meteor of benediction, dissipating the clouds, and warming the hearts of the
beholders to charity on earth, that they might be fitted for
glory in heaven!

---

63. The Son's Return.

GERALD GRIFFIN.

1. On a sudden, she heard voices outside the window.
Alive to the slightest circumstance that was unusual, she
arose, all dark as it was, threw on her simple dress in haste,
and groped her way to the front door of the dwelling. She
recognized the voice of a friendly neighbor, and opened the
door, supposing that he might have some interesting intelligence to communicate. She judged correctly.

"Good news! good news! Mrs. Reardon; and I give you
joy of them this morning. What will you give me for telling
who is in that small boat at the shore?"

"That small boat!—what?—where?"

2. "Below there, ma'am, where I'm pointing my finger
Don't you see them coming up the crag towards you?"

"I cannot—I cannot, it is so dark," the widow replied
endeavoring to penetrate the gloom.

"Dark!—and the broad sun shining down upon them this
whole day!"

"Day!—the sun! O my Almighty Father! save me."

"What's the matter? Don't you see them, ma'am?"

3. "See them?" the poor woman exclaimed, placing her

hands on her eyes, and shrieking aloud in her agony : "Oh! I shall never see him more ! I am dark and blind !"

The peasant started back and blessed himself. The next instant the poor widow was caught in the arms of her son.

"Where is she ? My mother ! O my darling mother ! I am come back to you. Look ! I have kept my word."

4. She strove, with a sudden effort of self-restraint, to keep her misfortune secret, and wept without speaking, upon the neck of her long-absent relative, who attributed her tears to an excess of happiness. But when he presented his young wife, and called her attention to the happy, laughing faces and healthful cheeks of their children, the wandering of her eyes and the confusion of her manner left it no longer possible to retain the secret.

5. "My good, kind boy," said she, laying her hand heavily on his arm, "you are returned to my old arms once more, and I am grateful for it—but we cannot expect to have all we wish for in this world. O my poor boy! I can never see you—I can never see your children ! I am blind."

The young man uttered a horrid and piercing cry, while he tossed his clenched hands above his head, and stamped upon the earth in sudden anguish. "Blind! my mother! O Heaven! is this the end of all my toils and wishes ? To come home, and find her dark forever ! Is it for this that I have prayed and labored ? Blind and dark ! O my poor mother ! O Heaven ! O mother, mother !"

6. "Hold, now, my boy—where are you ? What way is that for a Christian to talk ? Come near me, and let me touch your hands. Don't add to my sorrows, Richard, my child, by uttering a word against the will of Heaven. Where are you ? Come near me. Let me hear you say that you are resigned to this and all other visitations of the great Lord of all light. Say this, my child, and your virtue will be dearer to me than my eyes ? Ah, my good Richard! you may be sure the Almighty never strikes us except it is for our sins, or for our good. I thought too much of you, my child, and the Lord saw that my heart was straying to the world again, and e has struck me for the happiness of both. Let me hear that

you are satisfied. I can see your heart still, and that is dearer
to me than your person. Let me see it as good and dutiful
as I knew it before you left me."

7. The disappointed exile supported her in his arms. "Well,
well, my poor mother," he said, "I am satisfied. Since you
are the chief sufferer, and show no discontent, it would be too
unreasonable that I should murmur. The will of Heaven be
done! but it is a bitter—bitter stroke." Again he folded
his dark parent to his bosom, and wept aloud; while his wife,
retiring softly to a distance, hid her face in her cloak. Her
children clung with fear and anxiety to her side, and gazed
with affrighted faces upon the afflicted mother and son.

8. But they were not forgotten. After she had repeatedly
embraced her recovered child, the good widow remembered
her guests. She extended her arms towards that part of the
room at which she heard the sobs and moanings of the
younger mother. "Is that my daughter's voice?" she asked—
"place her in my arms, Richard. Let me feel the mother of
your children upon my bosom." The young woman flung
herself into the embrace of the aged widow. "Young and
fair, I am sure," the latter continued, passing her wasted fingers over the blooming cheek of the good American. "I can
feel the roses upon this cheek, I am certain. But what are
these? Tears? My good child, you should dry our tears
instead of adding to them. Where are your children? Let
me see—ah! my heart—let me *feel* them, I mean—let me
take them in my arms. My little angels! Oh! if I could
only open my eyes, for one moment, to look upon you all—but
for one little instant—I would close them again for the rest
of my life, and think myself happy. If it had happened only
one day—one hour after your arrival—but the will of Heaven
be done! perhaps even this moment, when we think our
selves most miserable, He is preparing for us some hidden
blessing."

9. Once more the pious widow was correct in her conjec
ture. It is true, that day, which all hoped should be a day of
rapture, was spent by the reunited family in tears and mourning. But Providence did not indeed intend that creatures'

who had served him so faithfully should be visited with more than a temporary sorrow, for a slight and unaccustomed transgression.

10. The news of the widow's misfortune spread rapidly through the country, and excited universal sympathy—for few refuse their commiseration to a fellow-creature's sorrow, even of those who would accord a tardy and measured sympathy to his good fortune. Among those who heard with real pity the story of their distress, was a surgeon who resided in the neighborhood, and who felt all that enthusiastic devotion to his art, which its high importance to the welfare of mankind was calculated to excite in a generous mind. This gentleman took an early opportunity of visiting the old widow when she was alone in the cottage. The simplicity with which she told her story, and the entire resignation which she expressed, interested and touched him deeply.

64 THE SON'S RETURN—*continued.*

1. "It is not over with me yet, sir," she concluded, "for still, when the family are talking around me, I forget that I am blind; and when I hear my son say something pleasant, I turn to see the smile upon his lips; and when the darkness reminds me of my loss, it seems as if I lost my sight over again !"

2. The surgeon discovered, on examination, that the blindness was occasioned by a disease called cataract, which obscures, by an unhealthy secretion, the lucid brightness of the crystalline lens (described in a former chapter), and obstructs the entrance of the rays of light. The improvements which modern practitioners have made in this science render this disease, which was once held to be incurable, now comparatively easy of removal The surgeon perceived at once, by the condition of the eyes, that, by the abstraction of the injured lens, he could restore sight to the afflicted widow.

3 Unwilling, however, to excite her hopes too suddenly

or prematurely, he began by asking her whether, for a chance
of recovering the use of her eyes, she would submit to a little
pain ?

The poor woman replied, "that if he thought he could once
more enable her to behold her child and his children, she would
be content to undergo any pain which would not endanger her
existence."

4. "Then," replied her visitor, "I may inform you, and I
have the strongest reasons to believe, that I can restore your
sight, provided you agree to place yourself at my disposal for
a few days. I will provide you with an apartment in my
house, and your family shall know nothing of it until the cure
is effected."

5. The widow consented ; and on that very evening the
operation was performed. The pain was slight, and was endured by the patient without a murmur. For a few days after,
the surgeon insisted on her wearing a covering over her eyes,
until the wounds which he had found it necessary to inflict
had been perfectly healed.

6. One morning, after he had felt her pulse and made the
necessary inquiries, he said, while he held the hand of the
widow :—

"I think we may now venture with safety to remove the
covering. Compose yourself now, my good old friend, and
suppress all emotion. Prepare your heart for the reception
of a great happiness."

7. The poor woman clasped her hands firmly together, and
moved her lips as if in prayer. At the same moment the
covering fell from her brow, and the light burst in a joyous
flood upon her soul. She sat for an instant bewildered, and
incapable of viewing any object with distinctness. The first
upon which her eyes reposed was the figure of a young man
bending his gaze with an intense and ecstatic fondness upon
hers, and with his arms outstretched as if to anticipate the
recognition. The face, though changed and sunned since she
had known it, was still familiar to her. She started from her
seat with a wild cry of joy, and cast herself upon the bosom
of her son.

8. She embraced him repeatedly, then removed him to a distance, that she might have the opportunity of viewing him with greater distinctness, and again, with a burst of tears, flung herself upon his neck. Other voices, too, mingled with theirs. She beheld her daughter and their children waiting eagerly for her caress. She embraced them all, returning from each to each, and perusing their faces and persons as if she would never drink deep enough of the cup of rapture which her recovered sense afforded her. The beauty of the young mother—the fresh and rosy color of the children—the glossy brightness of their hair—their smiles—their movements of joy —all afforded subjects for delight and admiration, such as she might never have experienced, had she never considered them in the light of blessings lost for life. The surgeon, who thought that the consciousness of a stranger's presence might impose a restraint upon the feelings of the patient and her friends, retired into a distant corner, where he beheld, not without tears, the scene of happiness which he had been made instrumental in conferring.

9. "Richard," said the widow, as she laid her hand upon her son's shoulder, and looked into his eyes, "did I not judge aright when I said that even when we thought ourselves the most miserable, the Almighty might have been preparing for us some hidden blessing ? Were we in the right to murmur ?"

The young man withdrew his arms from his mother, clasped them before him, and bowed down his head in silence.

---

65. THE CHERWELL WATER-LILY.

FABER.

1. How often doth a wild flower bring
   Fancies and thoughts that seem to spring
     From inmost depths of feeling !
   Nay, often they have power to bless
   With their uncultured loveliness,
   And far into the aching breast

There goes a heavenly thought of rest
  With their soft influence stealing.
How often, too, can ye unlock,
Dear wild flowers, with a gentle shock,
  The wells of holy tears !
While somewhat of a Christian light
Breaks sweetly on the mourner's sight,
  To calm unquiet fears !
Ah ! surely such strange power is given
To lowly flowers like dew from heaven ;
For lessons oft by them are brought,
Deeper than mortal sage hath taught,
Lessons of wisdom pure, that rise
From some clear fountains in the skies.

2 Fairest of Flora's lovely daughters
That bloom by stilly-running waters,
Fair lily ! thou a type must be
Of virgin love and purity !
Fragrant thou art as any flower
That decks a lady's garden-bower.
But he who would thy sweetness know,
Must stoop and bend his loving brow
To catch thy scent, so faint and rare,
Scarce breathed upon the Summer air.
And all thy motions, too, how free,
And yet how fraught with sympathy !
So pale thy tint, so meek thy gleam,
Shed on thy kindly father-stream !
Still, as he swayeth to and fro,
  How true in all thy goings,
As if thy very soul did know
  The secrets of his flowings.

3. And then that heart of living gold,
Which thou dost modestly infold,
And screen from man's too searching view,
Within thy robe of snowy hue !

To careless man thou seem'st to roam
   Abroad upon the river,
In all thy movements chain'd to home,
   Fast-rooted there forever :
Link'd by a holy, hidden tie,
Too subtle for a mortal eye.
Nor riveted by mortal art,
Deep down within thy father's heart

4. Emblem in truth thou art to me
Of all a daughter ought to be !
How shall I liken thee, sweet flower,
That other men may feel thy power,
May seek thee on some lovely night,
And say how strong, how chaste the night,
   The tie of filial duty,
How graceful, too, and angel-bright,
   The pride of lowly beauty !
Thou sittest on the varying tide
As if thy spirit did preside,
With a becoming, queenly grace,
As mistress of this lonely place ;
A quiet magic hast thou now
To smooth the river's ruffled brow,
   And calm his rippling water,
And yet, so delicate and airy,
Thou art to him a very fairy,
   A widow'd father's only daughter.

----

66. Edward the Confessor.

LINGARD.

John Lingard, D. D., was born, in England. in 1771; died in 1851. With the completion of the "History of England," in ten volumes, the literary fame of Dr. Lingard became established throughout Europe. Cardinal Wiseman speaks of this history, and its learned author, in the following terms :—" It is a Providence that in history we have had given to the nation a writer like Lingard, whose gigantic merit will be better appreciated in each successive generation, as it sees his work standing calm and erect amidst the shoals of petty pretenders to usurp his station.   When Hume shall have fairly taken his place among the classical writers of our tongue, and Macaulay shall have been transferred to the shelves of romances and poets, and each thus have received his due meed of praise, then Lingard will be still more conspicuous as the only impartial historian of our country."

1. IF we estimate the character of a sovereign by the test of popular affection, we must rank Edward among the best princes of his time.   The goodness of his heart was adored by his subjects, who lamented his death with tears of undissembled grief, and bequeathed his memory as an object of veneration to their posterity.   The blessings of his reign are the constant theme of our ancient writers : not, indeed, that he displayed any of those brilliant qualities which attract admiration, while they inflict misery.

2. He could not boast of the victories which he had achieved, but he exhibited the interesting spectacle of a king, negligent of his private interests, and wholly devoted to the welfare of his people ; and, by his labors to restore the dominion of the laws, his vigilance to ward off foreign aggression, his constant, and ultimately successful, solicitude to appease the feuds of his nobles,—if he did not prevent the interruption, he secured, at least, a longer duration of public tranquillity, than had been enjoyed in England for half a century.

3. He was pious, kind, and compassionate ; the father of the poor, and the protector of the weak ; more willing to give than to receive, and better pleased to pardon than to punish. Under the preceding kings, force generally supplied the place of justice, and the people were impoverished by the rapacity of the sovereign.   But Edward enforced the laws of his Saxon predecessors, and disdained the riches that were wrung from the labors of his subjects.

4. Temperate in his diet, unostentatious in his person, pursuing no pleasures but those which his hawks and hounds afforded, he was content with the patrimonial demesnes of the crown ; and was able to assert, even after the abolition of that fruitful source of revenue, the Danegelt, that he possessed a greater portion of wealth than any of his predecessors had enjoyed.   To him, the principle that the king can do no wrong,

was literally applied by the gratitude of his people, who, if
they occasionally complained of the measures of the govern
ment, attributed the blame not to the monarch himself, of
whose benevolence they entertained no doubt, but to the
ministers, who had abused his confidence, or deceived his
credulity.

5. It was, however, a fortunate circumstance for the memory
of Edward, that he occupied the interval between the Danish
and Norman conquests. Writers were induced to view his
character with more partiality, from the hatred with which
they looked upon his successors and predecessors. They were
foreigners; he was a native: they held the crown by conquest;
he by descent: they ground to the dust the slaves whom they
had made; he became known to his countrymen only by his
benefits. Hence he appeared to shine with purer light amid
the gloom with which he was surrounded; and whenever the
people under the despotism of the Norman kings, had any
opportunity of expressing their real wishes, they constantly
called for "the laws and customs of the good King Edward."

---

67. CÆSAR'S OFFER OF AMNESTY TO CATO.

ADDISON.

JOSEPH ADDISON—One of the best of a class of writers known as "the
writers of Queen Anne's time." His writings were chiefly essays published
in the 'Spectator," "Tatler," and "Guardian." He died 1719.

Decius. Cæsar sends health to Cato.
Cato.   Could he send it
To Cato's slaughter'd friends, it would be welcome.
Are not your orders to address the senate?
Decius. My business is with Cato: Cæsar sees
The straits to which you're driven; and as he knows
Cato's high worth, is anxious for his life.
Cato. My life is grafted on the fate of Rome:
Would he save Cato, bid him spare his country.
Tell your dictator this; and tell him, Cato
Disdains a life which he has power to offer.

Decius. Rome and her senators submit to Cæsar;
Her generals and her consuls are no more,
Who check'd his conquests, and denied his triumphs.
Why will not Cato be this Cæsar's friend?

   Cato. Those very reasons thou hast urged, forbid it

   Decius. Cato, I've orders to expostulate,
And reason with you as from friend to friend.
Think on the storm that gathers o'er your head,
And threatens every hour to burst upon it;
Still may you stand high in your country's honors,
Do but comply, and make your peace with Cæsar
Rome will rejoice; and casts its eyes on Cato,
As on the second of mankind.

   Cato.   No more!
I must not think of life on such conditions.

   Decius. Cæsar is well acquainted with your virtues,
And therefore sets this value on your life:
Let him but know the price of Cato's friendship,
And name your terms.

   Cato.   Bid him disband his legions,
Restore the commonwealth to liberty,
Submit his actions to the public censure,
And stand the judgment of a Roman senate.
Bid him do this,—and Cato is his friend.

   Decius. Cato, the world talks loudly of your wisdom—

   Cato. Nay, more,—though Cato's voice was ne'er
     employ'd
To clear the guilty, and to varnish crimes,
Myself will mount the rostrum in his favor,
And strive to gain his pardon from the people.

   Decius. A style like this becomes a conqueror.

   Cato. Decius, a style like this becomes a Roman.

   Decius. What is a Roman, that is Cæsar's foe?

   Cato. Greater than Cæsar; he's a friend to *virtue*

   Decius. Consider, Cato, you're in *Utica;*
And at the head of your own little senate:
You don't now thunder in the capitol,
With all the mouths of Rome to second you.

Cato. Let *him* consider that, who drives us hither.
'Tis Cæsar's sword hath made Rome's senate little,
And thinn'd its ranks. Alas! thy dazzled eye
Beholds this man in a false, glaring light,
Which conquest and success have thrown upon him.
Didst thou but view him right, thou'dst see him black
With murder, treason, sacrilege, and crimes
That strike my soul with horror but to name them.
I know thou look'st on me, as on a wretch
Beset with ills, and cover'd with misfortunes;
But, Decius, mark my words,—millions of worlds
Should never buy me to be like that Cæsar.

Decius. Does Cato send *this* answer back to Cæsar,
For all his generous cares, and proffer'd friendship?

Cato. His cares for me are insolent and vain.
Presumptuous man! the gods take care of Cato.
Would Cæsar show the greatness of his soul,
Bid him employ his care for these my friends,
And make good use of his ill-gotten power,
By sheltering men much better than himself.

Decius. Your high, unconquer'd heart makes you
forget
That you're a man. You rush on your destruction—
But I have done. When I relate hereafter
The tale of this unhappy embassy,
All Rome will be in tears.

---

68. THE DISCONTENTED MILLER.

GOLDSMITH.

OLIVER GOLDSMITH was born, 1731, at Pallasmore, county Longford, Ireland. As a poet, essayist, dramatist, and novelist, Goldsmith occupies a high position among the English classics. His novel of "The Vicar o. Wakefield," his poems of "The Traveller" and "Deserted Village," and his drama, "She Stoops to Conquer," are each models in their kind. His historical writings are chiefly compilations, and not very reliable as authorities. Died April 4th, 1774.

1. WHANG, the miller, was naturally avaricious; nobody loved money better than he, or more respected those who had

It.   When people would talk of a rich man in company, Whang
would say, " I know him very well; he and I have been long
acquainted ; he and I are intimate." But, if ever a poor
man was mentioned, he had not the least knowledge of the
man; he might be very well for aught he knew; but he was
not fond of making many acquaintances, and loved to choose
his company.

2.   Whang, however, with all his eagerness for riches, was
poor.   He had nothing but the profits of his mill to support
him; but, though these were small, they were certain; while
it stood and went he was sure of eating; and his frugality was
such that he every day laid some money by, which he would at
intervals count and contemplate with much satisfaction.   Yet
still his acquisitions were not equal to his desires; he only
found himself above want, whereas he desired to be possessed
of affluence.

3.   One day, as he was indulging these wishes he was informed that a neighbor of his had found a pan of money under
ground, having dreamed of it three nights running before.
These tidings were daggers to the heart of poor Whang.
" Here am I," says he, " toiling and moiling from morning
till night for a few paltry farthings, while neighbor Thanks
only goes quietly to bed and dreams himself into thousands
before morning. Oh, that I could dream like him ! With what
pleasure would I dig round the pan !   How slyly would I carry
it home! not even my wife should see me: and then, oh! the
pleasure of thrusting one's hand into a heap of gold up to the
elbow !"

4.   Such reflections only served to make the miller unhappy;
he discontinued his former assiduity; he was quite disgusted
with small gains, and his customers began to forsake him
Every day he repeated the wish, and every night laid himsel
down in order to dream.   Fortune, that was for a long tim
unkind, at last, however, seemed to smile on his distresses, and
indulged him with the wished-for vision.   He dreamed that
under a certain part of the foundation of his mill there was
concealed a monstrous pan of gold and diamonds, buried deep
in the ground, and covered with a large flat stone.

5. He concealed his good luck from every person, as is usual in money-dreams, in order to have the vision repeated the two succeeding nights, by which he should be certain of its truth. His wishes in this, also, were answered; he still dreamed of the same pan of money in the very same place. Now, therefore, it was past a doubt; so, getting up early the third morning, he repaired alone, with a mattock in his hand, to the mill, and began to undermine that part of the wall to which the vision directed him.

6. The first omen of success that he met was a broken ring; digging still deeper, he turned up a house-tile, quite new and entire. At last, after much digging, he came to a broad flat stone, but then so large that it was beyond a man's strength to remove it. "Here!" cried he, in raptures, to himself; "here it is; under this stone there is room for a very large pan of diamonds indeed. I must e'en go home to my wife, and tell her the whole affair, and get her to assist me in turning it up."

7. Away, therefore, he goes, and acquaints his wife with every circumstance of their good fortune. Her raptures on this occasion may easily be imagined. She flew round his neck and embraced him in an ecstasy of joy; but these transports, however, did not allay their eagerness to know the exact sum; returning, therefore, together to the same place where Whang had been digging, there they found—not, indeed, the expected treasure—but the mill, their only support, undermined and fallen.

69. LORD JAMES OF DOUGLAS.

AYTOUN.

WM. EDMONDSTOUNE AYTOUN, was born at Fife, in Scotland, in 1813. His writings have chiefly appeared in *Blackwood's Magazine*. From his national and historical ballads, published in that periodical, the volume of "The Lays of the Scottish Cavaliers," has been made up. We know of no ballads in our tongue, more spirit-stirring or ennobling in sentiment, than "The Execution of Montrose," "Burial March of Dundee," "Edinburgh after Flodden," "The Heart of the Bruce," &c.

1. " THE Moors have come from Africa
      To spoil and waste and slay,
    And King Alonzo of Castile
      Must fight with them to-day."

   " Now shame it were," cried good Lord James,
      " Shall never be said of me
    That I and mine have turn'd aside
      From the Cross in jeopardie !

2. " Have down, have down, my merry men all—
      Have down unto the plain ;
    We'll let the Scottish lion loose
      Within the fields of Spain !"

   " Now welcome to me, noble lord,
      Thou and thy stalwart power ;
    Dear is the sight of a Christian knight.
      Who comes in such an hour !

3. " Is it for bond or faith you come,
      Or yet for golden fee ?
    Or bring ye France's lilies here,
      Or the flower of Burgundie !"

   " God greet thee well, thou valiant king,
      Thee and thy belted peers—
    Sir James of Douglas am I call'd,
      And these are Scottish spears.

4. " We do not fight for bond or plight,
      Nor yet for golden fee ;
    But for the sake of our blessed Lord,
      Who died upon the tree.

   " We bring our great king Robert's heart
      Across the weltering wave,
    To lay it in the holy soil
      Hard by the Saviour's grave.

5. " True pilgrims we, by land or sea,
   Where danger bars the way ;
   And therefore are we here, Lord King,
   To ride with thee this day !"

70. THE JESUITS.

MRS. SADLIER.

MARY A. SADLIER—born in Coote Hill, county Cavan, Ireland. Mrs. Sadlier emigrated to America in early life, but not before she had acquired that thorough knowledge of the Irish people which has enabled her to draw so many truthful pictures of the different classes among them. She has been a contributor to several of our leading Catholic journals in the United States and the Canadas. Her translations from the French are numerous, and some of them valuable. Her fame chiefly rests, however, on her original stories of Irish life at home and abroad. " New Lights," " Willy Burke," " The Blakes and Flanagans," " The Confessions of an Apostate," " Elinor Preston," &c., are well known to the Catholics of America. Her last and greatest work, " The Confederate Chieftains," is a work of much labor and research.

1. THE world never saw such an order as the Jesuits, never dreamed of such a mission as theirs, until it sprang into sudden existence from the divine genius of Ignatius Loyola, at the very moment when Christendom most needed such a powerful auxiliary. When the revolutionary doctrines of the Reformation were sweeping like a torrent over many of the countries of Europe, and men were asking themselves in fear and terror when and where was the devastating flood to be arrested in its course, the Almighty, ever watching over the interests of his Church, suddenly raised up a mighty dyke in presence of the great waters, and all at once they rolled back to their centre in the far north, and the fairest climes of old Europe were saved from their ravages.

2. This new bulwark of the Everlasting Church was no other than the Society of Jesus, one of the grandest conceptions that ever emanated from the brain of mortal man So admirably fitted for the task before it, so well versed in all human science, yet so simple and so humble in their religious character, so full of the loftiest and most chivalrous devotion, and so utterly detached from earthly things, did the Jesuits appear before the world, that its dazzled vision could

scarce comprehend what manner of men they were, those first
disciples of Ignatius, the nucleus and foundation of that
heroic order since so well known in every quarter of the
habitable globe.

3. The martial character of its founder, who had fought
with distinction in the Spanish wars, impressed itself on his
order, and gave to it that lofty sentiment of heroism which
distinguished it from all other monastic institutions then ex-
isting. It was to combat the pernicious innovations of the
great heresy of the sixteenth century that the Jesuits were
called into existence; and as instruments for that chosen work,
they were from the first endowed with every quality that
might insure success.

4. The arch-heretics of the day professed to unshackle the
human intellect by leading it into all science, and far beyond
the range prescribed by *Romish tyranny.* The Jesuits met
them more than half way, with the open volume of science in
their hand. The heretics professed to be learned; the Jesuits
were more learned than they, for they mastered all knowledge,
sacred and profane, which could tend to elevate mankind, and
in every branch of science and literature they soared to heights
where the enemies of religion might not follow.

5. They combated the foe with his own arms, and the
world saw, with amazement, that the sons of Ignatius were
the true enlighteners of the age, for the light which their
genius threw on human learning came direct from the source
of truth. The heretics were world-seeking and world-wor-
shipping; the Jesuits trampled the world under their feet, and
crucified the ancient Adam within them. Many of the earlier
Jesuits were the sons of noble, and some even of princely,
families; among others, St. Ignatius himself, St. Francis Xavier, St. Francis Borgia, St. Louis Gonzaga, and St. Stanis
laus Kotska.

6. But they cheerfully resigned the world, and enlisted under the banner of Christ in the Society which bore his name
Armed only with the cross, their standard at once and their
weapon, they went forth to fight and to conquer, strong in
faith, humility, and charity; strong, too, in the gift of elo-

quence, and radiant with the light of science. The first Jesuits were men mighty in word and work, endowed even with the gift of miracles, like unto the first Apostles, and that for a similar purpose,—to bear testimony of the truth before the heretic and the unbeliever, and to establish the authority of God's Church on earth.

7. Animated with the spirit which descended on Ignatius during his lone night-watch in the chapel of Our Lady of Montserrat, the Jesuits were everywhere seen in the thickest of the contest, then raging all over Europe, between truth and religion on the one side, and error and heresy on the other. Wherever the Church needed their powerful succor, wherever human souls were in danger, there were the sons of Loyola seen, with lance in rest, to rescue and to save. The burning plains of Africa, the idolatrous countries of Asia, the wilds of the New World, and the swarming cities of old Europe, all were alike the scenes of the Jesuits' herculean labors.

8. They taught, they preached, they guided the councils of kings, they knelt with the penitent criminal in his cell, they consoled the poor man in his sorrows and privations, they traversed unknown regions in search of souls to save, they ate with the Indian in his wigwam, and slept on the cold earth, with only the sky for a covering, and often, very often, they suffered tortures and death at the hands of the ruthless savage. East, west, north, and south, the earth has been saturated with their blood, and Christianity sprang up everywhere in the footprints washed with their blood.

---

71. EDUCATION.

DIGBY.

1. THE ancients say that the essential things in the education of the young are to teach them to worship the gods, to revere their parents, to honor their elders, to obey the laws, to submit to rulers, to love their friends, to be temperate in refraining from pleasures—objects not one of which the moderns would

think of entering into a philosophic plan of education; since it is notorious that with them the direction of the energies and passions is always excluded from it.

2. The moderns have determined, practically at least, that the whole of education consists in acquiring knowledge, and that the only subject of deliberation is respecting the mode best calculated to further that end in the shortest time, and with the least possible expenditure. With them, the person who can speak or argue on the greatest number of subjects, with the air of knowing all about each of them, is the best educated.

3. The moderns generally applaud that system of public education which nourishes what they call a manly spirit, by which the boy is made bold and insolent, and constantly ready to fight or contend with any one that offers the smallest opposition to his will; which makes him resemble the son of Strepsiades returning from the school of the Sophists, of whom his father says, with joy, "In the first place, I mark the expression of your countenance: your face indicates at once that you are prepared to deny and to contradict. Yours is the Attic look."

4. Hence, many of their young men are like those who were disciples of the Sophists, of whom Socrates says, they were fair and of good natural dispositions—what the moderns would term of polished manners, but insolent through youth. The rules given to youth for conversation, in his treatise on the manner in which men should bear, approaches nearer to the mildness and delicacy of Christian charity than, perhaps, any other passage in the heathen writers. He inculcates what approaches to its modesty, its patience, in attending to others, and waiting for the voluntary self-corrections of those with whom they converse, and its slowness to contradict and give offence.

5. But all this falls very short, and indeed can yield not the slightest idea, of the effects of education upon the young in the ages of faith, when the Catholic religion formed its basis, and directed its whole system in all its objects, manners, and details "The soul of the child," says St. Jerome, "is to be

educated with the view of its becoming a temple of God. It should hear nothing but what pertains to the fear of God. Let there be letters of ivory," he continues, "with which it may play—and let its play be instruction. No learned man or noble virgin should disdain to take charge of its instruction."

6. These observations will have prepared us to feel the beauty of the following examples:—We read of St. Blier, that while a child he gave admirable signs of piety and grace Nothing could be imagined more sweet, benign, gentle, and agreeable than his whole manner: he seemed like a little angel in human flesh, who used to pray devoutly, visit holy places, converse with saints, and obey the commandments of God with the utmost diligence.

7. Christine de Pisan says of Louis, duc d'Orléans, son of King Charles V., that the first words which were taught him were the Ave-Maria, and that it was a sweet thing to hear him say it, kneeling, with his little hands joined, before an image of our Lady; and that thus he early learned to serve God, which he continued to do all his life. And Dante, in the "Paradise," commemorating the youthful graces of St. Dominic, says of him,

"Many a time his nurse, on entering, found
That he had risen in silence, and was prostrate,
As who should say, ' My errand was for this.' "

8. The old writers love to dwell upon the description of this age. Thus the young Archduke Leopold of Austria is described as having the looks, as well as the innocence, of an angel; and it is said that the mere sight of him in Church used to inspire people with devotion. The young St. Francis Regis, while at college at Puy, was known to all the inhabitants of the town under the title of the Angel of the College. There might have been seen a young nobleman employed in collecting the poor little boys of the town, and explaining to them the Christian doctrine! What school of ancient philosophy ever conceived any thing like this?

72. EDUCATION—*continued.*

1. IN the first place then let it be remembered, that the mind of the young must ever be devoted either to an idea or to sense,—either to an object of faith (and youth is peculiarly qualified for possessing faith), or to that visible form of good which ministers to animal excitement. If the citadels of the souls of the young be left void of pure and noble images, they will be taken possession of by those that are contrary to them; if not guarded by the bright symbols of beauteous and eternal things, error and death, moral death, with all its process of intellectual degradation, will plant their pale flag there.

2. As with the intellectual direction, so it is with the manners, and intercourse of youth; for these will ever be directed after one of two types—either by the spirit of sweetness and love, or that of insolence and malignity. All systems of education that are merely human, and under the guidance of rationalism, will never nourish and fortify, when they do not even recognize and extol the latter; for being formed on merely natural principles, all that belongs to man's unkindness will have free scope to be developed within their dominions; and, therefore, disobedience, dissipation, the will and ability to oppress weaker companions, will entitle the youth, who has sufficient tact, to know how far precisely these qualities may be exercised with the applause of animal minds, to the enviable character of possessing a *manly* spirit. He will discover, too, that his father has only one desire respecting him, like that of Jason in the tragedy, whose sole prayer for his sons is, that he may see them grow to manhood, well nourished and vigorous, that they may be a defence to him against his enemies.

3. In studies also, emulation will be carried to an excess, which renders the youthful mind obnoxious to all the worst attendants of ambition, so that under these modern systems, while education conduces to victory, their victory, as Socrates says, will often undo the work of education.

4. Plato had so sublime a sense of just education, that he

acknowledges, that the good when young, will appear to be weak and simple, and that they will be easily deceived by the unjust—and he, too, would not allow the young to acquire that knowledge of the world, which was so carefully excluded from Catholic schools—but which is now thought so essential to children.

5. ' He is only good who has a good soul ; which he cannot possess who has a personal acquaintance with evil."[1]

6. Are we disposed to question this proposition! Hear what Fuller acknowledges, "Almost twenty years since," says he, "I heard a profane jest, and still remember it."

7. The old poet, Claude de Morenne, acknowledges in one of his pieces, that he had read certain poems in his youth, which had done an injury to his imagination and his heart, which nothing could repair. This is the dreadful effect of renouncing the ancient discipline. Such is the stain which reading of this description impresses upon the mind, that the moral consequences seem among those which never may be cancelled from the book wherein the past is written.

---

73. St. Agnes.

TENNYSON.

A. Tennyson, the present poet laureate of England, is a popular and voluminous writer. He has a rich yet delicate taste in the use of language, and a descriptive power unparalleled by any other living poet.

1. Deep on the convent-roof the snows
    Are sparkling to the moon;
My breath to heaven like vapor goes;
    May my soul follow soon !
The shadows of the convent-towers
    Slant down the snowy sward,
Still creeping with the creeping hours
    That lead me to my Lord.
Make Thou my spirit pure and clear
    As are the frosty skies,

---

[1] Plato de Repub., lib. iii.

Or this first snow-drop of the year
    That in my bosom lies.

2 As these white robes are soil'd and dark,
    To yonder shining ground;
As this pale taper's earthly spark,
    To yonder argent round;
So shows my soul before the Lamb,
    My spirit before Thee;
So in mine earthly house I am,
    To that I hope to be.
Break up the heavens, O Lord! and far,
    Through all yon starlight keen,
Draw me, thy bride, a glittering star,
    In raiment white and clean.

3. He lifts me to the golden doors;
    The flashes come and go;
All heaven bursts her starry floors,
    And strews her lights below,
And deepens on and up! the gates
    Roll back, and far within
For me the Heavenly Bridegroom waits,
    To make me pure of sin.
The sabbaths of Eternity,
    One sabbath deep and wide—
A light upon the shining sea—
    The Bridegroom with his bride!

---

74. Infidel Philosophy and Literature.

ROBERTSON.

Robertson—a distinguished writer and lecturer of the day. He is a native of Scotland, and at present holds the honorable position of Professor of History in the Irish University.

1. The infidel philosophy of the last age was the child of the Reformation. Towards the close of the sixteenth century,

a sect of deists had sprung up in Protestant Switzerland. As early as the reign of James the First, Lord Herbert, of Cherbury, commenced that long series of English deists, consisting of Chubb, Collins, Shaftesbury, Toland, Bolingbroke, the friend of Voltaire. Bayle, who at the commencement of he eighteenth century, introduced infidelity into France, was Protestant; and so was Rousseau, the eloquent apostle of leism, and who did nothing more than develop the principles of Protestantism.

2. Voltaire and his fellow-conspirators against the Christian religion, borrowed most of their weapons from the arsenal of the English deists; and the philosopher of Ferney was, in his youth, the friend and guest of Bolingbroke. So Protestantism, which often, though falsely, taunts the Catholic Church with having given birth to unbelief, lies, itself, clearly open to that imputation. Let us take a glance at the character of the leaders of the great anti-Christian confederacy in France.

3. Bayle was a writer of great erudition, and extreme subtlety of reasoning. His "Dictionnaire Philosophique" is, even at the present day, often consulted. Montesquieu, one of the most manly intellects of the eighteenth century, unfortunately devoted to the wretched philosophy of the day the powers which God had given him for a nobler purpose. His strong sense, indeed, and extensive learning, guarded him against the wilder excesses of unbelief; but the absence of strong religious convictions left him without a compass and a chart on the wide ocean of political and ethical investigations.

4. Rousseau was a man of the most impassioned eloquence and vigorous reasoning; but a mind withal so sophistical, that, according to the just observation of La Harpe, even truth itself deceives us in his writings. His firm belief in the existence of the Deity, and the immortality of the soul, as well as in the necessity of virtue for a future state of happiness, and some remarkable tributes to the Divinity, and the blessed influences of the Christian religion, give, at times, to the pages of Rousseau a warmth and a splendor we rarely find in the other infidel writers of the last century.

5. Inferior to Rousseau in eloquence and logical power, the

sophist of Ferney possessed a more various and versatile tal
ent. Essaying philosophy and history, and poetry—tragic,
comic, and epic; the novel, the romance, the satire, the epi-
gram, he directed all his powers to one infernal purpose—the
spread of irreligion, and thought his labor lost as long as
Christ retained one worshipper! Unlike the more impassioned
sophist of Geneva, rarely do we meet in his writings with a
generous sentiment or a tender emotion. But all that ele-
vates and thrills humanity—the sanctities of religion, the nobleness of virtue, the purity of the domestic hearth, the ex-
pansiveness of friendship, the generosity of patriotism, the
majesty of law, were polluted by his ribald jest and fiend-like
mockery. "Like those insects that corrode the roots of the
most precious plants, he strives," says Count de Maistre, "to
corrupt youth and women."

6. And it is to be observed that, despite the great progress
of religion in France within the last fifty years; though the
aristocracy of French literature has long rejected the yoke of
Voltaire, he still reigns in its lower walks, and the novel, and
the satire, and the ballad, still feel his deadly influence. The
only truth which this writer did not assail was, the existence
of God; but every other dogma of religion became the butt
of his ridicule.

7. A more advanced phase of infidelity was represented by
D'Alembert, Diderot, and others; they openly advocated materialism and atheism. In the Encyclopedia they strove to
array all arts and sciences against the Christian religion. It
was, indeed, a tower of Babel, raised up by man's impiety
against God. It was a tree of knowledge without a graft
from the tree of life. In mathematics and physics only did
D'Alembert attain to a great eminence. Diderot was a much
inferior intellect, that strove to make up by the phrenetic violence of his declamation for the utter hollowness of his ideas.
It was he who gave to Raynal that frothy rhetoric, and those
turgid invectives against priests and kings, which the latter
wove into his history of the European settlements in the East
and West Indies.

75. INFIDEL PHILOSOPHY, ETC.—*continued.*

1. THE great Buffon, though he condescended to do homage to the miserable philosophy of his day, yet, by the nobleness of his sentiments, as well as by the majesty of his genius, often ~se superior to the doctrine he professed.

Bernardine de St. Pierre was another great painter of nature. His better feelings at times led him to Christianity, but his excessive vanity drove him back to the opposite opinions. What shall I say of the remaining wretched herd of materialists and atheists,—a Baron d'Holbach, a Helvetius, a La Mettrie, a Cabanis, and others? It has been well said by a great writer, that materialism is something below humanity. And while debasing man to a level with the brute, it takes from him all the nobler instincts of his own nature; it fails to give him in return those of the lower animals. So deep a perversion of man's moral and intellectual being we cannot conceive.

2. We cannot realize (and happily for us we cannot), that awful eclipse of the understanding which denies God. We have a mingled feeling of terror and of pity, when we contemplate those miserable souls, that, as the great Italian poet, Dante, says, have lost the supreme intelligential bliss: When that great idea of God is extinguished in the human mind, what remains to man?

Nature abhors a vacuum, said the old naturalists; with what horror then must we recoil from that void which atheism creates?—a void in the intelligence, a void in the conscience, a void in the affections, a void in society, a void in domestic life. The human mind is swung from its orbit; it wanders through trackless space; and the reign of chaos and old night returns.

3 What a lamentable abuse of all the noblest gifts of intellect, wit, and eloquence, imagination and reasoning! And for the accomplishment of what purpose? For the overthrow of religion, natural and revealed religion, the guide of existence, the great moral teacher, which solves all the prob-

lens of life, which tells our origin and destiny, our duties to
our Creator and our fellow-creatures, the foundation of the
family and of the State,—religion, the instructress of youth,
and the prop of age; the balm of wounded minds, and the
moderator of human joys; which controls the passions, yet
imparts a zest to innocent pleasures; which survives the illusions of youth, and the disappointments of manhood; consoles
us in life, and supports us in death.

4. Such were the blessings that perverted genius strove to
snatch from mankind. Yet the time was at hand, when the
proud Titans, who sought to storm Heaven, were to be driven
back by the thunderbolts of Almighty wrath, and hurled down
into the lowest depths of Tartarus.

But, even in regard to literature and science, the influence
of this infidel party was most pernicious. How could *they*
understand nature, who rested their eyes on its surface only,
but never pierced to its inner depths? How could they understand the philosophy of history, who denied the providence of
God, and the free will of man? How could they comprehend
metaphysics, who disowned God, and knew nothing of man's
origin, nor of his destiny? And, was an abject materialism
compatible with the aspirations of poetry?

5. Classical philology, too, shared the fate of poetry and
of history; and in education was made to give place to mathematics and the natural sciences. Hence, from this period
dates the decline of philological studies in France. The men
of genius of whom infidelity could boast, like Montesquieu,
Voltaire, Rousseau, Buffon, and D'Alembert, were men who
had been trained up in a Christian country, had received a
Christian education, and whose minds had been imbued with
the doctrines and the ethics of Christianity, and had partially
retained these sentiments in the midst of their unbelief. But,
let unbelief sink deep into a nation's mind—let it form its
morals, and fashion its manners—and we shall soon see how
barbarism of taste and coarseness of habits will be associated
with moral depravity and mental debasement. Look at the
goddess literature of the French Republic from 1790 to 1802,
and at that of the Empire down to 1814. What contempt

ible mediocrity of intellect ; what wretched corruption of taste !

6. But in the Catholic literature, which, after a long sleep revives under Napoleon, and afterwards under the Bourbons, what fulness of life, what energy do we not discover ! What brilliancy of fancy and fervor of feeling in Chateau'riand ! What depth of thought and majesty of diction in the philosopher, De Bonald ! What profound intuitions—what force and plausibility of style in the great Count de Maistre ! What vigorous ratiocination—what burning eloquence, in De Lamennais before his fall ! What elevation of feeling and harmony of numbers in the lyric poet, Lamartine ! Except in the semi-Pantheistic school, represented by Victor Cousin and his friends, French infidelity in the present age, whether in literature or in philosophy, has no first-rate talent to display. Yet of this school, Jouffroy died repenting his errors, and Victor Cousin himself has lately returned to the bosom of the Church.

----•----

76. The Dying Girl.

WILLIAMS.

RICHARD DALTON WILLIAMS is by birth an Irishman. At present, he is Professor of *Belles Lettres* in the Catholic College, Mobile. "He writes with equal ability on all subjects, whether they be grave or gay, pathetic or humorous."—*Hayes's Ballads of Ireland.*

1. FROM a Munster vale they brought her,
    From the pure and balmy air,
An Ormond peasant's daughter,
    With blue eyes and golden hair.
They brought her to the city,
    And she faded slowly there ;
Consumption has no pity
    For blue eyes and golden hair.

2. When I saw her first reclining,
    Her lips were moved in prayer,
And the setting sun was shining
    On her loosen'd golden hair. ·

When our kindly glances met her,
  Deadly brilliant was her eye ;
And she said that she was better,
  While we knew that she must die

3. She speaks of Munster valleys,
  The patron, dance, and fair,
And her thin hand feebly dallies
  With her scattered golden hair.
When silently we listen'd
  To her breath, with quiet care,
Her eyes with wonder glisten'd,
  And she ask'd us what was there

4. The poor thing smiled to ask it,
  And her pretty mouth laid bare,
Like gems within a casket,
  A string of pearlets rare.
We said that we were trying
  By the gushing of her blood,
And the time she took in sighing,
  To know if she were good.

5. Well, she smiled and chatted gayly,
  Though we saw, in mute despair,
The hectic brighter daily,
  And the death-dew on her hair.
And oft, her wasted fingers
  Beating time upon the bed,
O'er some old tune she lingers,
  And she bows her golden head.

6. At length the harp is broken,
  And the spirit in its strings,
As the last decree is spoken,
  To its source, exulting, springs.
Descending swiftly from the skies,
  Her guardian angel came,

He struck God's lightning from her eyes,
And bore him back the flame.

7. Before the sun had risen
　　Through the lark-loved morning air,
Her young soul left its prison,
　　Undefiled by sin or care.
I stood beside the couch in tears,
　　Where, pale and calm, she slept,
And though I've gazed on death for years,
　　I blush not that I wept.
I check'd with effort pity's sighs,
　　And left the matron there,
To close the curtains of her eyes,
　　And bind her golden hair.

---

77. MARIE ANTOINETTE.

BURKE.

EDMUND BURKE, born in Dublin, 1728; died, 1797. As a statesman and an orator, the world has, perhaps, never seen a greater than Edmund Burke. A great orator of our own day, says of him: "No one can doubt that enlightened men in all ages will hang over the works of Mr. Burke. He was a writer of the first class, and excelled in almost every kind of prose composition."—*Lord Brougham.*

"In the three principal questions which excited his interest, and called forth the most splendid displays of his eloquence—The contest with the American Colonies, the impeachment of Warren Hastings, and the French Revolution—we see displayed a philanthropy the most pure, illustrated by a genius the most resplendent. . . He was ever the bold and uncompromising champion of justice, mercy, and truth."—*Allibone's "Dictionary q Authors."*

As a writer, Burke has bequeathed to our times, some of the most perfect models of literary composition. His "Treatise on the Sublime and Beautiful," has never been exceeded in any language. He was, in every sense, a truly great and good man, and hence "the deep reverence with which his character is regarded in the present day." Indeed, the empire of Britain has no name more prized, than that of Edmund Burke, the son of a Dublin attorney.

1. HISTORY, who keeps a durable record of all our acts, and exercises her awful censure over the proceedings of all sorts of sovereigns, will not forget either those events or the era of this liberal refinement in the intercourse of mankind

History will record, that on the morning of the 6th of October, 1789, the King and Queen of France, after a day of confusion, alarm, dismay, and slaughter, lay down, under the pledged security of public faith, to indulge nature in a few hours of respite, and troubled, melancholy repose.

2. From this sleep the queen was first startled by the voice of the sentinel at her door, who cried out to her, to save herself by flight—that this was the last proof of fidelity he could give—that they were upon him, and he was dead. Instantly he was cut down. A band of cruel ruffians and assassins, reeking with blood, rushed into the chamber of the queen, and pierced with a hundred strokes of bayonets and poniards the bed, from whence this persecuted woman had but just time to fly almost naked, and, through ways unknown to the murderers, had escaped to seek refuge at the feet of a king and husband, not secure of his own life for a moment.

3. This king, to say no more of him, and this queen, and their infant children (who once would have been the pride and hope of a great and generous people), were then forced to abandon the sanctuary of the most splendid palace in the world, which they left swimming in blood, polluted by massacre, and strewed with scattered limbs and mutilated carcasses. Thence they were conducted into the capital of their kingdom. Two had been selected from the unprovoked, unresisted, promiscuous slaughter, which was made of the gentlemen of birth and family, who composed the king's body-guard. These two gentlemen, with all the parade of an execution of justice, were cruelly and publicly dragged to the block, and beheaded in the great court of the palace.

4. Their heads were stuck upon spears, and led the procession; while the royal captives, who followed in the train, were slowly moved along, amidst the horrid yells, and thrilling screams, and frantic dances, and infamous contumelies, and all the unutterable abominations of the furies of hell, in the abused shapes of the vilest of women. After they had been made to taste, drop by drop, more than the bitterness of death, in the slow torture of a journey of twelve miles, protracted to six hours, they were, under a guard, composed of those very

soldiers who had thus conducted them through this famous triumph, lodged in one of the old palaces of Paris, now converted into a Bastile for kings. . . . . .

5. It is now sixteen or seventeen years since I saw the Queen of France, then the Dauphiness, at Versailles; and surely never lighted on this orb, which she hardly seemed to touch, a more delightful vision. I saw her just above the horizon, decorating and cheering the elevated sphere she just began to move in,—glittering like the morning star, full of life, and splendor, and joy. Oh! what a revolution! and what a heart I must have, to contemplate without emotion that elevation and that fall! Little did I dream, when she added titles of veneration, to those of enthusiastic, distant respectful love, that she should ever be obliged to carry the sharp antidote against disgrace, concealed in that bosom; little did I dream that I should have lived to see such disasters fallen upon her in a nation of gallant men, in a nation of men of honor, and of cavaliers.

6. I thought ten thousand swords must have leaped from their scabbards, to avenge even a look that threatened her with insult. But the age of chivalry is gone. That of sophisters, economists, and calculators, has succeeded: and the glory of Europe is extinguished forever. Never, never more shall we behold that generous loyalty to rank and sex, that proud submission, that dignified obedience, that subordination of the heart, which kept alive, even in servitude itself, the spirit of an exalted freedom. The unbought grace of life, the cheap defence of nations, the nurse of manly sentiment and heroic enterprise, is gone! It is gone, that sensibility of principle, that chastity of honor, which felt a stain like a wound, which inspired courage, while it mitigated ferocity, which ennobled whatever it touched, and under which vice itself lost half its evil, by losing all its grossness.

78. The Old Émigré.

MISS MITFORD.

MARY RUSSELL MITFORD—born at Almford, in England, 1786; died 1855. Miss Mitford's sketches of rural life are inimitable in their kind, and her style is a model for such compositions. Her series of sketches entitled "Our Village," and "Belford Regis," form very readable volumes.

1. THE first occupant of Mrs. Duval's pleasant apartments was a Catholic priest, an *émigré*, to whom they had a double recommendation,—in his hostess's knowledge of the French language and French cookery (she being, as he used to affirm, the only Englishwoman that ever made drinkable coffee); and in the old associations of the precincts ("piece of a cloister"), around which the venerable memorials of the ancient faith still lingered, even in decay. He might have said, with Antonio, in one of the finest scenes ever conceived by a poet's imagination,—that in which the echo answers from the murdered woman's grave:

2. "I do love these ancient ruins;
   We never tread upon them but we set
   Our foot upon some reverend history;
   And, questionless, here in this open court
   (Which now lies open to the injuries
   Of stormy weather) some do lie interr'd,
   Loved the Church so well, and gave so largely to't,
   They thought it should have canopied their bones,
   Till doomsday. But all things have their end:
   Churches and cities (which have diseases like to men)
   Must have like death that we have."

   WEBSTER—*Duchess of Malfi.*

3. The Abbé Villaret had been a cadet of one of the oldest families in France, destined to the Church as the birthright of a younger son, but attached to his profession with a seriousness and earnestness not common among the gay *noblesse* of the old *régime*. This devotion, had, of course, been greatly increased by the persecution of the Church which distinguished the commencement of the Revolution. The good Abbé had been marked as one of the earliest victims, and had escaped, through the gratitude of an old servant, from the fate which swept off sisters and brothers, and almost every individual, except himself, of a large and flourishing family.

4. Penniless and solitary, he made his way to England, and found an asylum in the town of Belford, at first assisted by the pittance allowed by our government to those unfortunate foreigners, and subsequently supported by his own exertions as assistant to the priest of the Catholic chapel in Belford, and as a teacher of the French language in the town and neighborhood; and so complete had been the ravages of the Revolution in his own family, and so entirely had he established himself in the esteem of his English friends, that, when the short peace of Amiens restored so many of his brother *émigrés* to their native land, he refused to quit the country of his adoption, and remained the contented inhabitant of the Priory Cottage.

5. The contented and most beloved inhabitant, not only of that small cottage, but of the town to which it belonged, was the good Abbé. Everybody loved the kind and placid old man, whose resignation was so real and so cheerful, who had such a talent for making the best of things, whose moral alchemy could extract some good out of every evil, and who seemed only the more indulgent to the faults and follies of others because he had so little cause to require indulgence for his own.

6. From the castle to the cottage, from the nobleman whose children he taught, down to the farmer's wife who furnished him with eggs and butter, the venerable Abbé was a universal favorite. There was something in his very appearance—his small, neat person, a little bent, more by sorrow than age, his thin, white hair, his mild, intelligent countenance, with a sweet, placid smile, that spoke more of courtesy than of gayety, his gentle voice, and even the broken English which reminded one that he was a sojourner in a strange land —that awakened a mingled emotion of pity and respect.

7. His dress, too, always neat, yet never seeming new, contributed to the air of decayed gentility that hung about him; and the beautiful little dog who was his constant attendant, and the graceful boy who so frequently accompanied him, formed an interesting group on the high roads which he frequented; for the good Abbé was so much in request as a teacher, and

the amount of his earnings was so considerable, that he might
have passed for well-to-do in the world, had not his charity
to his poorer countrymen, and his liberality to Louis and to
Mrs Duval, been such as to keep him constantly poor.

---

79. THE SISTER OF CHARITY.

GERALD GRIFFIN.

1. SHE once was a lady of honor and wealth,
   Bright glow'd on her features the roses of health;
   Her vesture was blended of silk and of gold,
   And her motion shook perfume from every fold:
   Joy revell'd around her—love shone at her side,
   And gay was her smile, as the glance of a bride;
   And light was her step in the mirth-sounding hall,
   When she heard of the daughters of Vincent de Paul

2. She felt, in her spirit, the summons of grace,
   That call'd her to live for the suffering race;
   And heedless of pleasure, of comfort, of home,
   Rose quickly like Mary, and answer'd, "I come."
   She put from her person the trappings of pride,
   And pass'd from her home, with the joy of a bride,
   Nor wept at the threshold, as onwards she moved—
   For her heart was on fire in the cause it approved,

3. Lost ever to fashion—to vanity lost,
   That beauty that once was the song and the toast—
   No more in the ball-room that figure we meet,
   But gliding at dusk to the wretch's retreat,
   Forgot in the halls is that high-sounding name,
   For the Sister of Charity blushes at fame;
   Forgot are the claims of her riches and birth,
   For she barters for heaven the glory of earth.

4. Those feet, that to music could gracefully move,
   Now bear her alone on the mission of love;

Those hands that once dangled the perfume and gem,
Are tending the helpless, or lifted for them ;
That voice that once echo'd the song of the vain,
Now whispers relief to the bosom of pain ;
And the hair that was shining with diamond and pearl,
Is wet with the tears of the penitent girl.

5   Her down bed—a pallet; her trinkets—a bead;
Her lustre—one taper that serves her to read;
Her sculpture—the crucifix nail'd by her bed;
Her paintings—one print of the thorn-crowned head,
Her cushion—the pavement that wearies her knees ;
Her music—the psalm, or the sigh of disease ;
The delicate lady lives mortified there,
And the feast is forsaken for fasting and prayer.

6. Yet not to the service of heart and of mind,
Are the cares of that heaven-minded virgin confined.
Like Him whom she loves, to the mansions of grief
·She hastes with the tidings of joy and relief.
She strengthens the weary—she comforts the weak,
And soft is her voice in the ear of the sick ;
Where want and affliction on mortals attend,
The Sister of Charity *there* is a friend.

7. Unshrinking where pestilence scatters his breath,
Like an angel she moves, 'mid the vapor of death ;
Where rings the loud musket, and flashes the sword,
Unfearing she walks, for she follows the Lord.
How sweetly she bends o'er each plague-tainted face,
With looks that are lighted with holiest grace ;
How kindly she dresses each suffering limb,
For she sees in the wounded the image of Him.

8. Behold her, ye worldly! behold her, ye vain !
Who shrink from the pathway of virtue and pain ;
Who yield up to pleasure your nights and your days,
Forgetful of service, forgetful of praise.

Ye lazy philosophers—self-seeking men,—
Ye fireside philanthropists, great at the pen,
How stands in the balance your eloquence weigh'd
With the life and the deeds of that high-born maid?

80. SIR THOMAS MORE TO HIS DAUGHTER.

SIR THOMAS MORE, a celebrated chancellor of England, who succeeded Cardinal Wolsey, as Lord High Chancellor, in 1530, and filled the office for three years with scrupulous integrity. For his conscientious scruples to take the oath of supremacy in favor of that brutal king, Henry VIII., he was beheaded in 1535, at the age of fifty-five. He was the author of the celebrated political romance of "Utopia." Dr. Johnson pronounced the works of More to be models of pure and elegant style. The following letter is addressed to his favorite child, Margaret Roper.

1. THOMAS MORE sendeth greeting to his dearest daughter, Margaret:

My Dearest Daughter—There was no reason why you should have deferred writing to me one day longer, though your letters were barren of any thing of interest, as you tell me. Even had it been so, your letters might have been pardoned by any man, much more, then, by a father, to whose eyes even the blemishes in his child's face will seem beautiful. But these letters of yours, Meg, were so finished both in style and manner, that not only was there nothing in them to fear your father's censure, but Momus himself, though not in his best humor, could have found nothing in them to smile at in the way of censure.

2. I greatly thank our dear friend, Mr. Nicols, for his kindness. He is a man well versed in astronomy; and I congratulate you on your good fortune in learning from him in the space of one month, and with so small labor of your own, so many and such high wonders of that mighty and eterna Workman, which were found only after many ages, and by watching so many long and cold nights under the open sky Thus, you have accomplished, in a short time, what took the labor of years of some of the most excellent wits the world has ever produced.

3. Another thing which you write me, pleaseth me exceedingly, that you have determined with yourself to study philoso

phy so dilligently, that you will regain by your diligence what
your negligence had lost you. I love you for this, my dear
Meg, that, whereas I never found you a loiterer—your proficiency evidently showing how painfully you have proceeded
therein—yet, such is your modesty, that you had rather still
accuse yourself of negligence, than make any vain boast
Except you mean this, that you will hereafter be so diligent,
that your former endeavors, though praiseworthy, may, as
compared to your future diligence, be called negligence.

4. If this you mean—as I verily think you do—nothing can
be more fortunate for me, nothing, my dearest daughter, more
happy for you. I have earnestly wished that you might spend
the rest of your days in studying the Holy Scriptures, and the
science of medicine : these offer the means for fulfilling the end
of our existence, which is, to endeavor to have a sound mind
in a sound body. Of these studies you have already laid some
foundation, nor will you ever want matter to build upon. In
nothing are the first years of life so well bestowed as in humane
learning and the liberal arts.

5. By these we obtain that our after age can better struggle
with the difficulties of life ; and if not acquired in youth, it is
uncertain whether at any other time we shall have the advantage of so careful, so loving, and so learned a master. I could
wish, my dear Meg, to talk long with you about these matters,
but here they are bringing in the supper, interrupting me and
calling me away. My supper will not be so sweet to me, as
this my speech with you is ; but then, we have others to mind
as well as ourselves.

6. Farewell, my dearest daughter, and commend me kindly
to your husband, my loving son ; who, it rejoices me to hear,
is studying the same things you do. You know I always
counselled you to give place to your husband ; but, in this
respect, I give you full license to strive and be the master,
more especially in the knowledge of the spheres. Farewell,
again and again. Commend me to all your school-fellows, but
to your master especially. From your father who loves you,

THOMAS MORE.

81. Influence of Catholicity on Civil Liberty.

DR. SPALDING.

M. J. Spalding, D. D., bishop of Louisville, born in Kentucky in the early part of the present century. This distinguished prelate and profound theologian, is also an accomplished scholar, and an eminent writer, who counts nothing foreign to his purpose, that affects the welfare of men. His reviews, essays, and lectures, are replete with the information most requisite in our age. His "Evidences of Catholicity," "Review of D'Aubigné's History of the Reformation," "Sketches of the early Catholic Missions in Kentucky," and his "Miscellanies," are among our standard works.

1. Of the old Catholic republics, two yet remain, standing monuments of the influence of Catholicity on free institutions. The one is imbosomed in the Pyrenees of Catholic Spain, and the other is perched on the Apennines of Catholic Italy. The very names of Andorra and San Marino are enough to refute the assertion, that Catholicity is opposed to republican governments. Both of these little republics owed their origin *directly* to the Catholic religion. That of Andorra was founded by a Catholic bishop, and that of San Marino, by a Catholic monk, whose name it bears. The bishops of Urgel have been, and are still, the protectors of the former; and the Roman Pontiffs of the latter.

2. Andorra has continued to exist, with few political vicissitudes, for more than a thousand years; while San Marino dates back her history more than fifteen hundred years, and is therefore not only the oldest republic in the world, but perhaps the oldest government in Europe. The former, to a territory of two hundred English square miles, has a population of fifteen thousand; while the latter, with half the population, has a territory of only twenty-one square miles. Both of them are governed by officers of their own choice; and the government of San Marino in particular, is conducted on the most radically democratic principles.

3. The legislative body consists of the Council of Sixty, one half of whom at least are, by law, to be chosen from the plebeian order; and of the *Arrengo*, or general assembly, summoned under extraordinary circumstances, in which all the families of the republic are to be represented. The executive is lodged

in two *capitanei regyenti*, or governors, chosen every six months, and holding jurisdiction, one in the city of San Marino, and the other in the country ;—so jealous are these old republicans of placing power in the hands of one man ! The judiciary department is managed by a commissary, who is required by law to be a foreigner,—a native of some other part of Italy,—in order that, in the discharge of his office, he may be biassed by no undue prejudices, resulting from family connections.

4. When Addison visited the republic in 1700, he "scarcely met with any in the place who had not a tincture of learning." He also saw the collection of the laws of the republic, published in Latin, in one volume folio, under the title : "Statuta illustrissimæ reipublicæ Sancti Marini." When Napoleon, at the head of his victorious French troops, was in the neighborhood of San Marino, in 1797, he paused, and sent a congratulatory deputation to the republic, "which expressed the reverence felt by her young sister, France, for so ancient and free a commonwealth, and offered, besides an increase of territory, a present of four pieces of artillery." The present was gratefully accepted, but the other tempting offer was wisely declined !

5. The good old Catholic times produced patriots and heroes, of whom the present age might well be proud. William Wallace, defeated at Buscenneth, fell a martyr to the liberty of his native Scotland in 1305. Robert Bruce achieved what Wallace had bled for not in vain,—the independence of his country. He won, in 1314, the decisive battle of Bannockburn, which resulted in the expulsion of the English invaders from Scotland. Are the Hungarians, and Poles, and Spaniards, and French, who fought for centuries the battles of European independence against the Saracens and Turks, to be set down as enemies of freedom ? Are the brave knights of St. John, who so heroically devoted themselves for the liberty of Europe at Rhodes and at Malta, also to be ranked with the enemies of human rights ?

6. We might bring the subject home to our own times and country, and show that the Catholics of the colony of Mary-

land, were the first to proclaim universal liberty, civil and religious, in North America; that in the war for independence with Protestant England, Catholic France came generously and effectually to our assistance; that Irish and American Catholics fought side by side with their Protestant fellow-citizens in that eventful war; that the Maryland line which bled so freely at Camden with the Catholic Baron de Kalb, while Gates and his Protestant militia were consulting their safety by flight, was composed to a great extent of Catholic soldiers; that there was no Catholic traitor during our revolution; that the one who perilled most in signing the Declaration of Independence, and who was the last survivor of that noble band of patriots, was the illustrious Catholic, Charles Carroll of Carrollton; that half the generals and officers of our revolution—Lafayette, Pulaski, Count de Grasse, Rochambeau, De Kalb, Kosciuszko, and many others were Catholics; and that the first commodore appointed by Washington to form our infant navy, was the Irish Catholic—BARRY. These facts, which are but a few of those which might be adduced, prove conclusively that Catholicity is still, what she was in the middle ages, the steadfast friend of free institutions.

7. To conclude: Can it be that Catholicity, which saved Europe from barbarism and a foreign Mohammedan despotism,—which in every age has been the advocate of free principles, and the mother of heroes and of republics,—which originated *Magna Charta* and laid the foundation of liberty in every country in Europe,—and which in our own day and country has evinced a similar spirit,—is the enemy of free principles? We must blot out the facts of history, before we can come to any such conclusion! If history is at all to be relied on, we must conclude, that THE INFLUENCE OF THE CATHOLIC CHURCH HAS BEEN FAVORABLE TO CIVIL LIBERTY

82. The Ministry of Angels.

SPENSER.

Edmund Spenser—one of the brightest of that galaxy of poets who shed lustre on the reign of Elizabeth. The poetry of Spenser belongs to the first order. There is a salutary purity and nobleness about it. He is a connecting link between Chaucer and Milton; resembling the former in his descriptive power, his tenderness, and his sense of beauty, though inferior to him in homely vigor and dramatic insight into character. His 'Fairy Queen" is the chief representative in English poetry of the romance which once delighted hall and bower. Notwithstanding his polemical allegory of Duessa, a sorry tribute to the age, nothing is more striking than the Catholic tone that belongs to Spenser's poetry. The religion and the chivalry of the Middle Ages were alike the inspirers of his song. He belongs to the order of poets who are rather the monument of a time gone by than an illustration of their own.

1. And is there care in heaven? And is there love
In heavenly spirits to these creatures base,
That may compassion of their evils move?
There is :—else much more wretched were the case
Of men than beasts : but oh ! th' exceeding grace
Of highest God, that loves his creatures so,
And all his works with mercy doth embrace,
That blessed angels he sends to and fro,
To serve to wicked man, to serve his wicked foe !

2. How oft do they their silver bowers leave
To come to succor us, that succor want !
How oft do they, with golden pinions cleave
The flitting skies, like flying pursuivant,
Against foul fiends to aid us militant !
They for us fight, they watch and duly ward,
And their bright squadrons round about us plant ;
And all for love, and nothing for reward :
Oh ! why should heavenly God to men have such regard ?

Sonnet.

3. Sweet is the rose, but grows upon a brere ;
Sweet is the juniper, but sharp his bough ;
Sweet is the eglantine, but pricketh near ;
Sweet is the firbloom, but his branches rough ;

Sweet is the cyprus, but his rind is tough ;
Sweet is the nut, but bitter is his pill ;
Sweet is the broom flower, but yet sour enough ;
And sweet is moly, but his root is ill :
So, every sweet with sour is temper'd still ; ·
That maketh it be coveted the more :
For easy things, that may be got at will,
Most sorts of men do set but little store.
Why, then, should I account of little pain
That endless pleasure shall unto me gain ?

---

83. THE CHOICE.

MILES.

George H. Miles, native of Baltimore, professor now at Mt. St. Mary's
College, his Alma Mater, one of our most gifted writers in poetry and
prose. His two published tales of "The Governess," and "Loretto; or,
The Choice," and still more his tragedy of "Mahomet," prove him possessed of a high order of talent.

1. "WHAT do you think of the world, Agnes ? rather a nice
place after all—eh ? Oh, I have had my time in it !"

"And so have I," said Agnes.

"You ought to see more of it, my girl."

"No, thank you ; I have seen quite enough."

"Why, you jade you, what have you seen in a month ? It
takes one years to see the world as it is, in all its majestically
accumulating glory and versatile interest. Poh !" continued
the Colonel, "what have *you* seen ?"

2. "I have seen," returned Agnes, with provoking calmness,
"that its standard of morality is not God's standard ; that
wealth and impudence are its virtues ; poverty and modesty
its vices ; that money is its god, its grand governing principle,
to which all else is subservient ; that happiness is measured
by the purse, and that a comfortable if not luxurious settlement in life is the grand goal, in the chase of which eternity
is lost sight of."

"Poh !" ejaculated the Colonel. ·

3. "I have seen Catholics almost universally ashamed of the first principles of their faith, and artfully smoothing them over to attract their dissenting brethren. I have seen them dressing so indecently, even when priests are invited, that their pastors are put to the blush."

"That's the priest's fault," mumbled the Colonel.

4. "I have seen," continued Agnes, smiling at the interruption, "that your happy, merry men and women, are only so because they have a false conscience, which has ceased to accuse them; I have seen all who have virtue enough to feel, living in perpetual fear of the temptations by which they are surrounded. I have seen that society is but a hollow farce, in which there is neither love nor friendship. I have seen the idol of a thousand worshippers left without a single friend when touched by poverty."

5. The Colonel groaned and looked away from Lel.

"And I have seen," said Agnes, taking her uncle's hand, and modulating her voice to a whisper, "I have seen that, in spite of all this, the world is dazzlingly beautiful, winning, enchanting. And oh, my dear, good uncle, it is not *God* that makes it so! I have felt its insidious fascination. I tell you, uncle, that I have been wandering along the brink of a precipice; that I could no more live in the world than can the moth live in the candle; that my only salvation is in that Convent!"

6. The old man knocked the ashes carefully from his cigar, slowly brushed a tear from his eye, and put his arm around Lel's neck.

"Thank God, *you* are not a Catholic!" he exclaimed. "There are no Protestant convents to take *you* from me."

With tears streaming down her cheeks, Lel leaned her head on his shoulder. A horrible suspicion ran through the Colonel's mind. He raised her head in the clear moonlight, and mutely questioned her, with such a fearful, timid gaze, that her heart bled for him, as she said—

"Yes, uncle, I *am* a Catholic!"

7. The cigar fell from his hand—his cane rolled on the porch—his broad chest swelled as if his heart was bursting—

11

had they both been dead at his feet, he could scarcely have shown more grief, than at this overthrow of all his plans, this defeat of his best diplomacy.

"CHECK-MATED !" he sobbed in uncontrolled agony ; repulsed them sternly from his side, and then, spreading his arms, snatched them both to his bosom. "Check-mated Check-mated !"

8. One word: the sermon just preached by Agnes against he world, has nothing new in it; Solomon put it all in a nutshell long ago; it will be found better expressed in every prayer-book. To the Colonel, it was perfectly puerile, the same old song which saints and misanthropists have been singing together from time immemorial. Only by constant meditation do we comprehend that life is but a préparation for death; and unless this great truth is realized, where is the folly in living as if time were the main thing and eternity a trifle?

9. The visible present, though brief, and bounded by the grave, is apt to be more important than the invisible future. Without strong *faith*, men *must* live as they do; and all who reprove them for neglecting their souls, in over devotion to their bodies, will seem only fools, or very good people, who have not weighed well the difficulty of what they propose. Every day we witness the same spectacle—a world, for whom Jod died upon the cross, devoting all their time, all their thoughts, to obtain material comfort and avoid sorrow: a prayer at night, an ejaculation in the morning—the rest of the day sacred to the body.

10. We see this every day; we do not wonder at it ; it is all right, all in the order of Providence : the only mystery is, that some weak, pious souls are absurd enough to quit the world, and devote the greater part of their lives to religious exercises; this is the singular part of it. It would be an unnatural state of things, indeed, if all mankind were to make business secondary to religion, and spend as much time in praising God, as they do in making money.

11. Why, the best instructed, the most edifying Catholic parents, cannot help preferring an auspicious alliance with

man for their daughters, to an eternal union with God in the solitary cloister; and how can we expect the worldly-minded Colonel, who has not seen a confessional for forty years, to consider the choice made by Agnes, as any thing else than a burning shame, a living death?

12. How many of us have realized, by prayer and meditation, that heaven is all and earth nothing? How many of us are truly sick of the vanity of life, much as we pretend to be, and do not sagely conclude that our neighbors and ourselves are all doing our duty, taking our share of enjoyment with sufficient gratitude, and bearing our just proportion of affliction with exemplary resignation?

13. There was a time when monasteries and chapels were as numerous as castles; when the Christian world seemed ambitious to live a Christian life; when self-denial and self-castigation were honored; when the consecration of a cathedral was of more moment than the opening of a railroad; when there was something nobler than science, and dearer than profit; when the security of government was in the humility of the people; when the security of the people was in the firmness and purity of the Church; when there was not, as now, a groundwork of ignorance, pride, and envy, which is either a withering master or a dangerous slave. Yes! there was a time when all this was, and when Agnes might not have been laughed at; but it was in the dark ages, reader, in those terrible nights before the sunlight of newspapers had illumined the earth.

---

84. THE CHOICE—*continued.*

1. MUST it be told that, within a month after her return from the city, Agnes entered the convent as a candidate; that three months later, her long hair was cut to suit the brown cap of the novice? Until her hair was cut, the Colonel had cherished a hope that she would repent her girlish haste; but when he saw the ruin caused by those envious shears, he could not help saying—"It is all over—all over!"

2. And ye who have clung to Agnes, in the hope that she would be induced to marry Melville, or incline to Mr. Almy, or that some romantic young gentleman would appear upon the carpet, invested with every virtue and every grace, between whom and our young novice, a sweet sympathy might be established, which should ultimately lead to better things than the cloister, and supply a chapter or two of delicious sentiment,— leave us, we beseech you,—for her CHOICE is made, though the vows are not yet taken.

3. Yes! she is lost to the world! that sweet, beautiful girl, who laughed so merrily with her load of premiums in her arms; the milk-white lamb among those green hills; the friend who had gone to change Lel, and who did change her, though she nearly perished in the effort; the kind protectress who had comforted little Clarence and the Wanderer; the keen-sighted woman who had penetrated the secret of Mr. Almy's face; who had conquered Melville, and reigned supreme in the ball-room, eclipsing all the practised belles of the season!

4. *She was lost to the world!* that sweet, beautiful girl, who was so well fitted to delight and adorn it; lost before the first bloom of youth had passed from her cheeks, before experience had dried the first bright waters of hope and trust that are born in our hearts; lost before there was any need to seek a refuge from the ills of life in that last resource, a convent! *She is lost to the world,* and what matters it what she has gained—what heaven has won!—so thought the Colonel.

5. Yet, what was his love for Agnes, compared to her mother's—the mother who remembered her baptism, her first cries, her first words, her first caresses; who had counted her first smiles, and treasured them in her heart; who remembered every incident of her youth, her first lisping prayers, her first songs, her first visit to mass, her first confession, her first communion, her confirmation: what was his bereavement to hers?

6. Agnes was her only child, her only companion in prayer, her jewel, her treasure, her all on earth; a thousand uncles could not have loved her as she did; their lives had been one, and now they are called upon to live apart. Oh, not apart!

Who shall say apart! When they are repeating, day after day, and night after night, the same dear litanies, when they are appealing to the same saints, the same angels, the same Blessed Mother, the same Father, Son, and Holy Ghost; when they are living together in God, who shall say they are iving apart!

7. And thus thought Mrs. Cleveland, and she missed not ner daughter's long, dark hair; and if she shed floods of natu ral tears, it was not because her daughter was clad in the plain livery of heaven. And so thought Lel, and she was glad of the CHOICE, though she had now to sit and sew alone, though she had to walk alone, though she had to watch the sun rise and set, and play Beethoven, and listen to the birds and pluck wild flowers, and muse under the old oak-trees without Agnes at her side.

8. O God! how beautiful must the soul be when entering heaven! The plainest face, when lit with sanctity, is sublime, and prince and peasant bow down before it, or if they smite, it is in envy. No rouge shall ever tinge thy pale cheek, Sister Agnes; no ring shall ever glitter on thy white hand; thy hair shall never be twined into lockets; thy foot shall never twinkle in the dance!

9. Thou art the child of God, Sister Agnes! And who will dare to claim thee for the world, as thou kneelest there before the altar, or say that thou wert made for man? Who would snatch thee thence, thou young companion of the angels, as if thou wert to be pitied and saved? There is the likeness to God, which the children of earth have lost, and who would bid it vanish?

---

85. THE FATE OF ANDRÉ.

HAMILTON.

ALEXANDER HAMILTON, at the age of seventeen, during the first days of the Revolution, commenced his public career. He was engaged in the first act of armed opposition, and during the war was Washington's principal and confidential aid. He was the author of three-fourths of the Nos. of the "Federalist." These essays constitute one of the most profound and lucid treatises on politics that has ever been written. The melancholy circum-stances of the close of his life are still remembered. He was killed in a duel, by Aaron Burr, at Weehawken, near New York, in 1804. There has been but one other instance of such profound and universal mourning throughout the United States. His assassin, then in the second office of the republic, and the favorite of a powerful party, became a fugitive and a vagabond.

1. NEVER, perhaps, did any man suffer death with more justice, or deserve it less. The first step he took, after his capture, was to write a letter to General Washington, conceived in terms of dignity without insolence, and apology without meanness. The scope of it was to vindicate himself from the imputation of having assumed a mean character for treacherous or interested purposes ; asserting that he had been involuntarily an impostor; that, contrary to his intention, which was to meet a person for intelligence on neutral ground, he had been betrayed within our posts, and forced into the vile condition of an enemy in disguise ; soliciting only, that, to whatever rigor policy might devote him, a decency of treatment might be observed, due to a person who, though unfortunate, had been guilty of nothing dishonorable.

2. His request was granted in its fullest extent ; for, in the whole progress of the affair, he was treated with the most scrupulous delicacy. When brought before the Board of Officers, he met with every mark of indulgence, and was required to answer no interrogatory which could even embarrass his feelings. On his part, while he carefully concealed every thing that might involve others, he frankly confessed all the facts relating to himself ; and, upon his confession, without the trouble of examining a witness, the board made their report. The members of it were not more impressed with the candor and firmness, mixed with a becoming sensibility, which he displayed, than he was penetrated with their liberality and politeness.

3. He acknowledged the generosity of the behavior towards him in every respect, but particularly in this, in the strongest terms of manly gratitude. In a conversation with a gentleman who visited him after his trial, he said he flattered himself he had never been illiberal ; but if there were any remains of prejudice in his mind, his present experience must obliterate them. In one of the visits I made to him (and I saw him several

times during his confinement), he begged me to be the bearer
of a request to the general, for permission to send an open letter to Sir Henry Clinton.

4. "I foresee my fate," said he, "and though I pretend not
to play the hero, or to be indifferent about life, yet I am reconciled to whatever may happen, conscious that misfortune, not
guilt, has brought it upon me. There is only one thing that
disturbs my tranquillity. Sir Henry Clinton has been too good
to me; he has been lavish of his kindness. I am bound to him
by too many obligations, and love him too well, to bear the
thought that he should reproach himself or that others should
reproach him, on the supposition of my having conceived myself obliged, by his instructions, to run the risk I did.

5. "I would not, for the world, leave a sting in his mind
that should imbitter his future days." He could scarce finish
the sentence, bursting into tears in spite of his efforts to suppress them; and with difficulty collected himself enough afterwards to add: "I wish to be permitted to assure him, I did
not act under this impression, but submitted to a necessity imposed upon me, as contrary to my own inclination as to his
orders." His request was readily complied with; and he wrote
the letter annexed, with which I dare say you will be as much
pleased as I am, both for the diction and sentiment.

6. When his sentence was announced to him, he remarked,
that since it was his lot to die, there was still a choice in the
mode, which would make a material difference in his feelings;
and he would be happy, if possible, to be indulged with a pro-
fessional death. He made a second application, by letter, in
concise but persuasive terms. It was thought this indulgence,
being incompatible with the customs of war, could not be
granted; and it was therefore determined, in both cases, to
evade an answer, to spare him the sensations which a certain
knowledge of the intended mode would inflict.

7. In going to the place of execution, he bowed familiarly,
as he went along, to all those with whom he had been acquainted in his confinement. A smile of complacency expressed the
serene fortitude of his mind. Arrived at the fatal spot, he
asked, with some emotion, "Must I then die in this manner?"

He was told it had been unavoidable. "I am reconciled to my fate," said he, "but not to the mode." Soon, however, recollecting himself, he added : "It will be but a momentary pang ;" and, springing upon the cart, performed the last offices to himself, with a composure that excited the admiration and melted the hearts of the beholders. Upon being told the final moment was at hand, and asked if he had any thing to say, hê answered, "Nothing, but to request you will witness to the world, that I die like a brave man." Among the extraordinary circumstances that attended him, in the midst of his enemies, he died universally esteemed and universally regretted.

8. There was something singularly interesting in the character and fortunes of André. To an excellent understanding, well improved by education and travel, he united a peculiar elegance of mind and manners, and the advantage of a pleasing person. 'Tis said he possessed a pretty taste for the fine arts, and had himself attained some proficiency in poetry, music, and painting. His knowledge appeared without ostentation, and embellished by a diffidence that rarely accompanies so many talents and accomplishments ; which left you to suppose more than appeared.

9. His sentiments were elevated, and inspired esteem . they had a softness that conciliated affection. His elocution was pleasing ; his address easy, polite, and insinuating. By his merit, he had acquired the unlimited confidence of his general, and was making a rapid progress in military rank and reputation. But in the height of his career, flushed with new hopes from the execution of a project, the most beneficial to his party that could be devised, he was at once precipitated from the summit of prosperity, and saw all the expectations of his ambition blasted, and himself ruined.

10. The character I have given of him is drawn partly from what I saw of him myself, and partly from information. I am aware that a man of real merit is never seen in so favorable a light as through the medium of adversity : the clouds that surround him are shades that set off his good qualities. Misfortune cuts down the little vanities that, in prosperous times, serve as so many spots in his virtues ; and gives a tone of

humility that makes his worth more amiable. His spectators, who enjoy a happier lot, are less prone to detract from it, through envy, and are more disposed, by compassion, to give him the credit he deserves, and perhaps even to magnify it.

11. I speak not of André's conduct in this affair as a philosopher, but as a man of the world. The authorized maxims nd practices of war are the satires of human nature. They countenance almost every species of seduction as well as violence; and the general who can make most traitors in the army of his adversary, is frequently most applauded. On this scale we acquit André; while we could not but condemn him, if we were to examine his conduct by the sober rules of philosophy and moral rectitude. It is, however, a blemish on his fame, that he once intended to prostitute a flag: about this a man of nice honor ought to have had a scruple; but the temptation was great; let his misfortunes cast a veil over his error

---

86. MELROSE ABBEY AS IT IS.

SCOTT.

SIR WALTER SCOTT, is one of the men of whom Scotland is justly proud. It is the peculiar merit of Scott's writings to have revived something of that chivalrous sentiment, without which society rusts in sordid pursuits, and to have turned back the eyes of a self-conceited age to the "olden time." With the frank nature and cordial humor which belonged to Chaucer and Shakspeare, Scott possessed also much of their dramatic power.

1 If thou wouldst view fair Melrose aright,
    Go, visit it by the pale moonlight;
    For the gay beams of lightsome day
    Gild but to flout the ruins gray.
    When the broken arches are black in night,
    And each shafted oriel glimmers white;
    When the cold light's uncertain shower
    Streams on the ruin'd central tower;
    When buttress and buttress alternately
    Seem framed of ebon and ivory;
    When silver edges the imagery,
    And the scrolls that teach thee to live and die;

11*

When distant Tweed is heard to rave,
And the owlet to hoot o'er the dead man's grave,
Then go ; but go alone the while—
Then view St. David's ruin'd pile :
And, home returning, soothly swear,—
Was never scene so sad and fair !

2. Again on the knight look'd the churchman old,
    And again he sighèd heavily ;
For he had himself been a warrior bold,
    And fought in Spain and Italy.
And he thought on the days that were long since by,
When his limbs were strong and his courage was high:
Now, slow and faint, he led the way,
Where, cloister'd round, the garden lay ;
The pillar'd arches were over their head,
And beneath their feet were the bones of the dead.

3. Spreading herbs and flowrets bright
Glisten'd with the dew of night !
Nor herb nor floweret glistened there
But was carved in the cloister-arches as fair.
    The monk gazed long on the lovely moon,
        Then into the night he lookèd forth;
     And red and bright the streamers light
       Were dancing in the glowing north.
  So had he seen, in fair Castile,
     The youth in glittering squadrons start ;
  Sudden the flying jennet wheel,
     And hurl the unexpected dart.
He knew, by the streamers that shot so bright,
That spirits were riding the northern light.

4. By a steel-clench'd postern-door
    They enter'd now the chancel tall ;
The darken'd roof rose high aloof
    On pillars lofty, and light, and small ;

The keystone, that lock'd each ribbèd aisle,
Was a fleur-de-lys,. or a quatre-feuille ;
The corbells were carved grotesque and grim ;
And the pillars, with cluster'd shafts so trim,
With base and with capitol flourish'd around,
Seem'd bundles of lances which garlands had bound.

5. Full many a scutcheon and banner riven
Shook to the cold night-wind of heaven
   Around the screenèd altar's pale !
And there the dying lamps did burn
Before thy low and lonely urn,
O gallant chief of Otterburne,
   And thine, dark knight of Liddesdale !
O fading honors of the dead !
O high ambition, lowly laid !

6. The moon on the east oriel shone
Through slender shafts of shapely stone
   By foliaged tracery combined ;
Thou wouldst have thought some fairy's hand
'Twixt poplars straight the osier wand,
   In many a freakish knot, had twined ;
Then framed a spell, when the work was done,
And changed the willow wreaths to stone,
The silver light, so pale and faint,
Show'd many a prophet and many a saint,
   Whose image on the glass was dyed.
Full in the midst, his cross of red—
Triumphant Michael brandishèd,
   And trampled the apostate's pride.
The moonbeam kiss'd the holy pane,
And threw on the pavement a bloody stain.

87 THE FIRST SOLITARY OF THE THEBAIS.

CHATEAUBRIAND.

The name of CHATEAUBRIAND stands distinguished among the literary men of modern France, and his vivid imagination and poetical fervor would have made him conspicuous in any age. His masterpiece is the "Genius of Christianity," which contains more brilliant and varied eloquence than any work of the kind produced by the present century.

1. "To the east of this vale of palms arose a high mountain. I directed my course to this kind of Pharos, that seemed to call me to a haven of security, through the immovable floods and solid billows of an ocean of sand. I reached the foot of the mountain, and began to ascend the black and calcined rocks, which closed the horizon on every side. Night descended. Thinking I heard some sound near me, I halted, and plainly distinguished the footsteps of some wild beast, which was wandering in the dark, and broke through the dried shrubs that opposed his progress. I thought that I recognized the lion of the fountain.

2. "Suddenly he sent forth a tremendous roar. The echoes of these unknown mountains seemed to awaken for the first time, and returned the roar in savage murmurs. He had paused in front of a cavern whose entrance was closed with a stone. I beheld a light glimmering between the crevices of this rock, and my heart beat high with hope and with wonder. I approached and looked in, when, to my astonishment, I really beheld a light shining at the bottom of the cavern.

" 'Whoever thou art,' cried I, 'that feedest the savage beasts, have pity on a wretched wanderer.'

" Scarcely had I pronounced these words, when I heard the voice of an old man who was chanting one of the Scripture canticles. I cried in a loud tone :

" 'Christian, receive your brother.'

3. " Scarcely had I uttered these words, when a man approached, broken with age ; his snowy beard seemed whitened with all the years of Jacob, and he was clothed in a garment formed of the leaves of the palm.

" 'Stranger,' said he, 'you are welcome. You behold a

man who is on the point of being reduced to his kindred dust. The hour of my happy departure is arrived : yet still I have a few moments left to dedicate to hospitality. Enter, my brother, the grotto of Paul.'

" Overpowered with veneration, I followed this founder of Christianity in the deserts of the Thebais.

4. " A palm-tree, which grew in the recess of the grotto, entwined its spreading branches along the rock, and formed a species of vestibule. Near it flowed a spring remarkable for its transparency ; out of this fountain issued a small rivulet, that had scarcely escaped from its source before it buried itself in the bosom of the earth. Paul seated himself with me on the margin of the fountain, and the lion that had shown me the Arab's well, came and crouched himself at our feet.

5. " 'Stranger,' said the anchorite, with a happy simplicity, 'how do the affairs of the world go on? Do they still build cities? Who is the master that reigns at present? For a hundred and thirteen years have I inhabited this grotto? and for a hundred years I have seen only two men—yourself, and Anthony, the inheritor of my desert ; he came yesterday to visit me, and will return to-morrow to bury me.'

6. " As he said this, Paul went and brought some bread of the finest kind, from the cavity of the rock. He told me that Providence supplied him every day with a fresh quantity of this food. He invited me to break the heavenly gift with him. We drank the water of the spring in the hollow of our hands ; and after this frugal repast, the holy man inquired what events had conducted me to this inaccessible retreat. After listening to the deplorable history of my life :

7. " 'Eudorus,' said he, 'your faults have been great ; but there is no stain which the tears of penitence cannot efface. It s not without some design that Providence has made you a witness of the introduction of Christianity into every land. You will also find it here in this solitude, among the lions, beneath the fires of the tropic, as you have encountered it amidst the bears and the glaciers of the pole. Soldie of Jesus Christ, you are destined to fight and to conquer for the faith. O God ! whose ways are incomprehensible, it is thou that hast

conducted this young confessor to my grotto, vaat I might
unveil futurity to his view ; that by perfecting him in the
knowledge of his religion, I might complete in him by grace
the work that nature has begun ! Eudorus, repose here for
the rest of the day ; to-morrow, at sunrise, we will ascend the
mountain to pray, and I will speak to you before I die.'

8. "After this, the holy man conversed with me for a long
time on the beauty of religion, and on the blessings it should
one day shed upon mankind. During this discourse the old
man presented an extraordinary contrast ; simple as a child
when left to nature alone, he seemed to have forgotten every-
thing, or rather to know nothing, of the world, of its grandeurs,
its miseries, and its pleasures ; but when God descended into
his soul, Paul became an inspired genius, filled with experience
of the present, and with visions of the future. Thus in his
person two opposite characters seemed to unite : still it was
doubtful which was the more admirable, Paul the ignorant, or
Paul the prophet ; since to the simplicity of the former was
granted the sublimity of the latter.

9. "After giving me many instructions full of a wisdom
intermingled with sweetness, and a gravity tempered with
cheerfulness, Paul invited me to offer with him a sacrifice of
praise to the Eternal ; he arose, and placing himself under the
palm-tree, thus chanted aloud :

"'Blessed be thou, the God of my fathers, who hast had
regard to the lowliness of thy servant !

"'O solitude, thou spouse of my bosom, thou art about to
lose him for whom thou didst possess unfading charms !

"'The votary of solitude ought to preserve his body in
chastity, to have his lips undefiled, and his mind illuminated
with divine light.

"'Holy sadness of penitence, come, pierce my soul like a
needle of gold, and fill it with celestial sweetness !

"'Tears are the mother of virtue, and sorrow is the footstool to heaven.'

10. "The old man's prayer was scarcely finished, when I fell
into a sweet and profound sleep. I reposed on the stony
couch which Paul preferred to a bed of roses. The sun was on

the point of setting when I again opened my eyes to the light. The hermit said to me :

" ' Arise and pray ; take your refreshment, and let us go to the mountain.'

" I obeyed him, and we departed together. For more than six hours we ascended the craggy rocks ; and at daybreak we had reached the most elevated point of Mount Colzim.

11. "An immense horizon stretched around us. To the east arose the summits of Horeb and Sinai; the desert of Sûr, and the Red Sea, lay stretched in boundless expanse below; to the south the mountains of the Thebais formed a mighty chain ; the northern prospect was bounded by the northern plains, over which Pharoah pursued the Hebrews ; while to the west, stretching far beyond the sands amidst which I had been lost, lay the fertile valley of Egypt.

12. "The first rays of Aurora, streaming from the horizon of Arabia Felix, for some time tinged this immense picture with softened light. The zebra, the antelope, and the ostrich ran rapidly over the desert, while the camels of a caravan passed gently in a row, headed by a sagacious ass, which acted as their conductor. The bosom of the Red Sea was checkered with many a whitening sail, that wafted into its ports the silks and the perfumes of the East, or perhaps bore some intelligent voyager to the shores of India. At last the sun arose, and crowned with splendor this frontier of the eastern and western worlds ; he poured a blaze of light on the heights of Sinai— a feeble, yet brilliant image of the God that Moses contemplated on the summit of this sacred mount !"

88. The First Solitary—concluded.

1. "My hoary conductor now broke silence :

" ' Confessor of the faith,' said he 'cast your eyes around you. Behold this eastern clime, where all the religions, and all the revolutions of the earth, have had their origin; behold this Egypt, whence your Greece received her elegant divinities, and India her monstrous and misshapen gods; in these same regions Jesus Christ himself appeared, and the day shall come when a descendant of Ishmael shall re-establish error beneath the Arab's tent.   The first system of morality that was committed to writing, was also the production of this fruitful soil.

2.   "'It is worthy of your attention, that the people of the East, as if in punishment for some great rebellion of their fore-'athers, have almost always been under the dominion of tyrants; hus, as a kind of miraculous counterpoise, morality and religion have sprung up in the same land that gave birth to slavery and misfortune.   Lastly, these same deserts witnessed the march of the armies of Sesostris and Cambyses, of Alexander and Cæsar.   Ye too, ye future ages, shall send hither armies equally numerous, and warriors not less celebrated! All the great and daring efforts of the human species have either had their origin here, or have come hither to exhaust their force.   A supernatural energy has ever been preserved in these regions wherein the first man received life; something miraculous seems still attached to the cradle of creation and the source of light and knowledge.

3.   "'Without stopping to contemplate those scenes of human grandeur that have long been closed in endless night, or to consider those epochs so renowned in history, but which have passed away like the fleeting vapor, it is to the Christian, above all others, that the East is a land of wonders.

"'You have seen Christianity, aided by morality, penetrate the civilized countries of Italy and Greece ; you have seen it introduced by means of charity among the barbarous nations of Gaul and Germany; here, under the influence of an atmosphere that weakens the soul while rendering it obstinate, among a people grave by its political institutions, and trifling by its climate, charity and morality would be insufficient.

4.   "'The religion of Jesus Christ can only enter the temples of Isis and Ammon under the veil of penitence.   To luxury and effeminacy it must offer examples of the most rigid privation, to the knavery of the priests, and the lying illusions of false divinities, it must oppose real miracles and the oracles of truth: scenes of extraordinary virtue alone can tear away the crowd from the enchantments of the theatre and the circus·

when men have been guilty of great crimes, great expiations are necessary, in order that the renown of the latter may efface the celebrity of the former.

5. "'Such are the reasons for which those missionaries were established, of whom I am the first, and who will be perpetuated in these solitudes. Admire in this the conduct of our divine chief, who knows how to arrange his armies according to the places and the obstacles they have to encounter. Contemplate these two religions, about to struggle here hand to hand until one shall have humbled the other in the dust. The ancient worship of Osiris, whose origin is hidden in the night of time, proudly confident in its traditions, its mysteries, and its pomps, rests securely upon victory.

6. "'The mighty dragon of Egypt lies basking in the midst of his waves, and exclaims : "The river is mine." He believes that the crocodile shall always receive the incense of mortals, and that the ox, which is slaughtered at the crib, shall never cease to rank as the first of divinities. No, my son, an army shall be formed in these deserts, and shall march to conquest under the banners of truth. From the solitudes of Thebais and of Scetis shall it advance: it is composed of aged saints, who carry no other weapon than their staffs to besiege the ministers of error in their very temples.

7. "'The latter occupy fertile plains, and revel amidst luxury and sensual gratifications ; the former inhabit the burning sands of the desert, and patiently endure all the rigors of life. Hell, that foresees the destruction of its power, attempts every means to insure its victory: the demons of voluptuousness, of riches, and of ambition, seek to corrupt these faithful soldiers of the cross ; but heaven comes to the succor of its children, and lavishes miracles in their favor. Who can recount the names of so many illustrious recluses—the Anthonies, the Serapions, the Macariuses, the Pacomiuses? Victory declares in their favor. The Lord gathers Egypt about him, as a shepherd gathers round him his mantle.

8. "'Where error once dictated the oracles of falsehood, the voice of truth is now heard ; wherever the false divinities had instituted a superstitious rite, there Jesus had placed a saint.

The grottoes of the Thebais are inhabited, the catacombs of the dead are peopled with the living who are dead to all the passions of the world. The gods, banished from their temples, return to the river and the plough. A burst of triumphant joy resounds from the pyramids of Cheops even to the tomb o! Osymandyas. The posterity of Joseph enters into the land of Goshen; and this victory, purchased by the tears of its victors costs not one tear to the vanquished!'

9 "Paul, for a moment, interrupted his discourse, and then again addressed me.

"'Eudorus,' said he, 'never more abandon the ranks of the soldiers of Jesus Christ. If you are not a rebel to the cause of Heaven, what a crown awaits you! what enviable glory will be yours! My son, what are you still seeking among men? Has the world still charms for you? Do you wish, like the faithless Israelite, to lead the dance around the golden calf? You know not the ruin that awaits this mighty empire, so long the terror and the destroyer of the human race ; know, then, that the crimes of these masters of the world are hastening the day of vengeance.

10. "'They have persecuted the faithful followers of Jesus; they have been drunk with the blood of his martyrs.'

"Here Paul again interrupted his discourse. He stretched forth his hands toward Mount Horeb ; his eyes sparkled with animation, a flame of glory played around his head, his wrinkled forehead seemed invested with all the gracefulness of youth : like another Elias, he exclaimed in accents of rapture:

11. "'Whence come those fugitive families that seek an asylum in the cave of the solitary? Who are those people tha flock from the four regions of the earth ? Do you see yonde terrific horsemen, the impure children of the demons and of th sorcerers of Scythia?'[1] The scourge of God conducts them. Their horses vie with the leopard in speed : numberless as th sands of the desert, their captives flock before them. What seek these kings, clad in the skins of wild beasts, their heads covered with rude hats, and their faces tinged with green.'[3] Why

---

[1] The Huns.   [2] Attila.   [3] The Goths and Lombards.

do these naked savages butcher their prisoners under the walls
of the besieged city?[1] Hold! yon monster has drunk the blood
of the Roman who fell beneath his hand![2]

12. "'They all pour from their native deserts: they march
towards this new Babylon. O, queen of cities! how art thou
fallen! How is the beauty of thy capitol effaced! How are
thy plains deserted, and how dreadful is the solitude that
reigns around! But, lo! astonishing spectacle! the cross
appears elevated above the scene of surrounding desolation!
It takes its station upon new-born Rome, and marks each
magnificent edifice as it rises from the dust. Paul, thou father
of anchorites, exult with joy ere thou diest! Thy children
shall inhabit the ruined palaces of the Cæsars; the porticos
whence the sentence of exterminating wrath was pronounced
against the Christians, shall be converted into religious cloisters;[3] and penitence shall consecrate the spots where crimes
once reigned triumphant.'"

---

89. HORATIUS.

MACAULAY.

Thomas Babington Macaulay was born at the beginning of the present
century, and died in 1860. As an essayist, he is remarkable for his brilliant rhetorical powers, splendid tone of coloring, and happy illustrations.
Macaulay has also written "Lays of Ancient Rome," which are full of
animation and poetic fervor. At the time of his death he was engaged in
writing the "History of England;" but the volumes of this work published, partake more of the character of a brilliant romance, than of true
and dignified history.

1. ALONE stood brave Horatius,
 But constant still in mind;
 Thrice thirty thousand foes before,
 And the broad flood behind.
"Down with him!" cried false Sextus,
 With a smile on his pale face;

---

[1] The Franks and Vandals.   [2] The Saracen.
[3] The Thermæ of Diocletian, now inhabited by the Carthusians.

"Now yield thee," cried Lars Porsena,
 "Now yield thee to our grace."

2. Round turn'd he, as not deigning·
 Those craven ranks to see ;
 Naught spake he to Lars Porsena,
 To Sextus naught spoke he ;
 But he saw on Palatinus
 The white porch of his home ;
 And he spake to the noble river
 That rolls by the towers of Roma.

3. "O Tiber ! father Tiber !
 To whom the Romans pray,
 A Roman's life, a Roman's arms,
 Take thou in charge this day !"
 So he spake, and speaking sheathed
 The good sword by his side,
 And, with his harness on his back,
 Plunged headlong in the tide.

4. No sound of joy or sorrow
 Was heard from either bank;
 But friends and foes in dumb surprise,
 With parted lips and straining eyes,
 Stood gazing where he sank:
 And when above the surges
 They saw his crest appear,
 All Rome sent forth a rapturous cry,
 And even the ranks of Tuscany
 Could scarce forbear to cheer.

5 But fiercely ran the current,
 Swollen high by months of rain;
 And fast his blood was flowing ;
 And he was sore in pain,
 And heavy with his armor,
 And spent with changing blows ;

And oft they thought him sinking,
  But still again he rose.

6. Never, I ween, did swimmer,
    In such an evil case,
  Struggle through such a raging flood
    Safe to the landing-place.
  But his limbs were borne up bravely
    By the brave heart within,
  And our good father Tiber
    Bare bravely up his chin.

7 "Curse on him!" quoth false Sextus;
    "Will not the villain drown?
  But for this stay, ere close of day
    We should have sack'd the town!"
  "Heaven help him!" quoth Lars Porsena,
    "And bring him safe to shore;
  For such a gallant feat of arms
    Was never seen before."

8. And now he feels the bottom;
    Now on dry earth he stands;
  Now round him throng the fathers
    To press his gory hands;
  And now with shouts and clapping,
    And noise of weeping loud,
  He enters through the river-gate,
    Borne by the joyous crowd.

9. When the goodman mends his armor,
    And trims his helmet's plume;
  When the goodwife's shuttle merrily
    Goes flashing through the loom;
  With weeping and with laughter
    Still is the story told,
  How well Horatius kept the bridge
    In the brave days of old.

90. THE EXILE'S RETURN.

MRS. SADLIER.

1. MANY changes have passed over the face of the Green Isle since I left its rocky shores,—changes public and changes private have taken place among its people—the friends whom I loved and cherished have passed away, ay! every soul; so that, with the aid of my altered appearance, I can pass myself off for a stranger, yet there is something in the very atmosphere which breathes of *home*. The warm hearts and loving eyes that cheered my boyhood are gone,—the *living* friends are lost to sight, and I miss their enlivening presence, oh! how much!—but the inanimate friends—the old familiar scenes remain.

2. I have taken up my abode in the very house of my nativity—ruined it is, and desolate, yet it is the shell which contained the kernel of my affections. The fields are as green, the sky as changeful, the mountains as grand, the sacred valley as lone and solemn, and, above all, the faith and piety of the people is still the same, simple, earnest, nothing doubting, all-performing.

3. Oh! I am not alone here, one cannot be alone here, with the monuments of ages of faith around, and the same faith ever living and acting among the people. I can go and kneel by the graves of my parents, and pray that my end may be like theirs, and I feel that the penitent tears I shed are acceptable to God, and that the spirits of those over whose ashes I weep, may one day welcome me in glory, when the last trace of my guilt is effaced by whatever process God pleases.

4. Here, amid the solitude of the desert city, I meditate on the years I passed in a foreign land, and rejoice that the feverish dream is over. Where I herded my goats, a peasant boy, I muse, an old and wrinkled man, on the path of life I have trodden. I stand at the opposite end of existence, and ask myself what is the difference. I have had since what is called "position," I have wealth still—ay! a fortune, but what of

that—I am old, friendless, childless, and *alone*, burdened with
harrowing recollections, and ready to sink into the grave, un-
honored and unknown.

5. I was poor· and unlearned in those days which I now
look back on with regret, but I had many hearts to love
me ; "now," said I bitterly to myself, " I dare not breathe my
ame to any hereabouts, for the memory of my crime is tra-
ditional among the people, and, did they recognize me, all the
wealth I have would not bribe them to look with kindness on
him who was once AN APOSTATE.

91. MOUNT ORIENT.

GERALD GRIFFIN.

1. THE M'Orients of Mount Orient, gentle reader, were
looked upon in our neighborhood as people of high fashion,
unbounded literary attainments, and the most delicate sensibility. They had, until within the last two years, spent the
greater portion of their life "abroad" (a word which has a
portentous sound in our village). On their return to Mount
Orient, they occasioned quite a revolution in all our tastes
and customs : they introduced waltzing, smoking cigars, &c.
I have seen their open carriage sometimes driving by my window, Miss Mimosa M'Orient seated on the coach-box, and
Mr. Ajax M'Orient, her brother, occupying the interior in a
frieze jacket and a southwester.

2. But what added most to their influence was that both
were considered prodigies of intellect. Ajax M'Orient had
written poems in which "rill" rhymed to "hill," "beam" to
"stream," "mountain" to "fountain," and "billow" to "wil-
ow." Nay, it was even whispered that he had formed a
design of immortalizing Robert Burns, by turning his poems
into good English, and had actually performed that operation
upon Tam O'Shanter, which was so much changed for the
better, that you would hardly know it again. So that he
passed in these parts for a surprising genius.

3. He was likewise a universal critic, one of those agreeable persons, who know every thing in the world better than anybody else. He would ask you what you thought of that engraving, and on your selecting a particular group for admiration, he would civilly inform you that you had praised the only defect in the piece. Like the host in Horace, who used to analyze his dishes with his praises in such a manner as to deprive his guests of all inclination to taste them, Ajax would afflict you with pointing out the beauties of a picture, until you began to see no beauty in it.

4. Nor did nature escape him : walk out with him, and he would commend every lake, and rock, and river, until you wished yourself under ground from him. The wind, the sun, the air, the clouds, the waters, nothing was safe from the taint of his villanous commendation. And then his metaphysics, it was all well until he grew metaphysical: so jealous was he of originality on these subjects, that if you assented too hastily to one of his own propositions, ten to one but he would wheel round and assail it, satisfied to prove himself wrong, provided he could prove you wrong also. The navigation of the Red Sea was not a nicer matter than to get through a conversation with Mr. Ajax M'Orient without an argument.

5. On the other hand, Miss Mimosa M'Orient was very handsome, a great enthusiast, an ardent lover of Ireland (unlike her brother, who affected the aristocrat, and curled his lip at O'Connell); with a mind all sunshine and a heart all fire ; a soul innocence itself—radiant candor—heroic courage —a glowing zeal for universal liberty—a heart alive to the tenderest feelings of distress—and a mind, to judge by her conversation, imbued with the deepest sentiments of virtue.

6. Miss M'Orient had a near relative living under her protection, named Mary de Courcy, who did not seem to have half her advantages. She was rather plain, had no enthusiasm whatever, very seldom talked of Ireland, had so much common sense in her mind that there was no room for sunshine ; and as to fire in her bosom, the academy of Lagoda alone, to all appearance, could have furnished artists capable of extracting it. She might be candid, but she had too much reserve to

thrust it forth as if for sale; and she might have an innocent
heart, but she was not forever talking of it. Of courage she
did not boast much; and as to universal liberty, Mary de
Courcy, like the knife-grinder,

"——seldom loved to meddle
With politics, sir."

7. Of her feelings she never spoke at all, and on the subject
of virtue she could not compete in eloquence with Miss
M'Orient.

Still it was a riddle, that while everybody liked Miss de
Courcy, the M'Orients seemed to be but little esteemed or
loved by those who knew them well and long. Indeed, some
looked upon them as of that class of individuals who in our
times have overrun society, enfeebling literature with false
sentiment, poisoning all wholesome feeling, turning virtue into
ostentation, annulling modesty, corrupting the very springs of
piety itself by affectation and parade, and selfishly seeking to
engross the world's admiration by wearing their virtues (false
as they are) like their jewels, all outside.

8. Thus, while Miss M'Orient and her brother were rhyming
and romancing about "green fields," and "groves," and "lang
syne," and "negroes," and "birds in cages," and "sympathy,"
and "universal freedom," they were such a pair of arrant
scolds and tyrants in their own house, that no servant could
stay two months in their employment. While Miss M'Orient
would weep by the hour to hear a blackbird whistle Paddy
Carey outside a farmer's cottage, she would see whole families, nay whole nations, reduced to beggary, without shedding
a tear, nor think of depriving herself of a morocco album to
save a starving fellow-creature's life.

9. It was during one of those seasons of distress, which so
frequently afflict the peasantry of Ireland, that Mary de
Courcy happened one morning to be watering some flowers
that graced the small inclosure in front of Mount Orient
House, when a female cottager, accompanied by a group o.
helpless children, presented themselves before her. Miss de
Courcy and Mimosa both had known the woman in better
times, and the former was surprised at her present destitution.

12

10 "Ah! Miss Mary!" said she, "'tis all over with a now, since the house and the man that kept it up are gone together. Hush, child! be quiet! You never again will come over to us now, Miss Mary, in the summer days, to sit down inside our door, an' to take the cup of beautiful thick milk from Nelly, and to talk so kindly to the children. That's all over now, miss—them times are gone."

11. Moved by the poor woman's sorrow, Miss de Courcy for the first time keenly felt her utter want of fortune. She determined, however, to lay before Miss M'Orient in the course of the day the condition of their old cottage acquaintance, and conceived that she entered the room in happy time, when she found her tender-hearted friend dissolved in tears, and with a book between her hands. Still better, it was a work on Ireland, and Mimosa showed her *protégée* the page, still moistened from the offerings of her sympathy, in which the writer had drawn a very lively picture of the sufferings of her countrymen during a period of more than usual affliction.

12. "Such writing as this, dear Mary!" she exclaimed, in ecstasy of woe, "would move me were the sketch at the Antipodes; but being taken in Ireland, beloved Ireland! imagine its effect upon my feelings—I, who am not myself—I have nothing for you, my good man, go about your business [to an old beggar-man who presented himself with a low bow at the window]—who am not myself when Ireland is the theme! the heart must be insensible indeed that such a picture could not move to pity.

13. "Ah! if the poor Irish—[I declare there are three more beggars on the avenue! Thomas, did not your master give strict orders that not a single beggar should be allowed to set foot inside the gate?]—ah! if the poor—[let some one go and turn them out this instant— we must certainly have the dogs let loose again]—if the Irish poor had many such advocates, charity would win its burning way at length even into cold recesses—"

"There's a poor woman wants a dhrop of milk, ma'am," said a servant, appearing at the door.

14. "I haven't it for her—let me not be disturbed [was

servant]—into the cold recesses of even an absentee landlord's heart. The appeal, dear Mary, is perfectly irresistible; nor can I conceive a higher gratification than that of lending a healing hand to such affliction."

"I am glad to hear you say so, Mimosa, my dear," said Mary, "for I have it in my power to give you the gratification you desire."

"How, Miss de Courcy?" said the sentimental lady in an altered tone, and with some secret alarm.

15. Mary de Courcy was not aware how wide a difference there is, between crying over human misery in hot-pressed small octavo, and relieving it in common life; between sentimentalizing over the picture of human woe, and loving and befriending the original. She did not know that there are creatures who will melt like Niobe at an imaginary distress, while the sight of actual suffering will find them callous as a flint. She proceeded, therefore, with a sanguine spirit, to explain the circumstances of their old neighbors, expecting that all her trouble would be in moderating the extent of her enthusiastic auditor's liberality.

16. But she could not get a shilling from the patriotic Miss M'Orient. That young lady had expended the last of her pocket-money on this beautiful book on Irish misery, so that she had not a sixpence left for the miserable Irish. But then she felt for them! She talked, too, a great deal about "her principles." It was not "*her* principle," that the poor should ever be relieved by money. It was by forwarding "the march of intellect," those evils should be remedied. As the world became enlightened, men would find it was their interest that human misery should be alleviated in the persons of their fellow-creatures, a regenerative spirit would pervade society, and peace and abundance would shed their light on every land, not even excepting dear, neglected, and down-trodden Ireland.

17. But, as for the widow, she hadn't a sixpence for her. Besides, who knew but she might drink it? Misfortune drives so many to the dram-shop. Well, if Miss de Courcy would provide against that, still, who could say that she was

not an impostor! Oh, true, Miss M'Orient knew the woman well. But she had a great many other older and nearer acquaintances; and it was "*her* principle," that charity was nothing without order. In vulgar language, it should always begin at home. At all events, she could and would do nothing.

"Ah, Mimosa," said Mary, "do you think that vulgar rule has never an exception?"

"Never—Mary—never. Send in luncheon" [to a servant].

---

92. The Crusades.

WORDSWORTH.

WILLIAM WORDSWORTH was born in England in 1770, and died in 1850; he belonged to what is called the "*Lake*-School" of poets. He has left no poem of any length worthy of admiration throughout; but many of his shorter pieces are unsurpassed in the English language.

1. FURL we the sails, and pass with tardy oars
    Through these bright regions, casting many a glance
    Upon the dream-like issues, the romance
Of many-color'd life that fortune pours
Round the Crusaders, till on distant shores
    Their labors end: or they return to lie,
    The vow perform'd, in cross-legg'd effigy,
Devoutly stretch'd upon their chancel-floors.
Am I deceived? Or is their requiem chanted
    By voices never mute when Heaven unties
    Her inmost, softest, tenderest harmonies?
Requiem which earth takes up with voice undaunted,
    When she would tell how brave, and good, and wise,
For their high guerdon not in vain have panted.

2. As faith thus sanctified the warrior's crest,
    While from the papal unity there came
    What feebler means had fail'd to give, one aim
Diffused through all the regions of the west;
So does her unity its power attest

By works of art, that shed on the outward frame
Of worship, glory and grace, which who shall blame
That ever look'd to Heaven for final rest?
Hail, countless temples, that so well befit
    Your ministry! that, as ye rise and take
Form, spirit, and character from holy writ,
    Give to devotion, wheresoe'er awake,
    Pinions of high and higher sweep, and make
The unconverted soul with awe submit!

THE VIRGIN.

3 MOTHER! whose virgin bosom was uncross'd
    With the least shade of thought to sin allied;
    Woman! above all women glorified,
Our tainted nature's solitary boast;
Purer than foam on central-ocean tost,
    Brighter than eastern skies at daybreak strewn
    With fancied roses, than the unblemish'd moon
Before her vane begins on heaven's blue coast,
Thy image falls to earth. Yet some, I ween,
    Not unforgiven, the suppliant knee might bend,
    As to a visible power, in which did blend
    All that was mix'd and reconciled in thee
Of mother's love with maiden purity,
Of high with low, celestial with terrene.

---

93. DUTIES OF THE AMERICAN CITIZEN.

WEBSTER.

HON. DANIEL WEBSTER—born at Salisbury, New Hampshire, in 1782; died, 1852. As an orator and a statesman, the New World has as yet produced no man greater than he. His works are published in six octavo volumes, and his name shall live as long as the American nation lasts.

1. LET us cherish, fellow-citizens, a deep and solemn conviction of the duties which have devolved upon us. This lovely land, this glorious liberty, these benign institutions, the

dear purchase of our fathers, are ours; ours to enjoy, ours to preserve, ours to transmit. Generations past, and generations to come, hold us responsible for this sacred trust.

2. Our fathers, from behind, admonish us, with their anxious paternal voices; posterity calls out to us from the bosom of the future; the world turns hither its solicitous eyes—all, all conjure us to act wisely and faithfully in the relation which we sustain. We can never, indeed, pay the debt which is upon us; but by virtue, by morality, by religion, by the cultivation of every good principle and every good habit, we may hope to enjoy the blessing through our day, and leave it unimpaired to our children.

3. Let us feel deeply how much of what we are, and of what we possess, we owe to this liberty, and these institutions of government. Nature has, indeed, given us a soil which yields bounteously to the hands of industry; the mighty and fruitful ocean is before us, and the skies over our heads shed health and vigor. But what are lands, and seas, and skies, to civilized men, without society, without knowledge, without morals, without religious culture? and how can these be enjoyed, in all their extent, and all their excellence, but under the protection of wise institutions and a free government?

4. Fellow-citizens, there is not *one* of us, there is not one of us here present, who does not at this moment, and at every moment, experience in his own condition, and in the condition of those most near and dear to him, the influence and the benefit of this liberty, and these institutions.

5. Let us, then, acknowledge the blessing; let us feel it deeply and powerfully; let us cherish a strong affection for it, and resolve to maintain and perpetuate it. The blood of our fathers—let it not have been shed in vain; the great hope of posterity— let it not be blasted.

94. THE CATACOMBS.

MANAHAN.

Rev. Ambrose Manahan, D. D., born in New York city. He finished his studies at the Propaganda, in Rome, and was ordained priest for the diocese of New York. He has recently made a valuable contribution to Catholic literature, in his work entitled "The Triumph of the Catholic Church."

1 It was in the year 1599 that Bosius, anxious to discover some of the many subterranean cemeteries mentioned by ancient writers as situated near the Via Appia and the Ardeatina, went out of the Capena gate, along the Appian road, to the place where our Lord appeared to Peter—thence going along the Ardeatina way to where it is crossed by a road leading from St. Sebastian's to St. Paul's Church—he carefully examined that whole ground in search of some hole that would give him admission into the subterranean city.

2. He perceived, at last, in the middle of a field, some arches that led him to suspect he had come upon the object of his desires. He managed to effect an entrance, and made his way down until he found himself standing in the habitations of the dead. Numberless monuments cut out of the clay tell him this at a glance. He hastens along this first road, to its terminus, where he finds two others striking off in different directions : he enters the one to the right—it is encumbered and choked up with ruins ;—he returns and starts upon the one to the left, along which he journeys until he discovers in the ground, under his feet, a small hole or passage.

3. He creeps into this opening, and almost snake-like keeps moving forwards until delighted with, at last, the sight of high cryptæ into which he is ushered from his narrow winding Here, in wide halls and endless corridors, he beholds on every side closet-like openings carved out of the side walls for the reception of dead bodies ; some of nobler appearance are decorated with arches so as to give each its own alcove. He remarks but few sepulchres in the ground-floor, only placed there, no doubt, when no more unoccupied room was left in the walls.

4. The greater part of the tombs are shut with marble

slabs, or closed up with brick-work ; some gape wide open, and there lie the remains of his forefathers of the first ages of the church ; short tombs for children are interspersed among 'he larger ; the same difference appears in the size of the bones ;—some of them are hard and seem almost petrified, while others fall to ashes when touched. Far on in the most hidden recesses he came upon three or four chambers that seemed to have had their walls once whitened, though no paintings were visible on them ; fragments of inscriptions lay scattered all around the chapels.

5. He more than once found himself in large round halls, from which a number of roads started out in every direction, like lines from the centre towards the superficies of a circle, or like the spokes in a wheel. These stretched away endlessly as far as he ever ascertained, and induced him to call this place a labyrinth indeed ! Again and again he returned to his exploring expedition, and, often wearied but never satiated, his admiration gave the palm to this above all the other cemeteries which he had visited in all the course of his forty years' search. He calls it, in size, beauty and splendor, the chief one of all the catacombs.

6. With all his patience and enthusiasm he could not say that he had ever reached the utmost bounds of this vast and extraordinary place, although he often spent whole days and nights travelling around through its interminable windings. Every day new outlets made their appearance,—new roads were discovered,—leading out of his best-known districts. It was his belief that these roads and those under St. Sebastian's not only communicated together, but kept on over to St. Paul's, extended to the Annunziata and out to the Three Fountains, and even stretched back as far as the walls of Rome ; and in every thing concerning these catacombs Bosius is a sure guide.

7. And yet, more wonderful to relate ! this sepulchral city —already so far down beneath the surface of the earth—has its own immense underways, which, laid out on a similar plan, underlie its excavated streets no one knows how far. Stairs cut out of the clay invite the astonished visitor to go down from the level of this first *souterrain* into a second maze of

streets and corridors, furnished, like the former, with their
ranges of tombs (*loculi*), their chambers and chapels. Brick
walls are here found supporting many parts of these sub-sub-
terranean establishments.

8. Most of the roads have been rendered impassable by the
clay that has fallen in and encumbered them. They may pe
chance be cleared one day by some unterrified adventurer
but only when those above them shall have first become exhausted by his long researches. Even this second underground
district has its own under-works still deeper in the bosom of
the earth. Short and small steps in the clay take you down.
from the lower to this lowest of the excavated cemeteries. Upper
apartments, basement-rooms and sub-cellar vaults in a house
are familiar ideas, but our minds can hardly realize the conception carried out as it is here.

9. I can state, however, that I have personally verified the
exactness of these discoveries, and stood even in that third,
lowest tier of routes, one below the other. Only few roads are
opened in the lowest range ; there do not appear to be many
simple tombs there as in the upper catacombs, but a number
of larger chambers reserved, one would suppose, for the burial
of distinguished families.

10. Far away in the outskirts of this subterranean city,—
in the most hidden recesses of the catacombs, perpetual fountains of limpid water gleam under the light of the visitor's
taper : in one sequestered corner, several steps cut in the earth,
lead you down to drink of abundant streams of sweet and
salubrious water,—streams where, no doubt, many a martyr
washed his wounds, and many a pursued and fainting fugitive
came, like the panting deer, to be refreshed. These waters
have. doubtless, flowed on the head of many a valorous neo-
phyte, who sleeps among the martyrs in this subterranean
dormitory.

11. In these deepest corridors you behold the outlines only
of some tombs or graves marked in the clay walls, as if ready
for the work of being dug out for the next burial. Why was
the work suspended ? Were the diggers arrested here by the
glorious news of the appearance of the cross in the skies, and

led to fling away their tools and their garments of sadness by Constantine's call to the Catholic faithful to come up in joy and freedom out of their dismal places of refuge, and drive the remnants of heathen superstition from the city of the Cæsars?

12. So it seemed to me when, filled with the spirit of the place and its memories, I stood and looked upon those unfinished graves. Then the Church of God came forth in her deep-dyed purple robes from the catacombs, and fastened the Cross of Christ on the imperial banner, and took her seat on the Vatican mount, our holy Sion hill. When Israel no longer pitched her tents around the ark in the wilderness, Jerusalem rehearsed, amid the splendors of Solomon's temple, the wonders of the land of bondage, the passage over the sea and through the desert.

13. The Rome of to-day shows how her enduring faith has carried along with it safely, through all vicissitudes, the shrines and tombs and relics of her martyrs. The rites of the Roman Catholic Church shall forever keep alive a grateful, universal and festival remembrance of the pristine scenes of her trials and triumph. Do not the very lights of our altars burn more brightly to our eyes when we recall the fortitude and devotion that knelt in their first gleam through those dismal chambers? and do not our censers perfume the sanctuary with recollections of the fragrance of piety that mingled with the first blest incense which they flung around through the foulness and damp airs of our primeval temples? Throughout the whole world treasures from the catacombs enrich the altar-stones of our sacrifice.

14. A faithless world looks with amazement on the unfading Roman scarlet, and the pomp and magnificence displayed in the Catholic ceremonial. The most gorgeous embellishments of our solemn services but faintly express the sombre and sublime grandeur in which our minds call up those ancient solemnities from which our decorations and our ritual took their rise : when the first Popes administered our sacraments to candidates for the palm of martyrdom, and the august and tremendous sacrifice of the mass was offered up in those excavated sanctuaries—whose purple hangings were cloths tinged

from the veins of the followers of the Lamb—whose most rare
and precious ornaments were the blood-stained sponges and
vials and instruments of torture—while the venerable bodies
of the slaughtered flock upheld the altar on which the divine
sacrifice was offered up to God.

---

95. THE RELIGIOUS MILITARY ORDERS.

ARCHBISHOP PURCELL.

JOHN B. PURCELL, D. D., Archbishop of Cincinnati, was born 17th of
February, 1800, in Mallow, County Cork, Ireland. Emigrated when a boy
to America; studied in Mount St. Mary's, Emmettsburg; went to Paris,
and followed up his theological studies at St. Sulpice, where he was ordained priest. On his return to the United States, Dr. Purcell became
Professor of Theology in his Alma Mater, at Emmettsburg and was subsequently appointed President of that noble institution. He was consecrated Bishop of Cincinnati on the 13th of October, 1855, and was since
made Archbishop of that province. Although this eminent prelate has not
found time amid the onerous duties of his high office to apply himself to
literary pursuits, proofs are not wanting that he might attain distinction
in the walks of literature. Soon after his consecration as Bishop of Cincinnati, he was called upon to defend the doctrines of the Church in a protracted discussion with the Rev. Mr. Campbell, founder of the Campbell-
ites, in which he distinguished himself as well by his skill in dialectics, as
his profound scholastic attainments. The archbishop's lectures, delivered
on various subjects, are admirable specimens of such composition, and
have done much for the diffusion of valuable information. What he has
done and achieved for the cause of religion is well known to the Catholics
of America; and when future historians trace the fortunes of the Church
in the New World, the name of *Purcell* shall be held in honor, as one of
the first great patriarchs of the West.

1. By the religious military orders, I mean, 1. The Knights
of St. John of Jerusalem, or Hospitallers, or of Rhodes, or of
Malta, as the same order has been successively designated.
2. The Templars. 3. The Teutonic Knights; leaving out of
this view the Knights of the Holy Sepulchre, of Calatrava,
of St. Jago, of the Sword, and others, which cannot be regarded as strictly religious orders, have no such name in
story, nor rendered such important services to Christendom as
those which I have first named.

*   *   *   *   *

2 In the middle of the eleventh century, the merchants of
Amalphi, in the kingdom of Naples, who traded with Egypt

in rich merchandise and works of art, and who had often ex
perienced in their visits to the Holy Land the cruelty of
Greeks and Saracens, purchased, by costly presents to the
Caliph and his courtiers, permission for the Latin Christians
to have two hospitals in Jerusalem, one for men and the other
for women. The chapels attached to these hospitals were
dedicated, respectively, to St. John the Almoner, and St.
Magdalen. They were served by self-appointed seculars,
whose charity induced them to forego the pleasure of home
and friends, to devote themselves to the care of the sick, the
poor, and the stranger, in the Holy City. This was the cradle
of the Knights Hospitallers.

*   *   *   *   *

3. The Hospitallers were divided into three bodies, or classes.
1st. Those distinguished by birth, or the rank they had held
in the army of the Crusaders. 2d. Ecclesiastics who were to
superintend the hospitals, and serve as chaplains to the army
in peace and war. 3d. Lay-brothers, or servants. A new
classification was afterwards made from the seven different
languages spoken by the Knights—*i. e.*, those of Provence,
Auvergne, France, Italy, Aragon; a little later including
Castile and Portugal, and England, until she apostatized.

4. The government was aristocratic. The supreme authority was vested in a council, of which the Grand Master
was president. The different houses of the Order were administered by preceptors, or overseers, removable at pleasure,
and who were held to a strict accountability. The same austerities were practised by all, and the necessity of bearing
arms was not suffered to interfere with the strict observances
of the convent. Purity of life, and prompt obedience to orders, and detachment from the world, were the distinguishing
virtues of the soldier monks.

5. THE TEMPLARS were founded by Hugh de Payens and
eight others, all natives of France, to protect the pilgrims on
their way to and from Jerusalem, and to unite with the Hospitallers and aid the king of Jerusalem in repelling the incur-
sions, humbling the pride, and chastising the audacity of the

infidels. They were too proud to serve in hospitals. Their costume was a white mantle, with a red cross on the left breast. Their name was derived from their residence near the Temple. They were approved by Honorius II. Their rule was given them by St. Bernard, by order of the Council of Troyes. Their exemption from what was considered the degrading, or ignoble, obligation of waiting on the sick, drew to the new Order a vast multitude of the richest lords and princes of Europe, so that the Templars soon outshone the Hospitallers in the splendor of wealth—but never in that of virtue. Nevertheless, they continued for centuries to render essential services to Christendom in checking the aggressions of Mohammedanism.

6. THE TEUTONIC KNIGHTS commenced their existence on the plain before Ptolemais, or St. Jean d'Acre. Many of these brave Germans, who had followed their gallant Emperor, Frederick I., and his son, the Duke of Suabia, to the holy wars, when wounded in the frequent sorties of the garrison, lay helpless on the battle-field, unable to communicate their wants and sufferings in a language unknown to their brethren in arms. A few Germans, who had come by sea from Bremen and Lubeck, commiserating the hard fate of their countrymen, took the sails of their ships and made tents, into which they collected the wounded, and served them with their own hands. Forty of the chiefs of the same nation united with them in the work of charity, and from this noble association sprang a new religious and military order like to those of the Templars and Hospitallers. They were approved by Pope Celestine III., at the prayer of Henry VI. of Germany, in 1192, receiving the name of the Teutonic Knights of the House of St. Mary of Jerusalem. They got this name from the fact of a German having built in Jerusalem a hospital and oratory under the invocation of the blessed Virgin, for the sick pilgrims from his fatherland. Their uniform was a white mantle, with a black cross; they were bound by the three vows, like the Hospitallers and Templars. Before being admitted to the Order, they were required to make oath that they were Germans, of noble birth, and that they engaged for

ufe in the care of the poor and sick, and the defence of the
Holy Places. These were the three orders on which Christendom relied, more than on the irregular efforts of the Crusaders,
for the protection of the Holy Land.

---

96. MARY MAGDALEN.

CALLANAN.

CALLANAN was born in Ireland in 1795; died in 1829. During his life,
he was one of the popular contributors to 'Blackwood's Magazine." His
reputation as a poet is well established.

1. To the hall of that feast came the sinful and fair;
   She heard in the city that Jesus was there;
   She mark'd not the splendor that blazed on their board,
   But silently knelt at the feet of her Lord.

2. The hair from her forehead, so sad and so meek,
   Hung dark o'er the blushes that burn'd on her cheek;
   And so still and so lowly she bent in her shame,
   It seem'd as her spirit had flown from its frame.

3. The frown and the murmur went round through them all
   That one so unhallow'd should tread in that hall;
   And some said the poor would be objects more meet,
   For the wealth of the perfumes she shower'd at his feet

4. She mark'd but her Saviour, she spoke but in sighs,
   She dared not look up to the heaven of his eyes;
   And the hot tears gush'd forth at each heave of he
        breast,
   As her lips to his sandals she throbbingly press'd.

5. On the cloud after tempests, as shineth the bow,
   In the glance of the sunbeam, as melteth the snow,
   He look'd on that lost one—her sins were forgiven;
   And Mary went forth in the beauty of heaven.

97. DIALOGUE WITH THE GOUT

FRANKLIN.

BENJAMIN FRANKLIN was born in Boston in 1706. In early life he was a printer. He was a prominent politician before, during, and after the Revolutionary War, a member of the Continental Congress, and subsequently Minister of the United States to France, having at an earlier date, been the agent of the Colonies in England. But he was particularly distinguished for his philosophical discoveries, especially that of the identity of lightning and electricity. He died in 1790.

1. *Franklin.* Eh ! Oh ! Eh ! What have I done to merit these cruel sufferings ?

Gout. Many things : you have ate and drank too freely, and too much indulged those legs of yours in their indolence

Franklin. Who is it that accuses me ?

Gout. It is I, even I, the Gout.

Franklin. What ! my enemy in person ?

Gout. No ; not your enemy.

Franklin. I repeat it, my enemy ; for you would not only torment my body to death, but ruin my good name. You reproach me as a glutton and a tippler : now all the world that knows me will allow that I am neither the one nor the other.

2. *Gout.* The world may think as it pleases. It is always very complaisant to itself, and sometimes to its friends ; but I very well know that the quantity of meat and drink proper for a man who takes a reasonable degree of exercise would be too much for another who never takes any.

Franklin. I take—Eh ! Oh !—as much exercise—Eh !—as I can, Madam Gout. You know my sedentary state ; and on that account, it would seem, Madam Gout, as if you might spare me a little, seeing it is not altogether my own fault.

3. *Gout.* Not a jot: your rhetoric and your politeness ar thrown away: your apology avails nothing. If your situation in life is a sedentary one, your amusements, your recreations, at least, should be active. You ought to walk or ride ; or if the weather prevents that, play at something.

But let us examine your course of life. While the mornings are long, and you have leisure to go abroad, what do you do ? Why instead of gaining an appetite for breakfast, by salutary exercise, you amuse yourself with books, pamphlets, or newspapers, which commonly are not worth the reading. Yet you eat an inordinate breakfast: four dishes of tea, with cream, one or two buttered toasts, with slices of hung beef; which I fancy are not things the most easily digested.

4. Immediately afterwards, you sit down to write at your desk, or converse with persons who apply to you on business. Thus the time passes till one, without any kind of bodily exercise. But all this I could pardon, in regard, as you say, to your sedentary condition; but what is your practice after dinner? Walking in the beautiful gardens of those friends with whom you have dined would be the choice of men of sense; yours is to be fixed down to chess, where you are found engaged for two or three hours.

5. This is your perpetual recreation: the least eligible of any for a sedentary man, because, instead of accelerating the motion of the fluids, the rigid attention it requires helps to retard the circulation and obstruct internal secretions. Wrapt in the speculations of this wretched game, you destroy your constitution. What can be expected from such a course of living but a body replete with stagnant humors, ready to fall a prey to all kinds of dangerous maladies, if I, the Gout, did not occasionally bring you relief by agitating those humors, and so purifying or dissipating them? Fie, then, Mr. Franklin! But, amidst my instructions, I had almost forgot to administer my wholesome corrections; so take that twinge, and that.

6. *Franklin.* Oh! Eh! Oh! Oh! As much instruction as you please, Madam Gout, and as many reproaches; but pray, Madam, a *truce* with your corrections!

Gout. No, sir, no; I will not abate a particle of what is so much for your good, therefore—

Franklin. Oh! Eh! It is not fair to say I take no exercise, when I do, very often, go out to dine, and return in my carriage.

7. *Gout.* That, of all imaginable exercises, is the most slight and insignificant, if you allude to the motion of a carriage suspended on springs. By observing the degree of heat

obtained by different kinds of motion, we may form an estimate of the quantity of exercise given by each. Thus, for example, if you turn out to walk in winter with cold feet, in an hour's time you will be in a glow all over; ride on horseback, the same effect will scarcely be perceived by four hours' round trotting; but if you loll in a carriage, such as you have mentioned, you may travel all day, and gladly enter the last inn to warm your feet by a fire.

8. Flatter yourself, then, no longer, that half an hour's airing in your carriage deserves the name of exercise. Providence has appointed few to roll in carriages, while he has given to all a pair of legs, which are machines infinitely more commodious and serviceable. Be grateful, then, and make a proper use of yours.

---

98. Magnanimity of a Christian Emperor.

SCHLEGEL.

Frederic Von Schlegel was born in 1772; died in 1829. Schlegel was one of the most distinguished writers of Germany—as a poet, critic, essayist, and historian. In 1808 he became a Catholic. For many years of his life, in connection with his brother, Augustus William, he was engaged in the publication of the "Athenæum," a critical journal, which did much towards establishing a more independent spirit in German literature.—*Cyclopedia of Biography.*

1. After the downfall of the Carlovingian family, the empire was restored to its pristine vigor by the election of the noble Conrad, duke of the Franconians. This pious, chivalrous, wise, and valiant monarch, had to contend with many difficulties, and fortune did not always smile upon his efforts. But he terminated his royal career with a deed, which alone exalts him far above other celebrated conquerors and rulers and was attended with more important consequences to aftertimes, than have resulted from many brilliant reigns; and this single deed, which forms the brightest jewel in the crown of glory that adorns those ages, so clearly reveals the true nature of Christian principles of government, and the Christian idea of political power, that I may be permitted to notice it briefly.

2. When he felt his end approaching, and perceived that of the four principal German nations, the Saxons alone, by their superior power, were capable of bringing to a successful issue the mighty struggle in which all Europe was at that critical period involved, he bade his brother carry to Henry, duke of Saxony, hitherto the rival of his house, and who was as magnanimous as fortunate, the holy lance and consecrated sword of the ancient kings, with all the other imperial insignia. He thus pointed him out as the successor of his own choice, and in his regard for the general weal, and in his anxiety to maintain a great pacific power capable of defending the common interests of Christendom, he disregarded the suggestions of national vanity, and sacrificed even the glory of his own house.

3. So wise and judicious, as well as heroic, a sacrifice of all selfish glory, for what the interests of society and the necessities of the times evidently demanded, is that principle which forms the very foundation, and constitutes the true spirit, of all Christian governments. And by this very deed Conrad became, after Charlemagne, the second restorer of the western empire, and the real founder of the German nation; for it was this noble resolve of his great soul, which alone saved the Germanic body from a complete dismemberment. The event fully justified his choice. The new king, Henry, victorious on every side, labored to build a great number of cities, to restore the reign of peace and justice, and to maintain the purity of Christian manners and Christian institutions; and prepared for his mightier son, the great. Otho, the restoration of the Christian empire in Italy, whither the latter was loudly and unanimously called.

---

99. THE MARTYRDOM OF ST. AGNES.

DE VERE.

SIR AUBREY DE VERE—an English poet of the present day, has written a volume of beautiful poems, distinguished by their true spirit of Catholic devotion.

Angels.

1. BEARING lilies in our bosom,
   Holy Agnes, we have flown

Mission'd from the Heaven of Heavens
   Unto thee, and thee alone.
We are coming, we are flying,
To behold thy happy dying.

Agnes.

2. Bearing lilies far before you,
   Whose fresh odors, backward blown,
Light those smiles upon your faces,
   Mingling sweet breath with your own,
Ye are coming, smoothly, slowly,
To the lowliest of the lowly.

Angels.

3. Unto us the boon was given;
   One glad message, holy maid,
On the lips of two blest spirits,
   Like an incense-grain was laid.
As it bears us on like lightning,
Cloudy skies are round us brightening

Agnes

4. I am here, a mortal maiden;
   If our Father aught hath said,
Let me hear His words and do them.
   Ought I not to feel afraid,
As ye come, your shadows flinging
O'er a breast, to meet them springing?

Angels.

5. Agnes, there is joy in Heaven;
   Gladness, like the day, is flung
O'er the spaces never measured,
   And from every angel's tongue
Swell those songs of impulse vernal,
All whose echoes are eternal.

6. Agnes, from the depth of Heaven
      Joy is rising, like a spring
   Borne above its grassy margin,
      Borne in many a crystal ring;
   Each o'er beds of wild flowers gliding,
   Over each low murmurs sliding.

7. When a Christian lies expiring,
      Angel choirs, with plumes outspread,
   Bend above his death-bed, singing;
      That, when Death's mild sleep is fled,
   There may be no harsh transition
   While he greets the Heavenly Vision.

Agnes.

8. Am I dreaming, blessed angels?
      Late ye floated two in one;
   Now, a thousand radiant spirits
      Round me weave a glistening zone.
   Lilies, as they wind extending,
   Roses with those lilies blending.

9. See! th' horizon's ring they circle;
      Now they gird the zenith blue;
   And now, o'er every brake and billo
      Float like mist and flash like dew.
   All the earth, with life o'erflowing,
   Into heavenly shapes is growing!

10 They are rising! they are rising!
      As they rise, the veil is riven!
   They are rising! I am rising—
      Rising with them into Heaven!—
   Rising with those shining legions
   Into life's eternal regions!

100. EUROPEAN CIVILIZATION.

BALMEZ.

Abbé J. BALMEZ, born at Vich, in Catalonia, Spain, in 1910; died, 1848. .n lofty eloquence, sound philosophy, solid and profound erudition, this illustrious Spanish author of the present century stands unrivalled. His work on the "Civilization of Europe," should be familiar to every intelligent mind. His more recent work on "Fundamental Philosophy" (ad mirably translated by Henry F. Brownson), is the best work on Christian Philosophy of which the English language can boast.

1. IT is a fact now generally acknowledged, and openly confessed, that Christianity has exercised a very important and salutary influence on the development of European civilization. If this fact has not yet had given to it the importance which it deserves, it is because it has not been sufficiently appreciated. With respect to civilization, a distinction is sometimes made between the influence of Christianity and that of Catholicity; its merits are lavished on the former, and stinted to the latter, by those who forget that, with respect to European civilization, Catholicity can always claim the principal share; and, for many centuries, an exclusive one; since during a very long period, she worked alone at the great work. People have not been willing to see that when Protestantism appeared in Europe, the work was bordering on completion; with an injustice and ingratitude which I cannot describe, they have reproached Catholicity with the spirit of barbarism, ignorance, and oppression, while they were making an ostentatious display of the rich civilization, knowledge, and liberty, for which they were principally indebted to her.

2. If they did not wish to fathom the intimate connection between Catholicity and European civilization,—if they had not the patience necessary for the long investigations into which this examination would lead them, at least it woul have been proper to take a glance at the condition of countrie where the Catholic religion has not exerted all her influence during centuries of trouble, and compare them with those in which she has been predominant. The East and the West, both subject to great revolutions, both professing Christianity, but in such a way that the Catholic principle was weak and

vacillating in the East, while it was energetic and deeply rooted in the West ; these, we say, would have afforded two very good points of comparison to estimate the value of Christianity without Catholicity, when the civilization and the existence of nations were at stake.

3. In the West, the revolutions were multiplied and fearful; the chaos was at its height ; and, nevertheless, out of chaos came light and life. Neither the barbarism of the nations who inundated those countries, and established themselves there, nor the furious assaults of Islamism, even in the days of its greatest power and enthusiasm, could succeed in destroying the germs of a rich and fertile civilization. In the East, on the contrary, all tended to old age and decay ; nothing revived ; and, under the blows of the power which was ineffectual against us, all was shaken to pieces. The spiritual power of Rome, and its influence on temporal affairs, have certainly borne fruits very different from those produced under the same circumstances, by its violent opponents.

4. If Europe were destined one day again to undergo a general and fearful revolution, either by a universal spread of revolutionary ideas, or by a violent invasion of social and proprietary rights by pauperism ; if the Colossus of the North, seated on its throne of eternal snows, with knowledge in its head, and blind force in its hands, possessing at once the means of civilization and unceasingly turning towards the East, the South, and the West, that covetous and crafty look which in history is the characteristic march of all invading empires ; if, availing itself of a favorable moment, it were to make an attempt on the independence of Europe, then we should perhaps have a proof of the value of the Catholic principle in a great extremity; then we should feel the power of the unity which is proclaimed and supported by Catholicity, and while calling to mind the middle ages, we should come to acknowledge one of the causes of the weakness of the East and the strength of the West.

5. Then would be remembered a fact, which, though but of yesterday, is falling into oblivion, viz. : that the nation whose heroic courage broke the power of Napoleon was proverbially

Catholic ; and who knows whether, in the attempts which the Vicar of Jesus Christ has deplored in such touching language,— who knows whether it be not the secret influence of a presentiment, perhaps even a foresight, of the necessity of weakening that sublime power, which has been in all ages, when the cause of humanity was in question, the centre of great attempts? But let us return.

6. It cannot be denied that, since the sixteenth century, European civilization has shown life and brilliancy ; but it is a mistake to attribute this phenomenon to Protestantism. In order to examine the extent and influence of a fact, we ought not to be content with the events which have followed it ; it is also necessary to consider whether these events were already prepared ; whether they are any thing more than the necessary result of anterior facts ; and we must take care not to reason in a way which is justly declared to be sophistical by logicians, *post hoc, ergo propter hoc:* after that, therefore on account of it. Without Protestantism, and before it, European civilization was already very much advanced, thanks to the labors and influence of the Catholic religion ; that greatness and splendor which it subsequently displayed were not owing to it, but arose in spite of it.

---

101. St. Francis de Sales' last Will and Testament.

ST. FRANCIS DE SALES.

St. Francis de Sales, Bishop of Geneva, was one of the most accomplished noblemen of Savoy. Possessed of great personal attractions and brilliant talents, his friends saw the most distinguished worldly career opened for him; but deaf to their remonstrances and entreaties, he embraced the ecclesiastical state. He died in 1622, aged fifty-six. During his life he converted seventy-two thousand unbelievers. He was celebrated as a preacher. His writings are full of beauties. But his greatest work —the fruits of which we see around us in America as well as in Europe —was the establishment of the Order of the Visitation. This religious order —so zealously devoted to the education of youth—is a true type of the piety, learning, and zeal of its saintly founder.

1. After being beat about on the boisterous ocean of this world, and experiencing so many dangers of shipwreck, from storms, tempests, and rocks of vanity, I present myself before

thee, O my God! to account for the talents thy infinite goodness has intrusted to my charge. I am now within the sight of land. How I pity the lot of those I leave behind, still exposed to such imminent dangers! How treacherous are the attractions of life, how strong its charms, how fascinating its blandishments! Where are you, O devout souls? I could wish to have your company in this my passage, or to join you in your holy exercises. Prepare to go to the celestial Jerusalem.

2. Behold the effect of life! Life can produce no other work than death; while solid devotion produces eternal life. It is the autumn season, in which fruits are gathered for eternity. This plant, which has received its increase from heaven, will soon be removed, and mortals will see no more of it than its roots, the sad spoils of corruption. The flower, which the sun has decorated with such brilliant colors, speedily fades. Consider that life flies like a shadow, passes as a dream, evaporates as smoke, and that human ambition can embrace nothing solid. Every thing is transitory.

3. The sun, which arises above our horizon, precipitates his course to tread on the heels of night; while darkness solicits the return of light, to hasten the most beautiful parts of our universe to destruction. Rivers are continually rushing to the sea, their centre, as if they were there to find rest. The moon appears in the firmament, sometimes full, at other times decreasing, and seems to take a pleasure, as if her task and career were soon to end. Winter robs the trees of their foliage, to read us a lesson of mortality. No tie, no affection whatever, holds me now to this earth. I have resigned my will entirely into thy hands.

4. Thou hast, O Lord! long since taught me how to die. My inclinations to the world have been long dead. Mortifications have deadened my body, my soul wishes to shake off this coil, and I only value and esteem that life which is found in thee. In proportion as I feel my body weaken, my spirit grows stronger. I am ready to burst from my prison. I here see, as in a mirror, what beatitude is. How unspeakable are the delights of a soul in the grace of God! Sensual

pleasures being satiety and disgust, true pledge of inanity and imperfection; while pleasurable enjoyments of the soul are infinite, and never pall upon the palate. Let us then quit this world, and ascend through the aid of God's mercy, to heaven.

5. And you, Christian souls, are you not content to accompany me? Do you fear the passage? Are you not already dead to the world, that you may live to God? Can you fear the pains of dissolution, when you reflect what your Saviour has suffered for the love of you? · Keep your conscience in a fit state to give a satisfactory account of your actions: imagine the judgments of God are at every hour suspended over your head; that life holds by a single thread, by a nothing; and that in the gardens of this world death lurks under every rose and violet, as the serpent under the grass.

6. Now that I am quitting this world, Christian souls, what legacy can I leave you? Earthly possessions you have renounced, and holy poverty you have embraced. I therefore bequeath to you humility, the true *lapis lydius*, or touchstone of devotion, which can discriminate piety from hypocrisy; she is the mother of all virtues, ever occupied in reforming our lives and actions, and always walks accompanied by charity. Oh, devout souls! how much more difficult is the task of acquiring this Christian humility than the other virtues! Oh! how does nature suffer, when you are told to humble your mind, to make yourselves little, to pardon your enemies!

7. What a struggle does it cost to break down and totally destroy that tender love of self, the mortal enemy to humiliations and abjection. This legacy of *humility*, I trust you will both receive and practise. As for thee, my God! I shall not leave thee my soul; it has long been thine; thou hast redeemed it with the price of thy blood, and withdrawn it from the captivity of sin and death; it will be happy, if, pardoning its faults, thou wilt receive it into thy embraces! Now I must give in my accounts, the thought of divine justice makes me tremble, but the thought of divine mercy gives me hope, I throw myself into thy arms, O Lord, to solicit pardon, I will

cast myself at thy feet to bathe them with my tears, to pray
for me ; and through thy infinite goodness, I may receive the
effects of thy infinite mercies.

———◆———

92. Arch Confraternity of S. Giovanni Decollato.

MAGUIRE.

John Francis Maguire, a distinguished Irish member of the British
Parliament, and editor of the "Cork Examiner." Within the last few
years, Mr. Maguire has attained considerable distinction as a true patriot,
an orator, and a man of letters. His work on "Rome, its Ruler, and its
Institutions," is a valuable addition to Catholic literature, and is the best
defence of the Roman government that has yet appeared.

1. Morichini gives an interesting account of this confraternity, whose mission is one of singular charity,—to bring comfort
and consolation to the last moments of the condemned. It
appears that on the 8th day of May, 1488, some good Floren-
tines, then in Rome, considering that those who died by the
hand of justice had no one to visit and comfort them in their
last hours, instituted a confraternity which was at first called
Della Misericordia, and afterwards by its present name, from
the church of their patron. Pope Innocent VIII. granted
the society a place under the Campidolio, in which they erected
a church to St. John the Baptist ; and here they were allowed
to bury the remains of those who had been executed. Their
objects were sympathized with, and their efforts assisted, by
successive Pontiffs. Tuscans only, or their descendants to the
third generation are received into the society.

2. On the day previous to the execution of a criminal, they
invite, by public placard, prayers for his happy passage to the
other life. In the night of that day, the brothers, some half
dozen in number, including priests, assemble in the church of
S. Giovanni di Fiorentini, not far from the New Prisons. Here
they recite prayers, imploring the Divine assistance in the melancholy office which they are about to perform. They then proceed to the prisons, walking, two by two, in silence, some of
the brothers bearing lanterns in their hands. On entering the
chamber called *conforteria*, they assume the sack and cord, in

which they appear to the prisoner as well as to the public. They divide between them the pious labors. Two perform the office of consolers; one acts as the *sagrestano;* and another makes a record of all that happens from the moment of the intimation of the sentence to that of the execution. These dismal annals are carefully preserved.

3. At midnight, the guardians of the prison go to the cell of the condemned, and lead him, by a staircase, to the chapel of the *conforteria.* At the foot of the stairs, the condemned is met by the notary, who formally intimates to him the sentence of death. The unhappy man is then delivered up to the two "comforters," who embrace him, and, with the crucifix and the image of the Sorrowful Mother presented to him, offer all the consolation which religion and charity can suggest in that terrible moment. The others assist in alleviating his misery, and, without being importunate, endeavor to dispose him to confess, and receive the Holy Communion.

4. Should he be ignorant of the truths of Christianity, they instruct him in them in a simple manner. If the condemned manifest a disposition to impenitence, they not only themselves use every effort which the circumstances of his case render necessary, but call in the aid of other clergymen. The other members of the confraternity employ the hours preceding the execution in the recital of appropriate prayers, and confess and communicate at a mass celebrated two hours before dawn.

5. Clad in the *sacco*, they proceed, two by two, to the prison, the procession being headed by a cross-bearer with a great cross, and a torch-bearer at each side, carrying a torch of yellow wax. The procession having arrived at the prison, the condemned descends the steps; the first object which meets his gaze being an image of the Blessed Virgin, before which he kneels, and, proceeding on, does the same before the crucifix, which is near the gate that he now leaves forever. Here he ascends the car which awaits him, accompanied by the "comforters," who console and assist him to the last; and the procession moves on to the place of execution, the members of the confraternity going in advance.

6. Arrived at the fatal spot, the condemned descends from

the car, and is led into a chamber of an adjoining building, which is hung with black, where the last acts of devotion are performed, or, if he be impenitent, where the last efforts are made to move him to a better spirit. The hour being come, the executioner bandages his eyes, and places him upon the block; and thus, while supported by his *confortori*, and repeating the sacred name and invoking the mercy of Jesus, the axe descends upon the criminal, and human justice is satisfied. The brothers then take charge of the body, lay it on a bier, and, carrying it to their church, decently inter it. Finally, they conclude their pious work by prayer.

---

103. THE CONFRATERNITY "DELLA MORTE."

MAGUIRE.

1. FREQUENTLY, towards night, does the stranger in Rome hear in the streets the sad chant of the *Miserere*; and on approaching the place whence the solemn sounds proceed, he beholds a long procession of figures clad entirely in black, and headed by a cross-bearer; many of the figures bearing large waxen torches, which fling a wild glare upon the bier, on which is borne the body of the deceased. It is the Confraternity *della Morte*, dedicated to the pious office of providing burial for the poor. It was first instituted in 1551, and finally established by Pius IV. in 1560.

2. It is composed mostly of citizens of good position, some of whom are of high rank. The members are distinguished by a habit of black, and a hood of the same color, with apertures for the eyes. When they hear of a death, they meet, and having put on their habits, go out in pairs; and when they arrive at the house where the body lies, they place it on a bier, and take it to a church, singing the *Miserere* as the mournful procession winds through the streets.

3. Even should they be apprised of a death which had occurred twenty, or even thirty, miles distant from Rome, no matter what may be the time or the season, the burial of their

poor fellow-creature is at once attended by this excellent society. In the Pontificate of Clement VIII., a terrible inundation was caused by the rise of the Tiber—a calamity ever to be dreaded, and ever attended with the greatest misery and danger to the poor—and the brethren were seen employed, as far as Ostia and Fiumicino, in extricating dead bodies from the water.

4. Another confraternity—*della Perseveranza*—which is composed of pious men, visit and relieve poor strangers who are domiciled in inns and lodging-houses, and minister to their different wants. This confraternity was established under Alexander VII., in 1663; and besides its duty of ministering to the necessities of the living, it also provides decent sepulture for the dead—poor strangers being in both cases the objects of their special care.

5. A fatal accident, which occurred near Tivoli, in September, 1856, afforded a melancholy occasion for the exercise of the charity of one of those institutions, and severely tested the humanity and courage of its brotherhood. An Irish clergyman, whose name it is not necessary to mention, was unfortunately drowned while bathing in the sulphur lake below Tivoli. After three days, the body was recovered ; but it was found to be in an advanced state of decomposition, in a great measure owing to the highly impregnated character of the water.

6. The members of the confraternity *della Morte*, established in the church of the Carita, in Tivoli, laid the body in a coffin, which they had provided for the purpose; and though the day was intensely hot, and the odor from the body was in the highest degree offensive, they bore it, for a distance of five miles, to the cathedral, where, after the last offices of religion being paid to it, it was buried in the grave set apart for the deceased canons of the church.

7. Here were a number of men, the majority of them artisans, encountering this fearful danger, and undergoing this perilous toil, beneath the raging heat of an Italian sun ; not only without hope of fee or reward, but freely sacrificing their day's employment to the performance of a pious work. The number of the brethren to whom this duty was allotted was twenty-four ; and they relieved each other by turns—those not

engaged in bearing the body chanting sacred hymns, the dirge-like tones of which fall upon the ear of the stranger with such solemn effect.

------

104. Lament of Mary, Queen of Scots.

BURNS.

Robert Burns was born in Scotland in 1758; died in 1796. In poetic genius he has been surpassed by few in any age. Born of the people, he sang of the people, and his songs are the genuine expression of Scottish feeling; hence it is that his name is identified with the Scottish nation.

1. Now nature hangs her mantle green
　　On every blooming tree,
　And spreads her sheets o' daisies white
　　Out o'er the grassy lea ;
　Now Phœbus cheers the crystal streams,
　　And glads the azure skies ;
　But naught can glad the weary wight
　　That fast in durance lies.

2. Now lav'rocks wake the merry morn,
　　Aloft on dewy wing ;
　The merle, in his noontide bower,
　　Makes woodland-echoes ring ;
　The mavis wild, wi' many a note,
　　Sings drowsy day to rest ;
　In love and freedom they rejoice,
　　Wi' care nor thrall opprest.

3. Now blooms the lily by the bank,
　　The primrose down the brae ;
　The hawthorn's budding in the glen,
　　And milk-white is the slae ;
　The meanest hind in fair Scotland
　　May rove their sweets among ;
　But I, the queen of a' Scotland,
　　Maun lie in prison strong.

4. I was the queen o' bonnie France,
    Where happy I hae been ;
Full lightly rose I in the morn,
    As blithe lay down at e'en ;
And I'm the sovereign o' Scotland,
    And mony a traitor there ;
Yet here I lie, in foreign bands,
    And never-ending care.

5. But as for thee, thou false woman,'
    My sister and my foe !
Grim vengeance, yet, shall whet a sword
    That through thy soul shall go ;
The weeping blood in woman's breast
    Was never known to thee ;
Nor the balm that drops on wounds of woe
    Frae woman's pitying e'e.

6 My son !² my son ! may kinder stars
    Upon thy fortune shine ;
And may those pleasures gild thy reign
    That ne'er wad blink on mine !
God keep thee frae thy mother's foes,
    Or turn their hearts to thee ;
And where thou meet'st thy mother's friend,
    Remember him for me !

7 Oh, soon, to me, may summer suns
    Nae mair light up the morn !
Nae mair, to me, the autumn winds
    Wave o'er the yellow corn !
And in the narrow house of death
    Let winter round me rave ;
And the next flowers that deck the spring
    Bloom on my peaceful grave.

Elizabeth, queen of England, who unjustly detained her in prison.
² James the First, king of England.

105. THE PLAGUE OF LOCUSTS.

FROM NEWMAN'S "CALLISTA."

1. THE plague of locusts, one of the most awful visitations
to which the countries included in the Roman Empire were
exposed, extended from the Atlantic to Ethiopia, from Arabia
to India, and from the Nile and Red Sea to Greece and the
north of Asia Minor. Instances are recorded in history of
clouds of the devastating insect crossing the Black Sea to
Poland, and the Mediterranean to Lombardy. It is as numerous in its species as it is wide in its range of territory.
Brood follows brood, with a sort of family likeness, yet with
distinct attributes, as we read in the prophets of the Old Testament, from whom Bochart tells us it is possible to enumerate
as many as ten kinds.

2. It wakens into existence and activity as early as the
month of March; but instances are not wanting as in our
present history, of its appearance as late as June. Even one
flight comprises myriads upon myriads, passing imagination, to
which the drops of rain, or the sands of the sea, are the only
fit comparisons; and hence it is almost a proverbial mode of expression in the East (as may be illustrated by the sacred pages
to which we just now referred), by way of describing a vast invading army, to liken it to the locusts. So dense are they, when
upon the wing, that it is no exaggeration to say that they hide the
sun, from which circumstance, indeed, their name in Arabic is
derived. And so ubiquitous are they when they have alighted
on the earth, that they simply cover or clothe its surface.

3. This last characteristic is stated in the sacred account of
the plagues of Egypt, where their faculty of devastation is also
mentioned. The corrupting fly and the bruising and prostrat-
ing hail preceded them in the series of visitations, but they
came to do the work of ruin thoroughly. For not only the
crops and fruits, but the foliage of the forest itself, nay, the
small twigs and the bark of the trees, are the victims of their
curious and energetic rapacity. They have been known
even to gnaw the door-posts of the houses. Nor do they

execute their task in so slovenly a way, that, as they have succeeded other plagues, so they may have successors themselves.

4. They take pains to spoil what they leave. Like the
harpies, they smear every thing that they touch with a miserable slime, which has the effect of a virus in corroding, or, as
some say, in scorching and burning. And then, perhaps, as
if all this were too little, when they can do nothing else, they
die, as if out of sheer malevolence to man, for the poisonous
elements of their nature are then let loose and dispersed abroad,
and create a pestilence; and they manage to destroy many more
by their death than in their life.

5. Such are the locusts,—whose existence the ancient heretics brought forward as their primary proof that there was an
evil creator; and of whom an Arabian writer shows his national
horror, when he says that they have the head of a horse, the
eyes of an elephant, the neck of a bull, the horns of a stag, the
breast of a lion, the belly of a scorpion, the wings of an eagle,
the legs of a camel, the feet of an ostrich, and the tail of a
serpent.

6. And now they are rushing upon a considerable tract of
that beautiful region of which we have spoken with such admiration. The swarm to which Juba pointed, grew and grew,
till it became a compact body, as much as a furlong square;
yet it was but the vanguard of a series of similar hosts, formed,
one after another, out of the hot mould or sand, rising into the
air like clouds, enlarging into a dusky canopy, and then discharged against the fruitful plain. At length, the huge,
innumerous mass was put into motion, and began its career,
darkening the face of day.

7 As became an instrument of divine power, it seemed to
have no volition of its own; it was set off, it drifted with the
wind, and thus made northwards, straight for Sicca. Thus
they advanced, host after host, for a time wafted on the air,
and gradually declining to the earth, while fresh broods were
carried over the first, and neared the earth, after a longer flight,
in their turn. For twelve miles did they extend, from front to
rear, and their whizzing and hissing could be heard for six
miles on every side of them.

8. The bright sun, though hidden by them, illumined their bodies, and was reflected from their quivering wings; and as they heavily fell earthward, they seemed like the innumerable flakes of a yellow-colored snow. And like snow did they descend, a living carpet, or rather pall, upon fields, crops, gardens, copses, groves, orchards, vineyards, olive woods, orangeries, palm plantations, and the deep forests, sparing nothing within their reach, and, where there was nothing to devour, lying helpless in drifts, or crawling forward obstinately, as best they might, with the hope of prey.

9. They could spare their hundred thousand soldiers, twice or thrice over, and not miss them; their masses filled the bottoms of the ravines and hollow ways, impeding the traveller as he rode forward on his journey, and trampled by thousands under his horse's hoofs. In vain was all this overthrow and waste by the roadside; in vain their loss in river, pool, and water-course. The poor peasants hastily dug pits and trenches as their enemy came on; in vain they filled them from the wells or with lighted stubble. Heavily and thickly did the locusts fall; they were lavish of their lives; they choked the flame and the water, which destroyed them the while. and the vast, living hostile armament still moved on.

106. The Plague of Locusts—*continued.*

1. They moved on like soldiers in their ranks, stopping at nothing, and straggling for nothing; they carried a broad furrow, or weal, all across the country, black and loathsome, while it was as green and smiling on each side of them, and in front, as it had been before they came. Before them, in the language of the prophets, was a paradise, and behind them a desert. They are daunted by nothing; they surmount walls and hedges, and enter inclosed gardens or inhabited houses.

2. A rare and experimental vineyard has been planted in a sheltered grove. The high winds of Africa will not commonly allow the light trellis or the slim pole; but here the lofty poplar of

Campania has been possible, on which the vine-plant mounts so many yards into the air, that the poor grape-gatherers bargain for a funeral pile and a tomb as one of the conditions of their engagement. The locusts have done what the winds and lightning could not do, and the whole promise of the vintage, leaves and all, is gone, and the slender stems are left bare.

3. There is another yard, less uncommon, but still tended with more than common care ; each plant is kept within due bounds by a circular trench around it, and by upright canes on which it is to trail; in an hour the solicitude and long toil of the vine-dresser are lost, and his pride humbled. There is a smiling farm; another sort of vine, of remarkable character, is found against the farm-house. This vine springs from one root, and has clothed and matted with its many branches the four walls. The whole of it is covered thick with long clusters, which another month will ripen. On every grape and leaf there is a locust.

4. In the dry caves and pits, carefully strewed with straw, the harvest-men have (safely, as they thought just now) been lodging the far-famed African wheat. One grain or root shoots up into ten, twenty, fifty, eighty, nay, three or four hundred stalks; sometimes the stalks have two ears apiece, and these shoot off into a number of lesser ones. These stores are intended for the Roman populace; but the locusts have been beforehand with them. The small patches of ground belonging to the poor peasants up and down the country, for raising the turnips, garlic, barley, and water-melons, on which they live, are the prey of these glutton invaders as much as the choicest vines and olives.

5. Nor have they any reverence for the villa of the civil decurion, or the Roman official. The neatly arranged kitchen-garden, with its cherries, plums, peaches, and apricots, is a waste; as the slaves sit around, in the kitchen in the first court, at their coarse evening meal, the room is filled with the invading force, and the news comes to them that the enemy has fallen upon the apples and pears, in the basement, and is at the same time plundering and sacking the preserves of quince and

pomegranate, and revelling in the jars of precious oil of Cyprus and Mendes in the store-rooms.

6. They come up to the walls of Sicca, and are flung against them into the ditch. Not a moment's hesitation or delay; they recover their footing, they climb up the wood or stucco, they surmount the parapet, or they have entered in at the windows, filling the apartments, and the most private and luxurious chambers, not one or two, like stragglers at forage, or rioters after a victory, but in order of battle, and with the array of an army. Choice plants or flowers about the *impluvia* and *xysti*, for ornament or refreshment—myrtles, oranges, pomegranates, the rose, and the carnation—have disappeared.

7. They dim the bright marbles of the walls and the gilding of the ceiling. They enter the *triclinium* in the midst of the banquet; they crawl over the viands, and spoil what they do not devour. Unrelaxed by success and by enjoyment, onward they go; a secret, mysterious instinct keeps them together, as if they had a king over them. They move along the floor in so strange an order that they seem to be a tessellated pavement themselves, and to be the artificial embellishment of the place; so true are their lines, and so perfect is the pattern they describe.

8. Onward they go, to the market, to the temple sacrifices, to bakers' stores, to the cook-shops, to the confectioners, to the druggists; nothing comes amiss to them; wherever man has aught to eat or drink there are they, reckless of death, strong of appetite, certain of conquest.

They have passed on; the men of Sicca sadly congratulate themselves, and begin to look about them and to sum up their losses. Being the proprietors of the neighboring districts, and the purchasers of its produce, they lament over the devastation, not because the fair country is disfigured, but because income is becoming scanty, and prices are becoming high.

9. How is a population of many thousands to be fed? Where is the grain? where the melons, the figs, the dates, the gourds, the beans, the grapes, to sustain and solace the multitudes in their lanes, caverns, and garrets? This is another weighty consideration for the class well-to-do in the world

The taxes, too, and contributions, the capitation tax, the percentage upon corn, the various articles of revenue due to Rome, how are they to be paid? How are the cattle to be provided for the sacrifices and the tables of the wealthy? One-half, at least, of the supply of Sicca is cut off.

10. No longer slaves are seen coming into the city from the country in troops, with their baskets on their shoulders, or beating forward the horse, or mule, or ox overladen with its burden, or driving in the dangerous cow or the unresisting sheep. The animation of the place is gone; a gloom hangs over the Forum, and if its frequenters are still merry there is something of sullenness and recklessness in their mirth. The gods have given the city up; something or other has angered them. Locusts, indeed, are no uncommon visitation, but at an earlier season. Perhaps some temple has been polluted, or some unholy rite practised, or some secret conspiracy has spread.

11. Another, and a still worse, calamity. The invaders, as we have already hinted, could be more terrible still in their overthrow than in their ravages. The inhabitants of the country had attempted, where they could, to destroy them by fire and water. It would seem as if the malignant animals had resolved that the sufferers should have the benefit of this policy to the full, for they had not got more than twenty miles beyond Sicca when they suddenly sickened and died. When they thus had done all the mischief they could by their living, when they thus had made their foul maws the grave of every living thing, next they died themselves and made the desolated land their own grave. They took from it its hundred forms and varieties of beautiful life, and left it their own fetid and poisonous carcasses in payment.

12. It was a sudden catastrophe; they seemed making for the Mediterranean, as if, like other great conquerors, they had other worlds to subdue beyond it; but, whether they were over-gorged, or struck by some atmospheric change, or that their time was come and they paid the debt of nature, so it was that suddenly they fell, and their glory came to naught, and all was vanity to them as to others, and "their stench

rose up, and their corruption rose up, because they had done proudly."

13 The hideous swarms lay dead in the most steaming underwood, in the green swamps, in the sheltered valleys, in the ditches and furrows of the fields, amid the monuments of their own prowess, the ruined crops and the dishonored vineyards. A poisonous element, issuing from their remains, mingled with the atmosphere and corrupted it. The dismayed peasants found that a plague had begun; a new visitation, not confined to the territory which the enemy had made its own, but extending far and wide as the atmosphere extends in all directions. Their daily toil, no longer claimed by the fruits of the earth, which have ceased to exist, is now devoted to the object of ridding themselves of the deadly legacy which they have received in their stead.

14. In vain; it is their last toil; they are digging pits, they are raising piles, for their own corpses, as well as for the bodies of their enemies. Invader and victim lie in the same grave, burn in the same heap; they sicken while they work, and the pestilence spreads. A new invasion is menacing Sicca, in the shape of companies of peasants and slaves, with their employers and overseers, nay, the farmers themselves and proprietors, the panic having broken the bonds of discipline, rushing from famine and infection as to a place of safety. The inhabitants of the city are as frightened as they, and more energetic. They determine to keep them at a distance; the gates are closed; a strict cordon is drawn; however, by the continual pressure, numbers contrive to make an entrance, as water into a vessel, or light through the closed shutters, and any how the air can not be put in quarantine, so the pestilence has the better of it, and at last appears in the alleys and in the cellars of Sicca.

107. An Hour at the Old Play-Ground.

ANON.

1. I sat an hour to-day, John,
   Beside the old brook stream;
   Where we were school-boys in old times,
   When manhood was a dream;
   The brook is choked with falling leaves,
   The pond is dried away,
   I scarce believe that you would know
   The dear old place to-day!

2. The school-house is no more, John;
   Beneath our locust-trees,
   The wild-rose by the window side
   No more waves in the breeze;
   The scatter'd stones look desolate,
   The sod they rested on
   Has been plough'd up by stranger hands,
   Since you and I were gone.

3. The chestnut-tree is dead, John,
   And what is sadder now,
   The broken grape-vine of our swing,
   Hangs on the wither'd bough;
   I read our names upon the bark,
   And found the pebbles rare,
   Laid up beneath the hollow side,
   As we had piled them there.

4. Beneath the grass-grown bank, John,
   I look'd for our old spring,
   That bubbled down the alder path,
   Three paces from the swing;
   The rushes grow upon the brink,
   The pool is black and bare,
   And not a foot, this many a day,
   It seems, has trodden there.

5. I took the old blind road, John.
That wander'd up the hill,
'Tis darker than it used to be,
And seems so lone and still;
The birds sing yet upon the boughs,
Where once the sweet grapes hung,
But not a voice of human kind,
Where all our voices rung

6. I sat me on the fence, John,
That lies as in old time,
The same half pannel in the path
We used so oft to climb;
And thought how o'er the bars of life
Our playmates had pass'd on,
And left me counting on the spot,
The faces that are gone.

----

108. CHRISTIAN AND PAGAN ROME.

DR. NELIGAN.

REV. WILLIAM H. NELIGAN, LL. D., was born in Clonmel, County Tipperary, Ireland. Formerly a minister of the Church of England—became a convert in 1858; studied in Rome, and was ordained priest in New York by Archbishop Hughes in 1857. His work on "Rome, its churches, &c.," gives a striking and correct picture of the Eternal City. He has also written an edifying work entitled "Saintly Characters," with others of less note.

1. ROME is a city of contrasts. Like Rebecca, she bears within her two worlds opposed to each other. It is agreeable to pass from one to the other. Having spent the morning in Christian Rome, we would now take a glimpse at ancient Rome. This makes the chief happiness of the pilgrim. It seems to multiply his existence. We sat down on the eastern part of the Palatine Hill, as the sun was casting his declining rays on the scene before us.

2. This seems to me to be a place which Jeremias would select, to meditate on the ruins of the city. Seated upon the

dust of the palace of Nero and Augustus, he could have uttered one of his plaintive meditations on the ruins of departed greatness. Soon would it change its tone to one of triumphant rejoicing, as he thought how the city of Nero became the city of Peter, the Prince of the Apostles, and that "the glory of this last city should be more than that of the first." Before you, are the arch of Titus, the Coliseum, and the arch of Constantine, which form a triangle, and which were built on the boundaries of the ancient and the Christian world, when Paganism and Judaism were disputing with the rising church the empire of mankind.

8. The arch of Titus, by its inscription on both sides, recalls to us the prophecy of Daniel and the prophecy of Christ, with respect to the destruction of the city, and shows to all generations the effect of these words, "His blood be upon us and upon our children.". The second is the Coliseum, a witness of the degradation of humanity at the era of Christianity, of the struggle of paganism, and of the cruelty which she exercised against the Church. It is also a witness of the victory of the weak over the strong, and of the suffering victims over those who persecuted them. This was the battle-field where the martyrs were crowned. In this amphitheatre, erected by the hands of Jews and pagans, the most glorious triumphs of Christianity were gained. But the scene draws to a close.

4. The arch of Constantine is the witness of the conquest of Catholicity over the territory through which paganism reigned. It was erected to the "liberator of the city, and to the founder of peace." These the finger of God seems to have kept in such a state of preservation, to be his witnesses to the end of all ages. Viewed by the eye of Christian philosophy, the ruins of the Eternal City speak with a wondrous eloquence There God and man meet; Christianity the conqueror, and paganism the conquered, are present everywhere. As the work of man, the city presents to us the ruins of temples, of palaces, aqueducts, and mutilated mausoleums—all mingled together in the dust; as the work of God, the city of St. Peter and of Pio Nono is always radiant with youth.

5. The cross has crowned the Capitol for a longer period

than the imperial eagle. Everywhere you see a privileged ruin of paganism coming to shelter itself under the wing of religion, to escape from utter destruction. Like captives, who find any conditions acceptable, should their lives be spared, the old glories of Rome have submitted themselves to any use .hat may be made of them. They have become Christian temples, tombs of martyrs, columns, pedestals, and even the pavement in the houses of the victors. They are satisfied if the daughter of heaven deign to touch them with her finger. It is to them an assurance of immortality. They seem to remember the treatment which they received from the hands of the barbarians, and, to escape fresh ravages, they are desirous of being adopted by that poor church, whose blood they drank in the day of their glory.

6. How often is the Catholic pilgrim delighted with these obelisks, which were formerly erected to some of the great men of the world! At their base you find inscribed the name of the hero to whom they were erected; above this, the name of the Pontiff, the successor of the fisherman of Galilee, who dedicated them to St. Peter, St. Paul, or the Mother of God, and placed their statues on the summit of the pillar. Here both history and poetry seem united together. This aspect of defeat and victory, which is to be met with at every step in the Eternal City, affords much instruction.

7. It is to the serious mind a lesson which makes him despise all that is of earth, and admire all that is from God. If with feelings like these, the traveller, the artist, and the pilgrim behold all these monuments of antiquity, and if they be the means of detaching him from all that is changing around him, and of uniting him to the things which change not, h may indeed say he has seen Rome.

109. ROSEMARY IN THE SCULPTOR'S STUDIO.

HUNTINGTON.

J. V. HUNTINGTON, born in New York in 1815, formerly an Episcopalian minister; since his conversion to Catholicity entirely devoted to literary pursuits. He is best known as a novelist, but has published a volume of poetry and a good many fugitive pieces. His novels indicate an intimate acquaintance with the better and more cultivated portion of American society. His novel of "Rosemary" is a work of considerable dramatic power, colored with the warm tints of a poet's fancy. His "Pretty Plate" is one of the best juvenile stories with which we are acquainted.

1. ROSEMARY sat with her back to the countess, and her face to the old brilliant picture of the glorious Coming, with its angels in sky-blue robes and saints with gilded halos.

" A very interesting picture," Rory said.

" Very ! I can hardly take my eyes off from it."

" Very well, as you must look at some point in particular, suppose that you look at that picture."

" Is the position in which I sit of any consequence ?"

" As long as you do not lean back, and continue to look at the picture, it is of no consequence. You may change it whenever you like. Be quite unconstrained in that respect."

" I am glad you allow me to sit. I supposed the sitting would be a standing."

" Not to-day. Another time I may try your patience further."

2. While Rosemary sat thus, her eyes fastened on the picture, and scarcely seeing O'Morra, who stood near his pile of clay, working it with an instrument into shape, he conversed with her in a tranquil tone. She was pleased though surprised at this, for from the rigid silence he had imposed on the countess, she had counted on more than usual taciturnity on his part. First, he gave her a history of the picture, painted by a monk in the fifteenth century. Thence he naturally passed to the subject of which it treated.

3. All representations of so great a theme, the crowning event of human history, but lying beyond the domain of human experience, were unsatisfactory. Rosemary thought so too. Insensibly he diverged to the mighty scene itself. His language, remarkably calm and unexcited but admirably chosen,

became soon the outline of a meditation on the Final Judg
ment.   Circumstance after circumstance taken from Holy Writ
came in to heighten the tremendous word-picture, and in the
midst of the scene Rosemary and himself were placed as assistants and spectators.

4. " We may suppose that our purgation will not have ceased
before, as it will certainly cease then.   What feelings must be
ours, in such a case, when we shall have burst the prison of
the tomb, to behold the tomb itself, the solid earth, crumble
and melt, and yet feel in our own risen bodies the throb of
eternal life !   What a moment !   the wedding again of the
flesh and spirit instantaneously co-glorified ; a fact of which
we shall take note with perfect intellectual clearness, even in
the same instant that the Beatific Vision breaks upon us with
its infinite vistas of entrancing splendor !"

5. Rosemary's beautiful face kindled like a vase lighted from
within ; she leaned a little forward and raised one fair arm
towards the old picture, as if she would have spoken.

"The resurrection of the flesh, its glorification, its divini
sation almost, is to me one of the most consoling dogmas of
our faith.   That body is immortal already in my opinion ; it
shall breathe and pulsate, shall see and hear, have motion and
force and splendor, while God shall be God.   What is the
grave ?   You have lain in it once, yet now you live !   What
has happened to you in a figure shall happen to us all in reality.   You ought to feel this vividly—you, once the motionless
tenant of a tomb !"

6. From that time O'Morra worked on in silence.   At last
Rosemary timidly glanced at him—for she was weary.   He
was not looking at her at all ; his bright eye was fixed on vacancy, and his fingers worked, like a blind man's, in the plastic
clay.   It was a rude human figure, feminine vaguely, nude, black,
dripping wet ; in the body the posture was nearly all that was
evident, and that was roughly outlined ; the head was mas-
sively brought out, and under the clay hair, clotted and lumped,
was a noble face, upturned to heaven with an expression of
wonder, awe, joy, and earnest gazing, as upon some marvellous
glory.

110. STELLA MATUTINA, ORA PRO NOBIS.[1]

HUNTINGTON.

1. GLEAMING o'er mountain, coast, and wave,
   What splendor IT, foretokening, gave
   The front of shadow-chasing morn!
   And, ere the day-star was re-born,
   With borrow'd but auspicious light
   Gladden'd the night-long watcher's sight!

2. Fair herald of a brighter sun,
   And pledge of Heaven's own day begun,
   When th' ancient world's long night was o'er,
   So shone, above death's dreaded shore,
   And life's now ever-brightening sea,
   The lowly MAID of GALILEE.

3. Lost now in His effulgent ray,
   Bathed in the brightness of His day,
   O Morning Star! still sweetly shine
   Through that dim night which yet is mine,
   Precede for me His dawning light,
   Who only puts all shades to flight!

---

111. RELIGIOUS ORDERS.

LEIBNITZ.

Wm. G. LEIBNITZ was born in Leipsic in 1646; died in 1716. His scientific and philosophical attainments entitle him to be placed among the highest mathematicians and philosophers of the age.

1. SINCE the glory of God and the happiness of our fellow-creatures may be promoted by various means, by command or by example, according to the condition and disposition of

---

[1] *Stella Matutina, ora pro nobis. Morning Star, pray for us;*—one of the suffrages in the Litany of Loretto.

each, the advantages of that institution are manifest by which, besides those who are engaged in active and every-day life, there are also found in the Church ascetic and contemplative men, who, abandoning the cares of life, and trampling its pleasures under foot, devote their whole being to the contemplation of the Deity, and the admiration of his works; or who freed from personal concerns, apply themselves exclusively to watch and relieve the necessities of others; some by instructing the ignorant or erring; some by assisting the needy and afflicted.

2. Nor is it the least among those marks which commend to us that Church, which alone has preserved the name and the badges of Catholicity, that we see her alone produce and cherish these illustrious examples of the eminent virtues and of the ascetic life.

Wherefore, I confess, that I have ardently admired the religious orders, and the pious confraternities, and the other similar admirable institutions; for they are a sort of celestial soldiery upon earth, provided, corruptions and abuses being removed, they are governed according to the institutes of the founders, and regulated by the supreme Pontiff for the use of the universal Church.

3. For what can be more glorious than to carry the light of truth to distant nations, through seas and fires and swords, —to traffic in the salvation of souls alone,—to forego the allurements of pleasure, and even the enjoyment of conversation and of social intercourse, in order to pursue, undisturbed, the contemplation of abstruse truths and divine meditation,—to dedicate one's self to the education of youth in science and in virtue,—to assist and console the wretched, the despairing the lost, the captive, the condemned, the sick,—in squalor, in chains, in distant lands,—undeterred even by the fear of pestilence from the lavish exercise of these heavenly offices of charity!

4. The man who knows not, or despises these things, has but a vulgar and plebeian conception of virtue; he foolishly measures the obligations of men towards their God by the perfunctory discharge of ordinary duties, and by that

3. In his way thither, he passed through Ghent : and after stopping there a few days, to indulge that tender and pleasing melancholy, which arises in the mind of every man in the decline of life, on visiting the place of his nativity, and viewing the scenes and objects familiar to him in his early youth, he pursued his journey, accompanied by his son Philip, his daughter the archduchess, his sisters the dowager queens of France and Hungary, Maximilian his son-in-law, and a numerous retinue of the Flemish nobility.

4. Before he went on board, he dismissed them, with marks of his attention or regard ; and taking leave of Philip with all the tenderness of a father who embraced his son for the last time, he set sail under convoy of a large fleet of Spanish, Flemish, and English ships.

5. His voyage was prosperous, and agreeable ; and he arrived at Laredo in Biscay, on the eleventh day after he left Zealand. As soon as he landed, he fell prostrate on the ground ; and considering himself now as dead to the world, he kissed the earth, and said, "Naked came I out of my mother's womb, and naked I now return to thee, thou common mother of mankind."

6. From Laredo he proceeded to Valladolid. There he took a last and tender leave of his two sisters ; whom he would not permit to accompany him to his solitude, though they entreated it with tears : not only that they might have the consolation of contributing, by their attendance and care, to mitigate or to soothe his sufferings, but that they might reap instruction and benefit, by joining with him in those pious exercises, to which he had consecrated the remainder of his days.

7. From Valladolid, he continued his journey to Plazencia in Estremadura. He had passed through that city a great many years before ; and having been struck at that time with the delightful situation of the monastery of St. Justus, belonging to the order of St. Jerome, not many miles distant from that place, he had then observed to some of his attendants, that this was a spot to which Diocletian might have retired with pleasure.

8. The impression had remained so strong on his mind, that he pitched upon it as the place of his retreat. It was seated in a vale of no great extent, watered by a small brook, and surrounded by rising grounds, covered with lofty trees. From the nature of the soil, as well as the temperature of the climate, it was esteemed the most healthful and delicious situation in Spain.

9. Some months before his resignation, he had sent an architect thither, to add a new apartment to the monastery, for his accommodation ; but he gave strict orders that the style of the building should be such as suited his present station, rather than his former dignity. It consisted only of six rooms, four of them in the form of friars' cells, with naked walls ; the other two, each twenty feet square, were hung with brown cloth, and furnished in the most simple manner.

10. They were all on a level with the ground ; with a door on one side into a garden, of which Charles himself had given the plan, and had filled it with various plants, which he proposed to cultivate with his own hands. On the other side, they communicated with the chapel of the monastery, in which he was to perform his devotions.

11. Into this humble retreat, hardly sufficient for the comfortable accommodation of a private gentleman, did Charles enter with twelve domestics only. He buried there, in solitude and silence, his grandeur, his ambition, together with all those vast projects, which, during half a century, had alarmed and agitated Europe ; filling every kingdom in it, by turns, with the terror of his arms, and the dread of being subjected to his power.

12. In this retirement, Charles formed such a plan of life for himself, as would have suited the condition of a private person of a moderate fortune. His table was neat but plain ; his domestics few ; his intercourse with them familiar ; all the cumbersome and ceremonious forms of attendance on his person were entirely abolished, as destructive of that social ease and tranquillity which he courted, in order to soothe the remainder of his days.

13. As the mildness of the climate, together with his deliv

srance from the burdens and cares of government, procured him, at first, a considerable remission from the acute pains with which he had been long tormented ; he enjoyed, perhaps, more complete satisfaction in this humble solitude, than all his grandeur had ever yielded him.

14. The ambitious thoughts and projects which had so long engrossed and disquieted him, were quite effaced from his mind. Far from taking any part in the political transactions of the princes of Europe, he restrained his curiosity even from any inquiry concerning them ; and he seemed to view the busy scene which he had abandoned, with all the contempt and in-difference arising from his thorough experience of its vanity, as well as from the pleasing reflection of having disentangled himself from its cares.

---

115. LETTER FROM PLINY TO MARCELLINUS.

MELMOTH.

1. I WRITE this under the utmost oppression of sorrow. The youngest daughter of my friend Fundanus is dead ! Never surely was there a more agreeable, and more amiable young person ; or one who better deserved to have enjoyed a long, I had almost said, an immortal life ! She had all the wisdom of age, and discretion of a matron, joined with youthful sweetness and virgin modesty.

2. With what an engaging fondness did she behave to her father! How kindly and respectfully receive his friends ! How affectionately treat all those who, in their respective offices, had the care and education of her! She employed much of her time in reading, in which she discovered great strength of judgment ; she indulged herself in few diversions, and those with much caution. With what forbearance, with what patience, with what courage, did she endure her last ill-ness !

3. She complied with all the directions of her physicians ; she encouraged her sister and her father ; and, when all her

strength of body was exhausted, supported herself by the single vigor of her mind. That indeed continued, even to her last moments, unbroken by the pain of a long illness, or the terrors of approaching death; and it is a reflection which makes the loss of her so much the more to be lamented. A loss infinitely severe! and more severe by the particular conjuncture in which it happened!

4. She was contracted to a most worthy youth; the wedding day was fixed, and we were all invited. How sad a change from the highest joy to the deepest sorrow! How shall I express the wound that pierced my heart, when I heard Fundanus himself (as grief is ever finding out circumstances to aggravate its affliction), ordering the money he had designed to lay out upon clothes and jewels for her marriage, to be employed in myrrh and spices for her funeral!

5. He is a man of great learning and good sense, who has applied himself, from his earliest youth, to the noblest and most elevated studies; but all the maxims of fortitude which he has received from books, or advanced himself, he now absolutely rejects; and every other virtue of his heart gives place to all a parent's tenderness.

6. We shall excuse, we shall even approve his sorrow, when we consider what he has lost. He has lost a daughter, who resembled him in his manners, as well as his person; and exactly copied out all her father. If his friend Marcellinus shall think proper to write to him, upon the subject of so reasonable a grief, let me remind him not to use the rougher arguments of consolation, and such as seem to carry a sort of reproof with them; but those of kind and sympathizing humanity.

7. Time will render him more open to the dictates of reason; for as a fresh wound shrinks back from the hand of the surgeon, but by degrees submits to, and even requires the means of its cure; so a mind, under the first impressions of a misfortune, shuns and rejects all arguments of consolation; but at length, if applied with tenderness, calmly and willingly acquiesces in them Farewell.

116. To ᴛʜᴇ Roʙɪɴ.

ELIZA COOK.

Eʟɪᴢᴀ Cooᴋ, an English poetess of some note, was born in London, in 818. There is a heartiness and a fresh good-nature ringing through every tanza of Miss Cook's poetry, that wins a way for it to every heart. She oves nature and makes others love it too.

1. I wɪsʜ I could welcome the spring, bonnie bird,
   With a carol as joyous as thine ;
   Would my heart were as light as thy wing, bonnie bird,
   And thine eloquent spirit-song mine !

   The bloom of the earth and the glow of the sky
   Win the loud-trilling lark from his nest ;
   But though gushingly rich are his pæans on high,
   Yet, sweet robin, I like thee the best.

2. I've been marking the plumes of thy scarlet-faced suit,
   And the light in thy pretty black eye,
   'Till my harpstring of gladness is mournfully mute,
   And I echo thy note with a sigh.

   For you perch on the bud-cover'd spray, bonnie bird,
   O'er the bench where I chance to recline,
   And you chatter and warble away, bonnie bird,
   Calling up all the tales of " lang syne."

3 They sung to my childhood the ballad that told
  Of " the snow coming down very fast ;"
  And the plaints of the robin, all starving and cold,
  Flung a spell that will live to the last.

  How my tiny heart struggled with sorrowful heaves,
  That kept choking my eyes and my breath ;
  When I heard of thee spreading the shroud of green
     leaves,
  O'er the little ones lonely in death.

14*

4. I stood with delight by the frost-checker'd pane,
     And whisper'd, "See, see, Bobby comes ;"
While I fondly enticed him again and again,
     With the handful of savory crumbs.

There were springes and nets in each thicket and glen,
     That took captives by night and by day;
There were cages for chaffinch, for thrush, and for wren,
     For linnet, for sparrow, and jay.

5. But if ever thou chanced to be caught, bonnie bird,
     With what eager concern thou wert freed:
Keep a robin enslaved! why, 'twas thought, bonnie bird,
     That "bad luck" would have follow'd the deed.

They wonder'd what led the young dreamer to rove,
     In the face of a chill winter wind;
But the daisy below, and the robin above,
     Were bright things that I ever could find.

6 Thou wert nigh when the mountain streams gladden'd
        the sight ;
     When the autumn's blast smote the proud tree;
In the corn-field of plenty, or desert of blight,
     I was sure, bonnie bird, to see thee.

I sung to thee then as thou sing'st to me now,
     And my strain was as fresh and as wild;
Oh, what is the laurel Fame twines for the brow,
     To the wood-flowers pluck'd by the child!

7 Oh, would that, like thee, I could meet with all change,
     And ne'er murmur at aught that is sent;
Oh, would I could bear with the dark and the fair,
     And still hail it with voice of content.

How I wish I could welcome the spring, bonnie bird,
   With a carol as joyous as thine ;
Would my heart were as light as thy wing, bonnie bird,
   And thy beautiful spirit-song mine !

---

117. The Religion of Catholics.

DR. DOYLE.

Right Reverend James Doyle, late bishop of Kildare and Leighlin, was born at New Ross, County Wexford, Ireland, in 1786; died in 1834. During the fifteen years of Dr. Doyle's episcopacy, he was continually engaged in defending, with voice and pen, the rights of the Church, and the interests of the people. He lived in a troubled period of Irish history, when the island was convulsed from end to end by the tithe question, and the oppressive exactions of the landlords—when the voice of oppressed millions was thundering in the ears of the British government for Catholic emancipation; and on all those great questions, Dr. Doyle exercised a powerful influence. His letters written over the signature of J. K. L., on all the great topics of the day, political and religious, are classed among the ablest documents of the kind ever written.

1. It was the creed, my lord, of a Charlemagne and of a St. Louis, of an Alfred and an Edward, of the monarchs of the feudal times, as well as of the Emperors of Greece and Rome; it was believed at Venice and at Genoa, in Lucca and the Helvetic nations in the days of their freedom and greatness; all the barons of the middle ages, all the free cities of later times, professed the religion we now profess. You know well, my lord, that the charter of British freedom, and the common law of England, have their origin and source in Catholic times.

2. Who framed the free constitutions of the Spanish Goths? Who preserved science and literature, during the long night of the middle ages? Who imported literature from Constantinople, and opened for her an asylum at Rome, Florence, Padua, Paris, and Oxford? Who polished Europe by art, and refined her by legislation? Who discovered the New World, and opened a passage to another? Who were the masters of architecture, of painting, and of music? Who invented the compass, and the art of printing? Who were the poets, the his-

torians, the jurists, the men of deep research, and profound literature ?

3. Who have exalted human nature, and made man appear
again little less than the angels ?   Were they not almost exclusively the professors of our creed ?   Were they who created
and possessed freedom under every shape and form, unfit for
her enjoyment ?   Were men, deemed even now the lights of
he world and the benefactors of the human race, the deluded
 ictims of a slavish superstition ?   But what is there in our
creed which renders us unfit for freedom ?

4. Is it the doctrine of passive obedience ?   No, for the
obedience we yield to authority, is not blind, but reasonable ; our religion does not create despotism ; it supports
every established constitution which is not opposed to the laws
of nature, unless it be altered by those who are entitled to
change it.   In Poland it supported an elective monarch ; in
France an hereditary sovereign ; in Spain, an absolute or con-
stitutional king indifferently ; in England, when the houses of
York and Lancaster contended, it declared that he who was
king *de facto*, was entitled to the obedience of the people.

5. During the reign of the Tudors, there was a faithful adherence of the Catholics to their prince, under trials the most
severe and galling, because the constitution required it ; the
same was exhibited by them to the ungrateful race of Stuart;
but since the expulsion of James (foolishly called an abdica-
tion), have they not adopted with the nation at large, the
doctrine of the Revolution : " that the crown is held in trust
for the benefit of the people ; and that should the monarch
violate his compact, the subject is freed from the bond of his
allegiance ?"   Has there been any form of government ever
devised by man, to which the religion of Catholics has no
 een accommodated ?

6. Is there any obligation, either to a prince, or to a con-
titution, which it does not enforce ?

What, my lord, is the allegiance of the man divided who
gives to Cæsar what belongs to Cæsar, and to God what belongs to God ?   Is the allegiance of the priest divided who
yields submission to his bishop and his king ?—of the son who

obeys his parent and his prince? And yet these duties are not more distinct than those which we owe our sovereign and our spiritual head. Is there any man in society who has not distinct duties to discharge?

7. May not the same person be the head of a corporation, and an officer of the king? a justice of the peace, perhaps, and a bankrupt surgeon, with half his pay? And are the duties thus imposed upon him, incompatible one with another? If the Pope can define that the Jewish sabbath is dissolved, and that the Lord's day is to be sanctified, may not this be believed without prejudice to the act of settlement, or that for the limitation of the crown? If the Church decree that on Fridays her children should abstain from flesh-meat, are they thereby controlled from obeying the king when he summons them to war?

118. The Wife.

WASHINGTON IRVING.

1. I HAVE often had occasion to remark the fortitude with which women sustain the most overwhelming reverses of fortune. Those disasters which break down the spirit of a man, and prostrate him in the dust, seem to call forth all the energies of the softer sex, and give such intrepidity and elevation to their character, that at times it approaches to sublimity.

2. Nothing can be more touching than to behold a soft and tender female, who had been all weakness and dependence, and alive to every trivial roughness, while treading the prosperous paths of life, suddenly arising in mental force to be the comforter and supporter of her husband under misfortune, and abiding, with unshrinking firmness, the most bitter blasts of adversity.

3. As the vine, which has long twined its graceful foliage about the oak, and been lifted by it into sunshine, will, when the hardy plant is rifted by the thunderbolt, cling around it with its caressing tendrils, and bind up its shattered boughs ;

so is it beautifully ordered by Providence, that woman, who
is the mere dependant and ornament of man in his happier
hours, should be his stay and solace when smitten with sudden calamity; winding herself into the rugged recesses of his
nature, tenderly supporting the drooping head, and binding up
the broken heart.

4. I was once congratulating a friend, who had around him
a blooming family, knit together in the strongest affection.
"I can wish you no better lot," said he, with enthusiasm,
" than TO HAVE A WIFE AND CHILDREN.   If you are prosperous,
there they are to share your prosperity ; if otherwise, there
they are to comfort you."

5. And, indeed, I have observed, that A MARRIED MAN, falling into misfortune, is more apt to retrieve his situation in the
world than A SINGLE ONE ; partly, because he is more stimu-
lated to exertion by the necessities of the helpless and beloved
beings who depend upon him for subsistence ; but chiefly, because his spirits are soothed and relieved by domestic endear-
ments, and his SELF-RESPECT kept alive by finding, that
though all abroad is darkness and humiliation, yet there is still
a little world of love at home, of which he is the monarch.

6. Whereas, A SINGLE MAN is apt to run to WASTE and
SELF-NEGLECT ; to fancy himself *lonely* and *abandoned*, and his
heart to fall to ruin, like some deserted mansion, for want of an
inhabitant.

------◆------

119. CHRISTMAS.

LORD JOHN MANNERS.

1 OLD Christmas comes about again,
        The blessed day draws near,
    Albeit our faith and love do wax
        More faint and cold each year.

    Oh ! but it was a goodly sound,
        In th' unenlighten'd days,
    To hear our fathers raise their song
        Of simple-hearted praise.

2. Oh ! but it was a goodly sight,
   The rough-built hall to see,
Glancing with high-born dames and men,
   And hinds of low degree.

To holy Church's dearest sons,
   The humble and the poor,
To all who came, the seneschal
   Threw open wide the door.

3. With morris-dance, and carol-song,
   And quaint old mystery,
Memorials of a holy-day
   Were mingled in their glee.

Red berries bright, and holly green,
   Proclaim'd o'er hall and bower
That holy Church ruled all the land
   With undisputed power.

4. O'er wrekin wide, from side to side,
   From graybeard, maid, and boy,
Loud rang the notes, swift flow'd the
   Of unrestrain'd joy.

And now, of all our customs rare,
   And good old English ways,
This one, of keeping Christmas-time,
   Alone has reach'd our days.

5. Still, though our hearty glee has gone
   Though faith and love be cold,
Still do we welcome Christmas-tide
   As fondly as of old.

Still round the old paternal hearth
   Do loving faces meet,
And brothers parted through the year
   Do brothers kindly greet.

6. Oh ! may we aye, whate'er betide,
   In Christian joy and mirth,
   Sing welcome to the blessed day
   That gave our Saviour birth !

---

120. THE TRUCE OF GOD.

FREDET.

FREDET—late professor of history in St. Mary's College, Baltimore, has with great impartiality and truthfulness, compiled an ancient and modern history for the use of schools.

1. ANOTHER excellent institution that owed its existence to the middle ages, and for which humanity was also indebted to the happy influence of religion, was the sacred compact usually termed the *Truce of God.* From the ninth to the eleventh century, the feudal system, however beautiful in many of its principles, had been a constant source of contentions and wars. Each petty chieftain arrogated to himself an almost unlimited use of force and violence to avenge his wrongs, and pursue his rights, whether real or pretended. As, moreover, vassals were obliged to espouse the quarrels of their immediate lords, rapine, bloodshed, and their attendant miseries were to be seen everywhere ; nor could the most pacific citizens depend on one moment of perfect security, either for their properties or their lives.

2. Religion, by her divine and universally revered authority, was alone capable of raising an efficacious barrier against this torrent of evils. Experience having already shown the impossibility of stemming it at once, prudent measures were taken gradually to diminish its violence. Several bishops ordered, under penalty of excommunication, that, every week, during the four days consecrated to the memory of our Saviour's passion, death, burial, and resurrection, viz., from the afternoon of Wednesday till the morning of the following Monday, whatever might be the cause of strife and quarrel, all private hostilities should cease.

3. Shortly after, the same prohibition was extended to the

whole time of Advent and Lent, including several weeks both after Christmas and after Easter-Sunday. This beneficial institution, which originated in France towards the year 1040, was adopted in England, Spain, etc., and was confirmed by several popes and councils : nor must it be thought that it remained a dead letter; its success, on the contrary, was so remarkable, that the pious age in which the experiment was made, hesitated not to attribute it to the interposition of Heaven

4. Thus, by the exertions of ecclesiastical authority, the horrors and calamities of *feudal war* began to be considerably lessened and abridged. *Its ravages* were restrained to three days in the week and to certain seasons of the year; during the intervals of peace, there was leisure for passion to cool, for the mind to sicken at a languishing warfare, and for social habits to become more and more deeply rooted. A considerable number of days and weeks afforded security to all, and all, being now shielded by the religious sanction of this sacred compact, could travel abroad, or attend to their domestic affairs, without danger of molestation.

5. Such was the splendid victory which the religion of Christ won over the natural fierceness of the ancient tribes of the north ; a victory whose completion was also due to her influence, when the Crusades obliged those restless warriors to turn against the invading hordes of the Saracens and Turks, those weapons which they had hitherto used against their fellow-christians.

---

121. THE HIGH-BORN LADYE.

MOORE.

THOMAS MOORE was born in Dublin, in 1780, died in 1852. No poet ever moulded the English tongue into softer or more melodious strains than Moore, and none, in any language, ever adorned his verse with more sparkling gems of wit, fancy, and sentiment. His "Lalla Rookh" has never been equalled in any tongue, and his "Irish Melodies" have been translated into almost every European language. Poetry must lose its charms when the lays of MOORE shall be unsought, unsung. His prose, however, is by no means equal to his poetry.

1. In vain all the knights of the Underwald woo'd her,
   Though brightest of maidens, the proudest was she ;
   Brave chieftains they sought, and young minstrels they
       sued her,
   But worthy were none of the high-born Ladye.

   "Whosoever I wed," said this maid, so excelling,
     "That knight must the conq'ror of conquerors be ;
   He must place me in halls fit for monarchs to dwell in ;—
     None else shall be Lord of the high-born Ladye !"

2. Thus spoke the proud damsel, with scorn looking round
       her
   On knights and on nobles of highest degree,
   Who humbly and hopelessly left as they found her,
     And worshipp'd at distance the high-born Ladye.

   At length came a knight from a far land to woo her,
     With plumes on his helm, like the foam of the sea ;   .
   His vizor was down—but, with voice that thrill'd through
       her,
   He whisper'd his vows to the high-born Ladye.

3 "Proud maiden ! I come with high spousals to grace thee
     In me the great conq'ror of conquerors see ;
   Enthroned in a hall fit for monarchs I'll place thee,
     And mine thou'rt forever, thou high-born Ladye !"

   The maiden she smiled, and in jewels array'd her,
     Of thrones and tiaras already dreamt she ;
   And proud was the step, as her bridegroom convey'd her
     In pomp to his home, of that high-born Ladye.

6 "But whither," she, starting, exclaims, "have you led
       me ?
   Here's naught but a tomb and a dark cypress-tree ;   . ·

Is *this* the bright palace in which thou wouldst wed me ?"
With scorn in her glance, said the high-born Ladye.

" 'Tis the home," he replied, " of earth's loftiest crea
. tures,"
Then lifted his helm for the fair one to see ;
But she sunk on the ground—'twas a skeleton's features,
And Death was the Lord of the high-born Ladye.

---

122. ADVICE TO A YOUNG LADY ON HER MARRIAGE.

JONATHAN SWIFT, a clergyman of the established church, and Dean of St
Patrick's, Dublin, was born in the same city in 1667 ; died, 1745. Of Swift's
voluminous writings, the greater part are political and satirical. " Gulli-
ver's Travels," " Tale of a Tub," and " The Battle of the Books " are best
known to the reading world. The purity of Swift's style renders it a
model of English composition.

1. THE grand affair of your life will be to gain and preserve
the friendship and esteem of your husband. You are married
to a man of good education and learning, of an excellent understanding, and an exact taste. It is true, and it is happy
for you, that these qualities in him are adorned with great
modesty, a most amiable sweetness of temper, and an unusual
disposition to sobriety and virtue ; but, neither good nature
nor virtue will suffer him to esteem you against his judgment;
and although he is not capable of using you ill, yet you will
in time grow a thing indifferent, and, perhaps, contemptible,
unless you can supply the loss of youth and beauty, with
more durable qualities. You have but a very few years to b
young and handsome in the eyes of the world, you must there
fore use all endeavors to attain to some degree of those 'ac
complishments, which your husband most values in other
people, and for which he is most valued himself.

2 You must improve your mind, by closely pursuing such
a method of study as I shall direct or approve of. You must
get a collection of history and travels, and spend some hours

every day in reading them, and making extracts from them, if
your memory be weak ; you must invite persons of knowledge
and understanding to an acquaintance with you, by whose
conversation you may learn to correct your taste, and judgment ; and when you can bring yourself to comprehend and
relish the good sense of others, you will arrive in time to
think rightly yourself, and to become a reasonable and agree-
ble companion.

3. This must produce in your husband a true rational love
and esteem for you, which old age will not diminish   He will
have a regard for your judgment and opinion in matters of the
greatest weight; you will be able to entertain each other
without a third person to relieve you by finding discourse.
The endowments of your mind will even make your person
more agreeable to him ; and when you are alone, your time
will not lie heavy upon your hands for want of some trifling
amusement.   I would have you look upon finery as a necessary folly, which all great ladies did whom I have ever known.
I do not desire you to be out of the fashion, but to be the last
and least in it.

4. I expect that your dress shall be one degree lower than
your fortune can afford ; and in your own heart I would wish
you to be a contemner of all distinctions which a finer petticoat can give you ; because it will neither make you richer,
handsomer, younger, better natured, more virtuous or wise,
than if it hung upon a peg.   If you are in company with men
of learning, though they happen to discourse of arts and sciences out of your compass, yet you will gather advantage by
listening to them ; but if they be men of breeding as well as
learning, they will seldom engage in any conversation where
you ought not to be a leader, and in time have your part.

5. If they talk of the manners and customs of the several
kingdoms of Europe, of travels into remoter nations, of the
state of your own country, or of the great men and actions of
Greece and Rome ; if they give their judgment upon English
and French writers, either in verse or prose, or of the nature
and limits of virtue and vice,—it is a shame for a lady not to
relish such discourses, not to improve by them, and endeavor

by reading and information to have her share in those enter-
tainments.

6. Pray, observe, how insignificant things are many ladies, when they have passed their youth and beauty ; how
contemptible they appear to men, and yet more contemptible
to the younger part of their own sex, and have no relief, but
in passing their afternoons in visits, where they are never ac
ceptable ; while the former part of the day is spent in spleen
and envy, or in vain endeavors to repair by art and dress the
ruins of time. Whereas, I have known ladies at sixty, to
whom all the polite part of the court and town paid their addresses, without any further view than that of enjoying the
pleasure of their conversation. I am ignorant of any one
quality that is amiable in a man, which is not equally so in a
woman ; I do not except even modesty and gentleness of nature. Nor do I know one vice or folly which is not equally
detestable in both.

7. There is, indeed, one infirmity which is generally allowed
you, I mean that of cowardice; yet there should seem to be
something very capricious, that when women profess their admiration of valor in our sex, they should fancy it a very graceful, becoming quality in themselves, to be afraid of their own
shadows ; to scream in a barge when the weather is calmest,
or in a coach at the ring ; to run from a cow at a hundred
yards distance ; to fall into fits at the sight of a spider, an
earwig, or a frog. At least, if cowardice be a sign of cruelty
(as it is generally granted), I can hardly think it an accomplishment so desirable as to be thought worth improving by
affectation.

----•----

123. A Catholic Maiden of the Old Times.

BOYCE.

Rev. J. Boyce—a native of the north of Ireland, for several years pastor
of the Catholic Church in Worcester, Mass. Under the name of *Paul
Peppergrass*, he has written " Shandy Maguire," an excellent story of Irish
life. " The Spaewife," and " Mary Lee."   Mr. Boyce is an agreeable writer
of fiction.

1. "Why dost thou look at me so pityingly, good pil

grim?" said Alixe. "Is my father dead? Speak, I entreat thee!"

The mendicant seemed not to hear her voice. He gazed at her as if she were a statue on a pedestal, bending forward and leaning on his long polestaff. At length, his lips began lightly to tremble, and then his eyes, which kept moving leisurely over her face and form, scanning every feature, became gradually suffused with tears.

2. "My father's dead!" said Alice, in a voice scarcely audible, as she saw the pilgrim's tears fall on his coarse gabardine.

The words, though but few, and uttered in almost the tone of a whisper, were yet so full of anguish and despair, that they instantly recalled the stranger's wandering thoughts.

Slowly the old man stretched out his hands, and gently laid them on the head of the fair girl, saying, in accents tremulous with emotion,—

3. "Thy father lives, my child, and sends thee his blessing by these hands; receive it, and that of an old outcast also, who loves thee almost as well."

Alice knelt and raised her eyes towards heaven in speechless gratitude. Then, taking the beggar by the hand, she imprinted a kiss on his hard, sunburnt fingers. "Hast seen my father?" she inquired.

4. "Ay, truly have I. He is still at Brockton, with the faithful Reddy, who seldom leaves him even for a moment. I informed him of thy place of refuge, and he will soon venture hither to see thee."

"How looks he? Is he much altered?"

5. "Nay, I cannot answer thee in that, my child, having but seen him for the first time in seventeen years. It will be seventeen years come Holentide since we parted at Annie's grave—I mean at his wife's grave. I shook his honest hand for the last time across her open tomb, ere the earth had entirely covered her coffin from my sight. And, since that day, we have been both learning to forget each other, and the world also—he in his little library at Brockton, whence he hath shut out all profane converse, and I in the woods and wilds

of England, a roaming outcast, without a shelter or a home."

6. "So thou didst know my mother, good man?" said Alice, laying her hand on the beggar's arm, and looking up wistfully in his face.

"Thy mother?—ay, I knew her—once," he replied, with uppressed emotion.

"Then speak to me of my mother. I long to hear some one speak of her. People say she was very kind and gentle. Alas! I never saw her. She died in giving me birth; and so there's a void in my heart I would fain fill up with her image. Say, pilgrim, canst paint her to my fancy? I will listen to thee most attentively."

7. The mendicant turned his head aside, and drew his hand quickly across his eyes.

"Pardon, me, good man," said Alice, as she saw the motion, and understood it; "I fear me I have awakened some painful recollection."

"Nay," replied the mendicant, "it is but a foolish weakness." And he raised himself up to his full height, and planted his staff firmly against the rock, as if to nerve himself for the trial.

8. Father Peter and Nell Gower were conversing at the farther end of the cell, and casting a look occasionally in the direction of the speakers.

"Nell saith I am somewhat like my mother. Good man, dost think so?" inquired Alice.

"Like thy mother, my fair child? Ay, thy face is somewhat like. But the face is only a small part—a hundred such faces were not worth a heart like hers."

"She was so good?"

9. "Ay, and so noble, and so grand of soul."

"Ah!"

"And yet so humble, so charitable, so pure, and so truly Catholic. Hold, I'll question thee as to the resemblance, and then tell thee, mayhap, in how much thou'rt like thy mother."

"Speak on," said Alice; "I'll answer thee right faithfully."

"Hast been good to the poor beggar who came to beg an alms and shelter? and didst give him the kind word at meeting, and the secret dole at parting?"

Alice hesitated.

10. "She hath," replied a deep voice from a distant corner of the chapel.

Alice started, somewhat surprised at the solemn sound, but the mendicant seemed not to notice it.

"Hast worshipped thy God in the night and in the morning?"

"She hath."

"Hast been frequent at the sacred confessional and the holy altar?"

"She hath," responded the same voice, a third time.

11. "Dost love thy religion better than thy life?" demanded the pilgrim, in a sterner tone, still leaning on his staff, and looking steadily at the young girl. "Answer for thyself, maiden."

"Methinks I do," she at length replied, casting her eyes bashfully on the ground, and playing with the chain of her cross. "But I'm only a simple country girl, and have not yet been greatly tempted."

"Good," said the mendicant. "And art ready to sacrifice thy life for thy faith?"

"Ay, willingly!" responded Alice, in a tone of increased confidence.

12. "Hearken to me, child. Thy religion is a low, mean, and contemptible thing. It is driven out from the royal courts and princely halls of thy native land, where it once ruled triumphant, to dwell with the ignorant and the poor. It is forced to seek shelter in woods and caves. It is banished the presence of the great and powerful, despised and scoffed at even by the learned; nay, it is flung from their houses like a ragged garment, and fit only to be worn by wretched beggars like myself! Ha, girl! thy religion is the scorn of thy compeers—like the Christian name in the times of the Dioeletians, it's a disgrace and dishonor to acknowledge it."

13. "I care not," said Alice; "was not my Redeemer despised for his religion?"

"And art bold enough to meet the contemptuous smiles, and withstand the winks and nods, of the enemies of thy faith, as thou passest them by?"

Alice answered not in words, but she raised the cross from her bosom, where it hung, and reverently kissed the lips of the image of the Saviour.

The mendicant understood the silent reply, and proceeded:

14. "But of thy father. Wouldst abandon him to pre serve thy faith? Wouldst see him dragged on a hurdle to the gallows, amid the shouts of the rabble, when thy apostasy would save him?"

"What! is he a prisoner?" she cried, fearing the mendicant had hitherto been only preparing her for some dreadful announcement.

"Nay, answer me, maiden. Wouldst save thy father by apostasy?"

15. "Never!" responded Alice, raising herself to her full height, and crossing her arms on her breast as she spoke. "Never! I love him as fondly as ever daughter loved a parent—nay, I would give my life cheerfully to save his; but I would see him hanging on the gallows at Tyburn till the wind and sun had bleached his bones, rather than renounce the religion of my God and the honors of my ancestors!"

"Ha! thou wouldst, girl?" said the mendicant, catching her hand, and gazing full in her face. "Then thou hast learnt to feel as a Catholic."

---

124. MARCO BOZZARIS.

HALLECK.

FITZ GREENE HALLECK—an American poet, born at Guilford, Connecticut, in 1795. His poetry is musical, and full of vigor, evincing a refined taste, and a heart alive to every generous and noble sentiment.

[Marco Bozzaris, the Epaminondas of modern Greece, fell in a night attack upon the Turkish camp at Laspi, the site of the ancient Platæa, August 20, 1823, and expired in the moment of victory.]

1. AT midnight, in his guarded tent,.
     The Turk was dreaming of the hour

When Greece, her knee in suppliance bent,
　　Should tremble at his power:
In dreams through camp and court he bor'
The trophies of a conqueror;
　　In dreams his song of triumph heard;
Then wore his monarch's signet ring,—
Then press'd that monarch's throne,—a king;
As wild his thoughts, and gay of wing,
　　As Eden's garden bird.

2. An hour pass'd on,—the Turk awoke;
　　That bright dream was his last;
He woke, to hear his sentries shriek,—
"To arms! they come! the Greek! the Greek!
He woke, to die midst flame and smoke,
And shout, and groan, and sabre-stroke,
　　And death-shots falling thick and fast
As lightnings from the mountain cloud;
And heard, with voice as trumpet loud,
　　Bozzaris cheer his band:—
"Strike—till the last arm'd foe expires!
Strike—for your altars and your fires!
Strike—for the green graves of your sires!
　　God, and your native land!"

3 They fought, like brave men, long and well;
　　They piled the ground with Moslem slain;
They conquer'd; but Bozzaris fell,
　　Bleeding at every vein.
His few surviving comrades saw
His smile, when rang their proud hurrah,
　　And the red field was won;
Then saw in death his eyelids close,
Calmly, as to a night's repose,
　　Like flowers at set of sun.

4 Come to the bridal chamber, Death!
　　Come to the mother's when she feels

For the first time her first-born's breath;
  Come when the blessèd seals
That close the pestilence are broke,
And crowded cities wail its stroke;
Come in consumption's ghastly form,
The earthquake shock, the ocean storm;
Come when the heart beats high and warm,
  With banquet song, and dance, and wine,—
And thou art terrible: the tear,
The groan, the knell, the pall, the bier,
And all we know, or dream, or fear,
  Of agony, are thine.

5 But to the hero, when his sword
  Has won the battle for the free,
Thy voice sounds like a prophet's word,
And in its hollow tones are heard
  The thanks of millions yet to be.
Bozzaris! with the storied brave
  Greece nurtured in her glory's time,
Rest thee: there is no prouder grave,
  Even in her own proud clime.
  We tell thy doom without a sigh;
For thou art Freedom's now, and Fame's,—
One of the few, the immortal names,
  That were not born to die!

---

125. MRS. CAUDLE ON LATE HOURS.

DOUGLAS JERROLD.

Douglas Jerrold, born in Sheerness, Kent, England, in 1803; died, 1857.
As a dramatic and humorous writer, Jerrold was unsurpassed among his
contemporaries. He was one of the principal contributors to "Punch,"
and wielded a pen of considerable power in lashing the follies of the age.

1. PERHAPS, Mr. Caudle, you'll tell me where this is to end
Though, goodness knows, I needn't ask *that*. The end is plain
enough. Out, out, out! Every night, every night!

Oh dear! I only hope none of my girls will ever be the slave their poor mother is; they shan't if I can help it. What do you say? *Nothing?*

Well, I don't wonder at that, Mr. Caudle; you ought to be ashamed to speak; I don't wonder that you can't open your mouth.

2. I'm only astonished that at such hours you have the confidence to knock at your own door. Though I'm your wife, I must say it, I do sometimes wonder at your impudence.

What do you say? *Nothing?* Ha! you are an aggravating creature, Caudle; sitting there like a mummy of a man, and never so much as opening your lips to one. Just as if your own wife wasn't worth answering!

Oh, no! elsewhere you can talk fast enough; here, there's no getting a word from you. A pretty way of treating your wife!

3. Out,—out every night! What? *You haven't been out this week before?* That's nothing at all to do with it. You might just as well be out all the week as once, just!

And I should like to know what could keep you out till these hours? *Business?* Oh, yes; I dare say! Pretty business, out of doors at one in the morning!

What! *I shall drive you mad?* Oh, no; you haven't feelings enough to go mad. You'd be a better man, Caudle, if you had. *Will I listen to you?* What's the use? Of course, you've some story to put me off with. You can all do that, and laugh at us afterwards.

4. No, Caudle, don't say that. I'm not always trying to find fault,—not I. It's you. I never speak but when there's occasion; and what in my time I've put up with, there isn't anybody in the world knows. No, nor ever will.

Will I hear your story? Oh, you may tell it if you please, go on; only mind, I shan't believe a word of it. I'm not such a fool as that, I can tell you; no, not one word of it. There, now, don't begin to scold, but go on.

And that's your story, is it? That's your excuse for the hours you keep! That's your apology for undermining my health and ruining your family!

5. What do you think your children will say of you when they grow up, going and throwing away your money upon good-for-nothing bar-room acquaintance ?

He's not a bar-room acquaintance ? Who is he, then ? Come, you haven't told me that ; but I know,—it's that Prettyman. Yes, to be sure it is ! Upon my life ! Well, if I've hardly patience to live in the same house with you ! I've wanted a silver teapot these five years, and you must go and throw away as much money as — What ! *You haven't thrown it away ?* Haven't you ! Then my name's not Margaret, that's all I know.

6. A man gets arrested, and because he's taken from his wife and family and locked up, you must go and trouble your head with it ! And you must be mixing yourself up with sheriffs' officers, running from lawyer to lawyer to get bail, and settle the business, as you call it.

A pretty settlement you'll make of it, mark my words ! Yes ; and to mend the matter, to finish it quite, you must be one of the bail. That any man who isn't a born fool should do such a thing for another !

Do you think anybody would do as much for you ? *Yes ?* You say yes ? Well, I only wish,—just to show that I am right,—I only wish you were in a condition to try them. I should only like to see you arrested. You'd find the difference—*that* you would.

7. What's other people's affairs to you ? If you were locked up, depend upon it, there's not a soul would come near you. No ; it's all very fine now, when people think there isn't a chance of your being in trouble ; but I should only like to see what they'd say to you if *you* were in a watch-house. Yes, I should enjoy *that*, just to show you that I'm always right.

What do you say ? *You think better of the world ?* Ha ! that would be all very well if you could afford it ; but you're not in means, I know, to think so well of people as all that And of course they only laugh at you.

" Caudle is an easy fool," they cry,—I know it as well as if I heard them,—" Caudle's an easy fool ; anybody may lead him." Yes; anybody but his own wife, and she, of course, is nobody.

8. And now, everybody that's arrested will of course send to you. Yes, Mr. Caudle, you'll have your hands full now, no doubt of it. You'll soon know every watch-house and every sheriff's officer in London.

Your business will have to take care of itself; you'll have enough to do to run from lawyer to lawyer after the business of other people. Now, it's no use calling me a dear soul, not a bit ! No ; and I shan't put it off till to-morrow. It isn't often I speak, but I *will* speak now.

I wish that Prettyman had been at the bottom of the sea before— What? *It isn't Prettyman?* Ha ! it's very well for you to say so ; but I know it is ; it's just like him. He looks like a man that's always in debt—that's always in a watch-house.

9. Anybody might see it. I knew it from the very first time you brought him here, from the very night he put his dirty wet boots on my bright steel fender. Any woman could see what the fellow was in a minute. Prettyman ! A pretty gentleman, truly, to be robbing your wife and family !

Why couldn't you let him stop in the watch— Now don't call upon Heaven in that way, and ask me to be quiet, for I won't. Why couldn't you let him stop there ? He got himself in ; he might have got himself out again.

And you must keep me up, losing my sleep, my health, and, for what you care, my peace of mind. Ha ! everybody but you can see how I'm breaking. A great deal you care for that or your poor children !

And then you must be bail—you must be bound—for Mr Prettyman ! You may say bound ! Yes, you've your hand nicely tied, now. How he laughs at you—and serves you right, too !

10. Why, in another week he'll be in the East Indies ; o. course he will ! And you'll have to pay his debts ; yes, your children may go in rags, so that Mr. Prettyman— What do you say ? *It isn't Mr. Prettyman?* I know better.

Well, if it isn't Prettyman that's kept you out,—if it isn't

Prettyman you're bail for,—who is it, then ! I ask, who is
it, then? What? *My brother?* *Brother Tom?* O Caudle ! dear Caudle ——

It was too much for the poor soul ; she sobbed as if her
heart would break,—and Caudle left the room.

---

126. CARDINAL WOLSEY AND CROMWELL.[1]

SHAKSPEARE.

WILLIAM SHAKSPEARE was born at Stratford-on-Avon, Warwickshire, England, in 1564; died in 1616. Shakspeare possessed all the great qualities
of a poet, and united with them profound philosophical intellect. His expressions have become familiar, and it is through his plays that thousands
have grown acquainted with the history of England. It is deeply to be
regretted that an unpardonable license of language prevents many of his
works from being suitable reading for the pure minded and the young.
De Vere.

Wolsey. FAREWELL, a long farewell to all my greatness !
This is the state of man ; to-day he puts forth
The tender leaves of hope, to-morrow blossoms,
And bears his blushing honors thick upon him ;
The third day comes a frost, a killing frost ;
And—when he thinks, good easy man, full surely
His greatness is a ripening—nips his root,
And then he falls, as I do. I have ventured,
Like little wanton boys that swim on bladders,
This many summers in a sea of glory;
But far beyond my depth ; my high-blown pride
At length broke under me ; and now has left me,
Weary, and old with service, to the mercy
Of a rude stream, that must forever hide me.
Vain pomp, and glory of this world, I hate ye !
I feel my heart new opened ; Oh, how wretched
Is that poor man that hangs on princes' favors!
There is, betwixt that smile we would aspire to,

---

[1] Thomas Cromwell, a statesman of the time of Henry the Eighth
of England.

That sweet aspect[1] of princes, and their ruin,
More pangs and fears than wars or women have;
And when he falls, he falls like Lucifer,
Never to hope again.

Enter Cromwell, amazedly.

Why, how now, Cromwell?
   Cromwell. I have no power to speak, sir.
   Wol. What! amazed
At my misfortunes? Can thy spirit wonder,
A great man should decline? Nay, an'[2] you weep
I am fallen indeed.
   Crom. How does your Grace?
   Wol. Why, well;
Never so truly happy, my good Cromwell.
I know myself now: and I feel within me
A peace above all earthly dignities,—
A still and quiet conscience. The king has cured me,
I humbly thank his grace; and from these shoulders,
These ruin'd pillars, out of pity, taken
A load would sink a navy—too much honor:
Oh, 't is a burden, Cromwell, 't is a burden,
Too heavy for a man that hopes for heaven.
   Crom. I am glad, your Grace has made that right use of it
   Wol. I hope I have: I am able now, methinks,
(Out of a fortitude of soul I feel),
To endure more miseries, and greater far,
Than my weak-hearted enemies dare offer.
What news abroad?
   Crom. The heaviest and the worst
Is your displeasure with the king.
   Wol. God bless him!
   Crom. The next is, that Sir Thomas More is chosen
Lord Chancellor in your place.
   Wol. That's somewhat sudden:

---

[1] Shakspeare often puts the accent in *aspect* on the last syllable.
[2] *An.* by the old writers, is often used for *if*.

But he's a learned man. May he continue
Long in his highness' favor, and do justice
For truth's sake, and his conscience; that his bones,
When he has run his course, and sleeps in blessings,
May have a tomb of orphans' tears wept on 'em !
What more ?

Crom. That Cranmer is return'd with welcome
Install'd Lord Archbishop of Canterbury.

Wol. That's news, indeed.

Crom. Last, that the Lady Anne,
Whom the king hath in secrecy long married,
This day was view'd in open as his queen,
Going to chapel; and the voice is now
Only about her coronation.

Wol. There was the weight that pull'd me down.
        Cromwell !
The king has gone beyond me; all my glories
In that one woman I have lost forever :
No sun shall ever usher forth mine honors,
Or gild again the noble troops that waited
Upon my smiles.   Go, get thee from me, Cromwell :
I am a poor fallen man, unworthy now
To be thy lord and master : seek the king ;
That sun, I pray, may never set ! I have told him
What and how true thou art : he will advance thee ;
Some little memory of me will stir him
(I know his noble nature), not to let
Thy hopeful service perish too: good Cromwell,
Neglect him not ; make use now, and provide
For thine own future safety.

Crom. Oh, my lord,
Must I, then, leave you ?   Must I needs forego
So good, so noble, and so true a master ?
Bear witness, all that have not hearts of iron,
With what a sorrow Cromwell leaves his lord.
The king shall have my service ; but my prayers
Forever, and forever, shall be yours.

Wol. Cromwell, I did not think to shed a tear

In all my miseries; but thou hast forced me
Out of thy honest truth to play the woman.
Let's dry our eyes; and thus far hear me, Cromwell;
And, when I am forgotten,—as I shall be,—
And sleep in dull, cold marble, where no mention
Of me must more be heard of,—say, I taught thee;
Say, Wolsey, that once trod the ways of glory,
And sounded all the depths and shoals of honor,
Found thee a way, out of his wreck, to rise in;
A sure and safe one, though thy master miss'd it.
Mark but my fall, and that that ruin'd me.
Cromwell, I charge thee, fling away ambition;
By that sin fell the angels; how can man, then,
The image of his Maker, hope to win by't?
Love thyself last; cherish those hearts that hate thee;
Corruption wins not more than honesty;
Still in thy right hand carry gentle peace,
To silence envious tongues. Be just, and fear not:
Let all the ends thou aim'st at be thy country's,
Thy God's, and truth's; then if thou fall'st, O Cromwell!
Thou fall'st a blessed martyr. Serve the king:
And,——Prithee, lead me in:
There take an inventory of all I have,
To the last penny; 'tis the king's: my robe
And my integrity to Heaven, is all
I dare now call my own. O Cromwell, Cromwell!
Had I but served my God with half the zeal
I served my king, He would not in mine age
Have left me naked to mine enemies!

   Crom. Good sir, have patience.
   Wol. So I have. Farewell
The hopes of court! my hopes in heaven do dwell.

127. ROME SAVED BY FEMALE VIRTUE.

HOOK.

NATHANIEL HOOK, a native of England, died 1768. The date of his birth is unknown to us. He is the author of an excellent "History of Rome, from the building of Rome to the end of the Commonwealth." "Mr. Hook," says Allibone's "Dictionary of Authors," "was a Catholic, of whose life few particulars are known. He will always be remembered for his excellent Roman History, and as the friend of Alexander Pope, who brought the priest to his death-bed, to Bolingbroke's great disgust."

1. CORIOLANUS was a distinguished Roman senator and general, who had rendered eminent services to the republic. But these services were no security against envy and popular prejudices. He was at length treated with great severity and ingratitude, by the senate and people of Rome; and obliged to leave his country to preserve his life. Of a haughty and indignant spirit, he resolved to avenge himself; and with this view, applied to the Volscians, the enemies of Rome, and tendered them his services against his native country. The offer was cordially embraced, and Coriolanus was made general of the Volscian army.

2. He recovered from the Romans all the towns they had taken from the Volsci; carried by assault several cities in Latium; and led his troops within five miles of the city of Rome. After several unsuccessful embassies from the senate, all hope of pacifying the injured exile appeared extinguished; and the sole business at Rome was to prepare, with the utmost diligence, for sustaining a siege. The young and able-bodied men had instantly the guard of the gates and trenches assigned to them; while those of the veterans, who though exempt by their age from bearing arms, were yet capable of service, undertook the defence of the ramparts.

3. The women, in the mean while, terrified by these movements, and the impending danger, into a neglect of their wonted decorum, ran tumultuously from their houses to the temples. Every sanctuary, and especially the temple of Jupiter Capitolinus, resounded with the wailings and loud supplications of women, prostrate before the statues of their divinities In this general consternation and distress, Valeria (sister of

the famous Valerius Poplicola), as if moved by a divine im
pulse, suddenly took her stand upon the top of the steps of
the temple of Jupiter, assembled the women about her, and
having first exhorted them not to be terrified by the greatness
of the present danger, confidently declared, "That there was
yet hope for the republic; that its preservation depended upon
them, and upon their performance of the duty they owed their
country."

4. "Alas!" cried one of the company, "what resource can
there be in the weakness of wretched women, when our bravest
men, our ablest warriors themselves despair?"

"It is not by the sword, nor by strength of arms," replied
Valeria, "that we are to prevail; these belong not to our sex:
Soft moving words must be our weapons and our force. Let
us all in our mourning attire, and accompanied by our children,
go and entreat Veturia, the mother of Coriolanus, to intercede
with her son for our common country. Veturia's prayers will
bend his soul to pity. Haughty and implacable as he has
hitherto appeared, he has not a heart so cruel and obdurate,
as not to relent when he shall see his mother, his revered, his
beloved mother, a weeping suppliant at his feet."

5. This motion being universally applauded, the whole train
of women took their way to Veturia's house. Her son's wife
Volumnia, who was sitting with her when they arrived, and
greatly surprised at their coming, hastily asked them the
meaning of so extraordinary an appearance. "What is it,"
said she, "what can be the motive that has brought so
numerous a company of visitors to this house of sorrow?"

6. Valeria then addressed herself to the mother: "It is to
you, Veturia, that these women have recourse in the extreme
peril with which they and their children are threatened.
They intreat, implore, conjure you, to compassionate their distress, and the distress of our common country. Suffer not
Rome to become a prey to the Volsci, and our enemies to
triumph over our liberty. Go to the camp of Coriolanus:
take with you Volumnia and her two sons: let that
excellent wife join her intercession to yours. Permit these
women with their children to accompany you; they will

all cast themselves at his feet. O Veturia! conjure him to grant peace to his fellow-citizens. Cease not to beg till you have obtained. So good a man can never withstand your tears: our only hope is in you. Come then, Veturia; the danger presses; you have no time for deliberation; the enterprise is worthy of your virtue; Heaven will crown it with success; Rome shall once more owe its preservation to our ex. You will justly acquire to yourself an immortal fame, and have the pleasure to make every one of us a sharer in your glory."

7. Veturia, after a short silence, with tears in her eyes, answered: "Weak indeed is the foundation of your hope, Valeria, when you place it in the aid of two miserable women. We are not wanting in affection to our country, nor need we any remonstrance or entreaties to excite our zeal for its preservation. It is the power only of being serviceable that fails us. Ever since that unfortunate hour, when the people in their madness so unjustly banished Coriolanus, his heart has been no less estranged from his family than from his country. You will be convinced of this sad truth, by his own words to us at parting.

8. "When he returned home from the assembly, where he had been condemned, he found us in the depth of affliction, bewailing the miseries that were sure to follow our being deprived of so dear a son, and so excellent a husband. We had his children upon our knees. He kept himself at a distance from us; and, when he had awhile stood silent, motionless as a rock, his eyes fixed, and without shedding a tear; ''Tis done,' he said. 'O mother! and thou Volumnia, the best of wives, to you Marcius is no more! I am banished hence for my affection to my country, and the services I have done it.

9. "'I go this instant; and I leave forever a city where good men are proscribed. Support this blow of fortune with the magnanimity that becomes women of your high rank and virtue. I commend my children to your care. Educate them in a manner worthy of you, and of the race from which they come. Heaven grant they may be more fortunate than their

father, and never fall short of him in virtue; and may you
in them find your consolation!—Farewell.'

10. "We started up at the sound of this word, and with
loud cries of lamentation ran to him to receive his last embraces. I led his elder son by the hand; Volumnia had the
younger in her arms. He turned his eyes from us, and put
ting us back with his hand 'Mother,' said he, 'from this moment you have no son: our country has taken from you the
stay of your old age. Nor to you, Volumnia, will Marcius
be henceforth a husband; mayst thou be happy with another
more fortunate! My dear children, you have lost your father.'

* * *

128. ROME SAVED BY FEMALE VIRTUE—*continued.*

1. "He said no more, but instantly broke away from us.
He departed from Rome without settling his domestic affairs,
or leaving any orders about them; without money, without
servants, and even without letting us know to what part of
the world he would direct his steps. It is now the fourth
year since he went away; and he has never inquired after his
family, nor, by letter or messenger, given us the least account
of himself: so that it seems as if his mother and his wife, were
the chief objects of that general hatred which he shows to his
country.

2. "What success then can you expect from our entreaties
to a man so implacable? Can two women bend that stubborn
heart, which even all the ministers of religion were not able
to soften? And indeed what shall I say to him? What can
I reasonably desire of him?—that he would pardon ungrateful
citizens, who have treated him as the vilest criminal? that he
would take compassion upon a furious, unjust populace, which
had no regard for his innocence? and that he would betray a
nation, which has not only opened him an asylum, but has
even preferred him to her most illustrious citizens in the command of her armies?

3. "With what face can I ask him to abandon such generous

protectors, and deliver himself again into the hands of his most bitter enemies ? Can a Roman mother, and a Roman wife, with decency, exact, from a son and a husband, compliances which must dishonor him before both gods and men ? Mournful circumstance, in which we have not power to hate the most formidable enemy of our country ! Leave us therefore to our unhappy destiny ; and do not desire us to make it more unhappy, by an action that may cast a blemish upon our virtue."

4. The women made no answer but by their tears and entreaties. Some embraced her knees ; others beseeched Volumnia to join her prayers to theirs ; all conjured Veturia not to refuse her country this last assistance. Overcome at length by their urgent solicitations, she promised to do as they desired.

The very next day, all the most illustrious of the Roman women repaired to Veturia's house. There they presently mounted a number of chariots, which the consuls had ordered to be made ready for them ; and, without any guard, took the way to the enemy's camp.

5. Coriolanus, perceiving from afar that long train of chariots, sent out some horsemen to learn the design of it. They quickly brought him word, that it was his mother, his wife, and a great number of other women, and their children coming to the camp. He doubtless conjectured what views the Romans had in so extraordinary a deputation ; that this was the last expedient of the senate ; and, in his own mind, he determined not to let himself be moved.

6. But he reckoned upon a savage inflexibility that was not in his nature ; for going out with a few attendants to receiv the women, he no sooner beheld Veturia attired in mourning, her eyes bathed in tears, and with a countenance and motion that spoke her sinking under a load of sorrow, than he ran hastily to her; and not only calling her mother, but adding to that word the most tender epithets, embraced her, wept over her, and held her in his arms to prevent her falling. The like tenderness he presently after expressed to his wife, highly commending her discretion in having constantly remained with

his mother, since his departure from Rome.   And then, with
the warmest paternal affection, he caressed his children.

7. When some time had been allowed to those silent tears
of joy, which often flow plenteously at the sudden and unex
pected meeting of persons dear to each other, Veturia entered
upon the business she had undertaken.   After many forcible
ppeals to his understanding and patriotism, she exclaimed

What frenzy, what madness of anger transports my son:
Heaven is appeased by supplications, vows, and sacrifices:
shall mortals be implacable ?   Will Marcius set no bounds to
his resentment ?   But allowing that thy enmity to thy country
is too violent to let thee listen to her petition for peace ; yet
be not deaf, my son, be not inexorable, to the prayers and
tears of thy mother.

8. "Thou dreadest the very appearance of ingratitude towards the Volsci ; and shall thy mother have reason to accuse
thee of being ungrateful ?   Call to mind the tender care I
took of thy infancy and earliest youth ; the alarms, the anxiety, I suffered on thy account, when, entered into the state of
manhood, thy life was almost daily exposed in foreign wars;
the apprehensions, the terrors, I underwent; when I saw thee
so warmly engaged in our domestic quarrels, and, with heroic
courage, opposing the unjust pretensions of the furious pleb-
ians.   My sad forebodings of the event have been but too well
verified.   Consider the wretched life I have endured, if it may
be called life, the time that has passed since I was deprived
of thee.

9. "O Marcius, refuse me not the only request I ever made
to thee ; I will never importune thee with any other.   Cease
thy immoderate anger ; be reconciled to thy country ; this is
all I ask ; grant me but this, and we shall both be happy
Freed from those tempestuous passions which now agitate thy
soul, and from all the torments of self-reproach, thy days will
flow smoothly on in the sweet serenity of conscious virtue:
and as for me, if I carry back to Rome the hopes of an approaching peace, an assurance of thy being reconciled to thy
country, with what transports of joy shall I be received !   In
what honor, in what delightful repose, shall I pass the

remainder of my life! What immortal glory shall I have acquired!"

10. Coriolanus made no attempt to interrupt Veturia while she was speaking; and when she had ceased, he still continued in deep silence. Anger, hatred, and desire of revenge, balanced in his heart those softer passions which the sight and discourse of his mother had awakened in his breast. Veturia perceiving his irresolution, and fearing the event, thus renewed her expostulation : "Why dost thou not answer me, my son? Is there then such greatness of mind in giving all to resentment? Art thou ashamed to grant any thing to a mother who thus entreats thee, thus humbles herself to thee? If it be so, to what purpose should I longer endure a wretched life?" As she uttered these last words, interrupted by sighs, she threw herself prostrate at his feet. His wife and children did the same; and all the other women, with united voices of mournful accent, begged and implored his pity.

11. The Volscian officers, not able unmoved to behold this scene, turned away their eyes : but Coriolanus, almost beside himself to see Veturia at his feet, passionately cried out : "Ah! mother, what art thou doing?" And tenderly pressing her hand, in raising her up, he added, in a low voice, "Rome is saved, but thy son is lost!"

Early the next morning, Coriolanus broke up his camp, and peaceably marched his army homewards. Nobody had the boldness to contradict his orders. Many were exceedingly dissatisfied with his conduct; but others excused it, being more affected with his filial respect to his mother, than with their own interests.

---

129. THE FRIARS AND THE KNIGHT.

K. H. DIGBY.

1. Two friars of Paris, travelling in the depth of winter, came at the first hour of the night, fatigued, covered with mud, and wet with rain, to the gate of a house where they hoped to receive hospitality, not knowing that it belonged to

a knight who hated all friars, and who for twenty years had
never made his confession. The mother of the family replied
to their petition, " I know not, good fathers, what to do. If
I admit you under our roof, I fear my husband ; and if I send
you away cruelly in this tempestuous night, I shall dread the
indignation of God. Enter, and hide yourselves till my husband returns from hunting, and has supped, for then I shall
be able to supply you secretly with what is needful."

2. Shortly, the husband returns, sups joyfully, but, perceiving that his wife is sad, desires to know the cause. She
replies that she dares not disclose it. Pressed and encouraged, she at length relates what has happened, adding, that
she fears God's judgment, seeing that his servants are afflicted
with cold and hunger, while they are feasting at their ease.
The knight, becoming more gentle, orders them to be led
forth from their hiding-place, and to be supplied with food.

3. The poor friars came forth, and drew near the fire ; and
when he sees their emaciated faces, humid raiment, and their
feet stained with blood, the hand of the Lord is upon him,
and from a lion he becomes a lamb. With his own hands he
washes their feet, places the table, and prepares their beds,
bringing in fresh straw. After the supper, with altered look
and tone, he addresses the elder friar, and asks whether a
shameless sinner, who hath not confessed since many years,
can hope for pardon from God?

4. " Yea, in sooth," replied the friar ; " hope in the Lord
and do good, and he will deal with thee according to his
mercy ; for in whatever day the sinner repents, he will remember his iniquity no more." The contrite host declares that he
will not then defer any longer approaching the sacraments
" This very night," said he, " I will unburden my conscience
lest my soul should be required of me." The friar, however
little suspecting danger of death, advised him to wait til
morning. All retired to rest ; but during the night the friar
became alarmed, rose, prostrated himself on the earth, and
besought God to spare the sinner.

5. In the morning, however, the master of the house was
found dead. The man of God, judging from what had passed,

consoled the widow, declared that in his dreams he had been assured of the salvation of her husband; and the man was buried honorably, bells were tolled, and mass was sung, and the friars departed on their way.

6. It is to instances of this kind that St. Jerome alludes in his beautiful epistle to Lacta, where he says, "A holy and faithful family must needs sanctify its infidel chief. That man cannot be far from entering upon the career of faith, who is surrounded by sons and grandsons enlightened by the faith"

130. CATHOLIC RUINS.

CASWELL.

FATHER CASWELL is a convert from Anglicanism, and a priest of the Oratory of St. Philip Neri. He is a poet, calm, subdued, free from all turbulence, peaceful and serene. His poetry is of a very high order. —*Iв. Brownson.*

1. WHERE once our fathers offer'd praise and prayer,
   And sacrifice sublime;
Where rose upon the incense-breathing air
   The chant of olden time;—

Now, amid arches mouldering to the earth,
   The boding night-owl raves;
And pleasure-parties dance in idle mirth
   O'er the forgotten graves.

2. Or worse; the heretic of modern days
   Has made those walls his prize;
And in the pile our Faith alone could raise,
   That very Faith denies!

God of our fathers, look upon our woe!
   How long wilt thou not hear?
How long shall thy true vine be trodden low,
   Nor help from thee appear?

3　Oh, by our glory in the days gone by ;
　　　Oh, by thine ancient love ;
　　Oh, by our thousand Saints, who ceaseless cry
　　　Before thy throne above ;

　　Thou, for this isle, compassionate though just,
　　　Cherish thy wrath no more ;
　　But build again her temple from the dust,
　　　And our lost hope restore !

---

131. GIL BLAS AND THE PARASITE

LE SAGE.

ALAIN RENÉ LE SAGE, a celebrated French novelist and d　· ... write,
born in 1668, died in 1747.　He is principally remembered　als novel d
" Gil Blas," which first appeared in 1715.

1. WHEN the omelet I had bespoken was read; I sat down
to table by myself ; and had not yet swallowed the first
mouthful when the landlord came in, followed by the man
who had stopped him in the street.　This cavalier, who wore
a long sword, and seemed to be about thirty years of age, advanced towards me with an eager air, saying, " Mr. Student,
I am informed that you are that Signor Gil Blas of Santi-
lane, who is the link of philosophy, and ornament of Oviedo !
Is it possible that you are that mirror of learning, that sublime genius, whose reputation is so great in this country !
You know not," continued he, addressing himself to the innkeeper and his wife, " you know not what you possess !　You
have a treasure in your house !　Behold, in this young gentleman, the eighth wonder of the world !"　Then turning to
me, and throwing his arms about my neck, " Forgive," cried
he, " my transports !　I cannot contain the joy that your
presence creates."

2. I could not answer for some time, because he locked me
so closely in his arms that I was almost suffocated for want of
breath ; and it was not till I had disengaged my head from

his embrace that I replied, "Signor Cavalier, I did not think my name was known at Peñaflor." "How! known!" resumed he, in his former strain; "we keep a register of all the celebrated names within twenty leagues of us. You, in particular, are looked upon as a prodigy; and I don't at all doubt that Spain will one day be as proud of you as Greece was of her Seven Sages." These words were followed by a fresh hug, which I was forced to endure, though at the risk of strangulation. With the little experience I had, I ought not to have been the dupe of his professions and hyperbolical compliments.

3. I ought to have known, by his extravagant flattery, that he was one of those parasites who abound in every town, and who, when a stranger arrives, introduce themselves to him, in order to feast at his expense. But my youth and vanity made me judge otherwise. My admirer appeared to me so much of a gentleman, that I invited him to take a share of my supper. "Ah! with all my soul," cried he; "I am too much obliged to my kind stars for having thrown me in the way of the illustrious Gil Blas, not to enjoy my good fortune as long as I can! I have no great appetite," pursued he, "but I will sit down to bear you company, and eat a mouthful purely out of complaisance."

4. So saying, my panegyrist took his place right over against me; and, a cover being laid for him, he attacked the omelet as voraciously as if he had fasted three whole days. By his complaisant beginning I foresaw that our dish would not last long, and I therefore ordered a second, which they dressed with such dispatch that it was served just as we—or rather he—had made an end of the first. He proceeded o this with the same vigor; and found means, without losin one stroke of his teeth, to overwhelm me with praises during the whole repast, which made me very well pleased with my sweet self. He drank in proportion to his eating; sometimes to my health, sometimes to that of my father and mother, whose happiness in having such a son as I he could not enough admire.

5. All the while he plied me with wine, and insisted upon

my doing him justice, while I toasted health for health ; a cir
cumstance which, together with his intoxicating flattery, put
me into such good humor, that, seeing our second omelet half
devoured, I asked the landlord if he had no fish in the house.
Signor Corcuelo, who, in all likelihood, had a fellow-feeling
with the parasite, replied, "I have a delicate trout ; but those
who eat it must pay for the sauce ;—'tis a bit too dainty for
your palate, I doubt." "What do you call too dainty?"
said the sycophant, raising his voice ; "you're a wiseacre, indeed ! Know that there is nothing in this house too good for
Signor Gil Blas of Santillane, who deserves to be entertained
like a prince."

6. I was pleased at his laying hold of the landlord's last
words, in which he prevented me, who, finding myself offended,
said, with an air of disdain, "Produce this trout of yours,
Gaffer Corcuelo, and give yourself no trouble about the consequence." This was what the innkeeper wanted. He got it
ready, and served it up in a trice. At sight of this new dish,
I could perceive the parasite's eye sparkle with joy; and he
renewed that complaisance—I mean for the fish—which he
had already shown for the eggs. At last, however, he was
obliged to give out, for fear of accident, being crammed to the
very throat.

7. Having, therefore, eaten and drunk sufficiently, he thought
proper to conclude the farce by rising from table and accost-
ing me in these words : "Signor Gil Blas, I am too well satisfied with your good cheer to leave you without offering an important advice, which you seem to have great occasion for.
Henceforth, beware of praise, and be upon your guard against
everybody you do not know. You may meet with other people inclined to divert themselves with your credulity, and, perhaps, to push things still further ; but don't be duped again,
nor believe yourself (though they should swear it) the eighth
wonder of the world." So saying, he laughed in my face, and
stalked away.

182. THE DYING CHILD ON NEW YEAR'S EVE.

TENNYSON.

1　If you're waking, call me early, call me early, mother
　　　dear;
　　For I would see the sun rise upon the glad new year:
　　It is the last new year that ever I shall see;
　　Then you may lay me low i' the mould, and think no more
　　　o' me.

　　To-night I saw the sun set; he set and left behind
　　The good old year, the dear old time, and all my peace of
　　　mind;
　　And the new year's coming up, mother, but I shall never
　　　see
　　The may upon the blackthorn, the leaf upon the tree.

5　There's not a flower upon the hills; the frost is on the
　　　pane;
　　I only wish to live till the snow-drops come again:
　　I wish the snow would melt, and the sun come out on high,
　　I long to see a flower so before the day I die.

　　The building rook will caw from the windy, tall elm-tree,
　　And the tufted plover pipe along the fallow lea,
　　And the swallow will come back again with summer o'er
　　　the wave;
　　But I shall lie alone, mother, within the mouldering grave.

t　When the flowers come again, mother, beneath the waning
　　　light,
　　You'll never see me more in the long gray fields at night,
　　When from the dry dark wood the summer airs blow cool,
　　On the oat-grass, and the sword-grass, and the bulrush in
　　　the pool.

　　Ye'll bury me, my mother, just beneath the hawthorn
　　　shade;

And ye'll sometimes come and see me where I am lowly
  laid ;
I shall not forget ye, mother, I shall hear ye where ye
  pass,
With your feet above my head ·in the long and pleasant
  grass.

4 I have been wild and wayward; but you'll forgive me now
You'll kiss me, my own mother, upon my cheek and brow:
Nay, nay; you must not weep, nor let your grief be wild;
You should not fret for me, mother, you have another child

Oh, I will come again, mother, from out my resting-place ;
Though you'll not see me, mother, I shall look upon your
  face :
Though I cannot speak a word, I shall hearken what you
  say,
And be often, often with you, when you think I'm far away

5. Good-night, good-night !   When I have said good-night
  for evermore,
And ye see me carried out from the threshold of the door,
Don't let Effie come and see me till my grave be growing
  green ;
She'll be a better child to you than ever I have been.

She'll find my garden tools upon the granary floor ;
Let her take 'em, they are hers; I shall never garden
  more.
But tell her, when I'm gone, to train the rosebush that I
  set,
About the parlor window and the box of mignonette.

6. Good-night, sweet mother ! call me when it begins to
  dawn ;
All night I lie awake, but I fall asleep at morn.
But I would see the sun rise upon the glad new year ;
So, if you're waking, call me—call me early, mother dear !

123. Anecdote of King Charles II. of Spain.

.CATHOLIC WEEKLY INSTRUCTOR.

1. On the 20th of February, 1685, this king went to take a drive in the environs of Madrid. The day was remarkably fine, and the place was crowded with people. Suddenly, a priest in surplice, attended by only a boy, approached; and the king, doubting whether he was going to give the holy communion, or only extreme unction, questioned him, and was answered that he was bearing the holy Viaticum to a poor man in a cottage at some distance, and had been able to procure no better attendance, owing to the fineness of the day, which had left no one at home.

2. In an instant, the king opened the carriage-door, and leaping out, fell upon his knees and adored the Blessed Eucharist; then, with most respectful words, entreated the priest to take his place, shut the carriage-door, then walked at the side, with his hat in his hand. The way was long and tedious, but the good king went it cheerfully, and arrived at the cottage, opened himself the carriage, handed down the priest, and knelt while he passed. He entered into the poor house, and after the Holy Sacrament had been administered, went up to the bed, consoled with kind words the dying man, gave him an abundant alms, and made ample provision for an only daughter whom he left.

3. He now insisted on the priest again taking his place in the carriage. But the good curate, seeing how fatigued the king was, entreated him not to think of walking back, and at length, yielding to his importunities, he consented to go in the second carriage, while the priest went alone in the first. When they reached Madrid, the king got out, and again took his place, uncovered, by the carriage door.

4. But by this time the whole city was in commotion. The Confraternity of the Blessed Sacrament came forth with lighted tapers, and the nobility came forth in crowds, to follow the footsteps of their sovereign. In magnificent state, the procession reached the church of St. Mark, where benediction was given, and when the king came out, a vast multitude as-

sembled there, greeted him with a burst of enthusiastic ap
plause, which showed how far from lowering himself in his
subjects' eyes, is a sovereign who pays due homage to the
King of kings.

---

134. Spiritual Advantages of Catholic Cities.

K. H. DIGBY.

1. In a modern city men in the evening, leave their homes
for a banquet ; in a Catholic city they go out for the benediction. The offices of the Church, morning and evening, and
even the night instructions, were not wanting to those who
were still living in the world ; and if the intervals were passed
in study, or other intellectual exercise, it was a life scholastic
and almost monastical. The number of churches always open,
the frequent processions, and the repeated instructions of the
clergy, made the whole city like a holy place, and were, without doubt, the means of making multitudes to choose the strait
entrance, and to walk in the narrow way. There are many
who have no idea of the perfection in which great numbers, in
every rank of society, pass their lives in Catholic cities, not
even excepting that capital which has of late been made the
nurse of so much ill.

2. But wherever the modern philosophy has created, as it
were, an atmosphere, that which is spiritual is so confined,
closed, and isolated, that its existence is hardly felt or known.
The world appears to reign with undisputed possession, and
that, too, as if it had authority to reign. And yet there are
tender and passionate souls who have need of being unceasingly preserved in the path of virtue by the reign of religious
exercises, who, when deprived of the power of approaching at
the hour their inclinations may suggest to the sources of grace,
are exposed to great perils, and who perhaps sometimes do
incur in consequence, eternal death.

> " Ah me, how many perils do enfold
> The righteous man, to make him daily fall ?"

3. House of Prayer, why close thy gates? Is there an hour in all nature when the heart should be weary of prayer? when man whom God doth deign to hear in thee as his temple, should have no incense to offer before thy altar, no tear to confide to thee? Mark the manners, too, of the multitude that loiters in the public ways of every frequented town. See, how it meekly kneels to receive a benediction from the bishop who happens to pass by; and when the dusk comes on, and the lamp of the sanctuary begins to burn brighter, and to arrest the eye of the passenger through the opened doors of churches, hearken to the sweet sound of innumerable bells which rises from all sides, and see what a change of movement takes place among this joyous and innocent people :

4. The old men break off their conversation on the benches at the doors, and take out their rosaries; the children snatch up their books and jackets from the green in token that play is over; the women rise from their labor of the distaff; and all together proceed into the church, when the solemn litany soon rises with its abrupt and crashing peal, till the bells all toll out their last and loudest tone, and the adorable Victim is raised over the prostrate people, who then issue forth and retire to their respective homes in sweet peace, and with an expression of the utmost thankfulness and joy.

5. The moderns in vain attempt to account for the difference of manners in these Catholic cities, and in their own, by referring to their present prosperity and accumulation of wealth; these cities in point of magnificence incomparably surpassed theirs, and with respect to riches, they were not superior, for peace was in their strength, and abundance in their towers.

---

135. On Letter Writing.

BLACKWOOD'S MAGAZINE.

1. Epistolary as well as personal intercourse is, according to the mode in which it is carried on, one of the pleasantest

or most irksome things in the world. It is delightful to drop in on a friend without the solemn prelude of invitation and acceptance, to join a social circle, where we may suffer our minds and hearts to relax and expand in the happy conscious ness of perfect security from invidious remark and carping criticism ; where we may give the reins to the sportiveness of innocent fancy, or the enthusiasm of warm-hearted feeling ; where we may talk sense or nonsense, (I pity people who can not talk nousense), without fear of being looked into icicles by the coldness of unimaginative people, living pieces of clock-work, who dare not themselves utter a word, or lift up a little finger, without first weighing the important point in the hair balance of propriety and good breeding.

2. It is equally delightful to let the pen talk freely, and un-premeditatedly, and to one by whom we are sure of being un-derstood; but a formal letter, like a ceremonious morning visit, is tedious alike to the writer and receiver ; for the most part spun out with unmeaning phrases, trite observations, complimentary flourishes, and protestations of respect and at-tachment, so far not deceitful, as they never deceive anybody. Oh, the misery of having to compose a set, proper, well-worded, correctly-pointed, polite, elegant epistle ! one that must have a beginning, a middle, and an end, as methodically arranged and portioned out as the several parts of a sermon under three heads, or the three gradations of shade in a school-girl's first landscape !

3. For my part, I would rather be set to beat hemp, or weed in a turnip field, than to write such a letter exactly every month, or every fortnight, at the precise point of time from the date of our correspondent's last letter, that he or she wrote after the reception of ours ; as if one's thoughts bubbled up to the well-head, at regular periods, a pint at a time, to be bottled off for immediate use. Thought ! what has thought to do in such a correspondence ? It murders thought, quenches fancy, wastes time, spoils paper, wears out innocent goose-quills. " I'd rather be a kitten, and cry mew! than one of those same " prosing letter-mongers.

4. Surely in this age of invention something may be struck

set to obviate the necessity (if such necessity exists) of so tasking, degrading the human intellect. Why should not a sort of mute barrel-organ be constructed on the plan of those that play sets of tunes and country dances, to indite a catalogue of polite epistles calculated for all the ceremonious observances of good breeding? Oh, the unspeakable relief (could uch a machine be invented) of having only to *grind* out an answer to one of one's "dear, five hundred friends!"

5. Or, suppose there were to be an epistolary steam-engine. Ay, that's the thing. Steam does every thing now-a-days. Dear Mr. Brunel, set about it, I beseech you, and achieve the most glorious of your undertakings. The block machine at Portsmouth would be nothing to it. *That* spares manual labor; *this* would relieve mental drudgery, and thousands yet unborn . . . but hold! I am not so sure the female sex in general may quite enter into my views of the subject.

6. Those who pique themselves on the elegant style of their billets, or those fair scriblerinas just emancipated from boarding-school restraints, or the dragonism of their governess, just beginning to taste the refined enjoyments of sentimental, confidential, soul-breathing correspondence with some Angelina, Seraphina, or Laura Matilda; to indite beautiful little notes, with long-tailed letters, upon vellum paper, with pink margins, sealed with sweet mottoes, and dainty devices, the whole deliciously perfumed with musk and attar of roses; young ladies who collect "copies of verses," and charades, keep albums, copy patterns, make bread seals, work little dogs upon footstools, and paint flowers without shadow—oh! no! the epistolary steam-engine will never come into vogue with those dear creatures. *They* must enjoy the "feast of reason, and the flow of soul," and they must write—yes! and how they *do* write!

7. But for another genus of female scribes, unhappy innocents! who groan in spirit at the dire necessity of having to hammer out one of those aforesaid terrible epistles; who, having in due form dated the gilt-edged sheet that lies outspread before them in appalling whiteness, having also felicitously achieved the graceful exordium, "My dear Mrs. P,"

or "My dear Lady V," or "My dear —— any thing else," feel that they are *in for it*, and must say something ! Oh, that something that must come of nothing ! those bricks that must be made without straw! those pages that must be filled with words ! Yea, with words that must be sewed into sentences ! Yea, with sentences that must seem to mean something ; the whole to be tacked together, all neatly fitted and dovetailed so as to form one smooth, polished surface !

8. What were the labors of Hercules to such a task! The very thought of it puts me into a mental perspiration ; and, from my inmost soul, I compassionate the unfortunates now (at this very moment, perhaps) screwed up perpendicularly in the seat of torture, having in their right hand a fresh-nibbed patent pen, dipped ever and anon into the ink-bottle, as if to hook up ideas, and under the outspread palm of the left hand a fair sheet of best Bath post (ready to receive thoughts yet unhatched) on which their eyes are riveted with a stare of disconsolate perplexity infinitely touching to a feeling mind.

9. To such unhappy persons, in whose miseries I deeply sympathize. . . . Have I not groaned under similar horrors, from the hour when I was first shut up (under lock and key, I believe) to indite a dutiful epistle to an honored aunt ? I remember, as if it were yesterday, the moment when she who had enjoined the task entered to inspect the performance, which, by her calculation, should have been fully completed. I remember how sheepishly I hung down my head, when she snatched from before me the paper (on which I had made no farther progress than "My dear ant"), angrily exclaiming, "What, child! have you been shut up here three hours to call your aunt a pismire ?" From that hour of humiliation I have too often groaned under the endurance of similar penance, and I have learned from my own sufferings to compassionate those of my dear sisters in affliction. To such unhappy persons, then, I would fain offer a few hints (the fruit of long experience), which, if they have not already been suggested by their own observation, may prove serviceable in the hour of emergency.

10. Let them—or suppose I address myself to *one* particu

far sufferer; there is something more confidential in that manner of communicating one's ideas. As Moore says, "Heart
speaks to heart." I say, then, take always special care to
write by candlelight, for not only is the apparently unimport
ant operation of snuffing the candle in itself a momentary relief to the depressing consciousness of mental vacuum, but not
unfrequently that trifling act, or the brightening flame of the
taper, elicits, as it were, from the dull embers of fancy, a sym-
pathetic spark of fortunate conception. When such a one
occurs, seize it quickly and dexterously, but, at the same time,
with such cautious prudence, as not to huddle up and contract
in one short, paltry sentence, that which, if ingeniously handled, may be wiredrawn, so as to undulate gracefully and
smoothly over a whole page.

11. For the more ready practice of this invaluable art of
dilating, it will be expedient to stock your memory with a
large assortment of those precious words of many syllables,
that fill whole lines at once; "incomprehensibly, amazingly,
decidedly, solicitously, inconceivably, incontrovertibly." An
opportunity of using these, is, to a distressed spinster, as delightful as a copy all m's and n's to a child. "Command you
may, your mind from play." They run on with such delicious
smoothness!

------◆------

136. The Art of Book-Keeping.

THOMAS HOOD.

THOMAS HOOD, born in 1798; died, 1845. One of the best of the later
English humorists. His poetry is indeed characterized by the true marks
of genuine humor, which is ever based on real pathos and refined sensibility.

1. How hard, when those who do not wish to lend, thus lose,
    their books,
  Are snared by anglers,—folks that fish with literary
    Hooks,—
  Who call and take some favorite tome, but never read it
    through;—
  They thus complete their set at home, by making one at you.

I, of my "Spenser" quite bereft, last winter sore was
    shaken:
Of "Lamb" I've but a quarter left, nor could I save my
    "Bacon;"
And then I saw my "Crabbe," at last, like Hamlet, back-
    ward go ;
And as the tide was ebbing fast, of course I lost my
    "Rowe."

2 My "Mallet" served to knock me down, which makes me
    thus a talker;
And once, when I was out of town, my "Johnson" proved
    a "Walker."
While studying, o'er the fire, one day, my "Hobbes,"
    amidst the smoke,
They bore my "Colman" clean away, and carried off my
    "Coke."

They pick'd my "Locke," to me far more than Bramah's
    patent worth,
And now my losses I deplore, without a "Home" on earth:
If once a book you let them lift, another they conceal,
For though I caught them stealing "Swift," as quickly
    went my "Steele."

3 "Hope" is not now upon my shelf, where late he stood
    elated;
But what is strange, my "Pope" himself is excommuni-
    cated.
My little "Suckling" in the grave is sunk to swell the
    ravage ;
And what was Crusoe's fate to save, 'twas mine to love,
    —a "Savage."

Even "Glover's" works I cannot put my frozen hands
    upon;
Though ever since I lost my "Foote," my "Bunyan" has
    been gone.

My "Hoyle" with "Cotton" went oppress'd; my Tay-
    lor," too, must fail;
To save my "Goldsmith" from arrest, in vain I offer'd
    "Bayle."

4 1 "Prior" sought, but could not see the "Hood" so late
    in front;
And when I turned to hunt for "Lee," oh! where was my
    "Leigh Hunt"?
I tried to laugh, old care to tickle, yet could not "Tickle"
    touch;
And then, alack! I miss'd my "Mickle,"—and surely Mic-
    kle's much.

'Tis quite enough my griefs to feed, my sorrows to excuse,
To think I cannot read my "Reid," nor even use my
    "Hughes;"
My classics would not quiet lie, a thing so fondly hoped;
Like Dr. Primrose, I may cry, my "Livy" has eloped.

b. My life is ebbing fast away; I suffer from these shocks,
And though I fixed a lock on "Gray," there's gray upon
    my locks;
I'm far from "Young," am growing pale, I see my "But-
    ler" fly;
And when they ask about my ail, 'tis "Burton" I reply.

They still have made me slight returns, and thus my griefs
    divide;
For oh! they cured me of my "Burns," and eased my
    "Akenside."
But all I think I shall not say, nor let my anger burn,
For, as they never found me "Gay," they have not left
    me "Sterne."

16*

137. THE ALHAMBRA BY MOONLIGHT.

IRVING.

[The palace or castle called the Alhambra, consists of the remains of a very extensive and ancient pile of buildings in Spain, erected by the Moors when they were
rulers of the country.]

1. I HAVE given a picture of my apartment on my first taking possession of it: a few evenings have produced a thorough
change in the scene and in my feelings. The moon, which
then was invisible, has gradually gained upon the nights, and
now rolls in full splendor above the towers, pouring a flood of
tempered light into every court and hall. The garden beneath my window is gently lighted up ; the orange and cit-
ron trees are tipped with silver ; the fountain sparkles in the
moonbeams ; and even the blush of the rose is faintly visible

2. I have sat for hours at my window, inhaling the sweetness of the garden, and musing on the checkered features of
those whose history is dimly shadowed out in the elegant memorials around. Sometimes I have issued forth at midnight,
when every thing was quiet, and have wandered over the whole
building. Who can do justice to a moonlight night in such a
climate, and in such a place !

3. The temperature of an Andalusian midnight in summer,
is perfectly ethereal. We seem lifted up into a purer atmosphere : there is a serenity of soul, a buoyancy of spirits, an
elasticity of frame, that render mere *existence* enjoyment.
The effect of moonlight, too, on the Alhambra, has something
like enchantment. Every rent and chasm of time, every mouldering tint and weather-stain disappears ; the marble resumes
its original whiteness ; the long colonnades brighten in the
moonbeams ; the halls are illuminated with a softened radiance, until the whole edifice reminds one of the enchanted
palace of an Arabian tale.

4. At such a time, I have ascended to the little pavilion,
called the queen's toilet, to enjoy its varied and extensive
prospect. To the right, the snowy summits of the Sierra
Nevada would gleam, like silver clouds, against the darker
firmament and all the outlines of the mountains would be

softened, yet delicately defined. My delight, however, would
be to lean over the parapet of the Tecador, and gaze down
upon Granada, spread out like a map below me ; all buried
in deep repose, and its white palaces and convents sleeping,
as it were, in the moonshine.

5. Sometimes, I would hear the faint sounds of castanets
from some party of dancers lingering in the Alameda ; at
other times, I have heard the dubious tones of a guitar, and
the notes of a single voice rising from some solitary street,
and have pictured to myself some youthful cavalier serenading
his lady's window—a gallant custom of former days, but now
sadly on the decline, except in the remote towns and villages
of Spain.

6. Such are the scenes that have detained me for many an
hour loitering about the courts and balconies of the castle,
enjoying that mixture of reverie and sensation which steal
away existence in a southern climate, and it has been almost
morning before I have retired to my bed, and been lulled to
sleep by the falling waters of the fountain of Lindaraxa

---

188. BEST KIND OF REVENGE.
CHAMBERS.

ROBERT CHAMBERS, born in Peebles, Scotland, in 1802. He and his
brother William, have written numerous works in various departments of
literature. They are also known as eminent Scotch publishers.

1. SOME years ago, a warehouseman in Manchester, England, published a scurrilous pamphlet, in which he endeavored
to hold up the house of Grant Brothers to ridicule. William
Grant remarked upon the occurrence, that the man would live
to repent what he had done ; and this was conveyed by some
tale-bearer to the libeller, who said, " Oh, I suppose he thinks
I shall some time or other be in his debt ; but I will take good
care of that." It happens, however, that a man in business
cannot always choose who shall be his creditors. The pam-
phleteer became a bankrupt, and the brothers held an accept

ance of his which had been indorsed to them by the drawer, who had also become a bankrupt.

2. The wantonly-libelled men had thus become creditors of the libeller! They had it in their power to make him repent of his audacity. He could not obtain his certificate without their signature, and without it he could not enter into business again. He had obtained the number of signatures required by the bankrupt law, except one. It seemed folly to hope that the firm of "the brothers" would supply the deficiency. What! they, who had cruelly been made the laughing-stocks of the public, forget the wrong and favor the wrong-doer? He despaired. But the claims of a wife and children forced him at last to make the application. Humbled by misery, he presented himself at the counting-house of the wronged.

3. Mr. William Grant was there alone, and his first words to the delinquent were, "Shut the door, sir!"—sternly uttered. The door was shut, and the libeller stood trembling before the libelled. He told his tale, and produced his certificate, which was instantly clutched by the injured merchant. "You wrote a pamphlet against us once!" exclaimed Mr. Grant. The supplicant expected to see his parchment thrown into the fire. But this was not its destination. Mr. Grant took a pen, and writing something upon the document, handed it back to the bankrupt. He, poor wretch, expected to see "rogue, scoundrel, libeller," inscribed, but there was, in fair round characters, the signature of the firm.

4. "We make it a rule," said Mr. Grant, "never to refuse signing the certificate of an honest tradesman, and we have never heard that you were any thing else." The tears started into the poor man's eyes. "Ah," said Mr. Grant, "my saying was true. I said you would live to repent writing that pamphlet. I did not mean it as a threat. I only meant that some day you would know us better, and be sorry you had tried to injure us. I see you repent of it now." "I do, I do!" said the grateful man. "I bitterly repent it." "Well, well, my dear fellow, you know us now. How do you get on? What are you going to do?" The poor man stated that he

had friends who could assist him when his certificate was obtained. " But how are you off in the mean time ?"

5. And the answer was, that, having given up every farthing to his creditors, he had been compelled to stint his family of even common necessaries, that he might be enabled to pay the cost of his certificate. " My dear fellow, this will not do ; your family must not suffer. Be kind enough to take this ten-pound note to your wife from me. There, there, my dear fellow! Nay, don't cry; it will be all well with you yet. Keep up your spirits, set to work like a man, and you will raise your head among us yet." The overpowered man endeavored in vain to express his thanks : the swelling in his throat forbade words. He put his handkerchief to his face, and went out of the door crying like a child.

---

139. WHO IS MY NEIGHBOR ?

ANON.

1 THY neighbor ? It is he whom thou
    Hast power to aid and bless :
  Whose aching heart and burning brow
    Thy soothing heart may press.

  Thy neighbor ? 'Tis the fainting poor,
    Whose eye with want is dim ;
  Whom hunger sends from door to door ;
    Go thou and comfort him.

2. Thy neighbor ? 'Tis that weary man,
    Whose years are at their brim,
  Bent low with sickness, cares, and pain ;
    Go thou and comfort him.

  Thy neighbor ? 'Tis the heart bereft
    Of every earthly gem ;

Widow and orphan, helpless left ;
Go thou and shelter them.

3. Thy neighbor ? Yonder toiling slave,
Fetter'd in thought and limb,
Whose hopes are all beyond the grave ;
Go thou and ransom him.

Whene'er thou meet'st a human form
Less favor'd than thine own,
Remember 'tis thy neighbor worm,
Thy brother, or thy son.

4. Oh ! pass not, pass not heedless by ;
Perhaps thou canst redeem
The breaking heart from misery ;
Go share thy lot with him.

---

140. EDWIN, KING OF NORTHUMBRIA.

LINGARD.

1. ATTENDED by Paulinus, he entered the great council, requested the advice of his faithful witan, and exposed to them the reasons which induced him to prefer Christianity to the worship of paganism. Coiffi, the high priest of Northumbria, was the first to reply. It might have been expected, that prejudice and interest would have armed him with arguments against the adoption of a foreign creed ; but his attachment to paganism had been weakened by repeated disappointments, and he had learnt to despise the gods who had neglected to reward his services.

2 That the religion which he had hitherto taught was useless, he attempted to prove from his own misfortunes ; and avowed his resolution to listen to the reasons and examine the doctrine of Paulinus. He was followed by an aged thane, whose discourse offers an interesting picture of the simplicity

of the age. "When," said he, "O king, you and your ministers are seated at table in the depth of winter, and the cheerful fire blazes on the hearth in the middle of the hall, a sparrow
perhaps, chased by the wind and snow, enters at one door of
the apartment, and escapes by the other.

3 "During the moment of its passage, it enjoys the warmth;
when it is once departed, it is seen no more. Such is the nature of man. During a few years his existence is visible ; but
what has preceded, or what will follow it, is concealed from
the view of mortals. If the new religion offers any information on subjects so mysterious and important, it must be worthy of our attention." To these reasons the other members
assented.

4. Paulinus was desired to explain the principal articles of
the Christian faith ; and the king expressed his determination
to embrace the doctrine of the missionary. When it was
asked, who would dare to profane the altars of Woden, Coiffi
accepted the dangerous office. Laying aside the emblems of
the priestly dignity, he assumed the dress of a warrior ; and
despising the prohibitions of Saxon superstition, mounted the
favorite charger of Edwin. By those who were ignorant
of his motives, his conduct was attributed to temporary in-
sanity.

5. But disregarding their clamors, he proceeded to the
nearest temple, and bidding defiance to the gods of his fathers, hurled his spear into the sacred edifice. It stuck in the
opposite wall ; and, to the surprise of the trembling spectators,
the heavens were silent, and the sacrilege was unpunished.
Insensibly they recovered their fears, and, encouraged by the
exhortations of Coiffi, burnt to the ground the temple and th
surrounding groves

141. CLEANLINESS.

ADDISON.

1. CLEANLINESS may be defined to be the emblem of purity of mind, and may be recommended under the three following .eads : as it is a mark of politeness, as it produces affection, nd as it bears analogy to chastity of sentiment. First, it is a mark of politeness, for it is universally agreed upon, that no one unadorned with this virtue, can go into company without giving a manifold offence ; the different nations of the world are as much distinguished by their cleanliness, as by their arts and sciences ; the more they are advanced in civilization, the more they consult this part of politeness.

2. Secondly, cleanliness may be said to be the foster-mother of affection. Beauty commonly produces love, but cleanliness preserves it. Age, itself, is not unamiable while it is preserved clean and unsullied; like a piece of metal constantly kept smooth and bright, we look on it with more pleasure than on a new vessel cankered with rust. I might further observe, that as cleanliness renders us agreeable to others, it makes us easy to ourselves ; that it is an excellent preservative of health ; and that several vices, both of mind and body, are inconsistent with the habit of it.

3. In the third place, it bears a great analogy with chastity of sentiment, and naturally inspires refined feelings and passions ; we find from experience, that through the prevalence of custom, the most vicious actions lose their horror by being made familiar to us. On the contrary, those who live in the neighborhood of good examples, fly from the first appearance of what is shocking : and thus pure and unsullied thoughts are naturally suggested to the mind, by those objects that perpetually encompass us when they are beautiful and elegant in heir kind.

4. In the East, where the warmth of the climate makes cleanliness more immediately necessary than in colder countries, it is a part of religion ; the Jewish law (as well as the Mohammedan, which in some things copies after it), is filled

with bathings, purifications, and other rites of the like nature ; and we read several injunctions of this kind in the Book of Deuteronomy.

---

142. THERE WERE MERRY DAYS IN ENGLAND.

J. E. CARPENTER.

*" Go call thy sons : instruct them what a debt
They owe their ancestors ; and make them swear
To pay it—by transmitting down entire
Those sacred rights to which themselves were born."*

AKENSIDE.

1. THERE were merry days in England—and a blush is on my brow,
When I think of what our land has been, and what our homes are now ;
When our peasantry and artisans were good as well as brave,
And mildly heard the blessed truths the old religion gave.

There were merry days in England when a common lot we felt,
When at one shrine, and in one faith, the peer and peasant knelt ;
A faith that link'd in holy bonds the cottage and the throne,
Before a thousand priests uprose—with each a creed—*his own !*

2 There were merry days in England, when on the village green,
The good old pastor that they loved, amid his flock was seen ;
The parish church, that, even then, had seen an earlier day,
There only, like their forefathers, the people went to pray

There *were* merry days in England—*now* mark the Sabbath day,
How many scoff the fanes wherein their good forefathers lay ;
Some "new light" glitters in their path—but let the truth be told,
And who can say he's happier now than those who lived of old !

3 There were merry days in England—ere England's direst foes
To clamor forth sedition, in their wickedness arose ;
To riot in the scenes from which, once, Britons would recoil ;
To wreck a thousand hearths and homes, and—fatten on the spoil !

There were merry days in England—ere those traitors snapp'd the chord—
The bond of faith and truth that bound the poor man to the lord ;
When the people loved their rulers, their religion, and their laws,
And the welfare of the nation was to all a sacred cause.

4 There were merry days in England—there were joys we never knew,
Ere our poor men were so many, and our rich men were so few ;
When by honor and integrity our sires would stand o fall—
Before the great King MAMMON was the king that govern' all !

148. MEMORY AND HOPE.

PAULDING.

JAMES KIRKE PAULDING, born at Pawlings, on the Hudson, in 1779. Pauld-ing's writings are voluminous, and many of them of great interest. The best known, are " The Dutchman's Fireside," and " Westward Ho!"

1. HOPE is the leading-string of youth; memory the staff o, age. Yet, for a long time they were at variance, and scarcely ever associated together. Memory was almost always grave, nay, sad and melancholy. She delighted in silence and repose, amid rocks and waterfalls ; and whenever she raised her eyes from the ground, it was only to look back over her shoulder. Hope was a smiling, dancing, rosy boy, with sparkling eyes, and it was impossible to look upon him without being inspired by his gay and sprightly buoyancy. Wherever he went, he diffused gladness and joy around him ; the eyes of the young sparkled brighter than ever at his approach ; old age, as it cast its dim glances at the blue vault of heaven, seemed in-spired with new vigor ; the flowers looked more gay, the grass more green, the birds sung more cheerily, and all nature seemed to sympathize in his gladness. Memory was of mortal birth, but Hope partook of immortality.

2. One day they chanced to meet, and Memory reproached Hope with being a deceiver. She charged him with deluding mankind with visionary, impracticable schemes, and exciting expectations that led only to disappointment and regret; with being the *ignis fatuus* of youth, and the scourge of old age. But Hope cast back upon her the charge of deceit, and main-tained that the pictures of the past were as much exaggerated by Memory, as were the anticipations of Hope. He declared that she looked at objects at a great distance in the past, h in the future, and that this distance magnified every thing " Let us make the circuit of the world," said he, " and try the experiment." Memory reluctantly consented, and they went their way together.

3. The first person they met was a school-boy, lounging lazily along, and stopping every moment to gaze around, as if unwilling to proceed on his way. By and by, he sat down,

and burst into tears. "Whither so *fast*, my good lad?" asked Hope, jeeringly. "I am going to school," replied the lad, "to study, when I would rather, a thousand times, be at play; and sit on a bench with a book in my hand, while I long to be sporting in the fields. But never mind, I shall be a man soon, and then I shall be as free as the air." Saying this, he skipped away merrily in the hope of soon being a man. 'It is thus you play upon the inexperience of youth," said Memory, reproachfully.

4. Passing onward, they met a beautiful girl, pacing slowly and with a melancholy air, behind a party of gay young men and maidens, who walked arm in arm with each other, and were flirting and exchanging all those little harmless courtesies which nature prompts on such occasions. They were all gayly dressed in silks and ribbons; but the little girl had on a simple frock, a homely apron, and clumsy, thick-soled shoes. "Why do you not join yonder group," asked Hope, "and partake in their gayety, my pretty little girl?" "Alas!" replied she, "they take no notice of me. They call me a child. But I shall soon be a woman, and then I shall be so happy!" Inspired by this hope, she quickened her pace, and soon was seen dancing along merrily with the rest.

5. In this manner they wended their way from nation to nation, and clime to clime, until they had made the circuit of the universe. Wherever they came they found the human race, who, at this time, were all young (it being not many years since the first creation of mankind), repining at the present, and looking forward to a riper age for happiness. All anticipated some future good, and Memory had scarce any thing to do but cast looks of reproach at her young companion.

6. "Let us return home," said she, "to that delightful spot where I first drew my breath. I long to repose among its beautiful bowers; to listen to the brooks that murmured a thousand times more musically; to the birds that sung a thousand times more sweetly; and to the echoes that were softer than any I have since heard. Ah! there is nothing on earth so enchanting as the scenes of my early youth!" Hope

indulged himself in a sly, significant smile, and they proceeded on their return home.

7. As they journeyed but slowly, many years elapsed ere they approached the spot from which they had departed. It so happened one day, that they met an old man, bending un der the weight of years, and walking with trembling steps leaning on his staff. Memory at once recognized him as the youth they had seen going to school, on their first onset in the tour of the world. As they came nearer, the old man re clined on his staff, and looking at Hope, who, being immortal, was still a blithe, young boy, sighed, as if his heart was break ing. "What aileth thee, old man?" asked the youth. "What aileth me?" he replied, in a feeble, faltering voice. "What should ail me, but old age? I have outlived my health and strength; I have survived all that was near and dear; I have seen all that I loved, or that loved me, struck down to the earth like dead leaves in autumn; and now I stand like an old tree, withering, alone in the world, without roots, without branches, and without verdure. I have only just enough of sensation to know that I am miserable, and the recollection of the happiness of my youthful days, when, careless and full of blissful anticipations, I was a laughing, merry boy, only adds to the miseries I now endure."

8. "Behold!" said Memory, "the consequence of thy de ceptions," and she looked reproachfully at her companion. "Behold!" replied Hope, "the deception practised by thyself. Thou persuadest him that he was happy in his youth. Dost thou remember the boy we met when we first set out to gether, who was weeping on his way to school, and sighed to be a man?" Memory cast down her eyes, and was silent.

9. A little way onward they came to a miserable cottage at the door of which was an aged woman, meanly clad, and shaking with palsy. She sat all alone, her head resting on her bosom, and, as the pair approached, vainly tried to raise it up to look at them. "Good-morrow, old lady, and all happiness to you," cried Hope, gayly, and the old woman thought it was a long time since she had heard such a cheering saluta tion. "Happiness!" said she, in a voice that quivered with

weakness and infirmity. "Happiness! I have not known it since I was a little girl, without care or sorrow. Oh, I remember those delightful days, when I thought of nothing but the present moment, nor cared for the future or the past. When I laughed, and played, and sung, from morning till night, and envied no one, and wished to be no other than I was. But those happy times are passed, never to return. Oh, could I but once more return to the days of my childhood!" The old woman sunk back on her seat, and the tears flowed from her hollow eyes. Memory again reproached her companion, but he only asked her if she recollected the little girl they had met a long time ago, who was so miserable because she was so young? Memory knew it well enough, and said not another word.

10. They now approached their home, and Memory was on tiptoe with the thought of once more enjoying the unequalled beauties of those scenes from which she had been so long separated. But, some how or other, it seemed that they were sadly changed. Neither the grass was so green, the flowers so sweet and lovely, nor did the brooks murmur, the echoes answer, nor the birds sing half so enchantingly, as she remembered them in time past. "Alas!" she exclaimed, "how changed is every thing! I alone am the same!" "Every thing is the same, and thou alone art changed," answered Hope. "Thou hast deceived thyself in the past, just as much as I deceive others in the future."

11. "What are you disputing about?" asked an old man, whom they had not observed before, though he was standing close by them. "I have lived almost fourscore and ten years, and my experience may, perhaps, enable me to decide between you." They told him the occasion of their disagreement, and related the history of their journey round the earth. The old man smiled, and, for a few moments, sat buried in thought. He then said to them : "I, too, have lived to see all the hopes of my youth turn into shadows, clouds, and darkness, and vanish into nothing. I, too, have survived my fortune, my friends, my children; the hilarity of youth, and the blessing of health." "And dost thou not despair?" said Memory. "No,

I have still one hope left me."   "And what is that?"   "The hope of heaven!"

12 Memory turned towards Hope, threw herself into his arms, which opened to receive her, and, bursting into tears, exclaimed: "Forgive me, I have done thee injustice.   Let us never again separate from each other."   "With all my heart,' said Hope, and they continued forever after to travel together, hand in hand, through the world.

---

144. LOVE OF COUNTRY.

SCOTT.

1 BREATHES there the man, with soul so dead,
Who never to himself hath said,
   "This is my own, my native land!"
Whose heart has ne'er within him burn'd,
As home his footsteps he hath turn'd,
   From wandering on a foreign strand?
If such there breathe, go, mark him well;
For him no minstrel raptures swell:

    *   *   *   *   *

2. High though his titles, proud his name,
Boundless his wealth as wish can claim;
Despite those titles, power, and pelf,
The wretch, concentred all in self,
Living, shall forfeit fair renown;
And, doubly dying, shall go down
To the vile dust from which he sprung,
Unwept, unhonor'd, and unsung.

3 O Caledonia! stern and wild,
Meet nurse for a poetic child
Land of brown heath and shaggy wood
Land of the mountain and the flood.

Land of my sires; what mortal hand
Can e'er untie the filial band,
That knits me to thy ragged strand !

---

145. THE CHARMED SERPENT.

CHATEAUBRIAND.

FRANÇOIS AUGUSTE, VICOMTE DE CHATEAUBRIAND, born at St. Malo, France, in 1768; died in 1848. The name of Chateaubriand is one of those of which France will ever be justly proud. His writings are among the first of the modern French classics, and belong to a period which may be called the Christian Revival in France. His greatest works are the "Genius of Christianity," and "The Martyrs." Among his other literary achievements, Chateaubriand translated Milton's "Paradise Lost," into French.

1. ONE day, while we were encamped in a spacious plain on the bank of the Genesee River, we saw a rattlesnake. There was a Canadian in our party who could play on the flute, and to divert us he advanced toward the serpent with his new species of weapon. On the approach of his enemy, the haughty reptile curls himself into a spiral line, flattens his head, inflates his cheeks, contracts his lips, displays his envenomed fangs and his bloody throat. His double tongue glows like two flames of fire; his eyes are burning coals; his body, swollen with rage, rises and falls like the bellows of a forge; his dilated skin assumes a dull and scaly appearance; and his tail, which sends forth an ominous sound, vibrates with such rapidity as to resemble a light vapor.

2. The Canadian now begins to play on his flute. The serpent starts with surprise and draws back his head. In proportion as he is struck with the magic sound, his eyes lose their fierceness, the oscillations of his tail diminish, and the noise which it emits grows weaker, and gradually dies away. The spiral folds of the charmed serpent, diverging from the perpendicular, expand, and one after the other sink to the ground in concentric circles. The tints of azure, green, white, and gold, recover their brilliancy on his quivering skin, and, slightly turning his head, he remains motionless in the attitude of attention and pleasure

3. At this moment the Canadian advanced a few steps, producing with his flute sweet and simple notes. The reptile immediately lowers his variegated neck, opens a passage with his head through the slender grass, and begins to creep after the musician, halting when he halts, and again following him when he resumes his march. In this way he was led beyond the limits of our camp, attended by a great number of spectators, both savages and Europeans, who could scarcely believe their eyes. After witnessing this wonderful effect of melody, the assembly unanimously decided that the marvellous serpent should be permitted to escape.

146. Two Views of Nature.

CHATEAUBRIAND.

1. WE often rose at midnight and sat down upon deck, where we found only the officer of the watch and a few sailors silently smoking their pipes. No noise was heard, save the dashing of the prow through the billows, while sparks of fire ran with a white foam along the sides of the vessel. God of Christians! it is on the waters of the abyss and on the vast expanse of the heavens that thou hast particularly engraven the characters of thy omnipotence! Millions of stars sparkling in the azure of the celestial dome—the moon in the midst of the firmament—a sea unbounded by any shore—infinitude in the skies and on the waves—proclaim with most impressive effect the power of thy arm! Never did thy greatness strike me with profounder awe than in those nights, when, suspended between the stars and the ocean, I beheld immensity over my head and immensity beneath my feet!

2. I am nothing; I am only a simple, solitary wanderer, and often have I heard men of science disputing on the subject of a Supreme Being, without understanding them; but I have invariably remarked, that it is in the prospect of the sublime scenes of nature that this unknown Being manifests himself to the human heart. One evening, after we had reached the

17

beautiful waters that bathe the shores of Virginia, there was a profound calm, and every sail was furled. I was engaged below, when I heard the bell that summoned the crew to prayers. I hastened to mingle my supplications with those of my travelling companions. The officers of the ship were on the quarter-deck with the passengers, while the chaplain, with book in his hand, was stationed at a little distance before hem ; the seamen were scattered at random over the poop, we were all standing, our faces toward the prow of the vessel, which was turned to the west.

3. The solar orb, about to sink beneath the waves, was seen through the rigging, in the midst of boundless space; and, from the motion of the stern, it appeared as if it changed its horizon every moment. A few clouds wandered confusedly in the east, where the moon was slowly rising. The rest of the sky was serene ; and toward the north, a water-spout, forming a glorious triangle with the luminaries of day and night, and glistening with all the colors of the prism, rose from the sea, like a column of crystal supporting the vault of heaven.

4. He had been well deserving of pity who would not have recognized in this prospect the beauty of God. When my companions, doffing their tarpaulin hats, entoned with hoarse voice their simple hymn to Our Lady of Good Help, the patroness of the seas, the tears flowed from my eyes in spite of myself. How affecting was the prayer of those men, who, from a frail plank in the midst of the ocean, contemplated the sun setting behind the waves !

5. How the appeal of the poor sailor to the Mother of Sorrows went to the heart ! The consciousness of our insignificance in the presence of the Infinite,—our hymns, resounding to a distance over the silent waves,—the night approaching with its dangers,—our vessel, itself a wonder among so many wonders, a religious crew, penetrated with admiration and with awe,—a venerable priest in prayer,—the Almighty bending over the abyss, with one hand staying the sun in the west, with the other raising the moon in the east, and lending, through all immensity, an attentive ear to the feeble voice of

his creatures,—all this constituted a scene which no power of art can represent, and which it is scarcely possible for the heart of man to feel.

6. Let us now pass to the terrestrial scene.

I had wandered one evening in the woods, at some distance from the cataract of Niagara, when soon the last glimmering of daylight disappeared, and I enjoyed, in all its loneliness, the beauteous prospect of night amid the deserts of the New World.

7. An hour after sunset, the moon appeared above the trees in the opposite part of the heavens. A balmy breeze, which the queen of night had brought with her from the east, seemed to precede her in the forests, like her perfumed breath. The lonely luminary slowly ascended in the firmament, now peacefully pursuing her azure course, and now reposing on groups of clouds which resembled the summits of lofty, snow-covered mountains. These clouds, by the contraction and expansion of their vapory forms, rolled themselves into transparent zones of white satin, scattering in airy masses of foam, or forming in the heavens brilliant beds of down so lovely to the eye that you would have imagined you felt their softness and elasticity.

8. The scenery on the earth was not less enchanting: the soft and bluish beams of the moon darted through the inter-vals between the trees, and threw streams of light into the midst of the most profound darkness. The river that glided at my feet was now lost in the wood, and now reappearing, glistening with the constellations of night, which were reflected on its bosom. In a vast plain beyond this stream, the radiance of the moon reposed quietly on the verdure.

9. Birch-trees, scattered here and there in the savanna, and agitated by the breeze, formed shadowy islands which floated on a motionless sea of light. Near me, all was silence and repose, save the fall of some leaf, the transient rustling of a sudden breath of wind, or the hooting of the owl; but at a distance was heard, at intervals, the solemn roar of the Falls of Niagara, which in the stillness of the night, was prolonged from desert to desert, and died away among the solitary forests.

10. The grandeur, the astonishing solemnity of the scene, cannot be expressed in language; nor can the most delightful sights of Europe afford any idea of it. In vain does imagination attempt to soar in our cultivated fields; it everywhere meets with the habitations of men: but in those wild regions the mind loves to penetrate into an ocean of forests, to hover round the abysses of cataracts, to meditate on the banks of lakes and rivers, and, as it were, to find itself alone with God.

---

147. THE HOLY WELLS OF IRELAND.

FRASER.

JOHN FRASER, more generally known by his *nom de plume*, "J. De Jean," was born near Birr, in King's county, on the banks of the river Broana, and died in Dublin in 1849, about 40 years of age. He was an artisan—a cabinet-maker; a steady and unassuming workman,—enjoying the respect of his fellow-workmen, and the friendship of those to whom he was known by his literary and poetic talents. He possessed much mental power,—and had his means permitted him to cultivate and refine his poetic mind, he would have occupied a higher position as a poet than is now allotted him. As it is, he has clothed noble thoughts in terse and harmonious language: in his descriptive ballads he depicts, in vivid colors, the scenery of his native district, with all the natural fondness of one describing scenes hallowed by memories of childhood and maturer years.

1. THE holy wells—the living wells—the cool, the fresh, the pure—
   A thousand ages roll'd away, and still those founts endure,
   As full and sparkling as they flow'd, ere slave or tyrant trod
   The emerald garden set apart for Irishmen by God!
   And while their stainless chastity and lasting life have birth,
   Amid the oozy cells and caves of gross, material earth,
   The scripture of creation holds no fairer type than they—
   That an immortal spirit can be link'd with human clay!

2. How sweet, of old, the bubbling gush—no less to antlered race,
   Than to the hunter, and the hound, that smote them in the chase!

In forest depths the water-fount beguiled the Druid's love,
From that celestial fount of fire which warm'd from worlds
  above ;
Inspired apostles took it for a centre to the ring,
When sprinkling round baptismal life—salvation—from the
  spring ;
And in the sylvan solitude, or lonely mountain cave,
Beside it pass'd the hermit's life, as stainless as its wave.

3 The cottage hearth, the convent wall, the battlemented
     tower,
   Grew up around the crystal springs, as well as flag and
     flower ;
   The brooklime and the water-cress were evidence of health,
   Abiding in those basins, free to poverty and wealth :
   The city sent pale sufferers there the faded brow to dip,
   And woo the water to depose some bloom upon the lip ;
   The wounded warrior dragged him towards the unforgotten
     tide,
   And deemed the draught a heavenlier gift than triumph to
     his side.

4. The stag, the hunter, and the hound, the Druid and the
     saint,
   And anchorite are gone, and even the lineaments grown
     faint,
   Of those old ruins, into which, for monuments had sunk
   The glorious homes that held, like shrines, the monarch and
     the monk ;
   So far into the heights of God the mind of man has ranged,
   It learn'd a lore to change the earth—its very self it
     changed
   To some more bright intelligence ; yet still the springs en-
     dure,
   The same fresh fountains, but become more precious to the
     poor !

5 For knowledge has abused its powers, an empire to erect

For tyrants, on the rights the poor had given them to pro-
    tect ;
Till now the simple elements of nature are their *all*,
That from the cabin is not filch'd, and lavish'd in the hall—
And while night, noon, or morning meal no other plenty
    brings,
Nc beverage than the water draught from old, spontaneous
    springs,
They, sure, may deem them holy wells, that yield, from day
    to day,
One blessing which no tyrant hand can taint, or take away

---

148. WANTS.

PAULDING.

1. EVERYBODY, young and old, children and graybeards, has
heard of the renowned Haroun Al Raschid, the hero of Eastern history and Eastern romance, and the most illustrious of
the caliphs of Bagdad, that famous city on which the light of
learning and science shone, long ere it dawned on the benight-
ed regions of Europe, which has since succeeded to the diadem
that once glittered on the brow of Asia.   Though as the successor of the Prophet he exercised a despotic sway over the
lives and fortunes of his subjects, yet did he not, like the Eastern despots of more modern times, shut himself up within the
walls of his palace, hearing nothing but the adulation of his
dependants ; seeing nothing but the shadows which surrounded
him ; and knowing nothing but what he received through the
medium of interested deception or malignant falsehood.

2. That he might see with his own eyes, and hear with his
own ears, he was accustomed to go about through the streets
of Bagdad by night, in disguise, accompanied by Giafer the
Barmecide, his grand vizier, and Mesrour, his executioner ; one
to give him his counsel, the other to fulfil his commands
promptly, on all occasions.   If he saw any commotion among
the people, he mixed with them and learned its cause ; and if

m passing a house he heard the moanings of distress, or the complaints of suffering, he entered, for the purpose of administering relief. Thus he made himself acquainted with the condition of his subjects, and often heard those salutary truths which never reached his ears through the walls of his palace, or from the lips of the slaves that surrounded him.

3. On one of these occasions, as Al Raschid was thus perambulating the streets at night, in disguise, accompanied by his vizier and his executioner, in passing a splendid mansion he overheard, through the lattice of a window, the complaints of some one who seemed in the deepest distress, and silently approaching, looked into an apartment exhibiting all the signs of wealth and luxury. On a sofa of satin embroidered with gold, and sparkling with brilliant gems, he beheld a man richly dressed, in whom he recognized his favorite boon companion Bedreddin, on whom he had showered wealth and honors with more than Eastern prodigality. He was stretched out on the sofa, slapping his forehead, tearing his beard, and moaning piteously, as if in the extremity of suffering. At length, starting up on his feet, he exclaimed in tones of despair, "O Allah! I beseech thee to relieve me from my misery, and take away my life !"

4. The Commander of the Faithful, who loved Bedreddin, pitied his sorrows, and being desirous to know their cause, that he might relieve them, knocked at the door, which was opened by a black slave, who, on being informed that they were strangers in want of food and rest, at once admitted them, and informed his master, who called them into his presence and bade them welcome. A plentiful feast was spread before them, at which the master of the house sat down with his guests, but of which he did not partake, but looked on, sighing bitterly all the while.

5. The Commander of the Faithful at length ventured to ask him what caused his distress, and why he refrained from partaking in the feast with his guests, in proof that they were welcome. "Hath Allah afflicted thee with disease, that thou canst not enjoy the blessings he has bestowed ? Thou art surrounded by all the splendor that wealth can procure ; thy

dwelling is a palace, and its apartments are adorned with all the luxuries which captivate the eye, or administer to the gratification of the senses. Why is it then, O my brother, that thou art miserable ?"

6. "True, O stranger !" replied Bedreddin. "I have all these. I have health of body ; I am rich enough to purchase ll that wealth can bestow, and if I required more wealth and honors, I am the favorite companion of the Commander of the Faithful, on whose head lie the blessings of Allah, and of whom I have only to ask, to obtain all I desire, save one thing only."

7. "And what is that ?" asked the caliph. "Alas ! I adore the beautiful Zuleima, whose face is like the full moon, whose eyes are brighter and softer than those of the gazelle, and whose mouth is like the seal of Solomon. But she loves another, and all my wealth and honors are as nothing The want of one thing renders the possession of every other of no value. I am the most wretched of men ; my life is a burden, and my death would be a blessing."

8. "By the beard of the Prophet," cried the caliph, "I swear thy case is a hard one. But Allah is great and power-ful, and will, I trust, either deliver thee from thy burden, or give thee strength to bear it." Then thanking Bedreddin for his hospitality, the Commander of the Faithful departed with his companions.

---

149. WANTS—continued.

1. TAKING their way toward that part of the city inhabited by the poorer classes of people, the caliph stumbled over something, in the obscurity of night, and was nigh falling to the ground: at the same moment a voice cried out, " Allah, preserve me ! Am I not wretched enough already, that I must be trodden under foot by a wandering beggar like my-self, in the darkness of night !"

2. Mezrour the executioner, indignant at this insult to the Commander of the Faithful, was preparing to cut off his head,

when Al Raschid interposed, and inquired of the beggar his name, and why he was there sleeping in the streets at that hour of the night.

"Mashallah," replied he, "I sleep in the street because I have nowhere else to sleep ; and if I lie on a satin sofa, my pains and infirmities would rob me of rest. Whether on divans of silk, or in the dirt, all one to me, for neither by day nor by night do I know any rest. If I close my eyes for a moment, my dreams are of nothing but feasting, and I awake only to feel more bitterly the pangs of hunger and disease."

3. "Hast thou no home to shelter thee, no friends or kindred to relieve thy necessities, or administer to thy infirmities ?"

"No," replied the beggar; "my house was consumed by fire; my kindred are all dead, and my friends have deserted me. Alas ! stranger, I am in want of every thing—health, food, clothing, home, kindred, and friends. I am the most wretched of mankind, and death alone can relieve me."

4. "Of one thing, at least, I can relieve thee," said the caliph, giving him his purse. "Go and provide thyself food and shelter, and may Allah restore thy health."

The beggar took the purse, but instead of calling down blessings on the head of his benefactor, exclaimed, "Of what use is money? it cannot cure disease;" and the caliph again went on his way with Giafer his vizier, and Mesrour his executioner.

5. Passing from the abodes of want and misery, they at length reached a splendid palace, and seeing lights glimmering from the windows, the caliph approached, and looking through the silken curtains, beheld a man walking backward and forward, with languid step, as if oppressed with a load of cares. At length, casting himself down on a sofa, he stretched out his limbs, and yawning desperately, exclaimed, "O Allah ! what shall I do ! what will become of me ! I am weary of life ; it is nothing but a cheat, promising what it never purposes, and affording only hopes that end in disappointment, or, if realized, only in disgust."

6. The curiosity of the caliph being awakened to know the

cause of his despair, he ordered Mesrour to knock at the door; which being opened, they pleaded the privilege of strangers to enter for rest and refreshments. Again, in accordance with the precepts of the Koran and the customs of the East, the strangers were admitted to the presence of the lord of the palace, who received them with welcome, and directed refreshments to be brought. But though he treated his guests with kindness, he neither sat down with them, nor asked any questions, nor joined in their discourse, walking back and forth languidly, and seeming oppressed with a heavy burden of sorrows.

7. At length the caliph approached him reverently, and said: "Thou seemest sorrowful, O my brother! If thy suffering is of the body, I am a physician, and peradventure can afford thee relief; for I have travelled into distant lands, and collected very choice remedies for human infirmity."

"My sufferings are not of the body, but of the mind," answered the other.

"Hast thou lost the beloved of thy heart, the friend of thy bosom, or been disappointed in the attainment of that on which thou hast rested all thy hopes of happiness?"

8. "Alas! no. I have been disappointed, not in the means, but in the attainment of happiness. I want nothing but a want. I am cursed with the gratification of all my wishes, and the fruition of all my hopes. I have wasted my life in the acquisition of riches that only awakened new desires, and honors that no longer gratify my pride or repay me for the labor of sustaining them. I have been cheated in the pursuit of pleasures that weary me in the enjoyment, and am perishing for lack of the excitement of some new want. I have every thing I wish, yet enjoy nothing."

9. "Thy case is beyond my skill," replied the caliph; and the man cursed with the fruition of all his desires turned his back on him in despair. The caliph, after thanking him for his hospitality, departed with his companions, and when they had reached the street, exclaimed—

"Allah, preserve me! I will no longer fatigue myself in a vain pursuit, for it is impossible to confer happiness on such a perverse generation. I see it is all the same, whether a man wants one thing, every thing, or nothing. Let us go home and sleep."

---

150. VESUVIUS AND THE BAY OF NAPLES.

HASKINS.

REV. GEORGE FOXCROFT HASKINS, Rector of the House of the Angel Guardian, Boston. Mr. Haskins is a native of New England, and a convert to the Catholic faith. To his piety and zeal the Catholics of Boston are indebted for that truly valuable asylum for boys, the House of the Angel Guardian. His "Travels in England, France, Italy, and Ireland," is a pleasing and well-written volume, furnishing some interesting views of men and things in the countries visited by him.

1. ONE of our first promenades, after our arrival in Naples, was along the quay, in order to catch a distant view of Mount Vesuvius. There it was in all its grandeur, vomiting forth that eternal column of smoke; and as I stood contemplating it, I remembered well the feelings with which, many and many a time while I was a boy, I had read and heard of that same Vesuvius, and of its dreadful eruptions, and of the destruction of Pompeii and Herculaneum, and had in imagination seen the fiery floods, and the ashes, and the darkness, and felt the trembling of the earth, and fled with the terrified inhabitants.

2. Little did I then think that these eyes would ever behold that mount, or these feet stand on flags of that lava that had buried Herculaneum; yet here I was, traversing streets entirely paved with that same lava, and there, directly before me, in solemn grandeur, stood that same mountain caldron that had boiled over and ejected it. The evening was warm, and the sky serene and almost cloudless; and desirous of seeing the bay and mountain to greater advantage, we stepped into a boat, and bade the boatman row us off for one hour.

3. We glided softly over the glassy surface of the bay for that space of time, and then, having turned our boat's head towards Naples, we contemplated the scene before us with sentiments of admiration altogether indescribable. The sun was just setting in all that blaze of splendor so peculiar to an

Italian sunset. There were a few long, narrow strips of cloud above the horizon, just sufficient to catch and retain the richest of his tints.

4. The deep colorings and changing hues that melted one into the other, and cast their declining radiance on the bosom of the waters, and the peculiar transparency of the deep blue vault above, convinced me of that which before I never believed—that in an Italian sky and sunset there is something surpassingly beautiful, and such as is never witnessed elsewhere. The sunset, however, was not all. We were in the Bay of Naples, the. most magnificent in the world. Before us was that vast and beautiful city itself, numbering four hundred thousand inhabitants, forming a splendid amphitheatre. Its elegant quay, its castles, its palaces, its domes and minarets, fringed with sunset hues, afforded a spectacle of extraordinary beauty.

5. On the right, at the distance of about six miles, rose Vesuvius, the sun shining on its summit, and reddening with a fiery glow the volumes of smoke that were rolling perpendicularly from its mysterious crater. On the wide-extended plain at its foot, and within sight, lay those hapless cities that have so often and so fatally witnessed its terrible and devastating eruptions. There was Torre del Greco, that about fifty years since was completely buried with lava, and Portici, and Resini, and Torre del Annunciata. There also were Herculaneum and Pompeii, whose sad history is but too well known to all.

6. On the left rose the craggy promontory of Pausilippo, and farther distant that of Miseno, and the towns of Pozzuoli and Baia. There were also in view the islands of Ischia and Procida, and Capri and Nisida. All was classic ground, and each spot remarkable for some heroic achievement, or venerable association of a people long since extinct. We glided homeward in silence, and the regular stroke of the oars beat time to our meditations. About an hour after sunset we landed on the quay.

151. IRELAND.

HASKINS.

1. On the evening of the 24th day of July, we took passage at Liverpool, in the steamer "Iron Duke," for Dublin, where we arrived on the morning of the 25th. It was a lovely morning : the sun was shining brightly, illumining with pencil of fire the turrets, cottages, and princely mansions on either shore, and gilding with its mysterious tints the hill of Howth on one side, and the mountains of Wicklow on the other. There is not perhaps a bay in the world, if we except that of Naples, that is so beautiful, and altogether lovely, as the bay of Dublin. It is, moreover, vast, commodious, and perfectly safe. Frigates and merchantmen of the largest size, and yachts beautiful and buoyant as swans, may ride securely on the bosom of its waters.

2. As I stood on the deck of the Iron Duke, inhaling the fragrant land-breeze that rippled the glassy surface of the bay, thoughts kept crowding and crowding upon me—thoughts which I could not banish if I would, and would not if I could. Not so much the surpassing beauties of Dublin Bay ; not the lordly hill of Howth, and the glens and mountains of Wicklow, and the distant hills and verdant vales of Meath ; not the islands, and bluffs, and friendly lighthouses along the coast ; not the villas and gardens, that grew every instant more distinct and beautiful as we bowled along ; not the sandy beach, hard and clean as tidy housewife's floor ; nor steep banks and stately promontories ; not these, I say, so much engrossed my mind, as the single, solitary fact, that I was now at last, in good glorious old Ireland.

3. Ireland, all hail ! Thou art to me no stranger Full well I know thee. I have known and honored thee from my earliest childhood. Well do I remember the delight with which I read, and the ardor with which I learned, the speeches of thy orators, statesmen, and patriots—of Burke, and Grattan, and Curran, and Sheridan, and Emmet, and Russell, and Phillips ; and how afterwards, a student in a Protes

tant college, I gloated over the works of Dean Swift, and Sterne, and Tom Moore; and sympathized with thy bravest sons, in their repeated struggles for freedom; and admired the exploits of thy warriors and men-at-arms—thy Brian Boroimhes, and Malachys, and O'Briens, and O'Neils, and Sarsfields, and McCarthys, and Fitzgeralds, and O'Reillys.

4. Never can I forget the little Irish boy, my own pupil, who, in exchange for the letters I taught *him*, first taught *me* Christianity; nor the Irish servant in my paternal mansion, who first made me acquainted with a Catholic priest—the Rev. Mr. Taylor, whose memory is venerated in Boston; nor the Irishman in my father's employ, who lent me Catholic books, and a Catholic paper, printed in Hartford, and in whose house I made the acquaintance of the late William Wiley, who afterwards became my spiritual counsellor and father, and received me into the bosom of the Catholic Church, saying to me, as the Son of God said to the paralytic, "My child, be of good cheer; thy sins are forgiven thee."

5. Solomon says, "One may be rich, though he have nothing." This is true of thee, land of Erin. Outwardly thou art in rags, poverty-stricken, famine-stricken, and bleeding under blows inflicted by legal persecutors and unfeeling butchers; but within all bright and glorious, true as the needle to the pole, faithful even unto death, awaiting the crown of life. Truly thou art a land of saints; for I do believe that no nation on earth hath sent, and doth yearly send, so many saints to heaven.

6. Thou art a vast seminary for the education of bishops, priests, and apostolic men, who go forth into all the world and proclaim the gospel to every creature. Thou art a golden immortal flower, blooming amid thorns, and sending forth thy winged seeds, on every breeze, to gladden other nations, and to plant the faith in other lands.

152. THE AMERICAN FLAG.

DRAKE.

Joseph Rodman Drake, born in New York city in 1795; died, in 1850. His longest poem, "The Culprit Fay," was not published till after his death.

1. WHEN Freedom, from her mountain height,
    Unfurl'd her standard to the air,
  She tore the azure robe of night,
    And set the stars of glory there!
  She mingled with its gorgeous dyes
  The milky baldric of the skies,
  And striped its pure, celestial white,
  With streakings of the morning light;
  Then from his mansion in the sun
  She call'd her eagle-bearer down,
  And gave into his mighty hand
  The symbol of her chosen band!

2. Majestic monarch of the cloud!
    Who rear'st aloft thy regal form,
  To hear the tempest trumping loud,
    And see the lightning lances driven,
      When strive the warriors of the storm,
  And rolls the thunder-drum of heaven!
  Child of the sun! to thee 'tis given
    To guard the banner of the free,
  To hover in the sulphur smoke,
  To ward away the battle-stroke,
  And bid its blendings shine afar,
  Like rainbows on the cloud of war—
    The harbingers of victory!

3. Flag of the brave! thy folds shall fly,
  The sign of hope and triumph high,
  When speaks the signal trumpet tone,
  And the long line comes gleaming on.

Ere yet the life-blood, warm and wet,
Has dimm'd the glistening bayonet,
Each soldier's eye shall brightly turn
To where thy meteor glories burn ;
And as his springing steps advance,
Catch war and vengeance from the glance!
And when the cannon-mouthings loud
Heave in wild wreaths the battle-shroud,
And gory sabres rise and fall   ·
Like shoots of flame on midnight's pall;
There shall thy meteor glances glow,
   And cowering foes shall sink beneath
Each gallant arm that strikes below
   That lovely messenger of death.

4. Flag of the seas! on ocean wave
Thy stars shall glitter o'er the brave,
When Death, careering on the gale,
Sweeps darkly round the bellied sail,
And frighted waves rush wildly back,
Before the broadside's reeling rack;
Each dying wanderer of the sea
Shall look at once to heaven and thee,
And smile to see thy splendors fly,
In triumph o'er his closing eye.

5. Flag of the free heart's hope and home,
   By angel hands to valor given !
Thy stars have lit the welkin dome,
   And all thy hues were born in heaven.
. Forever float that standard sheet!
   Where breathes the foe but falls before us,
With Freedom's soil beneath our feet,
   And Freedom's banner streaming o'er us !

153 ABRAHAM AND THE FIRE-WORSHIPPER.

HOUSEHOLD WORDS.

SCENE—*The inside of a Tent, in which the Patriarch* ABRA-
HAM *and a* PERSIAN TRAVELLER, *a Fire-Worshipper, are
sitting awhile after supper.*

Fire-Worshipper [aside]. What have I said, or done,
      that by degrees
Mine host hath changed his gracious countenance,
Until he stareth on me, as in wrath!
Have I, 'twixt wake and sleep, lost his wise lore?
Or sit I thus too long, and he himself
Would fain be sleeping? I will speak to that.
[*Aloud.*] Impute it, O my great and gracious lord!
Unto my feeble flesh, and not my folly,
If mine old eyelids droop against their will,
And I become as one that hath no sense
Even to the milk and honey of thy words.—
With my lord's leave, and his good servant's help,
My limbs would creep to bed.
      Abraham [angrily quitting his seat]. In this tent, never
Thou art a thankless and an impious man.
      Fire-W. [rising in astonishment]. A thankless and an
            impious man! Oh, sir,
My thanks have all but worshipp'd thee.
      Abraham.   And whom
Forgotten? like the fawning dog I feed.
From the foot-washing to the meal, and now
To this thy cramm'd and dog-like wish for bed,
I've noted thee; and never hast thou breathed
One syllable of prayer, or praise, or thanks,
To the great God who made and feedeth all.
      Fire-W. Oh, sir, the god I worship is the Fire,
The god of gods; and seeing him not here,
In any symbol, or on any shrine,

I waited till he bless'd mine eyes at morn,
Sitting in heaven.

    Abraham.   O foul idolater !
And darest thou still to breathe in Abraham's tent ?
Forth with thee, wretch; for he that made thy god,
And all thy tribe, and all the host of heaven,
The invisible and only dreadful God,
Will speak to thee this night, out in the storm,
And try thee in thy foolish god, the Fire,
Which with his fingers he makes lightnings of.
Hark to the rising of his robes, the winds,
And get thee forth, and wait him.

                    . [*A violent storm is heard rising*
    Fire-W.   What! unhoused;
And on a night like this! me, poor old man,
A hundred years of age!

    Abraham [*urging him away*]. Not reverencing
The God of ages, thou revoltest reverence.

   . *Fire-W.* Thou hadst a father;—think of his gray hair,
Houseless, and cuff'd by such a storm as this.

    Abraham. God is thy father, and thou own'st not him

    Fire-W. I have a wife, as agèd as myself,
And if she learn my death, she'll not survive it,
No, not a day; she is so used to me;
So propp'd up by her other feeble self.
I pray thee, strike us not both down.

    Abraham [*still urging him*].   God made
Husband and wife, and must be own'd of them,
Else he must needs disown them.

    Fire-W.   We have children,—
One of them, sir, a daughter, who, next week,
Will all day long be going in and out,
Upon the watch for me; she, too, a wife,
And will be soon a mother. Spare, oh, spare her!
She's a good creature, and not strong.

    Abraham.   Mine ears
Are deaf to all things but thy blasphemy,
And to the coming of the Lord and God,

Who will this night condemn thee.

    [ABRAHAM *pushes him out; and remains alone, speaking*
                             For if ever
God came at night-time forth upon the world,
'Tis now this instant.   Hark to the huge winds,
The cataracts of hail, and rocky thunder,
Splitting like quarries of the stony clouds,
Beneath the touching of the foot of God !
That was God's speaking in the heavens,—that last
And inward utterance coming by itself.
What is it shaketh thus thy servant, Lord,
Making him fear, that in some loud rebuke
To this idolater, whom thou abhorrest,
Terror will slay himself ?   Lo, the earth quakes
Beneath my feet, and God is surely here.

               [*A dead silence; and then a still small voice*
The Voice. Abraham !
    Abraham. Where art thou, Lord? and who is it that
        speaks
So sweetly in mine ear, to bid me turn
And dare to face thy presence ?
    The Voice.   Who but He
Whose mightiest utterance thou hast yet to learn ?
I was not in the whirlwind, Abraham ;
I was not in the thunder, or the earthquake;
But I am in the still small voice.
Where is the stranger whom thou tookest in ?
    Abraham. Lord, he denied thee, and I drove him forth.
    The Voice. Then didst thou do what God himself forbore
Have I, although he did deny me, borne
With his injuriousness these hundred years,
And couldst thou not endure him one sole night,
And such a night as this ?
    Abraham.   Lord ! I have sinn'd,
And will go forth, and if he be not dead,
Will call him back, and tell him of thy mercies
Both to himself and me.
    The Voice.   Behold, and learn !

[*The Voice retires while it is speaking; and a fold of the
  tent is turned back, disclosing the* FIRE-WORSHIPPER, *wh:
  is calmly sleeping, with his head on the back of a house
  lamb.*

Abraham. O loving God! the lamb itself's his pillow,
And on his forehead is a balmy dew,
And in his sleep he smileth. I meantime,
Poor and proud fool, with my presumptuous hands,
Not God's, was dealing judgments on his head,
Which God himself had cradled!—Oh, methinks
There's more in this than prophet yet hath known,
And Faith, some day, will all in Love be shown.

* * *

154. PATRIOTISM AND CHRISTIANITY.

CHATEAUBRIAND.

1. BUT it is the Christian religion that has inⁿ sted pa
triotism with its true character. This sentiment 1 d to the
commission of crime among the ancients, because it was carried to excess ; Christianity has made it one of the principal
affections in man, but not an exclusive one. It commands us
above all things to be just ; it requires us to cherish the whole
family of Adam, since we ourselves belong to it, though our
countrymen have the first claim to our attachment.

2. This morality was unknown before the coming of the Christian lawgiver, who had been unjustly accused of attempting to
extirpate the passions : God destroys not his own work. The
gospel is not the destroyer of the heart, but its regulator. It
is to our feelings what taste is to the fine arts ; it retrenches
all that is exaggerated, false, common, and trivial ; it leaves
all that is fair, and good, and true. The Christian religion,
rightly understood, is only primitive nature washed from original pollution.

3. It is when at a distance from our country that we feel
the full force of the instinct by which we are attached to it.
For want of the reality, we try to feed upon dreams ; for the

heart is expert in deception, and there is no one who has been suckled at the breast of woman but has drunk of the cup of illusion. Sometimes it is a cottage which is situated like the paternal habitation; sometimes it is a wood, a valley, a hill, on which we bestow some of the sweet appellations of our native land. Andromache gives the name of Simois to a brook. And what an affecting object is this little rill, which recalls the idea of a mighty river in her native country! Remote from the soil which gave us birth, nature appears to us diminished, and but the shadow of that which we have lost.

4. Another artifice of the love of country is to attach a great value to an object of little intrinsic worth, but which comes from our native land, and which we have brought with us into exile. The soul seems to dwell even upon the inanimate things which have shared our destiny: we remain attached to the down on which our prosperity has slumbered, and still more to the straw on which we counted the days of our adversity. The vulgar have an energetic expression, to describe that languor which oppresses the soul when away from our country. "That man," they say, "is home-sick."

5. A sickness it really is, and the only cure for it is to return. If, however, we have been absent a few years, what do we find in the place of our nativity? How few of those whom we left behind in the vigor of health are still alive! Here are tombs where once stood palaces; there rise palaces where we left tombs. The paternal field is overgrown with briers, or cultivated by the plough of a stranger; and the tree beneath which we frolicked in our boyish days has disappeared.

6. Were we asked, what are those powerful ties which bind us to the place of our nativity, we would find some difficulty in answering the question. It is, perhaps, the smile of mother, of a father, of a sister; it is, perhaps, the recollection of the old preceptor who instructed us, and of the young companions of our childhood; it is, perhaps, the care bestowed upon us by a tender nurse, by some aged *domestic*, so essential a part of the household; finally, it is something most simple, and, if you please, trivial,—a dog that barked at night in the fields, a nightingale that returned every year to

the orchard, the nest of the swallow over the window, the village clock that appeared above the trees, the churchyard yew, or the Gothic tomb. Yet these simple things demonstrate the more clearly the reality of a Providence, as they could not possibly be the source of patriotism, or of the great virtues which it begets, unless by the appointment of the Almighty himself.

155. PETER THE HERMIT.

MICHAUD.

JOSEPH FRANCOIS MICHAUD—born at Albens, in Savoy, in 1767; died, 1839. His greatest claim to the attention of posterity is his "History of the Crusades." It is, indeed, the best work yet written on that period, and is justly considered one of the greatest historical works of modern times. Robson, the English translator, has disfigured the work by notes of a partisan and illiberal character, differing entirely from the spirit of the work.

1. PETER the Hermit traversed Italy, crossed the Alps, visited all parts of France, and the greatest portion of Europe, inflaming all hearts with the same zeal that consumed his own. He travelled mounted on a mule, with a crucifix in his hand, his feet bare, his head uncovered, his body girded with a thick cord, covered with a long frock, and a hermit's hood of the coarsest stuff. The singularity of his appearance was a spectacle for the people, while the austerity of his manners, his charity, and the moral doctrines that he preached, caused him to be revered as a saint wherever he came.

2. He went from city to city, from province to province, working upon the courage of some, and upon the piety of others; sometimes haranguing from the pulpits of the churches, sometimes preaching in the high-roads or public laces. His eloquence was animated and impressive, and filled with those vehement apostrophes which produce such effects upon an uncultivated multitude. He described the profanation of the holy places, and the blood of the Christians shed in torrents in the streets of Jerusalem.

3. He invoked, by turns, Heaven, the saints, the angels,

whom he called upon to bear witness to the truth of what he told them. He apostrophized Mount Sion, the rock of Calvary, and the Mount of Olives, which he made to resound with sobs and groans. When he had exhausted speech in painting the miseries of the faithful, he showed the spectators the crucifix which he carried with him; sometimes striking his reast and wounding his flesh, sometimes shedding torrents o. ears.

4. The people followed the steps of Peter in crowds. The preacher of the holy war was received everywhere as a messenger from God. They who could touch his vestments esteemed themselves happy, and a portion of hair pulled from the mule he rode was preserved as a holy relic. At the sound of his voice, differences in families were reconciled, the poor were comforted, the debauched blushed at their errors; nothing was talked of but the virtues of the eloquent cenobite; his austerities and his miracles were described, and his discourses were repeated to those who had not heard him, and been edified by his presence.

5. He often met, in his journeys, with Christians from the East, who had been banished from their country, and wandered over Europe, subsisting on charity.. Peter the Hermit presented them to the people, as living evidences of the barbarity of the infidels; and pointing to the rags with which they were clothed, he burst into torrents of invectives against their oppressors and persecutors.

6. At the sight of these miserable wretches, the faithful felt, by turns, the most lively emotions of pity, and the fury of vengeance; all deploring in their hearts the miseries and the disgrace of Jerusalem. The people raised their voices towards heaven, to entreat God to deign to cast a look of pity upon his beloved city; some offering their riches, others heir prayers, but all promising to lay down their lives for the deliverance of the holy places.

156. THE CELTIC CROSS.

T. D. McGEE.

1. THROUGH storm, and fire, and gloom, I see it stand,
       Firm, broad, and tall—
   The Celtic Cross that marks our Fatherland,
       Amid them all !
   Druids, and Danes, and Saxons, vainly rage
       Around its base ;
   It standeth shock on shock, and age on age,
       Star of a scatter'd race.

2. O Holy Cross ! dear symbol of the dread
       Death of our Lord,
   Around thee long have slept our Martyr-dead,
       Sward over sward !
   A hundred Bishops I myself can count
       Among the slain ;
   Chiefs, Captains, rank and file, a shining mount
       Of God's ripe grain.

3. The Monarch's mace, the Puritan's claymore,
       Smote thee not down ;
   On headland steep, on mountain summit hoar
       In mart and town ;
   In Glendalough, in Ara, in Tyrone,
       We find thee still,
   Thy open arms still stretching to thine own,
       O'er town, and lough, and hill.

4. And they would tear thee out of Irish soil,
       The guilty fools !
   How Time must mock their antiquated toil
       And broken tools !
   Cranmer and Cromwell from thy grasp retired
       Baffled and thrown :
   William and Anne to sap thy site conspired—
       The rest is known !

5. Holy Saint Patrick, Father of our Faith,
        Beloved of God !
Shield thy dear Church from the impending scathe ;
        Or, if the rod
Must scourge it yet again, inspire and raise
        To emprise high,
Men like the heroic race of other days,
        Who joy'd to die !

6 Fear !   Wherefore should the Celtic people fear
        Their Church's fate ?
The day is not—the day was never near—
        Could desolate
The Destined Island, all whose seedy clay
        Is holy ground—
Its cross shall stand till that predestined day,
        When Erin's self is drown'd !

---

157. Can the Soldier be an Atheist ?

CHATEAUBRIAND.

1. WILL the soldier who marches forth to battle—that child of glory—be an atheist?   Will he who seeks an endless life consent to perish forever?   Appear upon your thundering clouds, ye countless Christian warriors, now hosts of heaven ! appear !   From your exalted abode, from the holy city, proclaim to the heroes of our day that the brave man is not wholly consigned to the tomb, and that something more o him survives than an empty name.

2. All the great generals of antiquity were remarkable for their piety.   Epaminondas, the deliverer of his country, had the character of the most religious of men ; Xenophon, that philosophic warrior, was a pattern of piety; Alexander, the everlasting model of conquerors, gave himself out to be the son of Jupiter.   Among the Romans, the ancient consuls of the republic, a Cincinnatus, a Fabius, a Papirius Cursor, a Paulus

18

Æmilius, a Scipio, placed all their reliance on the deity of the Capitol ; Pompey marched to battle imploring the divine assistance ; Cæsar pretended to be of celestial descent ; Cato, his rival, was convinced of the immortality of the soul ; Brutus, his assassin, believed in the existence of supernatural powers ; and Augustus, his successor, reigned only in the name of the gods.

3 In modern times was tha' .aliant Sicambrian, the conueror of Rome and of the ƒ` .als, an unbeliever, who, falling at the feet of a priest, laid the foundation of the empire of France? Was St. Louis, the arbiter of kings,—revered by infidels themselves,—an unbeliever? Was the valorous Du Guesclin, whose coffin was sufficient for the capture of cities, —the Chevalier Bayard, without fear and without reproach, —the old Constable de Montmorenci, who recited his beads in the camp,—were these men without religion? But, more wonderful still, was the great Turenne, whom Bossuet brought back to the bosom of the Church, an unbeliever?

4. No character is more admirable than that of the Christian hero. The people whom he defends look up to him as a father ; he protects the husbandman and the produce of his fields ; he is an angel of war sent by God to mitigate the horrors of that scourge. Cities open their gates at the mere report of his justice ; ramparts fall before his virtue ; he is beloved by the soldier, he is idolized by nations ; with the courage of the warrior he combines the charity of the gospel; his conversation is impressive and instructing ; his words are full of simplicity; you are astonished to find such gentleness in a man accustomed to live in the midst of dangers. Thus the honey is hidden under the rugged bark of an oak which has braved the tempests of ages. We may safely conclude tha' i) respect whatever is atheism profitable for the soldier

158. JAPANESE MARTYRS.

CADDELL.

CECILIA MARY CADDELL—an English authoress, who has made many graceful and interesting contributions to the Catholic literature of our day. Among others, "Tales of the Festivals," "Miner's Daughter," "Blanche Leslie," and "Missions in Japan and Paraguay."

1. SCARCELY had the exiles reached this hospitable asylum ere another edict was published in Figo, commanding all the remaining Christians to repair to the house of a bonze appointed for the purpose, and in his presence to perform a certain ceremony, which was to be considered as a declaration of their belief in his teaching. Death was to be the penalty of a refusal; and two noblemen, named John and Simon, were chosen as examples of severity to the rest. Both were friends of the governor, to whom the order had been intrusted, and he did what he could to save them.

2. "If they would but *feign* compliance with the king's decree," or "have the ceremony privately performed at their own houses," or "bribe the bonze to allow it to be supposed he had received their recantation,"—each of these alternatives was as eagerly urged as it was indignantly rejected; and when a band of ruffians dragged John to the bonze's house, and set the superstitious book which was to be the token of his apostasy by main force upon his head, he protested so loudly and vehemently against the violence done to his will, that nothing remained but to sentence him to death. The execution took place in the presence of the governor; and from the chamber, still reeking with the blood of one friend, he went to the house of the other on a similar mission, and with equal reluctance.

3. Simon was quietly conversing with his mother when the governor entered; and the latter could not refrain from weeping as he besought that lady to have pity upon them both, and, by advising compliance with the king's commands, to spare herself the anguish of losing a son, and himself that of imbruing his hands in the blood of a friend. Touching as was the appeal, it was made in vain; for in her answer the Christian mother proved true to her faith; so that the governor

left the house, indignantly declaring that by her obstinacy she was guilty of the death of her son.

4. Another nobleman entered soon afterwards, charged with the personal execution of the sentence. This was no unusual method of proceeding, since every Japanese nobleman, strange to say, may at any moment be called upon to officiate in such cases, it being a favor often granted to persons of rank to die by the hand of a friend or a servant, rather than by that of the ordinary headsman. Jotivava was a friend of Simon's, and he proceeded with what heart he might to his sad and revolting duty.

5. Knowing his errand well, Simon received him with an affectionate smile, and then prostrated himself in prayer before an image of our Saviour crowned with thorns, while his wife and mother called for warm water that he might wash,—a ceremony the Japanese always observe upon joyful occasions. Tears of natural regret would flow, indeed, even in the midst of this generous exultation; and Agnes, falling upon her knees, besought her husband to cut off her hair, as a sign that she never would marry again.

6. After a little hesitation, he complied with this request; prophesying, however, that she and his mother would soon follow him to heaven; and then, accompanied by the three *Giffiaques*, or officers of the Confraternity of Mercy, whom he had summoned to be present at the execution, they all entered the hall where it was intended to take place. Michael, one of the Giffiaques, carried a crucifix; the other two bore lighted torches; and Simon walked between his wife and mother, while his disconsolate servants brought up the rear.

7. An unhappy renegade met them at the entrance, to take leave of Simon; but struck by the contrast between his own conduct and that of the martyr, he burst into tears, and was unable to speak. Most eloquently did Simon urge him to repentance, unconsciously using almost the very words of his Divine Master, as he bade him weep, "not for his own approaching fate, but for the fell apostasy by which he, a renegade, had rendered himself guilty of hell-fire;" then, distributing his rosaries and other objects of devotion as memorials

among his friends, he refused to give to the apostate a single bead, urgently as he besought it of him, unless he would make a solemn promise of repentance and amendment.

8. The condition was at length accepted, and Simon joyfully returned to his prayers. He and his friends recited the litany ; and then, bowing before a picture of our Saviour till nis forehead touched the ground, the nobleman who acted as executioner took off his head at a single blow. It fell at the feet of one of the Giffiaques ; but his mother, with the courage of a Machabee, took it in her hands, exclaiming, "Oh, dear head, resplendent now with celestial glory ! Oh, happy Simon, who hast had the honor of dying for Him who died for thee ! My God ! Thou didst give me Thy Son ; take now this son of mine, sacrificed for the love of Thee !"

9. After the mother came poor Agnes, weeping some softer tears over the relics of her husband ; and then, foreseeing that her own death would speedily follow upon his, she and he mother betook themselves to prayer, the three Giffiaques remaining in attendance, in order to be able to assist at their execution ; and, in fact, twenty-four hours had not elapsed before it was told them they were to die ; the officer who came to acquaint them with their sentence bringing with him Magdalen, the wife of John, and Lewis, a little child whom the latter had adopted as his own, both of whom were condemned to a similar fate.

159. JAPANESE MARTYRS—*continued.*

1. WITH eager joy the prisoners embraced each other, praising, blessing, and thanking God, not only that they were to suffer for Jesus, but also that they were to suffer on a cross like Jesus ; and then, robed in their best attire, they set off for the place of execution in palanquins which the guards had provided for the purpose. The Giffiaques walked at their side ; but small need had they to offer motives for constancy to these heroic souls, burning with the desire of martyrdom,

and eager to enter the path by which their nearest and dearest had already ascended to heaven.

2. Jane, the mother of Simon, besought the executioner to bind her limbs as tightly as possible, that she might thus share the anguish which the nails inflicted upon those of Jesus ; and she preached from her cross with so much force and eloquence, that the presiding officer, fearing the effects of her words upon the people, had her stabbed without waiting for the rest of the victims. Lewis and Magdalen were tied up next. They bound the child so violently that he could not refrain from shrieking ;. but when they asked him if he was afraid to die, he said he was not ; and so they took and set him up directly opposite his mother.

3. For a brief interval, the martyr and her adopted child gazed silently on each other; then, summoning all her strength, she said, "Son, we are going to heaven : take courage, and cry, 'Jesus, Mary !' with your latest breath." And again the child replied, as he had done before when, on leaving their own home, she had made him a similar exhortation, "Mother, you shall be obeyed !" The executioner struck at him first, but missed his aim ; and more than ever fearing for his constancy, Magdalen exhorted him from her cross, while Michael, standing at its foot spoke words of comfort to him.

4. But the child needed not their urging; he did not shriek again, nor did he shrink, but waited patiently until a second blow had pierced him through and through ; and the lance, yet reeking with his blood, was directly afterwards plunged into the heart of his mother, whose sharpest pang had probably already passed on the instant when the son of her love expired before her. And now the fair and youthful Agnes alone remained, kneeling, as when she first had reached the place of execution ; for no one had yet had the courage to approach her.

5. Like the headsman of her namesake, the loveliest child of Christian story, her very executioners could only weep that they were bid to mar the beauty of any thing so fair ; their hands were powerless to do their office ; and finding at last that no one sought to bind her, she went herself and laid her

rently and modestly down upon her cross. There she lay, waiting for her hour, calm and serene as if pillowed on an angel's bosom, until at length some of the spectators, induced partly by a bribe offered by the executioner, but chiefly by a bigoted hatred of her religion, bound her, and lifted up her cross, and then struck her blow after blow, until beneath their rude and unaccustomed hands she painfully expired.

6. For a year and a day the bodies were left to hang upon their crosses, as a terror to all others of the same religion, but Christians were not wanting to watch the blackening corpses, and, with a love like that of Respha, the mother of the sons of Saul, to drive from thence the fowls of the air by day, and the beasts of the field by night ; and finally, when the period of prohibition was expired, reverently to gather the hallowed bones to their last resting-place in the church of Nangasaki.

---

160. BOYHOOD'S YEARS.

MEEHAN.

REV. CHARLES MEEHAN, a gifted Irish priest, who has contributed some valuable works to the literature of his country. His "Confederation of Kilkenny," and "History of the Geraldines," are the best known. He has also written some very good poetry scattered here and there through the Irish periodicals.

1 Ah! why should I recall them—the gay, the joyous years,
  Ere hope was cross'd or pleasure dimm'd by sorrow and by tears?
  Or why should memory love to trace youth's glad and sunlit way,
  When those who made its charms so sweet are gather'd to decay?
  The summer's sun shall come again to brighten hill and bower—
  The teeming earth its fragrance bring beneath the balmy shower—

But all in vain will memory strive, in vain we shed our
tears—
They're gone away and can't return—the friends of boyhood's years !

2. Ah! why then wake my sorrow, and bid me now come
o'er
The vanish'd friends so dearly prized—the days to come
no more—
The happy days of infancy, when no guile our bosoms
knew,
Nor reck'd we of the pleasures that with each moment
flew ?
'Tis all in vain to weep for them—the past a dream appears :
·And where are they—the loved, the young, the friends of
boyhood's years ?

3 Go seek them in the cold churchyard—they long have stol'n
to rest ;
But do not weep, for their young cheeks by woe were ne'er
oppress'd ;
Life's sun for them in splendor set—no cloud came o'er
the ray
That lit them from this gloomy world upon their joyous
way.
No tears about their graves be shed—but sweetest flowers
be flung,
The fittest offering thou canst make to hearts that perish
young—
To hearts this world has never torn with racking hopes
and fears ;
For bless'd are they who pass away in boyhood's happy
years !

161. ON THE LOOK OF A GENTLEMAN.

HAZLITT.

WILLIAM HAZLITT, born in Maidstone, Ken., England, in 1778; died in 830. As an essayist and a critic, Hazlitt holds a high place among English authors. He is especially esteemed for the philosophical spirit of his criticisms. His largest work is the "Life of Napoleon;" but his fame chiefly rests on his essays and reviews. He was also distinguished as journalist.

1. WHAT it is that constitutes the look of a gentleman is more easily felt than described. We all know it when we see it; but we do not know how to account for it, or to explain in what it consists. Ease, grace, dignity, have been given as the exponents and expressive symbols of this look; but I would rather say, that an habitual self-possession determines the appearance of a gentleman. He should have the complete command not only over his countenance, but over his limbs and motions. In other words, he should discover in his air and manner a voluntary power over his whole body, which, with every inflexion of it, should be under the control of his will.

2 It must be evident that he looks and does as he likes, without any restraint, confusion, or awkwardness. He is, in fact, master of his person, as the professor of an art or science is of a particular instrument; he directs it to what use he pleases and intends. Wherever this power and facility appear, we recognize the look and deportment of the gentleman, that is, of a person who by his habits and situation in life, and in his ordinary intercourse with society, has had little else to do than to study those movements, and that carriage of the body, which were accompanied with most satisfaction to himself, and were calculated to excite the approbation of the beholder.

3. Ease, it might be observed, is not enough; dignity is too much There must be a certain *retenu*, a conscious decorum added to the first,—and a certain "familiarity of regard, quenching the austere countenance of control," in the second, to answer to our conception of this character. Perhaps, propriety is as near a word as any to denote the manners of the

gentleman ; elegance is necessary to the fine gentleman ; dignity is proper to noblemen ; and majesty to kings !

4. Wherever this constant and decent subjection of the body to the mind is visible in the customary actions of walking, sitting, riding, standing, speaking, &c., we draw the same conclusion as to the individual—whatever may be the impediments or unavoidable defects in the machine, of which he has the management. A man may have a mean or disagreeable exterior, may halt in his gait, or have lost the use of half his limbs; and yet he may show this habitual attention to what is graceful and becoming in the use he makes of all the power he has left—in the "nice conduct" of the most unpromising and impracticable figure.

5. A humpbacked or deformed man does not necessarily look like a clown or a mechanic ; on the contrary, from his care in the adjustment of his appearance, and his desire to remedy his defects, be for the most part acquires something of the look of a gentleman. The common nickname of *My Lord*, applied to such persons, has allusion to this—to their circumspect deportment, and tacit resistance to vulgar prejudice. Lord Ogleby, in the "Clandestine Marriage," is as crazy a piece of elegance and refinement, even after he is "wound up for the day," as can well be imagined ; yet in the hands of a genuine actor, his tottering step, his twitches of the gout, his unsuccessful attempts at youth and gayety, take nothing from the nobleman.

6. He has the *ideal* model in his mind, resents his deviations from it with proper horror, recovers himself from any ungraceful action as soon as possible : does all he can with his limited means, and fails in his just pretensions not from inadvertence, but necessity. Sir Joseph Banks, who was almost bent double, retained to the last the look of a privy-counsellor. There was all the firmness and dignity that could be given by the sense of his own importance to so distorted and disabled a trunk.

7. Sir Charles Bunbury, as he saunters down St. James's street, with a large slouched hat, a lack-lustre eye and aquiline nose, an old shabby drab-colored coat, buttoned across his

breast without a cape—with old top-boots, and his hands in his waistcoat or breeches' pockets, as if he were strolling along his own garden-walks, or over the turf at Newmarket, after having made his bets secure—presents nothing very dazzling, or graceful, or dignified to the imagination; though you can tell infallibly at the first glance, or even a bowshot off, that he is a gentleman of the first water.

8. What is the clue to this mystery? It is evident that his person costs him no more trouble than an old glove. His limbs are, from long practice, left to take care of themselves; they move of their own accord; he does not strut or stand on tip-toe to show

——"how tall
His person is above them all:"——

but he seems to find his own level, and wherever he is, to slide into his place naturally; he is equally at home among lords or gamblers; nothing can discompose his fixed serenity of look and purpose; there is no mark of superciliousness about him, nor does it appear as if any thing could meet his eye to startle or throw him off his guard; he neither avoids nor courts notice; but the *archaism* of his dress may be understood to denote a lingering partiality for the costume of the last age, and something like a prescriptive contempt for the finery of this

————◆————

162. Social Characters.

CHATEAUBRIAND.

1. Those characters which we have denominated *social*, are reduced by the poet to two—the *priest* and the *soldier*. Had we not set apart the fourth division of our work for the history of the clergy and the benefits which they confer, it would be an easy task to show here how far superior, in point of variety and grandeur, is the character of the Christian priest to that of the priest of polytheism.

2. What exquisite pictures might be drawn, from the pastor of the rustic hamlet to the pontiff whose brows are encir-

cled with the papal tiara ; from the parish priest of the city
to the anchoret of the rock ; from the Carthusian and the
inmate of La Trappe to the learned Benedictine ; from the
missionary, and the multitude of religious devoted to the al-
leviation of all the ills that afflict humanity, to the inspired
prophet of ancient Sion !

3 The order of virgins is not less varied or numerous, nor
less varied in its pursuits. Those daughters of charity who
consecrate their youth and their charms to the service of the
afflicted,—those inhabitants of the cloister who, under the
protection of the altar, educate the future wives of men, while
they congratulate themselves on their own union with a heavenly spouse,—this whole innocent family is in admirable correspondence with the nine sisters of fable. Antiquity presented
nothing more to the poet than a high-priest, a sorcerer, a ves-
tal, a sibyl. These characters, moreover, were but accidentally introduced ; whereas the Christian priest is calculated to
act one of the most important parts in the epic.

4. M. de la Harpe has shown in his *Melanie* what effects
may be produced with the character of a village curate when
delineated by an able hand. Shakspeare, Richardson, Goldsmith, have brought the priest upon the stage with more or
less felicity. As to external pomp, what religion was ever accompanied with ceremonies so magnificent as ours ? Corpus
Christi day, Christmas, Holy-week, Easter, All-souls, the funeral ceremony, the Mass, and a thousand other rites, furnish
an inexhaustible subject for splendid or pathetic descriptions.

5. The modern muse that complains of Christianity cannot
certainly be acquainted with its riches. Tasso has described
a procession in the *Jerusalem*, and it is one of the finest passages in his poem In short, the ancient sacrifice itself is not
banished from the Christian subject ; for nothing is more easy
than, by means of an episode, a comparison, or a retrospective
view, to introduce a sacrifice of the ancient covenant.

163. THE INDIAN BOAT.

MOORE.

1. 'TWAS midnight dark,
   The seaman's bark
Swift o'er the waters bore him,
   When, through the night,
   He spied a light
Shoot o'er the wave before him.
"A sail! a sail!" he cries;
   "She comes from the Indian shore,
And to-night shall be our prize,
   With her freight of golden ore;
   Sail on! sail on!"
   When morning shone,
He saw the gold still clearer;
   But, though so fast
   The waves he pass'd,
That boat seem'd never the nearer.

2. Bright daylight came,
   And still the same
Rich bark before him floated;
   While on the prize
   His wistful eyes
Like any young lover's doated:
"More sail! more sail!" he cries,
   While the waves o'ertop the mast;
And while his bounding galley flies,
   Like an arrow before the blast.
   Thus on, and on,
   Till day was gone,
And the moon through heaven did hie
   He swept the main,
   But all in vain,
That boat seem'd never the nigher.

3. And many a day
   To night gave way,
And many a morn succeeded :
   While still his flight,
   Through day and night,
That restless mariner speeded.
Who knows—who knows, what seas
   He is now careering o'er ?
Behind, the eternal breeze,
   And that mocking bark, before !
      For, oh, till sky
      And earth shall die,
And their death leave none to rue it,
      That boat must flee
      O'er the boundless sea,
And that ship in vain pursue it.

---

164. DEATH OF CHARLES II. OF ENGLAND.

ROBERTSON.

1. ON Monday, the 2d of February, 1685, the king, after a feverish and restless night, rose at an early hour. Though the remedies administered to him were attended with partial success, it soon became evident that the hour of his dissolution was rapidly approaching.

2. His brother, the Duke of York, whose persecution he had sometimes weakly consented to, was in his last illness destined to be his ministering angel of consolation. James knelt down by the pillow of the sick monarch, and asked if he might send for a Catholic priest. "For God's sake do," was the king's reply; but he immediately added, "Will it not expose you to danger ?"

3. James replied, "that he cared not for the danger," and sending out a trusty messenger, shortly afterwards introduced to his majesty the Rev. Mr. Huddleston, with these words—

"Sir, this worthy man comes to save your soul." The priest threw himself on his knees, and offered to the dying monarch the aid of his ministry.

4. To his inquiries Charles replied, "that it was his desire to die in the communion of the Roman Catholic Church ; that he heartily repented of all his sins, and in particular of having deferred his reconciliation to that hour ; that he hoped for salvation from the merits of Christ his Saviour ; that he pardoned all his enemies, asked pardon of all whom he had offended, and was in peace with all men ; and that he purposed, if God should spare him, to prove the sincerity of his repentance by a thorough amendment of life."

5. The Rev. Mr. Huddleston, having heard his confession, administered to him the holy viaticum, anointed him, and retired.   About two o'clock in the night, looking on the duke, who was kneeling at his bedside and kissing his hand, the monarch called him "the best of friends and brothers, desired him to forgive the harsh treatment which he had sometimes received, and prayed that God might grant him a long and prosperous reign"—words the truest which Charles had ever spoken, uttered on the threshold of that eternity, where all dissimulation is vain.

6. At noon on the following day, the 6th of February, 1685, the monarch calmly expired.

For this singular grace of a death-bed repentance, after a life so scandalous, I have often thought that Charles was indebted to the prayers of a holy priest whom, under peculiar circumstances, he had during his exile met with in Germany. The anecdote, with your permission, I will now state.

7. A few years before the restoration, Charles was on a visit to the ecclesiastical elector of Mayence.   In the course of conversation the elector said to the prince, "There is in my arch-diocese a saintly priest, called Holzhause, possessing the gifts of prophecy and miracle, and who, many years ago, and long before the event, foretold the tragic end of your royal father, and is deeply interested in English affairs : would you like to see him?"   "By all means," replied Charles.

8. The priest was accordingly sent for, and though the

night was stormy, he traversed in a boat, at the risk of his life, the Rhine from Bingen to Mayence. Having been introduced to the English prince, the latter questioned him much as to the prophecy relative to his father's death. All that passed in this secret interview, which was prolonged far nto the night, is not known.

9. But Holzhauser declared, that on taking leave. of the prince he invited him over to England, in case he should ever be restored to the throne of his ancestors. In reply, the holy man observed, he had long burned with the desire to preach the faith in England, and that if his duty to his congregation allowed him, he would accept the invitation. Charles shook hands with him in bidding him farewell, and he in turn strongly commended to the future king the protection of his English and Irish Catholic subjects.

---

165. RELIGION AN ESSENTIAL ELEMENT IN EDUCATION.

STAFF.

VERY REV. J. A. STAFF, a German priest, and Professor of Moral Theology. From his admirable work on ' The Spirit and Scope of Education " we extract the following :

1. To educate is not merely to awaken by some means or other the dormant faculties of the soul, and to give them any training which may happen to strike the educator's fancy. To educate a child, is to rescue the rising man from the perdition entailed upon him by Adam's fall, and to render him capable of attaining his true end in this world and in the next. As a citizen of this world, he has to fit himself for the sphere of ction in which Providence intends him to move ; and as a candidate for the kingdom of heaven, with his hopes in eternity, he has to produce fruits which will last forever.

2. To imagine that it is impossible to bring up a child at once for earth and for heaven, is to betray very little knowledge of things. God himself has placed us on earth as in a preparatory school and a place of probation, and it is His

will, that while we are here we should all, in our respective
callings, contribute our best exertions towards the welfare of
the whole. For this purpose He has bestowed certain talents
upon us, of the employment of which He will one day demand
a strict account. *Matt.* xxv. 15. If we wish, then, to attain
to our true and last end, which reaches from time into eternity, we must to the best of our power finish here on earth
the task allotted to us. "What things a man shall sow,
those also shall he reap." *Gal.* vi. 8.

3. The branch of education which has earth in view is
most intimately connected with the other, which aims at
heaven. The union between them is indissoluble. What is
here advanced, would only then involve contradiction, if in
speaking of a worldly education—of an education for earth,
such an education were meant as would fit youth for purely
temporal pursuits; just as if temporal welfare were man's
only end, and he had after death nothing either to fear or to
hope for. This opinion is, alas! but too prevalent among
men. Woe to the child whose educators entertain it, and who
is thereby kept in ignorance of its own true and eternal destiny! Woe to society did this opinion become universal!

4. For man, however, to rise to an intimate union of
friendship with God, it is absolutely necessary, under any circumstances, that God should *first* descend to him, in order to
instruct and enlighten him, to strengthen and to sanctify him
by light and grace from above. This is particularly requisite
in man's present fallen state, where he is of himself only an
object of the Divine displeasure, and moreover corrupted both
in mind and body.

5. It is a task beyond the power of finite being to accomplish, to rescue him now from the grasp of sin, to dissipate
the clouds which obstruct his mental vision, to restore him to
his former health and vigor, and to deliver his captive will
from the unholy fetters of sin and egotism. Omnipotence
alone could accomplish this great work, and Omnipotence did
accomplish it. The God-man, Jesus Christ, came in loving
obedience to the will of his Eternal Father, and delivered
himself a victim for man's redemption, establishing on earth a

new institution of salvation, which is to last unto the end of time.

6. Accordingly, there is no salvation for man possible unless through Christ. *Acts* iv. 12. Hence, if education is really intended to attain the one great and true object of education; if it is intended to furnish the rising generations, as they succeed one another on earth, with the means and assistance requisite for securing to them their eternal happiness; it must necessarily be Christian. It must be thoroughly imbued with the spirit of Christianity, breathing forth the life and soul of Christ's religion into the young beings intrusted to it, and not coldly mentioning it to them, as one among other institutions worthy of notice. Unless the educator conducts his little ones to Christ,—their Redeemer as well as his own,—he will inevitably lead them astray.

7. Nay, if the spirit of religion is banished from education, education will not so much as promote man's temporal welfare. Without religion, there is not such a thing as true love of one's self, or of one's neighbor; not such a thing as firm and enduring attachment to king and to country; not such a thing as a sincere union of heart and hand for the advancement of the common weal.

8. As Christianity alone unites man to God, so it alone unites man to man; and the good fruits which it produces, as mentioned by the Apostle (*Gal.* v. 22), are "charity, joy, peace, patience, benignity, goodness, longanimity, mildness, faith, modesty, continency, chastity." The more, on the other hand, man withdraws himself from its influence, the more disastrous are the works of the flesh, enumerated by the same Apostle. *Gal.* v. 19, &c. Compare *James*, iv. 1, &c.; and these works, who can deny it, are fraught with ruin both fo. time and eternity.

9. This profanation of education, the banishment and neglect of religion, the foolish attempt to raise and ennoble fallen man by the sole instrumentality of his fellow-man, is the greatest bane of modern times. Men may, indeed, be sent forth into the world with fine esthetic feelings, and with a fund of the most varied information, but they belong also

frequently to the class which St. Paul (*Rom.* i. 29, &c.) describes as filled with all iniquity, malice, fornication, covetousness, wickedness, full of envy, ... deceit, malignity, detractors, hateful to God, contumelious, proud, haughty, inventors of evil things, disobedient to parents, foolish, dissolute, without affection, without fidelity, &c., &c.

10. "In our schools," so writes a modern author, "Paganism predominates. Christianity has been either intentionally banished, or has been allowed to disappear, through indifference and neglect; or else, where it is still retained, it is treated as a subject of secondary importance. The atmosphere of the school is wholly that of the world. To educate, is now to make youth proficient in the arts, and to fit them for money-making. That is what is called forming good citizens; as if a man could be a good citizen without being at the same time a good Christian, and as if Christianity were not the true basis and the bulwark of Christian states and their constitutions.

------◆------

166. THE IMMORTAL SOUL OF MAN.

GEORGE, LORD BYRON, born in London in 1788; died in 1824. Of all the great English poets, Byron has attained the widest popularity, with the single exception of Shakspeare. If the moral tendency of his poems were only equal to their excellence, then, indeed, we could dwell on them as masterpieces of the art of poetry, but unfortunately, the contrary is the case with most of them. Still, Byron has left behind some exquisite verses on sacred and religious subjects, one of which we here give. It is one of his beautiful Hebrew Melodies.

1. WHEN coldness wraps this suffering clay,
    Ah, whither strays the immortal mind?
It cannot die, it cannot stay,
    But leaves its darken'd dust behind.
Then, unembodied, doth it trace
    By steps each planet's heavenly way?
Or fill at once the realms of space,
    A thing of eyes, that all survey?

2. Eternal. boundless, undecay'd,
    A thought unseen, but seeing all,
All, all in earth, or skies display'd,
    Shall it survey, shall it recall :
Each fainter trace that memory holds
    So darkly of departed years,
In one broad glance the soul beholds,
    And all, that was, at once appears

3 Before creation peopled earth,
    Its eye shall roll through chaos back ;
And where the farthest heaven had birth,
    The spirit trace its rising track ;
And where the future mars or makes,
    Its glance dilate o'er all to be,
While sun is quench'd or system breaks,
    Fix'd in its own eternity.

4. Above, or love, hope, hate, or fear,
    It lives all passionless and pure ;
An age shall fleet like earthly year;
    Its years as moments shall endure.
Away, away, without a wing,
    O'er all, through all, its thoughts shall fly;
A nameless and eternal thing,
    Forgetting what it was to die.

167. Books as Sources of Self-Cultivation.

STAFF.

1. The power of embodying and perpetuating thoughts and .eelings in visible signs is assuredly one of man's most precious ornaments. By means of it, those who are now living are enabled to conjure into their presence the ancient world, as well as the most distant scenes and events of the present day, and to enjoy friendly converse with the great and wise men of

every age. They may resuscitate into renewed life within
themselves the wisest, the best, and the most noble thoughts
and feelings which ever adorned the human mind. They have
the whole treasure of the world's experience at their own
disposal, and they may still follow the mightiest souls to the
heights of scientific, intellectual, and moral pre-eminence, of
which, without them, the world might never have had an idea.

2. Reading, however, is not unaccompanied with danger
Nay, in the present state of the literary world, abounding as
it does with bad books, reading may be the source of irrepar-
able evil. Accordingly, it is an essential duty for the educator to be most careful in his choice of books for the perusal
of the youth under his charge. Let him not be led astray by
fine-sounding names, and title-pages prodigal of promises, nor
by praise lavished in newspapers and reviews. On the contrary, he ought to lay it down as a rule, never to give his
pupils a book to read until he has himself read it quite
through, and found it, upon careful examination, to be suitable for them in an intellectual, as well as in a religious and
moral point of view.

3. This is a rule from which he should never depart. There
are books written intentionally for the perusal of youth, and
so arranged that the poison is all kept up for the last few
pages, at which stage of the work it necessarily produces the
most pernicious effects, since the unwary heart of the young
reader has already contracted a friendship with the author.
Even supposing that the latter is in every respect worthy of
confidence, as a man of principle and virtue, the teacher ought
not on that account to dispense himself from the rule above
mentioned. All works are not intended for all readers, and
no one can judge so well as he what is fit for his pupils, and
what not.

4. Besides taking this care in choosing their reading-book
while they are under his immediate guidance, he should, more
over, impress upon them, with all the urgency of true affection, the necessity which there is that they should in after-life
be guided by the opinion of a well-informed and conscientious
friend, and neither read nor purchase a book of which he dis-

approves. Common prudence demands this. A library, or a
bookseller's shop, is like a market, stocked not only with good
articles of food, but also with such as are unwholesome and
poisonous. In such a market-place, no rational being would
content himself with whatever came under his hand first, and
reedily devour it; but he would, on the contrary, be very
cautious in his purchases, in order not to buy a useless or
dangerous article.

5. Among the other maladies to which human nature is
subject, there is one which may be termed a *reading mania.*
Excess in reading is injurious in many respects.

Among other writings which are not suited for the perusal of the young, those should be named which are calculated
to distract their thoughts from serious occupations, and to
awaken in their hearts an excessive tenderness of feeling.
Even supposing the contents of such works are in themselves
of an edifying nature, they are very apt to give rise to a passion for reading; and then the taste, once corrupted and accustomed to a false beauty and sweetness of style, feels disgust
for wholesome nourishment, and seeks for food in silly and
dangerous novels and romances.

6. Whoever labors under an inordinate desire of reading
and who, accordingly, reads without distinction every book
which he can procure, will unavoidably come, sooner or later
upon bad and dangerous books. The hurried and superficial
manner in which he reads is also hurtful to the mental powers.
They are thereby overloaded with food, and like the body
under similar circumstances, become languid and unhealthy.
"Not many things, but much:" such was a maxim of the ancients on this subject.

7. Read not many books, but read one book well. It matters not how much or how little is read, but what *is* read
hould be so with a constant application of the mind. It is
far better and far more profitable for the reader to study one
book, so as to comprehend it thoroughly, and to see and
feel the spirit and tendency of the writer, than to peruse a
great number of books in such a manner as to touch only the
surface.

8. This inordinate desire of reading being one of the principal distempers of the present age, the teacher should accustom his pupils to read all books slowly and with reflection, so as to be able to follow the whole train of thought, and to retain in their memory, at least the more important points and divisions of the subject. In order to do this, he should strongly dvise them not to content themselves with one perusal of a book.

9. In perusing a work for the first time, the reader is too little acquainted with the author's turn of thought, and his peculiarities of character or style. He is as a traveller passing through a foreign country for the first time. The multitude and variety of new impressions he receives are apt to form only a dim and confused mass in the mind. This, however, is not the case at a second or third perusal of the same book.

10. He has already contracted an acquaintance with the author; he knows his spirit, and his manner of expressing himself; many things, which were at first dark and unintelligible, are now plain; many, which before escaped his notice altogether, now start up before him; what was clear at first becomes now more so, and is more deeply impressed upon the memory. When there is question of works of more than ordinary importance, the trouble of a third, or even more frequent perusal, is always amply repaid.

168. MAN'S DESTINY.

STAPF.

1. MAN's destiny is immeasurably exalted. His last end God. To rise nearer and nearer to God, not as an isolated being, but hand in hand with his fellow-men, in the bonds of brotherly love, and in the position in which Providence has placed him; such is his business here on earth. Hence the great command tells him, "Thou shalt love the Lord thy God with thy whole heart, and with thy whole soul, and with thy

whole mind, and thy neighbor as thyself. On these two commandments dependeth the whole law and the prophets." *Matt.* xxii. 37, &c.

2. The great duty of parents and educators is, then, to train up their young, and yet weak fellow-creatures, to this their noble end. No natural faculty dare be destroyed. Al should be developed, but developed in such a manner as to render them directly conducive to the one end in view, which is to raise man to God.

3. At all events, none should be hinderances or obstacles to this end. Did a man speak not merely with the tongues of men, but also with those of angels, did he know all mysteries, and all knowledge, and had not charity, he were nothing. And, again, what doth it profit a man, if he gain the whole world, and suffer the loss of his own soul! 1 *Cor.* xiii. 1, &c.; *Matt.* xvi. 26.

4. Man fell, and now, in his present state of corruption, groaning, as he does at his birth, under the load of original sin, he can find salvation nowhere but in and through his Divine Redeemer, Jesus Christ. In separation from him, there is no salvation. The name of Jesus is the only name in which mortal man can be rescued from perdition. *Acts* iv. 12.

5. Accordingly, the work of true education is to conduct youth to Jesus Christ. He has a right to them. He paid for them with his blood. He has made them the temples of the Holy Spirit by baptism. He intrusts them for a short time to parents and teachers, and when he asks them back, he expects to find them well prepared for the fulfilment of his all-wise and loving intentions.

6. Hence emanates the great truth, which cannot be too often repeated, that education should be thoroughly religious and Christian in its external forms, as in its inward spirit. If it is ever to restore to life, and to adorn with fresh blossoms and with wholesome fruits, the withered tree of fallen humanity, it must itself be animated in all its branches by the living and life-giving breath of Christianity. Accordingly, active charity, flowing from a lively faith, or the filial love of God, 's been, on every occasion, during the course of this treatise,

held up as the point most worthy of notice, as being the arcanum, or great secret in education.

7. The end of education is to insure man's happiness for time and for eternity. This, however, it cannot do without religion. For without religion there is not such a thing as true love of self, or of one's neighbor; and without this love no real happiness is attainable, even on this earth, either by individuals in particular, or by society in general.

8. Well, then, may the following words of an author, lately deceased, be repeated here in conclusion: "We should merit respect by our virtue; and to our virtue we should impart worth and duration by religion. Amid all the vicissitudes of life, let it be the guiding-star in our firmament. The shades of night may lower over us, rocks may surround us, still in its blessed light we will be ever able to steer on our course in safety!" Happy the world, if both educators and educated reduced this advice to practice!

---

169. Bingen on the Rhine.

HON. MRS. NORTON.

CAROLINE ELIZABETH SARAH NORTON, a grand-daughter of the famous Richard Brinsley Sheridan, is only second to Mrs. Hemans among the female poets of our age. She has been called "the Byron of female poets," and although her poetry may not have all the wild passion that breathes in Byron's, it is characterized by a depth and intensity of feeling that raise it far above what is usually written by females.

I.

A SOLDIER of the Legion lay dying in Algiers,
There was lack of woman's nursing, there was dearth o
    woman's tears;
But a comrade stood beside him, while his life-blood ebb'd
    away,
And bent, with pitying glances, to hear what he might say.
The dying soldier falter'd, as he took that comrade's hand,
And he said, "I never more shall see my own, my native
    land;

19

Take a message, and a token, to some distant friends of mine,
For I was born at Bingen—at Bingen on the Rhine.

II.

Tell my brothers and companions, when they meet and
    crowd around
To hear my mournful story in the pleasant vineyard ground,
That we fought the battle bravely, and when the day was
    done,
Full many a corse lay ghastly pale, beneath the setting sun.
And midst the dead and dying, were some grown old in wars,
The death-wound on their gallant breasts, the last of many
    scars ;
But some were young—and suddenly beheld life's morn de-
    cline ;
And one had come from Bingen—fair Bingen on the Rhine !

III.

"Tell my mother that her other sons shall comfort her old
    age,
And I was aye a truant bird, that thought his home a cage :
For my father was a soldier, and even as a child
My heart leap'd forth to hear him tell of struggles fierce and
    wild ;
And when he died, and left us to divide his scanty hoard,
I let them take whate'er they would, but kept my father's
    sword,
And with boyish love I hung it where the bright light used
    to shine,
On the cottage-wall at Bingen—calm Bingen on the Rhine !

IV.

" Tell my sister not to weep for me, and sob with drooping
    head,
When the troops are marching home again, with glad and
    gallant tread ;

But to look upon them proudly, with a calm and steadfast
  eye,
For her brother was a soldier, too, and not afraid to die.
And if a comrade seek her love, I ask her in my name
To listen to him kindly, without regret or shame;
And to hang the old sword in its place (my father's sword
  and mine),
For the honor of old Bingen—dear Bingen on the Rhine!

V.

"There's another—not a sister; in the happy days gone by,
You'd have known her by the merriment that sparkled in her
  eye;
Too innocent for coquetry,—too fond for idle scorning,—
Oh! friend, I fear the lightest heart makes sometimes heav-
  iest mourning;
Tell her the last night of my life (for ere the moon be risen
My body will be out of pain—my soul be out of prison),
I dream'd I stood with *her*, and saw the yellow sunlight
  shine
On the vine-clad hills of Bingen—fair Bingen on the Rhine!

VI.

"I saw the blue Rhine sweep along—I heard, or seem'd to
  hear,
The German songs we used to sing, in chorus sweet and clear;
And down the pleasant river, and up the slanting hill,
The echoing chorus sounded, through the evening calm and
  still;
And her glad blue eyes were on me as we passed with friendly
  talk
Down many a path beloved of yore, and well-remember'd
  walk,
And her little hand lay lightly, confidingly in mine:
But we'll meet no more at Bingen—loved Bingen on the
  Rhine!"

VII.

His voice grew faint and hoarser—his grasp was childish
    weak,—
His eyes put on a dying look,—he sigh'd and ceased to
    speak;
His comrade bent to lift him, but the spark of life had fled,—
The soldier of the Legion, in a foreign land—was dead!
And the soft moon rose up slowly, and calmly she look'd
    down
On the red sand of the battle-field, with bloody corpses
    strown;
Yea, calmly on that dreadful scene her pale light seem'd to
    shine,
As it shone on distant Bingen—fair Bingen on the Rhine!

---

170. On Good Breeding.

ANON.

1. As learning, honor, and virtue are absolutely necessary
to gain you the esteem and admiration of mankind, politeness
and good breeding are equally necessary to make you agreeable in conversation and common life. Great talents are
above the generality of the world, who neither possess them
themselves, nor judge of them rightly in others; but all people
are judges of the smaller talents, such as civility, affability,
and an obliging, agreeable address and manner, because they
feel the effects of them, as making society easy and pleasing.

2. Good sense must, in many cases, determine good breed
ing; but there are some general rules of it that always hold
true. For example, it is extremely rude not to give proper
attention, and a civil answer, when people speak to you; or to
go away, or be doing something else, while they are speaking
to you; for that convinces them that you despise them, and
do not think it worth your while to hear or answer what they
say. It is also very rude to take the best place in a room, or
to seize immediately upon what you like at table, without

offering first to help others, as if you considered nobody but yourself. On the contrary, you should always endeavor to procure all the conveniences you can to the people you are with.

3. Besides being civil, which is absolutely necessary, the perfection of good breeding is to be civil with ease, and in a becoming manner; awkwardness can proceed but from two causes, either from not having kept good company, or from not having attended to it. Attention is absolutely necessary for improving in behavior, as, indeed, it is for every thing else. If an awkward person drinks tea or coffee, he often scalds his mouth, and lets either the cup or the saucer fall, and spills the tea or coffee on his clothes.

4. At dinner his awkwardness distinguishes itself particularly, as he has more to do. There he holds his knife, fork, and spoon differently from other people; eats with his knife, to the great danger of his lips; picks his teeth with his fork; and puts his spoon, which has been in his mouth twenty times, into the dishes again. If he is to carve, he can never hit the joint; but, in his vain efforts to cut through the bone, scatters the sauce in everybody's face. He generally daubs himself with soup and grease, though his napkin is commonly stuck through a button-hole and tickles his chin. When he drinks, he coughs in his glass, and besprinkles the company...

5. Besides all this, he has strange tricks and gestures, such as snuffing up his nose, making faces, putting his fingers in his nose, or blowing it, so as greatly to disgust the company. His hands are troublesome to him when he has not something in them; and he does not know where to put them, but keeps them in perpetual motion. All this, I own, is not in any degree criminal; but it is highly disagreeable and ridiculous in company, and ought most carefully to be guarded against by every one that desires to please.

6. There is, likewise, an awkwardness of expression and words which ought to be avoided, such as false English, bad pronunciation, old sayings, and vulgar proverbs, which are so many proofs of a poor education. For example, if, instead of saying that tastes are different, and that every man has his

own peculiar one, you should repeat a vulgar proverb, and
say that "what is one man's meat is another man's poison,"
or else, "Every one to his liking, as the good man said when
he kissed his cow," the company would be persuaded that you
had never associated with any but low persons.

7. To mistake or forget names, to speak of "What-d'ye-
call-him," or "Thingum," or "How-d'ye-call her," is exces-
sively awkward and vulgar. To begin a story or narration
when you are not perfect in it, and cannot go through with it,
but are forced, possibly, to say in the middle of it, " I have
forgotten the rest," is very unpleasant and bungling. One
must be extremely exact, clear, and perspicuous in every thing
one says; otherwise, instead of entertaining or informing
others, one only tires and puzzles them.

8. The voice and manner of speaking, too, are not to be
neglected. Some people almost shut their mouths when they
speak, and mutter so that they are not to be understood;
others speak so fast, and sputter, that they are equally unintelligible. Some always speak as loud as if they were talking
to deaf people; and others so low that one cannot hear them.
All these, and many other habits, are awkward and disagreeable, and are to be avoided by attention. You cannot imagine how necessary it is to mind all these little things. I
have seen many people with great talents ill received for want
of having these little talents of good breeding; and others
well received only from their little talents, and who had no
great ones.

---

171. THE ANCIENT TOMBS.

FRANCES BROWN.

FRANCES BROWN was born in Stranorlar, county Donegal, in 1816. She
was afflicted with small-pox when about a year and a half old, by which
she lost her sight. At the age of seven years she began to educate herself, by asking of all her friends about her the meanings of words and
things. From hearing her brothers and sisters repeat their daily tasks in
grammar and spelling, she learnt the same lessons, and invariably knew
them before the others. Her memory was so retentive, that to induce her
friends to read for her the more thoughtful books for which they had no
taste, she used to relate stories of her own composition,—or do the house-

aold work which was allotted to them. The sight of the visible world having been shut against her, her clear natural intellect devised a mode by which she learned to see into the world of thought. The greater portion of her poems appeared in the "Athenæum,"—from the editor of which she has experienced kindness and encouragement.

1 THEY rise on isle and ocean shore,
   They stand by lake and stream,
And blend with many a shepherd's tale,
   And many a poet's dream;
Where darkly lowers the northern pine,
   Where the bright myrtle blooms,
And on the desert's trackless sands,
   Arise the ancient tombs.

2. The hands that raised them, long ago,
   In death and dust have slept,
And long the grave hath seal'd the fount
   Of eyes that o'er them wept ;
But still they stand, like sea-marks left
   Amid the passing waves
Of generations, that go down
   To their forgotten graves.

3. For many an early nation's steps
   Have pass'd from hill and plain ;
Their homes are gone, their deeds forgot,
   But still their tombs remain—
To tell, when time hath left no trace
   Of tower or storied page,
Our ancient earth how glorious was
   Her early heritage.

4. They tell us of the lost and mourn'd,
   When earth was new to tears ;
The bard that left his tuneful lyre,
   The chief that left his spears :
Ah! were their lights of love and fame
   On those dark altars shed,
To keep undimm'd through time and chang
   The memory of the dead ?

5. If so, alas for love's bright tears !
    And for ambition's dreams,
For earth hath kept their monuments
    But lost the sleepers' names :
They live no more in story's scroll,
    Or song's inspiring breath ;
For altars raised to human fame
    Have turn'd to shrines of·death.

6. But from your silence, glorious graves,
    What mystic voices rise,
That thus, through passing ages speak
    Their lessons to the wise !
Behold, how still the world rewards
    Her brightest, as of yore ;
For then she gave a nameless grave—
    And now she gives no more.

———————◆———————

172. Execution of Sir Thomas More.

[From the Historical Novel of ALICE SHERWIN.]

1. His beloved daughter Margaret, knowing she would not again be admitted within the precincts of the Tower, had paced the wharf for more than an hour ; when she at length perceived him, she burst through the billmen, and throwing herself on his neck, murmured, in a broken voice, "Oh, my father ! oh, my father !"

2. "Where is thy fortitude, my best jewel ?" said More, tenderly pressing his lips to her cheek. "Let this console thee, Margaret, that I suffer in innocence, and by the will of God ; to whose blessed pleasure, thou, my child, must accommodate thyself, and not only be patient under thy loss, but lead thy poor weak mother and thy sisters to follow thy example. And now retire ; I would not have thy best feelings become the scoff and jibe of a brutal guard."

3. His daughter prepared to obey; but had not proceeded ten steps, when, forgetful of all fortitude and self-control, she turned back, and falling on his neck, kissed him again and again. Sir Thomas did not speak; but notwithstanding his efforts at firmness tears fell rapidly from his eyes; neither was it until his adopted daughter, Margaret Clement, had loosened her arms by force, she could be separated from her father Dorothy Collie, her maid, who had been brought up in the family, also threw herself on her knees at her master's feet, covering his hand with kisses.

4. The space between his trial and execution was employed by More in prayer, meditation, and the severest corporal mortifications; he continually walked about with a sheet around him, so as to familiarize himself to the thought of death. He contrived to write a few lines with a coal to his daughter Margaret, expressing his earnest desire to suffer on the following day, which was the vigil of St. Thomas of Canterbury, and sending her his hair-shirt. Strange to say, early the next morning he received a visit from Sir Thomas Pope, who with much pain informed him he was to suffer at nine o'clock, adding that by the king's pardon his sentence was changed into beheading, because he had borne the highest office in the realm, and that he (Pope) was desired to be the messenger of the royal mercy.

5. "Well," said Sir Thomas, with his usual good humor, "God forbid the king should extend any more such mercy to those I hold dear, and preserve my posterity from similar pardons! For the rest, Master Pope, I thank you for your tidings; I am bound to his grace, who, by putting me here, has afforded me time and opportunity to prepare for my end I beseech you, my good friend, to move his majesty that my daughter Roper may be present at my burial."

6. "The king is content," said Pope, deeply moved, "tha all your family should attend, provided you use not many words on the scaffold."

"It is well I was informed," said More; "for I had purposed to have spoken; but I am ready to conform to his highness' pleasure. Nay, quiet yourself, good Master Pope,"

19°

he continued, as the other wrung his hand ; "for I trust shall yet live and love God together in eternal bliss."

7. When he was alone, More carefully attired himself in a gown of silk camlet, which he had received as a present from one Anthony Bonvise, a merchant of Lucca : it was so costly that Sir William Kingston advised him not to wear it, as he whose property it would become was but a *javill* (villain).

"Shall I account him a javill," said More, "who is this day to work me so singular a benefit ?   Nay, if it were cloth-of-gold, I should think it well bestowed.   Did not St. Cyprian, the martyred Bishop of Carthage, bestow on his executioner thirty pieces ? and shall I grudge a garment ?"

8. Kingston, however, persisted ; yet, although Sir Thomas yielded, he sent the headsman an angel out of his scanty store, to prove he bore him no ill-will.

When the crowd assembled round the scaffold on Tower Hill caught sight of their former favorite, his beard unshaved, his face pale and sharpened, and holding a red cross in his hand, they pressed eagerly around him, while audible expressions of indignation were heard on every side.   A poor woman pushed through the throng, offering him a cup of wine ; but he gently put her aside, saying, "Christ at His Passion drank not wine, but gall and vinegar."

He, however, met with many insults.   One female cried out that he had wrongfully judged her cause when lord chancellor ; to which he calmly replied, that "if he were now to give sentence, he would not alter his decision."

9. While preparing to mount the scaffold, an unwonted bustle took place at the very verge of the dense mass, and it was evident the guards were endeavoring to keep some person back ; their halberds, however, were beaten aside, and with almost superhuman strength a man forced himself through the press, grasping the prisoner's robe as he prepared to ascend the steps, and demanding with the voice and action of a maniac, "Do you know me, More ? do you know the man you rescued from the devil ?   Pray for me ! pray for me !   I have wandered round your prison ; if I had seen you, you had cured me again."

10. "It is John Hales of Winchester," said one of the guard. "He says Sir Thomas More cured him by his prayers of the black fever, and that since he has been in confinement the fits have returned worse than ever."

"He did more for me," said Hales, tenaciously retaining his hold, "than all the college of physicians. Pray for me, More! pray for me! Do you not remember me?"

"I do remember you," said More soothingly; "I will pray for you on the scaffold: go and live in peace; the fits will not return."

11. The man obeyed; when the prisoner finding himself too weak to ascend, said to Kingston, who was by his side, "I beseech you, see me safe up; my coming down I will take care of myself."

He then knelt, and recited the *Miserere*; after which he embraced the executioner, saying, "No mortal man could have done me a greater service than thou wilt this day. Pluck up thy spirit, and fear not to perform thy office. My neck is very short; take heed thou strike not awry, to save thy credit."

12. He covered his eyes himself, and laying his head on the block, removed his beard, saying, "This at least never committed treason."

There was a dull heavy sound, a gush of warm bright blood, and the soul of Sir Thomas More passed to God upon the very day which he had so earnestly desired.

---

173. THE INFLUENCE OF DEVOTION ON THE HAPPINESS OF LIFE.

BLAIR.

Dr. HUGH BLAIR, born in Edinburgh, in 1718; died in 1800. He is best known by his "Lectures on Rhetoric." Though somewhat hard and dry in style and manner, this work forms a useful guide to the young student. Dr. Blair is also known as the author of a learned and elaborate dissertation on MacPherson's "Poems of Ossian."

1. WHATEVER promotes and strengthens virtue, whatever calms and regulates the temper, is a source of happiness. De

votion produces these effects in a remarkable degree. It inspires composure of spirit, mildness, and benignity; weakens the painful, and cherishes the pleasing emotions; and, by these means, carries on the life of a pious man in a smooth and placid tenor.

2. Besides exerting this habitual influence on the mind, devotion opens a field of enjoyments to which the vicious are entire strangers; enjoyments the more valuable, as they peculiarly belong to retirement, when the world leaves us; and to adversity, when it becomes our foe. These are the two seasons, for which every wise man would most wish to provide some hidden store of comfort.

3. For let him be placed in the most favorable situation which the human state admits, the world can neither always amuse him, nor always shield him from distress. There will be many hours of vacuity, and many of dejection in his life. If he be a stranger to God, and to devotion, how dreary will the gloom of solitude often prove! With what oppressive weight will sickness, disappointment, or old age, fall upon his spirits.

4. But for those pensive periods, the pious man has a relief prepared. From the tiresome repetition of the common vanities of life, or from the painful corrosion of its cares and sorrows, devotion transports him into a new region; and surrounds him there with such objects as are the most fitted to cheer the dejection, to calm the tumults, and to heal the wounds of his heart. If the world has been empty and delusive, it gladdens him with the prospect of a higher and better order of things about to rise.

5. If men have been ungrateful and base, it displays before him the faithfulness of that Supreme Being, who, though every other friend fail, will never forsake him. Let us consult our xperience, and we shall find, that the two greatest sources of inward joy, are, the exercise of love directed towards a deserving object, and the exercise of hope terminating on some high and assured happiness. Both these are supplied by devotion; and therefore we have no reason to be surprised, if, on some occasions, it fills the hearts of good men with a satisfaction not to be expressed.

6. The refined pleasures of a pious mind are, in many respects, superior to the coarse gratifications of sense. They are pleasures which belong to the highest powers and best affections of the soul; whereas the gratifications of sense reside in the lowest region of our nature. To the latter, the soul stoops below its native dignity. The former, raise it above itself. The latter, leave always a comfortless, often a mortifying remembrance behind them. The former, are reviewed with applause and delight.

7. The pleasures of sense resemble a foaming torrent, which after a disorderly course, speedily runs out, and leaves an empty and offensive channel. But the pleasures of devotion resemble the equable current of a pure river, which enlivens the fields through which it passes, and diffuses verdure and fertility along its banks.

8. To thee, O Devotion! we owe the highest improvement of our nature, and much of the enjoyment of our life. Thou art the support of our virtue, and the rest of our souls, in this turbulent world. Thou composest the thoughts. Thou calmest the passions. Thou exaltest the heart. Thy communications, and thine only, are imparted to the low, no less than to the high; to the poor, as well as to the rich.

9. In thy presence worldly distinctions cease; and under thy influence, worldly sorrows are forgotten. Thou art the balm of the wounded mind. Thy sanctuary is ever open to the miserable; inaccessible only to the unrighteous and impure. Thou beginnest on earth the temper of heaven. In thee, the hosts of angels and blessed spirits eternally rejoice.

---

174. ON PRIDE.

POPE.

ALEXANDER POPE was born in London in 1688; died in 1744. As a poet, Pope holds a first place. In his "Rape of the Lock" he has blended the most delicate satire with the most lively fancy, and produced the finest and most brilliant mock-heroic poem in the world. His "Essay on Man," "Essay on Criticism," and "Temple of Fame," are each unsurpassed in beauty and elegance of style.

1. Or all the causes which conspire to blind
   Man's erring judgment, and misguide the mind,
   What the weak head with strongest bias rules,
   Is pride, the never-failing vice of fools.
   Whatever nature has in worth denied,
   She gives in large recruits of needful pride!
   For, as in bodies, thus in souls, we find
   What wants in blood and spirits, swell'd with wind
   Pride, where wit fails, steps in to our defence,
   And fills up all the mighty void of sense.

2. If once right reason drives that cloud away,
   Truth breaks upon us with resistless day.
   Trust not yourself; but, your defects to know,
   Make use of every friend—and every foe.
   A little learning is a dangerous thing;
   Drink deep, or taste not the Pierian spring:
   There shallow draughts intoxicate the brain;
   And drinking largely sobers it again.

3. Fired at first sight with what the muse imparts,
   In fearless youth we tempt the heights of arts,
   While, from the bounded level of our mind,
   Short views we take, nor see the lengths behind;
   But more advanced, behold, with strange surprise,
   New distant scenes of endless science rise!
   So, pleased at first the towering Alps we try,
   Mount o'er the vales, and seem to tread the sky;
   Th' eternal snows appear already past,
   And the first clouds and mountains seem the last;
   But, those attain'd, we tremble to survey
   The growing labors of the lengthen'd way;
   Th' increasing prospect tires our wondering eyes;
   Hills peep o'er hills, and Alps on Alps arise

175. ADHERENCE TO PRINCIPLE COMMANDS RESPECT.

MISS BROWNSON.

SARAH H. BROWNSON, daughter of Dr. O. A. Brownson, though still young in years, has already evinced considerable talent for literary composition. Her "Marian Elwood," published anonymously, with other smaller works which have only met the eyes of her friends, indicate a range of ability far in advance of the writer's age. "Marian Elwood" is the only one of Miss Brownson's works yet published, but it has a vigor of thought, and a richness of fancy, which must at once strike the reader.

1. WHEN Marian had finished her breakfast, she lounged carelessly to the windows, and after looking at her watch several times, went to her own room. At a quarter before nine, she appeared in the hall. "Where are you going?" asked Mr. Weston.

"To church. Am I not to have the pleasure of your escort as far at least as the door?"

2. "If you leave this house, and enter a papist temple, you shall never return to it."

"Polite, on my word. And what will you say to my mother?"

"What shall I say," he thundered, "what shall I say? I'll tell her you've come to bring dishonor on a respectable house, disgrace to an honorable man! What shall I say to her? I'll tell her of your insults—your—stay!"

3. "Uncle, listen a moment—listen to a little reason—"

"I'll hear nothing from you. Be still—"

"You must. Listen, I am a Roman Catholic."

"At home you may be; but in this house I have no idolaters."

"As a Roman Catholic I am bound to obey my Church"

"And her vile, crafty priests?"

"I have no time nor patience to hear your free, candid opinions," Marian said, her color rising. "I am willing to give you my reasons for acting as I am about to do; if you will listen, and show yourself a gentleman, and an enlightened one, very well; if you will not listen to what I wish to say, you will prove yourself prejudiced, bigoted, and narrow-minded." His very rage prevented him from answering.

4. "But," she continued, "you are none of the three. My religion, which I firmly believe, and am, therefore, bound in conscience to practise—my religion commands me to attend church every Sunday. And, think you, because the way is hard, I am to disobey? If I practise my religion when my mother's carriage drives me to the church door, and I have soft cushions to rest on, shall I desert it when I have a long walk to take, exposed to the wondering eyes of a handful of prejudiced country people? If I do that, do you think I am worthy the name of Catholic?"

5. "But it is no religion; it is the mask for crafty Jesuits, and—and—"

"Whatever this religion may be in your eyes, in mine it is my Redeemer's. If you believe it is a crime for you to—to —enter that parlor, and because I tell you it is absurd for you to imagine such a thing; if the whole world rises up and laughs at you for being afraid to enter your own parlor, and you, still believing you are committing a crime, should enter to avoid ridicule—"

6. "But that is not the same. You need not fancy you are about to commit a crime. You must know all our little town is on tiptoe to see you, and I intended satisfying their vulgar curiosity. If you are not with me, a thousand questions will be asked. I shall be forced to acknowledge that you went to—a—popish gathering. In an instant, you will be made a mark for scorn. You do not know the prejudice of our little village."

7. "'They are on tiptoe to see me!' Is a church then the place for me to exhibit myself? Am I then to break the laws of *my* church, listen not to the voice of my conscience, violate my duty to my God, because people want to look at me? Shame on you, uncle!"

"I did not mean that at all—but after meeting—"

8. "I will dress myself in my prettiest costume, and with Catherine as a guide, go to meet you, and I promise to endure, without a shade of scorn, the whole battery of your friends' eyes. If they ask questions, are you to shrink? Are you not man enough to say your niece follows her *own* con

science, in preference to *their* prejudices? They'll scorn me Let them. I should scorn myself had I not principle, religion, and character enough to do my duty in the face of a whole world's opposition. I know it is mortifying to you—I am sorry it is, but I must go."

9. "You are determined?"

"I am, sir."

"You are right," he answered, "and it shall never be said that James Weston could not appreciate firmness, though in an erring cause. I will go with you."

---

176. Mount Lebanon and its Cedars.

PATTERSON.

James Laird Patterson, M. A., an English gentleman, who a few years since made a visit to the Holy Land, and published an interesting account of his "Tour in Egypt, Palestine, and Syria." After visiting the holy places, Mr. Patterson became a convert to the Catholic faith.

1. ABOUT seven we were in motion, and had a most delightful ride over the crest of Lebanon. The view of the valley and Anti-Lebanon, and of the amphitheatre on the west side, is magnificent. We passed through several patches of snow, and found the air proportionately cold. From the crest of the mountain, the broad valley of B'scherri looks like a rocky glen: the village of that name, and Eden, appeared to the right. Higher up the valley spreads, and near the right flanking mountains the deep green cedars are nestled.

2. The cedars appear about two hundred in number, of which some eight or ten are very large. We measured three of the largest, and found them respectively thirty-seven feet ten inches, twenty-eight feet, and thirty-one feet in girth. On the north side of the four knolls on which the cedars stand (and in the midst of which our tent is pitched) is a deep ravine.

3. The general effect from here is beautiful. On the whole, I should say that the associations and the general effect of the cedars render them well worth a visit; but, in themselves, travellers have a little overrated them. This evening we have

been watching the sunset from one of the trees, in the fork of whose huge branches, or rather trunks, we sat. Between two of these we had a view of the valley and sea-horizon beyond, lit up by the changing sunset lights, and of one single bright star, among the delicate foliage of the trees, which I shall not easily forget.

4. We left the cedars with some regret that we had not resolved at once to stay there some days. I went up to the chapel, and the priest came to me, as I was going away, and gave me the benediction, laying the gospels on my head. He also made me a present of a small cornelian antique seal, which I shall cherish as a pleasant remembrance of him and his mountain charge.

5. At eight o'clock we started for Duman, a summer residence of the patriarch of the Maronites, where he now is. To reach it, we had to cross the head of the valley, and descend it for three or four miles on the south side. As we got lower, we found the ground more cultivated and very fertile, and the views most beautiful. Looking back, we saw the glen or ravine of gray limestone rocks, along which we were scrambling, terminated in an advanced amphitheatre of richly-tinted sandstone, above the centre of which the deep-green cedar grove was seen; while, far above, the grand semicircle of the highest range of Lebanon swept round. Its warm coloring was patched with snow here and there, contrasting with wonderful beauty with the deep sky above.

6. Looking before us, the winding glen yawned below. Its broken gray crags are set off by verdant patches of corn, and by vineyards and mulberry groves, and intersected in a thousand places by clear streams of water, glittering in the sun. But if nature, thus prodigal of beauty, charmed the way, much more was it beguiled by the moral aspect of the inhabitants of Lebanon. At every mile we saw the small chapel, neatly built of squared stones, surmounted by its modest bell-gable; at every turn the courteous but hearty greeting of the peasants, a cheery pleasant-faced race, reminded us that we were once more in a Catholic country.

www.ingramcontent.com/pod-product-compliance
Lightning Source LLC
Chambersburg PA
CBHW030327120726
47901CB00007B/1705